BEYOND THE END

THE LEGENDS -OF- ACALA

BEYOND THE END

MATTHEW MITTCHELL

HOLON
PUBLISHING

ISBN: 9780991528240
Published by **Holon Publishing & Collective Press**
Creative Collective of Authors, Artists, Businesses, and Non-profits.

www.Holon.co
@HolonPublishing
Holon@HolonPublishing.com

Curated by the Holon Creative Team
Front Cover Illustration by Kathryn L. Steele
Maps, Symbols, & Design by Jeremy Gotwals

Acknowledgments

There are so many more people who deserve mention here than I have space to mention them. I am truly blessed. First, I'd like to thank my parents for always encouraging my creativity and for letting me be weird. Thanks to Ms. Davis, my high school English teacher who convinced me that I had what it takes to be a writer. Thanks to the brilliant folks at The Dragon's Rocketship, whose advice and encouragement was indispensable. Thanks so much to my army of Beta-readers, whose feedback helped this book reach its full potential (Special shout out to Anwesha). Thanks to David, for his amazing computer-ninja skills. Thanks to my amazing editor Juliet, who makes me a better writer. And last, but most importantly, thanks to Kimberley, without whose patience and support, this book would literally not have been possible.

THE
LEGENDS
- OF -
ACALA

Table of Contents

Chapter One
Samara

The demon stared at me quizzically, head cocked to the side as if it didn't understand the question. Well, "stared" might be the wrong word considering it had no eyes. Its humanoid head was featureless and smooth like polished marble, as if it were a statue waiting for a sculptor to come along and finish it. Its alabaster face held only lines of multicolored gemstones arranged in a "T" shape that flickered and glowed seemingly at its whim. The rest of the Yaviya, the lowest class of Hell's denizens, was covered by a billowing cloak of purple fur that I assumed was made from the skin of some other unfortunate demon.

"I do not understand," the demon said in a vaguely feminine voice, despite having no mouth.

"Don't insult my intelligence, A'vish," I replied carefully in the Infernal tongue. The choppy guttural language always felt ill-suited for my mouth. "You're being deliberately evasive. You either know, or you don't know."

"It is not my intention to give insult," the Yaviya purred, "but I do not understand what you are asking. Perhaps if you rephrased the question?"

I stared down at the silvery-blue light of the summoning circle between us and took a deep breath to calm myself. The last thing I wanted to do was get sloppy when dealing with a demon, even one bound in a circle. I smoothed the front of my silk dress and brushed an errant red wisp of hair behind my ear. It was obvious my line of questioning made A'vish uncomfortable, but so bound, it couldn't lie to me, only remain silent or try to dance around the question. I tried again, "Do you know which Anaviya was summoned by Shakkar?"

"There were many summoned by him." Something about A'vish's tone made me think the Yaviya was toying with me, but it was tough to tell with demons.

"Are you familiar with the first one he summoned? The one who aided him in his understanding of your kind?"

"I cannot say."

"Because you don't know or you're not willing to tell me?"

"Yes."

"Yes..?"

The demon cocked its head to the side again.

"A'vish, which is it?"

"I cannot say."

"Do...you...know?" I said gnawing on the heavy Infernal words.

"I cannot give you a more satisfactory answer to the question, mage."

I relaxed my hands, which had balled themselves into fists, and rubbed the bridge of my nose. I had to change tactics. "Could you locate Shakkar's first Anaviya?"

The gemstones in A'vish's face started flickering in sequence. I'd noticed that behavior before when the demon was thinking very hard about something. "It is theoretically possible. But it will not help you."

"And why is that?"

The stones flickered again. "I am certain you would long be dust, as would many of your decedents, before I was able to locate what you ask for," A'vish said flatly.

That took me aback. Most demons were boastful of their abilities. It was unusual for one to downplay them, and I happened to know from experience that A'vish was quite talented at locating things. "I thought you could find anything in Hell?"

A'vish hesitated. "I can."

"Then what's the problem?"

The Yaviya just stood in silence, the gems in its face lighting up from the far points inward.

"Come now, Hell's not that large," I said.

"The size of Hell is constantly changing, based upon the will of the Rajasa—"

"You're sidestepping again. Why would it take you so long to find Shakkar's Anaviya?"

A'vish just remained silent, the gems on its empty face went dark.

Something finally occurred to me. "You've been commanded to find him before, haven't you? And you weren't able to, were you?"

The demon's smooth face lit up in rapid succession. "Did you think you were the first human to summon me for this purpose?"

Actually, I kind of did. It was a bit bruising to the pride to realize I wasn't quite as clever as I thought. When I took a step back from the situation, I realized I'd been naive. Doubtless, hundreds of mages over the years had tried exactly what I was doing. Oh, well. What was one more soul-crushing dead end in a day? I had learned one thing, though I drew no solace from it. Apparently the Anivaya I was looking for was hard even for other demons to find.

Five bells. I blew out a frustrated breath and glanced out the window at the late afternoon sun filtering through the stained glass of the West Library. The last ring faded from the distant bell tower. It was five bells past midday and I'd been poking through dusty tomes and scrolls since just after breakfast. I stood up and stretched my back, rubbing the crick that had formed in my neck and then smoothed out my wrinkled silk dress. Another day wasted without bringing me any closer to the answer. I was beginning to accept the sinking realization that what I was searching for wasn't likely to be found in any library in the Empire.

I stacked books and slid scrolls into their cases for the attendant to put away, placing my freshly bound copy of the *Sarga Paza* in my endless bag. It wasn't exactly "endless" of course, but the enchanted blue leather pouch was quite a bit larger on the inside than the outside. I grabbed my cloak off the peg by the door and strode out of the library with a familiar sense of frustration. The last of winter's chill was holding on stubbornly. I wrapped the cloak's warm velvet tighter around my shoulders as I entered the marble hallway bathed in the harsh light cast by the coldfire in their sconces.

My hair, which had been meticulously pinned up in the morning, was falling in uneven red tendrils. For a moment I was eight again and could hear my aunt saying, "A lady of House Arga should always *look* like a lady of House Arga." I sighed and began repining my errant locks using the reflection from the huge arched window.

When my hair was passable I stared down into the courtyard below. The Imperial Academy of Magic was always busy, especially near dinner. Students, both common and noble, scurried about making their way toward the dining hall, or off to finish some final preparations for a twilight summoning, or other obscure experiment. I was happy to be done with the years of tedious study it took to master the basics of magic. In fact, at nineteen, I was close to being the youngest Adept Mage in the history of the Academy, but that honor may very well slip through my fingers if I couldn't find what I was looking for.

My gaze slid to the center of the courtyard where a statue of Tarka towered over the students in marble splendor. As always depicted by Zuran craftsmanship, he was clad in scholarly robes and held an open scroll in one hand and a writing quill in the other. I squeezed the Tarka amulet that lay just above the hollow of my breasts and prayed silently.

Tarka, father of dragons, God of knowledge and magic, please lead your devotee to that which she seeks. All knowledge is sacred.

I stared down at the symbol carved into the medallion, an open book with an eye in the center, hoping he heard my prayer and cared enough to answer it. I pulled my cloak closed and headed out of the Western Hall. The air was damp and the southern wind had a fierce bite as I descended the stairs into the courtyard and the throngs of scurrying students. Spurred by the cold, I moved with purpose toward my destination on the other side of the vast campus.

The guardhouse was near the stables and there was a strong odor of horses, which reminded me of my special hiding spot in the barn on my father's estate. As I entered I was greeted by an attendant in apprentice robes who was quite handsome. Pretty, even.

"Lady Samara, are you ready to leave for the evening?" he said with full lips, blinking long lashes at me that concealed bright blue eyes. I'd been in the same class with his older brother Samir, and occasionally we'd warmed each other's beds. He was a commoner of course, but commoners could be fun to play with. Samir's eyes were hazel, but he had his brother's fair complexion and sandy hair. I couldn't help but wonder what else they shared in common.

"I am. Thank you, apprentice..?"

"Damir, m'lady. I'll have your carriage brought around while I inform your houseguards you're ready to depart." Damir gave a quick bow then disappeared down the hall toward the common room for a moment.

When he returned I asked, "How is Samir doing?"

Damir looked thoughtful for a moment, as if considering what to say. "He's performing his duties with the Twelfth Legion, m'lady."

That took me by surprise. "Samir? A battle mage? He doesn't...seem the type," I said, which was an understatement. Samir had always been more interested in the academic and theoretical sides of magic. In fact, he would have failed his practical exam if it wasn't for my aid.

Damir fidgeted, looking uncomfortable. "We all must serve where we're needed, m'lady."

"Of course," I replied, the reality sinking in. The Empire was on the brink of war with Moravar over some nonsense. Samir was a competent mage but he was hardly gifted, and he was just a commoner. He would be placed where he was needed to best serve the Empire. He didn't have the luxury of haunting dusty libraries trying to decipher ancient texts as I did.

"Well, when you talk to him tell him I said, '*Nir palam kil paykiratu'*."

He grinned, at that moment looking very much like his brother. "I will, m'lady."

"Just Samara, please."

"I will, m'lady Samara." I giggled at that as the assistant came in and indicated my carriage was ready.

I crossed out into the chilly waning sunlight. The two houseguards, wearing Arga blue and silver, bowed to me and ushered me into an enclosed carriage that matched their colors.

"To the manor, m'lady?"

"Yes. Thank you, Harold." He smiled and took the driver's seat while his companion Dirk took the seat next to him. It wasn't as if I even needed an escort. I was more than capable of taking care of myself, but House Arga had appearances to maintain.

The carriage lurched forward down the lane past the gate and out onto the streets of Imperia. It was maybe a quarter hour's walk from the Academy to House Arga's manor, so taking a carriage at all seemed a bit silly to me, but again appearances were important. Unlike some of the city's other districts, the wide streets of the College district were quite safe, as there was a member of the Civic Legion in gleaming brass-trimmed segmenta at practically every corner.

A breeze blowing through the windows brought the smell of the sea from the harbor. I closed my eyes and inhaled the scents of my adopted city, Imperia, the capital of the Empire of Zura. The crossroads of the world. Most called it by its ancient title, White Harbor, so named for the gleaming marble buildings visible from the sea.

The aroma of baking bread and spices from the market mingled with the smell of horse manure and fish from the docks, creating an odor that most probably found unpleasant, but to me it smelled like home. The evening sounds layered one on top of another, making it impossible to pick apart the cacophony. The city had a pulse, a life all its own and there was nowhere else in the world like it. I glanced out the window and took in the rosy sunset over the western buildings. Even the worldliest traveler would have a hard time denying the city's splendor.

All too soon we passed through gilded silver gates and behind the walls of the Arga estate. The Great Houses kept large estates in the capital near the palace, which dated back to the days of the Republic, before Zura became an Empire. The original structures had long since been destroyed by war and fires and the grounds had been expanded upon, but it gave me a comforting sense of symmetry to think that my ancestors had stood on this piece of ground for nearly two millennia.

The carriage came to a halt in front of the stairs to the main entrance, and Dirk opened the carriage door for me. "Will you be traveling anywhere else, m'lady?" Harold asked from the driver's seat.

"No, you may retire for the evening," I said, shivering against the damp breeze.

"Will you be spending another day at the Academy tomorrow, m'lady?" Harold asked, brows raised hopefully.

"I imagine so," I said glancing up at him with a grin. "Do try not to lose your entire week's pay dicing with the other houseguards." The Academy only had one guardhouse so all the Houses shared it. I could only guess the shenanigans those boys got up to while their charges were in class. I imagined it resembled a dockside tavern, day and night.

"It's cards for me, m'lady," Harold grinned broadly. He wasn't particularly handsome but he had a wonderful smile, one of those unashamed smiles that came from the bottom of his feet. "It's Dirk who's the dice man. He's the one who nearly lost his boots today." Dirk for his part actually blushed, staring pointedly down. It was adorable.

"Dirk, let's go get this cart squared away. Good evening, m'lady," Harold said, saving his friend from more embarrassment. Dirk gave a quick bow and returned to his seat on the carriage still red as a beet.

I made my way up the stairs past the large marble columns where a graying houseguard opened the door at my approach. The manor was warm and welcoming, and there was a fire crackling in the foyer as one of the servants took my cloak. "Welcome home, m'lady. Would you like to dine in the atrium or shall I have the meal sent to your room? "

Now that he'd mentioned food, I noticed the delicious aroma wafting from the kitchen and realized I was ravenous. "I'm rather tired. Just have it sent to my room," I said before making my way up the double staircase and heading down the long series of corridors toward my living quarters. At any given time, there were several hundred members of House Arga in White Harbor, and the manor had to be able to accommodate them, so the main building was enormous, larger than some castles.

I entered my quarters, home for the last seven years, set aside my bag and flopped down on the sofa, heaving a sigh. The room was small, quaint even compared to the one at my father's estate, but it was nicely appointed in rich amber hues, and doubtlessly larger than the one the Academy would have afforded me. Autumn came out of the small adjoining servant's room with a book of Verisian poetry in her hand. "Good evening, Mistress. Did you find anything useful?"

"No, nothing. Another wasted day," I huffed.

"It's out there, Mistress. You'll find it eventually," she said as she put her book away and knelt to remove my shoes, her auburn locks swaying. As Autumn looked up, her gaze settled on my hair.

"Oh, you tried to re-pin it yourself, I see," she said with the exact same expression my mother had when I was five and tried to demonstrate my bow-tying skills by tying her shoes in a knot.

"It's not that bad."

"Mistress," she said staring me in the eyes earnestly, "I'm afraid your gifts lie with working your will upon the fabric of the existence, not with hair styling." That got a chuckle out of me. "Here, I'll comb it out. Would you like something to drink?"

"Wine would be delightful."

She retrieved a steaming ewer of spiced wine and poured me a cup. The rich notes of cinnamon, clove, and cardamom danced on my tongue as the warmth of the wine flowed into to my bones. I turned sideways, leaning my shoulder against the back of the sofa as Autumn began removing the pins and gingerly combing through my hair. It was tangled but she had a gentle touch. It felt wonderful.

There was a knock on the door and an attendant came in with two platters of food and deposited them gracefully before departing with bow. The aroma of the stewed lamb roused my hunger again, and free from the burden of dinning with the rest of the family, I forwent manners and ate ravenously. I caught Autumn smiling at me over her own dinner. "I skipped lunch," I explained sheepishly.

She chuckled. "I'm just happy to see you eating, Mistress. You're far too thin. It's all the stress you've been under, no doubt."

"You always think I'm too thin."

"Compared to me, you're wasting away," she teased.

"You won't mind if I have your dessert then," I said, stabbing playfully at her fried apples. She quickly shoved the remainder of them in her mouth, which she then started fanning because they were too hot, eliciting giggles from both of us.

"Shall shall we go to the bath, Mistress?" Autumn said after the meal.

"Definitely."

My eyelids grew heavy as she departed and I'd nearly fallen asleep when she reappeared in the door. "Your bath is ready, Mistress," Autumn said stirring me from my reverie.

I set the blue jade bangle I wore on my left wrist and my amulet to Tarka in a gilded ivory box. Autumn helped me undress and put on a thick robe before doing so herself. There was a large communal bath that doubtlessly had dozens of Arga nobles, but I wasn't feeling particularly social, so we opted for one of the private baths. We drew aside the silk curtain to see steam rising from the sunken marble tub with rose petals floating along lazily.

We shed our robes and sank into warm inviting waters. With a belly full of lamb and wine, the ball of tension I'd been holding onto started to loosen as Autumn began washing me, chatting idly about the poetry she'd been reading. Autumn had been my handmaiden since I was a child. At twenty-two she was just three years older than me and technically my cousin, though by the wrong side of the bed. Her father was one of my uncles who had been careless with a local milkmaid. There was no denying the child was his, her polished gold irises were a trait possessed only by the noble families of Zura, but his wife wouldn't hear of adopting her. It was a situation all too common with the noble families, but my parents had made sure Autumn was looked after. We'd always been close, but after my mother's death nearly a decade ago, Autumn had become almost like a big sister.

She was pretty enough, though plain by noble standards, with fair skin and auburn curls. She had a lovely figure, curvy in all the right places with full breasts. Not for the first time I was jealous as I took note of my much more modest bust. I'd taken after my mother, who was slim and willowy. I'd also inherited her fair complexion and, unfortunately, her freckles, which my cousins had teased me endlessly about as children. I had every intention of developing a spell to get rid of them eventually...preferably without melting my face off in the process. I laid my head back against the edge of the tub and let the heat of the water soak through me until I nearly fell asleep.

We returned to my quarters and I had just slipped into my night gown when there was a knock. Autumn opened the door for an older servant woman.

"This came for you by courier, m'lady," she said handing me a scroll bearing the panther that was House Sena's symbol. My weariness forgotten, there was a quick flash of light as I broke the enchanted wax houseseal and began reading.

"*Initiate Mage Samara of House Arga,*

Apologies for the tardiness of my reply, I have taken to traveling since my retirement. If you still wish to discuss the academic issue put forth in your previous requests, you may meet with me at my home on the House Sena grounds in Imperia at noon two days hence. I look forward to our collaboration."

Sincerely,
Master Tertias Villias Harrias of House Sena.

I let out a squeal. "He's granting me a meeting! I was beginning to think he was going to just keep ignoring me until I stopped writing," I said, scanning the letter one more time.

I went to my desk, scrawled a quick response, and sealed it before handing it to the servant. "Have this sent by courier immediately," I said, turning to Autumn, my earlier weariness completely gone. "There's so much to do. I need to get my documents and research in order and review what I know. I'll need to get a letter from the Academy insisting on the importance of my research—"

"Mistress, you must also remember to breathe," Autumn said with a chuckle.

"As anyone who's ever worn a bodice can tell you, breathing is a luxury," I said as I scrawled down a quick list of things I needed her to do.

After a busy morning filled with preparations for my visit with Master Tertias, I was summoned to my uncle's private study. He had been a general in the legions before ascending to the Noble Council, the second highest position within House Arga, and his military organization showed. His study was neat and tidy with everything in its rightful place, all except for his desk, which was a mess of parchment. He was pouring over a large map, plotting points and measuring distances when I entered.

"Please, child, have a seat," he said indicating a pair of couches sitting across from each other with a low table between them. I bowed politely and took my seat. Once I was settled, he asked the servant who had escorted me to fetch a bottle of pear brandy.

High Councilor Decias Maximus Arga stood up from his desk. He was tall, a full head taller than most men, and unlike his weathered face and thin legion-cut white hair, his posture was untouched by age. He began arranging his papers into neat stacks. "Forgive the mess," he said to me. "This business with Moravar consumes all my time of late."

I'd been so busy with my research I'd hardly paid any attention to current events. "How do the negotiations go?"

"Not well I'm afraid. The blockade sank another one of our ships. Some of the Senators are starting to call for war. If Emperor Pullo was a bit younger, it likely would have already begun." When his desk was organized enough to meet standards, he made his way to the couch opposite me and sat down stiffly, as if his joints ached.

"I didn't realize it had escalated to that point."

He snorted. "The ironic thing is we don't even care about the islands they're claiming. It's nothing but a holdover from the old days of the Empire. But Moravar grows bolder and King Thaddeus is ambitious, so the Emperor believes to give up the 'tiresome little rock' would be to invite trouble."

"The Emperor is wise."

"I suppose he can be," my uncle replied, raising his eyebrows. "Despite being of House Vima."

"Of course." I said with a chuckle.

The servant arrived with a silver tray bearing a bottle and two delicate crystal brandy glasses with gold inlay. He sat the tray down and poured us each a glass. After dismissing the servant, my uncle took his glass and swirled the brandy before taking a sip. "So," he said, his sharp gaze falling over me. "How does your research go?"

I took a sip from my own glass. The sweet brandy was from my father's estate and it tasted like home, warming me despite its chill. I met my Uncle's gaze, his face an unreadable mask after a lifetime of politics, but there could be only one reason why he could have summoned me. "So far I've found nothing to aid my research in the libraries, but I have a promising meeting with Master Tertias Sena tomorrow."

"Really," he said seeming dispassionate, though it was a ruse. "I've heard the dusty old goat is the best linguist in the Empire."

"That's what I'm hoping." My uncle had ears everywhere. He probably knew about my meeting with Master Tertias before I did. He always had one eye on increasing the honor and prestige of the House.

Uncle Decias peered over his brandy. "I hear he's become somewhat of a hermit since he retired from the college. It must have taken some convincing."

"He was a bit difficult to pin down, but I appealed to his academic curiosity," I said, matching his gaze. "And a bit of flattery never hurts."

"Neither does bribery," he said, his thin lips curving into a shrewd smile.

I said nothing. I simply sipped my brandy with my most innocent face. The High Councilor's smile broadened. "Your father never did have a head for politics. You must have gotten that from your mother," he said, refilling our glasses. "You definitely inherited her smile."

I blushed, barely maintaining my demure composure. "Thank you, m'lord."

"Good luck tomorrow, child. I hope you find that which you seek," he raised his glass. "For the glory of the Empire."

"For the glory of House Arga," I replied raising mine.

"Indeed," High Councilor Decias Arga said, draining his brandy.

The House would be looking to arrange a marriage for me before long. If I was able to pull this off, it would be an enormous honor, so much so that it might be enough to keep me in House Arga, rather than married off to one of the other Houses as was usually the case. There was even a chance it might give me the leverage to actually choose who my betrothed would be.

The next day I rose before dawn, unable to sleep any longer due to my excitement over meeting Master Tertias. The manor was dark and quiet except for the servants moving about and the coldfire I'd summoned floated above my head bathing the halls in a pale blue. I found the atrium empty and peaceful, so I sat and performed my morning breathing meditation and hatha stretching. The house began to stir as I finished my exercises and went to wash up.

I chose a tasteful silver silk dress as Autumn put my hair up in a complicated but lovely arrangement, lined my eyes with a bit of kohl, and dabbed some carmine on my lips to finish. I packed the research materials and papers I needed in my endless bag. I went over everything one last time in my mind and rehearsed what I was going to say.

When it was time to leave, the houseguards brought the carriage around. It was only about a mile to the House Sena estate but again, appearances. As we arrived, a young man with a slave coin resting magically in the hollow of his throat led me to a dark haired woman with silver eyes who was flanked by servants. "Greetings, I'm Lucretia Sena," she said, kissing my cheeks in greeting. "You must be the persistent mage meeting with Master Tertias."

"Guilty as charged, I'm afraid," I said, trying to look demure.

She laughed. "Oh, darling please, tenaciousness is a virtue. He's been grouchy and tiresome since his retirement. My servant will take you to see him." One of the servant girls stepped forward obediently.

"Thank you, m'lady," I said inclining my head.

As Lucretia turned to walk back toward the manor house with the rest of the servants following in her wake, she said to me over her shoulder, "Oh, and don't drink his tea. It's *dreadful.*"

I laughed. "I appreciate the warning."

The servant led me around the manor. The Sena's estate in Imperia was roughly the same size as Arga's, but the manor house was much smaller. The area surrounding it was lined with modest but luxurious town homes. There were peacocks strutting the grounds, displaying their beautiful plumage despite the chilly weather. The songbirds also seemed immune to the cold, as their careless twitters mingled with the melody of some unseen fountain.

I was led to one of the town homes tucked back in the corner of the estate behind a copse of trees and bade to wait. The servant knocked on the door before announcing my arrival. After a moment, the door opened and she gestured for us to enter.

Tertias Sena stood in the modest foyer to greet us. He was long-limbed and rail-thin with short, jet black hair and bushy eyebrows. He had deep crow's feet at the corners of his eyes and his shoulders were somewhat hunched over, as if from a lifetime of squinting at dusty tomes by lamplight. "Greetings and well met, Initiate Samara." His voice was soft and high pitched. It was hard to envision him lecturing a class in the cavernous halls of the Imperial College.

"Well met, Master Tertias," I said returning his greeting as I bowed from the waist. "Thank you for making time to see me. It's an honor."

"Your…many letters intrigued me," he said with a polite smile. "Let us head up to the study," he said, dismissing the servant and turning to go up to the second floor. The house was tidy to the point it hardly looked lived in, and as far as I could tell, there were no servant accommodations.

The study turned out to be more of a library. It took up the entire top floor of the townhouse with shelves lining every wall, bearing thousands of neatly stowed books and scrolls. The high stained glass clerestory windows washed the room in soft diffused light. A long oak table and chairs in the middle of the room were the only other furniture.

"Please take a seat," Master Tertias said, gesturing near the head of the table. "How do you take your tea? I just brewed a pot of lovely Kalikara."

Remembering Lucretia's words I said, "Um, thank you, no." Not wanting him to take offense I added, "My stomach has been rather sensitive and I don't want to upset it." There was a touch of truth to that. I still had nervous butterflies.

"Suit yourself," he said pouring himself a cup from a teapot that looked old and delicate. I busied myself by gathering my documents and notes from my endless bag. Master Tertias took a seat across the table and sipped his tea. He leaned back in his chair and steepled his finger so that they were barely touching his lips and stared at me. The weight of his attention made my already knotted stomach squirm. "So, young mage," he said at length. "Why the sudden interest in dead languages?"

I took a centering breath and met the weight of his gaze. "Tell me, Master

Tertias, what do you know of summoning demons?" If the question took him aback, he hardly showed it. His bushy brow furrowed a bit, as he pondered over his fingers.

"Not much more than most I'm afraid. I speak Infernal, of course, but I was frankly never very interested in magic. Why do you ask?"

"Are you familiar with Shakkar?"

"Shakkar the Wise? If memory serves, he was a pre-Empire mage who authored a book on demon summoning."

"That's correct, master. He authored *the* book on demon summoning, the *Sarga Paza*, more commonly known as the 'Binding Book'. Before the Sarga Paza, mages could only summon the weakest of demons, the Yaviya, and even then it was dangerous. And they couldn't compel the demon to do their bidding, only bribe or trick them, as we do with Elementals."

Master Tertias took a sip of his tea and leaned forward a bit as I continued. "Mages have been summoning Yaviyas since the Dragon war, which was certainly a factor in humans actually prevailing, but summoning the Anaviya, the greatest demons, was completely beyond them. Not only were the summoning circles used inadequate to hold them, but an Anaviya's name must be used in order to summon it."

"And their names were unknown?" Master Tertias said, his bushy eyebrows raising.

I shook my head. "The Rajasa created the Anaviya *after* they were locked in Hell by the Gods. None had ever walked the earth before. No amount of bribery, threats, or trickery could compel the lesser demons to give up any of the Anaviyas' names. Keep in mind this was almost three millennia ago, and less was known about the theory and practice of magic in general. Many mages were probably unsure summoning such a powerful being was even possible, let alone survivable.

"And then came Shakkar," I said, excitement vibrating behind my breastbone. "By most accounts, he wasn't a particularly powerful mage, but he was quite clever. After questioning hundreds of demons he was able to get a general description of many of the Anaviya. He then began sending demons back to Hell to ask the Anaviya for permission to give up its name. Understandably most of them said no, not wanting to be potentially enslaved by a mage. But eventually, one said yes."

Master Tertias was listening intently so I continued with building confidence. "Now, bear in mind Shakkar couldn't even bind the weakest of demons, much less one as powerful as an Anaviya. He probably lacked the strength to banish it as well, so this was an extremely dangerous endeavor. There was a very real possibility that the demon would either destroy the circle it was trapped in outright, or at the very least, remain stuck in the circle with no way for Shakkar to banish it until the circle's power dissipated, at which point the demon could just walk out…presumably very angry. But Shakkar attempted the summoning anyway. No one knows exactly what happened, but he managed to both summon the Anaviya and somehow trick the demon into serving him."

Master Tertias smiled. "It sounds like he was either very clever, or very lucky."

"I would guess both," I said, returning the smile. "Unlike most of his kind, Shakkar's demon was more than willing to give up information on his fellows. It revealed the names of the other Anaviyas and, even more amazingly, taught Shakkar how to construct better circles so that the summoner could force the demon into service. With what he learned he was able to write the Sarga Paza."

"This knowledge allowed Shakkar to bind hundreds of demons into his service, enough to build him a palace, and eventually a kingdom. Mages from all across the world came to learn from him, and his book became the basis for all modern demon summoning."

"I see," Master Tertias said his bushy brows going up, clearly wondering what my story had to do with him.

"Seventy-one Anaviyas and the circles needed to safely summon and bind them are listed within the Sarga Paza, but the one that Shakkar first summoned is not among them. It's always been assumed by scholars that this was part of the price Shakkar agreed to in exchange for the demon's aid," I said.

"But?" Master Tertias prompted.

"But," I said opening one of the books on the table, "an ancient manuscript was recently uncovered under the ruins of an old temple. It appears to be an original copy of the Sarga Paza," I said, pausing for emphasis. "And it has an extra circle diagrammed in it."

I pointed to the open book. "This is an exact copy of the manuscript found." I opened my translated copy of the Sarga Paza setting them next to each other and pointed to a diagram in each book. "As you can see, except for the script, the various diagrams of the circles are exactly the same," I said tracing them for emphasis. "The earliest translations we have of the Sarga Paza are written in Avasitan, which was the scholarly language of the time, but I'm told that this is written in Vikatan. Can you verify that Master?" I asked, running my finger along the strange script and looking up questioningly.

Master Tertias leaned forward and squinted down at the parchment. "Yes. Yes, this is definitely Vikatan." A thrill shot up my spine.

"Shakkar was born in the Vikata region of Azanta, which means Vikatan would have been the language of his youth. I'm convinced that this is an original copy of Sarga Paza *before* it was translated to Avasitan, meaning that this," I said, turning to the last diagram in the manuscript, "must certainly be for the unnamed Anaviya, the one who Shakkar initially summoned," I said speaking faster. "If we could decipher this, we could summon it! Think of what we could learn? Think of what—"

Master Tertias heaved a deep sigh and shook his head. "I'm sorry, I can't translate this." My heart fell to my feet.

"What? Why?" I asked dumbfounded.

"It's a dead language, child. Hardly any examples of it exist. And it was only a regional language. When the Empire conquered Vikata and as its people were forced to learn the Common tongue, many such lesser dialects simply faded away."

"Well, perhaps you can decipher it...I mean...I have a copy of the Sarga Paza that's been translated into Common, perhaps you could use it to—"

He waved his hand, cutting me off. "Not only does no record of the script exist, no record of the spoken language exists either. Like many primitive tongues, you must be able to first speak Vikatan to understand the context to be able to read it. Otherwise it's illegible."

I felt suddenly faint. "Well...surely some record of Vikatan exists somewhere?"

"Not in Zura," he said firmly. "When I was younger, I studied dead languages extensively. If a text with what you need exists, then it's buried and forgotten in some museum or library." His bushy eyebrows drew tight as he looked at me with compassion in his deeply lined features. "I'm sorry, young Initiate. I know it's not what you wanted to hear, but without some further record there is nothing I can do."

"Perhaps if you study the text you'll find some pattern that allows you to—"

He drew himself up as high as his slouched shoulders would allow and spat, "I'm the foremost linguist in the Empire and I'm *quite* aware of my own abilities. I could study that text for a hundred years and still not be able to decipher it to the point you could use it to summon your demon. Am I mistaken to think that conducting a summoning with a partial translation would be rather dangerous?"

"No, you're not mistaken," I swallowed, shaking. "No, that would indeed be very dangerous. I'm sorry, Master. I meant no disrespect. I've just...it's just..." I grasped for something to say.

He blew out a breath, regaining his composure. "I understand, child. But what you're asking can't be done. Perhaps somewhere in Azanta, or Usna, or even Puravasu, some record of Vikatan still exists that may allow for its translation."

Perhaps there was some record in Azanta, but that lay half a world away. And then again, perhaps there wasn't. Perhaps the Vikatan tongue was just lost to the harsh embrace of time. I began gathering up my things and putting them in my bag, utterly defeated. "Thank you for your expertise, Master Tertias. I won't take up any more of your time."

He closed the Sarga Paza and slid it across the table toward me before he rose, stretching his hunched shoulders. "I always have time for a fellow devotee of Tarka," he said, touching his amulet which was an older more worn version of mine. "This was fascinating. If you find a way to translate the book, please do let me know. I'd be very interested."

"I will Master. And thank you again." I could feel tears welling up in my eyes and wanted to escape before I broke down crying. Just before I started down the stairs he cleared his throat.

"Good luck with your demon."

"Thank you," I said, making a hasty exit.

I strode numbly through the House Sena grounds. This was about the worst case scenario. The best linguist in the Empire, maybe the world, had no idea how to translate the only language that held the information to summon Shakkar's Anaviya, *if* indeed that's what the book even held. I felt my dreams falling away for the second time in a week. I approached the guardhouse and discovered that the carriage was already being brought around for me.

"Home, m'lady?" Harold finally asked. I thought about it. I thought about going home and crawling into bed and not stepping out again for a week. I thought about it hard. But that would be admitting defeat, and I wasn't quite ready to do that.

"No, to the Academy."

———————————

My mentor sat across from me, listening intently. His clear blue eyes stared evenly at me as I recounted my meeting with Tertias Sena. There was nothing special about his eyes, he was a commoner after all, but they were piercing. He listened with a serene face, not interrupting. I was beginning to compose myself. Master Carter's easy presence always had a calming effect on me. It was no doubt enhanced by the four cups of wine I'd had.

"So he said there's no way to translate it?"

"No, not with the understanding we currently have," I said, miserable.

"And you've exhausted your search of the libraries?" he said as he rose from his chair and strode across his spacious office to the window overlooking the courtyard. The long braid trailing after him retained the blackness of his youth, but his mustache and goatee were streaked with matching iron bands at the edges. Master Mage Delias Carter had a handsome face and he wore his five decades with grace.

"Yes. There's a few more I could try, but at this point it's really a shot in the dark." I stared down into my wine. "I suppose my next step will be to sail to Azanta and see if I can find anyone—"

"Have you ever heard of the Vija?" Master Carter asked out of the blue.

"Um…" The abrupt subject change caught me off guard, I flailed about mentally trying to think through the wine. "Aren't they some sort of primitive mystic?"

Master Carter smiled back over his shoulder. "Close.

They're seers of the Manu people."

"The Manu?" I strained trying to think back to my schooling.

"They live in Mystewood Forest, up in northern Sursum."

I vaguely remember learning about them. "Right…and?" I asked, trying to see the relevance.

"I met with one when I was hardly older than you," he said turning back to face me. "Perhaps a Vija could provide you with insight that could help you translate the book? Or at least point you in the right direction."

I looked at my mentor skeptically. "I mean no offense Master, but do you really think some backwoods witch is going have a better command of divination magic than someone at the Academy?"

Master Carter smiled patiently. "The Vija don't practice formal magic, they have some sort of innate gift. I was quite impressed by the one I met." From him, that was no small statement, He was one of the most knowledgeable mages in the world.

"And…you believe one of these Vija can help me?"

"I think it's possible. And Sursum is far closer than Azanta, and a far safer journey." Master Carter crossed back to stand before me. "I know you're willing to go to the ends of Acala to find what you seek. It's one of the things I admire about you. But perhaps you should, for once, try the easiest option first." He smirked broadly. "Though I know it goes against your nature."

I shot him an annoyed glance and tried to look sullen, but he had a point. Sursum was a closer and, as a territory of the Empire, far safer. It cost me little to search for my answers there first. And yes, maybe sometimes I did have a tendency to do things the hard way. I sighed. "I suppose if these Vija are as insightful as you claim it would be wise to consult one before traveling halfway across the world."

"Perhaps you can yet be taught," he said with a self-satisfied grin as he reclaimed his seat.

 I ignored the quip. "So how do I go about contacting this seer?"

 "I have absolutely no notion."

 I stared at him brows raised.

 "The one I met was ancient. He's doubtlessly been dead for years."

 "Ugh," I huffed, resting my face in my palm.

 My mentor smiled patiently.

 "That which is worth seeking is rarely easy to find."

Chapter Two
Darian

The Varaha charged. I knew to be careful near the Black Creek verge, yet still I was startled as it broke from the brush. It'd been several seasons since one of the troublesome beasts had been spotted.

"Keffa, get back and get some more Rangers to aid us," I shouted to my fellow scouts. "I'll try to draw its attention. Cayman, stay put and wait for a good shot. I'll try to turn it about."

"Wait, Darian—" Cayman started to say as I left at a full gallop, which blew the hood of my surcoat back and sent my hair dancing about my face.

I turned all my attention to the Varaha bearing down on me, confident in my fellow Rangers to do as commanded. Baleful red eyes stared out of what once might have been a boar before the verge twisted its form. Now it stood the height of a bull with the chitinous skin of a scorpion, flush with sharp metallic spines protruding along its back and sides. Like a grizzly, the beasts were deceptively fast. Fast enough to run down even a Manu horse. I knew from experience, however, their armor limited their mobility and caused them to turn poorly.

The beasts were neigh invulnerable from the front, event to obsidian arrowheads, so I didn't bother. Instead, I charged straight at it. If my horse, Tavas, felt panic at what I was doing he didn't show it. Bow in my left hand, reigns in the other, I stared the beast in the eye, waiting until the last moment to jerk hard to the right. The Varaha squealed in frustration as it tried in vain to swing its head to the side and gore Tavas with a wickedly curved tusk. The effort put the heavy creature off balance and it lost its footing on the loose scatter of pine nettles slamming hard to the ground.

I released the reins in my right hand, guiding the horse with my legs alone, and reached into my quiver, searching for the grooved shaft that denoted the obsidian tipped arrow. I found it, withdrew it, and in one swift motion, nocked the arrow and twisted in the saddle. The Varaha had already struggled to its feet and began to rise. I drew and, timing my shot at the height of the gallop, released the arrow at the only target I had available. The arrow pierced the thick armor of the creature's flank and sank to the fletching. The creature let out a metal-on-metal scream of hate that sounded nothing like a boar. I could only imagine it was how demons screamed.

That should slow him down.

I certainly had the monster's full attention. It rolled to its feet in one jerky motion and charged me again. Even with an arrow fletching-deep in its arse the thing was still fast. I turned about in the saddle, digging my heels in, urging Tavas back toward Cayman. I measured my pace, letting the monster gain on me. It screamed again, and I swear I could feel it's breath on my neck. As I drew closer to Cayman, I cut hard again to the creature's wounded side, and again it overextended and fell. Cayman's arrow caught a bad angle and slid under the creature's armored skin rather than penetrating. I had no time to fire an arrow this time before the beast was on me. I led it on a long circuit, before coming back around to give Cayman another shot.

Third time's a charm.

I tried to bring the creature around to its wounded side again, but apparently it had learned its lesson. The Varaha made a wide turn and charged at Cayman. He fired an arrow, but it was deflected harmlessly off the creature's thick skull. Now it was Cayman's turn to lead the merry chase, as I tried desperately to get alongside the beast for a clear shot.

If the Varaha was tiring it didn't show. But it was hobbled by its wounds, however minor, and I was closing on it. I watched in terror when Cayman's horse slipped on the wet nettles, and struggled to keep its footing. I had to act. Again, in one fluid motion, I drew and fired. The arrow flew true to the creature's heart…and shattered harmlessly on its armored plating. I must have drawn one of the steel-headed arrows in my haste.

The faulty arrow did however draw the Varaha's attention off of Cayman and back to me as it again turned to pursue me, with simmering hate in its crimson eyes. I'd become turned around in the chase, and not knowing which way the road and my allies were, I just picked a direction and dug my heels in, urging Tavas to give everything he had.

I led the abomination on a large arc to come back around to the road with the metallic scream driving my flight. I had to dodge around trees, brambles, and rocks so I wasn't entirely sure I was on course. On even ground I could have gained quite a lead but, things being as they were, I could only manage to stay a few lengths ahead of the monster.

Finally I came to a clearing that offered a little room to maneuver. I swung Tavas around in a tight circle, forcing the Varaha to turn to its injured side. I reached into my quiver, being sure to feel for the grooves this time, and knocked the arrow. The Varaha, favoring its wound, turned broad side to me for but a moment, but that was all I needed. Again I sent an arrow straight for its heart, this time striking true. The beast went down hard with a haunting scream, his slide cutting a deep furrow in the ground.

"Finally," I said coming to a stop, both Tavas and I breathing hard. "No one could accuse you of going down without a fight."

The Varaha began to rise. One of its tusks had broken in the fall, but it held the fire of a thousand suns in its eyes.

"Oh, surely the Gods jest?"

As if in response, the thing let out a shriek that nearly deafened me as it lumbered to its feet for another charge. Again I coaxed every ounce of strength Tavas yet possessed as we turned and resumed our flight. I fled the clearing in the direction I thought the road might be.

Cayman and I had both used up the two obsidian arrows we carried, which meant there was no reason to lead the beast back to him. I took a zig-zagging path, hoping my pursuer's stamina would give out or its wounds would finally catch up to it. Neither happened. The Varaha was every bit as determined, if a bit slower, than it had been when first he laid eyes on us.

Figuring I missed the road, I took a turn around a large boulder, hoping to lead the beast back the way we'd come. It was cleverer than I'd given it credit for I discovered, as I rounded the rock to find those hate-filled eyes were staring at me. I pulled hard on the reins, swinging Tavas's head away from the beast and earning a branch in the face for my efforts, as the Varaha's breath practically warmed my horse's tail.

I spit out blood as we tore through the brush that favored the Varaha. I had nowhere to maneuver and no trick left but speed. I broke out of the brush into another clearing that turned out to be the road. The Varaha screamed again, this time plaintively, as a dozen obsidian arrows struck the twisted beast. It fell for the last time, its massive thud sending up a cloud of dust. The thing's blood had a putrid, rotten smell to it, like a limb that needed to be amputated. Yet even with these grievous wounds, it screamed defiantly as the Rangers circled it, trying to gain its feet again and charge instead of looking for a way to escape as any natural creature would do. One last volley of obsidian ended the twisted monster's rage-filled cry.

I soon found myself surrounded by jovial Rangers patting my back and cheering as my mount and I caught our breath.

"Just had to steal all the fun, eh?" someone said.

"Yeah, 'fun'," Cayman replied joining the group. "The corpse will need to be burned so scavengers don't get sick feasting upon it. It already smells like it's been dead for a week," he said, making a show of sniffing the air.

As Rangers began looping ropes around the fallen beast to drag it from the road, Cayman came over to me. "I lost one of my packs in the chase. Help me look for it?" I nodded, exhausted.

We took the path that I'd cleared during my flight a few moments before breaking through the brush and coming to the furrow the Varaha's fall had left. Cayman eased his mount to a stop and turned to face me, fury in his normally careless posture. "What was that?" he asked in a voice tight with anger.

I ignored the note of accusation. "What was what?"

Frustrated, Cayman gestured toward the furrow.

"I dealt with the threat."

"And…you don't think soloing a Varaha is a bit reckless."

"I wasn't alone. I had your help," I said defensively.

"That's four obsidian arrows between us! When have you known *four* arrows to bring down one of those monsters?" He said holding up his fingers and gesturing wildly for emphasis.

"I thought…if the arrows were well placed we could at least lame it… anyway, I couldn't lead it back to the wagons," I said, getting angry.

"You could have led it away after you shot him it the flank. It never would have caught up to you on the road. Hell, you *charged* the bastard."

"They don't turn well," I countered. "I knew what I was doing."

"It missed you by two fingers!"

"That's called skill."

His nostrils flared. "Yeah and your skill lead it right after me. I was nearly pig food when my mount slipped."

At that I looked down guiltily. Absently, I noted the broken piece of tusk lying in the furrow and thought it should probably be burned with the rest. "I… admit it was more clever than I gave it credit for."

"If you want to die, that's one thing, but don't try to take me with you!"

The words stung as few in my life had. "I knew you could handle yourself. I thought we could bring it down without endangering anyone else."

"Are their lives worth more than yours?"

"As leader—"

"There were two dozen Rangers a few hundred yards behind us, they all know the risks. Being a leader means you lead! Not do it all by yourself. How do you think your mother would handle losing her only son? Don't you think she's suffered enough?"

I had nothing to say.

Cayman ran his fingers through his mess of chin-length braids. "By the Gods, you did everything you could. Are you ever going to stop blaming yourself?"

I still couldn't muster a response.

"Is it your wish to die?"

I started to answer out of reflex but I stopped and really considered the question. There was silence between us while Cayman waited for his answer. "No," I said at length, "but I don't know how much more suffering I can bare before I do."

He sucked in a deep breath, blowing out his anger and bluster. He looked as weary as I felt. "Come," he said at last, "let's return to the group. Perhaps a dragon will attack and you could try and handle that by yourself as well."

I frowned at him as I paused long enough to hop down and pick up the tusk before following.

Chapter Three
Samara

I gazed out the window of the carriage as it rocked along, and watched a pair of Senators in their traditional white togas stroll along the broad streets of the palace district with a trail of petitioners following like ducklings. It'd been a tumultuous couple of days since my meeting at the Sena estate. After a painful conversation with Uncle Decius, he'd dismissed me with disappointment in his eyes, which only added another rider to an already overburdened horse. As if I wasn't frustrated and despondent enough.

Autumn fidgeted in her seat next to me beaming a lovely smile. Normally when she was in a good mood it was infectious. Today, though, it was just grating.

"I see you're excited," I grumbled.

"Of course, Mistress. Aren't you? We're going on an adventure."

"Excited is not the word I would use."

"Really? After months of flipping through dusty tomes, I'm surprised you're not relishing the chance for a little fresh air."

"I'd be more excited if I knew for sure this journey wasn't all for naught."

Autumn shrugged. "We won't know until we get there. So as I see it, either we can enjoy our little adventure, or be sullen the whole trip. Either way it doesn't change your chance at success."

I shot her a grumpy glare but she was right. Sulking about like a child wouldn't help. I resolved to cast my dark mood aside with a sigh. "I suppose you're right. At least I have a place to start." After a moment I added, "And it does get me out of the stuffy libraries."

She beamed her smile at me again. "This will be fun, Mistress. You'll see."

"Mmhm," I mumbled skeptically.

The coach lurched to a stop and I glanced out the window. We had just passed the senate building and were still several blocks away from the Causeway. After a moment the driver stepped down from his seat and came to the window. "I'm sorry, m'lady. I'm afraid this is as close as we're going to be able to get."

"Why?" I asked surprised.

"The Legions are taking up the road," he said with an apologetic shrug. I leaned my head out of the carriage enough to see two long columns of soldiers.

"Apparently we're not the only one's using the Causeway today," I said, gathering my things. "It's not far. We'll just walk."

"Are you sure, m'lady?" Harold asked.

"Harold, I *am* capable of walking a few blocks. Besides, I have four capable houseguards, and by the looks of it, at least two legions as an escort."

"Of course, m'lady," he said, flashing that wonderful smile of his. We egressed from the carriage and gathered our belongings. I had only my endless bag with me, but Autumn had a small satchel and the guards all had rucksacks. Harold dismissed the carriage driver and my four houseguards formed up around Autumn and I as if we were walking some dangerous back alley. Appearances.

We walked the few blocks to our destination, going past a seemingly endless line of legionnaires. Soldiers with polished helmets and gleaming lorica segmenta and mages in their elegant burgundy robes all stood at attention managing to look both the picture of military organization and extremely bored. It made me remember Koto, my father's captain of the guard, saying, "The one thing ye're sure to learn in the Legions is how to stand in line." I wondered for a moment if my gentle bookworm Samir was in that procession.

All citizens and nobles were required to serve the Empire for at least two years, and for most that meant the legions. Not for the first time I thanked the Gods that my research for the Academy was considered important enough to count as my service. I didn't think I would have taken too well to the legions. I was certainly talented enough with battle magic, but I enjoyed a hot bath and a soft bed at the end of the day. And preferably someone to share it with.

We approached the large gated entrance to the Causeway complex and were met by a trio of elite Causeway guards, easily recognizable by their crimson and blue tabards. One of them stepped forward and said in a firm voice, "Hold. Please state your business on the Causeway."

Harold summoned his most formal voice. "Lady Samara of House Arga traveling to Summervale with an entourage of five."

One of the other Causeway guards began scribbling quickly on a tablet, quill moving furiously as the first one stepped forward and said in a humorless tone, "Your coin please, m'lady?"

I grabbed the chain around my neck, fishing my citizenship coin from under my cloak. I held the gold coin bearing my name and the eagle of House Arga as far as the chain would let me. "Samara Arga" I said clearly. The coin flared to life, emitting a soft yellow glow.

"Thank you, m'lady," he said as he waved us through seeming rushed. I glanced back at the long column of legionnaires. I supposed they were on a tight schedule.

We proceeded through the large courtyard and descended down the stairs toward what many considered to be the most amazing feat of magical engineering in the history of mankind. The Kardama Causeway was a direct route linking all six of the Empire's great cities. A few hundred years ago, some clever mages figured out a way to use the broken Realm of Kardama as a shortcut. One could now travel between any of the cities connected to the Causeway in barely half an hour.

We finally descended the steps onto the enormous Gateroom with its cavernous vaulted ceiling, easily large enough to hold a thousand people. Built into the far wall was a huge arch filled in with smooth moonstone. There were a hundred or so people milling about, couriers and merchants mostly, but there were a few nobles scattered here and there. Autumn took note of the vendors along the wall to the right.

"Mistress, would you care for some tea? I'm a bit parched."

"That would be lovely."

Autumn scurried off and returned a few minutes later with one of the vendors in tow bearing a tray with six cups of steaming chai and some small cakes. Autumn was always thoughtful of the guards. The tea was sweet and spicy but the cakes were a bit bland. We stood around for a few moments making idle chatter when Autumn noticed Dirk wasn't drinking his chai.

"Does the tea fail to meet you refined standards, Houseguard Dirk?" Autumn said with a raised eyebrow. She enjoyed tormenting him and he made it far too easy.

"Uh, no. The...the tea is fine," he said looking a bit pale.

Harold slapped him on the back. "I think my friend is a wee bit apprehensive about the Causeway," he said with a grin.

Autumn put her hand in front of her mouth in feigning shock. "What? Our fearless houseguard is scared of a little stroll down the Causeway?"

"It's not the walking that bothers me, it's the prospect of falling off the side forever," Dirk said indignantly.

"Oh, come now. Don't be dramatic," said Harold, "Even if you did fall off, you'd die of thirst in a few days."

"Perhaps not that long, I'm not sure the air off the Causeway is even breathable," I said with a smirk. Dirk blanched even farther as Autumn stifled a giggle.

"See there, that's not so bad. Just a panicked, terrifying death by suffocation. I can think of worse ways to go," Harold said with a smirk.

"Burned alive?" offered Autumn.

"Torn apart by ghouls?" I volunteered.

Harold tapped his chin thinking, "Ambushed by a pack of—a"

"Thank you. This conversation's been quite helpful," Dirk said in a flat voice as he set his tea cup on the merchant's tray. "I feel ever so much better." He cast a baleful glance at Harold, who ignored it and slapped him on the back again with one of his trademark smiles.

"Nobles and couriers to the front!" a Causeway guard shouted in a booming voice. My houseguards formed up around me again and we made our way toward the Causeway Gate. The raised platform that led to it was about the height of a man, seven yards across and nine long, ending at the arches of the gate. The landing resembled the rest of the Causeway in every detail, from the waist-high walls to the softly glowing runes etched into the bricks.

A small cadre of Causeway guards arranged us into a rough column and I found myself standing next to young boy who looked to be about seven, wearing the red and orange of House Paska. It was obviously his first trip to cross the Causeway and his copper eyes were wide with undimmed excitement as he took in the scene. The boy tugged at his sister's sleeve, pointing off to the left of the platform to a raised dais where several Causeway guards were working. "What is that thing?"

The girl, who was perhaps twelve and had the same copper eyes as her brother, heaved a labored sigh, signaling she was far too worldly to be impressed by the Causeway. "The key panel, of course."

"What does it do?"

"It opens the Causeway gate," she said as if it should be obvious.

"Yes, but how?"

"By…um…it uses…uh…when you turn…"

"You don't know how it works either."

"Yes I do! They turn those wheels and it causes the gate to open," the girl said indignantly.

"But *why* does that make it open?"

"Magic," said a clean shaven man with the same eyes.

The boy stared up at him. "Yes, Father, but *how*?"

The father smiled patiently and reached down to scoop up his son. "You see that glowing writing worked in the bricks?" he said pointing to the stairs leading up to the platform.

The boy squinted. "The blue squiggles?"

"Yes," he chuckled. "Every piece of the Causeway has a spell worked into it, just like the coldfire lanterns at home. And that key panel is how they control it. You see those rings? That controls the energy of the nexus we're on top of," he said pointing to the series of concentric copper rings set into the key platform.

The boy glanced down then started looking around. "Where?"

"You can't *see* it," the girl said with an exasperated eye-roll. "A nexus is where ley lines meet. Isn't that right, Father?" the girl said looking pleased with herself.

"That's right. Just like the blood in your body, energy doesn't flow evenly across the land. It collects in rivers and channels called ley lines," he said tracing a blue vein on the back of his son's hand, which elicited a giggle. "Where those rivers cross, energy builds and pools. That's a nexus."

"Well, if you can't see it, how do you know it's there?" the boy asked reasonably.

"How do you know the wind is there if you can't see it?"

"You can see the leaves blowing," the boy said.

"That's right. Just like the leaves rustling tells of the wind, there are things that tell of ley lines."

"You can also feel the wind on your skin," the girl added not to be outdone.

"Yes, and there's those who can feel ley lines the same way."

The boy furrowed his brow. "But why do you need a nexus to open the gate?" That was a very well thought-out question for a child. I could see myself teaching this boy at the Academy one day.

"Because it takes a vast amount of energy for the magic of the gate to open a path between this Realm and Kardama. The energy that pools at this nexus is used to open the gate, but there's only enough energy from the nexus to open the gate twice a day."

"What do they do if they need to open it more than that?" the boy asked. Again I was impressed by his inquisitiveness.

"They use specially prepared gems that store vast amounts of energy, but it's rarely done because of the expense."

The boy was quiet for a few moments, seemingly studying the ground looking for signs of the nexus. "Father, what is Kar-da-ma?" the boy said sounding it out carefully.

"It was the home of the Rajasa, but it was destroyed by the Gods when the Rajasa tried to invade our Realm. Now we just use it as a shortcut." He leaned in conspiratorially. "Like the one we take home from the market we don't tell your mother about." Both the children giggled.

After a moment the boy looked worried.

"What if the Rajasa see us on the Causeway?"

"The Gods locked the Rajasa in Hell long ago, son. There is nothing to be worried about."

Any further discussion was cut off when a voice boomed, "Quiet on the Causeway!" Once the noise died down to a dull murmur, he continued in a monotone voice. "Please stay to your right and don't dawdle," he said, holding up his right hand for emphasis. "Do not stand or set any objects on the guard wall as anything that falls over the side will be lost for good. Absolutely no violence or foolishness of any kind will be tolerated while on the Causeway. If you need assistance, just signal one of the Causeway guards and we will be there presently.

"When we get to the roundabout, please proceed to the right. If one of the Causeway Guards gives you an order, you will comply *immediately*. Remember, we are here to insure your safety. Please be ready to move at the fifth bell." He delivered the whole speech with almost no inflection. The Causeway Guards had a well-deserved reputation for being stern and humorless. They answered to no one but the Emperor and few were foolish enough to risk their wrath.

The guards at the Key station began rotating the dials. I could feel the pressure building in the room as the energy from the nexus was being shunted to the Gate as the first bell rang.

Clang. The runes at the base of the arch began to light up.

Clang. Excitement radiated from the boy's face like the sun's light.

Clang. A shudder ran up Dirk's spine and he looked like he was ready to lose his tea.

Clang. I put up my hood and wrapped my cloak tight, I knew what came next.

Clang.

The glowing runes running along the arch met at the top and intensified. The pearlescent moonstone that filled in the arch shimmered for a moment. Then it was simply gone. I turned my face aside as a blast of warm wind blew through the gate with gale force for a few seconds then subsided to a strong gust. Cloaks blew about and hats flew off. Pale purple light now bathed the chamber. The winds carried with them the distinctive smell of Kardama that is unlike anything in our Realm. The scent is sharp and sterile and, while not particularly unpleasant, it is oddly unsettling.

Four Causeway Guards started through the gate at a brisk march and the column filed in behind them. My entourage and I passed through the arch and into the Realm of Kardama. The Paska boy walked beside us in the same wide-eyed wonder I'm sure I had on my first stroll across the Causeway. Soft purple light, which originated from no obvious source, seemed to come from every direction while bits of debris and dust "fell" across our range of view with no obvious pattern, as if each item chose which way gravity would work on it. Every now and then something recognizable such as a bone would come into view, but mostly it was just rocks and dust, hardly anything larger than a helmet.

Then there was the wind. It whipped this way and that like a fickle cat. Sometimes it was as a gentle breeze, sometimes as a strong gust, though the magic worked into the bricks prevented the worst of it and kept debris from striking the Causeway. Sometimes the sky would be clear. Other times there would be huge clouds of dust in the distance, awash with lightning strikes though no thunder could be heard.

The magic worked into every stone imposed the laws of our Realm on all who tread on them, but if one were to fall over the guard wall, as Dirk so feared, they would be subject to Kardama's alien whims. That hadn't happened in decades, though in the early days of the Causeway there were problems. Animals who try to cross often spook or go mad, and every so often people do as well. But the Causeway Guards take their jobs very seriously, and few problems had occurred in my lifetime.

We reached the roundabout in perhaps a quarter hour. The guards leading us formed up on either side of the entrance and our column flowed onto the roundabout moving to the right. There were already people coming from other gates on the huge circle but we integrated seamlessly under the watchful eye of the guards.

We continued until we saw Summervale carved into the wall in the Common tongue. With nothing else to mark our bearings, this path was identical in every way to the one we took to the roundabout and I could see how being stuck in the Causeway could be maddening.

After another quarter hour, we approached the Gate to Zenith. As we got closer I noticed a very human looking bone falling mostly horizontally across the sky. I contemplated pointing it out to Dirk and making another joke, but one glance showed me my guard was trying very hard to maintain his composure and torturing him further would just be cruel, so I bit my tongue. We emerged from Kardama into a Gateroom that looked quite similar to the one in Imperiam, save that it was gilded in the blue and silver of house Arga instead of imperial purple.

We followed the stream of people through the Gateroom up the stairs and into the courtyard where another diligent set of Causeway guards took a record of everyone's arrival to make sure no one had managed to get left in Kardama.

Zenith was several hundred miles southeast of White Harbor, along the coast and apparently spring had already taken hold. The wet salty air was much warmer than in Imperia, but the clouds threatened the kind of rain that so often drenched the city in the morning only to disappear by midday.

A Causeway guard carrying a tablet waved us by as we approached. "Welcome back to Zenith, m'lady," he said, making notations. "There's a carriage waiting for you."

"Oh, thank you," I said a bit surprised. The guard made a stiff salute as he turned to the people behind us. Autumn raised her eyebrow at me in question and I simply shrugged. As we headed out onto the streets of Zenith, I glanced around for the carriage. The streets were much narrower than in White Harbor, making them seem busier. Dirk was the first to spot the blue and silver carriage at the end of the block.

The ominous clouds finally made good on their threat and burst into a drenching shower. I pulled up the hood of my cloak and we quickened our pace as much as the crowded street would allow. I was about to enter the carriage when a voice from within caught me off guard. "There you are, little Otter."

"Lucius?" My brother stepped out of the carriage and swept me up in a great embrace, twirling me about like a child, heedless of rain or decorum. I giggled like a fool. "How long have you been back?" I asked when he finally set me down.

"Just a few weeks. Father thought it best I be close to home in case we go to war and I'm called back into service." He held me at arm's length, looking me over. "By the Gods, you're so thin. Aren't they feeding you in White Harbor?" he said with a mischievous grin, his lilac eyes twinkling.

"Now and then," I said, ignoring the jab and looking him over as well. I'd barely seen my twin since he went into service with the Imperial Navy just over two years before and I hardly recognized him. His tenure in the navy had left him lean and hale. His skin, which used to be as pale as mine, was tanned a rich copper. His once-red hair was bleached strawberry blond by the sun and had grown nearly past his jawline, far longer than was fashionable for a noble. I ran my fingers through his dripping locks. "Have they no barbers in Zenith anymore?"

He stroked his neatly trimmed mustache and goatee, also out of fashion for a noble, and said, "The women in port find it fetching." I rolled my eyes at that and he gave a roguish grin. "Autumn what do you think?" he said, batting those lilac eyes that drove women mad.

"I…um…think it looks…I mean…" Autumn said blushing all the way to her ears.

"As I said." Lucius grinned wolfishly. Then he gestured toward the door. "Let's get out of this rain before you catch cold and Father blames me for it."

"Agreed," I said, stepping up into the carriage.

Autumn filed in behind me and Lucius barked a few orders before climbing in himself. "We'll head to the palace to grab horses for your guards and be off to the estate," Lucius said. "With any luck, we'll make it before dinner. Why are you here anyway?"

I was so excited at seeing my brother, the weight I'd been carrying in my gut was temporarily gone. "There will be plenty of time for that later. What have you been doing since you finished your service?"

"Father and Uncle Hadrian have me sailing with the House merchant ships, learning the particulars of the business. They want me to take over managing part of the fleet in a few years." Pride beamed on his face. My brother had never been very good at hiding his emotions, at least not from me.

"Lucius, that's wonderful! Look at you, all respectable." My brother had a well-earned reputation for being a bit of a rabble-rouser. At one point or another he'd been kicked out of half the taverns and brothels in White Harbor. "The House will be conspiring to arrange a marriage for you in no time," I said with a smug smile.

"Hopefully not for a while," he said with a sigh.

It was so nice to see Lucius again, we'd always been very close. Our other brother Tullias was ten years older and had always been somewhat distant from us. He had a very serious demeanor and never had "time to waste with childish things". Lucius and I, however, had plenty of time to waste on such endeavors. We'd nearly driven our parents and servants mad with our shenanigans.

We arrived at the palace grounds, larger and more splendid than the estate in Imperia. The palace itself was huge, with grand sweeping architecture, the oldest parts of which were built before even the founding of the Republic. It was beautiful and amazing, but in a distant way. It had never really felt homey to me.

"Give me a moment to make sure everything's in order then we'll head out," he said, stepping out of the carriage. I glanced out the window to see the rain had all but stopped, which was good because flooding could sometimes be a problem. Zenith had been built upon the numerous small islands that dotted the vast lagoon so that dozens of small canals crisscrossed the city. If the narrow streets were clogged with people it was often faster simply to take a boat to your destination, though thankfully that wasn't the case today.

Zenith wasn't as large as Imperia, nor as organized or ordered, but it had a wistful, almost ethereal quality to it. Gliding down the smooth canals between the colorful buildings on a pretty day made the city seem like a midsummer dream.

Zenith was the capital of Summervale, the southern most of the five states that made up Zura proper. The states had been independent kingdoms before coming together to form the Republic, and the Houses that ruled them before still governed them now, due to a series of compromises over the years. Now, the Senate and the Emperor make the laws, but the Noble Houses are responsible for enforcing them, and governing their states.

Lucius climbed back into the carriage, holding up a skin of wine and said, "This should aid us in passing the time." It did. We drank and chatted about the past few years and laughed at old stories. It was wonderful. By the time we reached the estate my spirits had undergone a much needed lift.

The sun was setting over the orchard when we arrived at the villa and the first pears of the season were barely visible on the branches. The smells of the villa washed over me, bringing with them memories of my childhood. It seemed like yesterday my mother stood in the foyer chiding me for getting my dress dirty.

Autumn's voice broke my reverie. "I'll go see to your room, Mistress. Shall I take your bag?"

"Yes, thank you," I said handing her my endless bag as she headed down one of the servant corridors.

"Too bad there's blood between us," Lucius said as Autumn rounded the corner.

"Like that's ever stopped you before," I said, raising an eyebrow.

Lucien covered his mouth in mock shock. "I have no idea what you mean, dear Otter."

"Hm, what about Flavianna Paska?"

"She's a second cousin and you have no proof of anything. Anyway you're one to talk, what about cousin Maximus?"

"He'a a *fourth* cousin and all we did was kiss. How do you even remember that? I was fifteen!"

"I was blessed with a sharp mind, and you were fourteen actually." It was his turn to raise an eyebrow and cast and accusatory glance. "And I heard that's not all he did with his mouth."

"Hardly. He was a good kisser though. Eager to please, as well. I imagine he would have been quite good at—"

"*Ugh*, enough!" Lucius said, dramatically covering his eyes. "I'm going to have to butcher a hog to get that image out of my mind."

One of the servants came to take our cloaks and I asked, "Is Father in the villa?"

"He and Master Tullias are in the atrium, I believe."

Lucius and I wove our way down the halls toward the atrium. Other than a few new frescos, it was exactly as I remembered it growing up. We rounded the hallway to find our father and eldest brother deep in conversation, no doubt over some boring detail regarding the management of the estate. My father may not have had a head for politics but he was brilliant with business. They were of similar height and shared the same light brown hair and deep purple eyes. Tullias was every bit the image of our father Gias, and given that Zuran nobles were slow to show their age, they looked more like brothers than father and son.

"Samara." Tullias inclined his head as he took note of my presence, which was about as much emotion as he ever showed.

"Brother," I said, adding, "You look well."

"Daughter!" Father said, closing the distance between us and taking me in his arms, then pushing me at arm's length like Lucius had. "Gods, but you show more of your mother's beauty every time I lay eyes on you." Which of course made me melt. "Has your research born fruit?"

The weight in the pit of my stomach had returned but I swallowed it down and forced myself to remain composed. I took a deep breath and filled them in on the road my research had taken.

Father spoke when I finished. "So your plan is to seek out one of these... Vija?"

"Yes. It's either that or book passage to Azanta."

Lucius chuckled. "You don't do things by half do you, Otter?"

Father shook his head in response. "She is her mother's daughter."

"How do you plan to get in contact with this Vija?" Tullias asked reasonably.

"I'll have to hire a Manu guide, I suppose."

Tullias snorted. "Have you any idea where to find one?"

"I might be able to help with that actually," Lucius interjected, stroking his unfashionable goatee. "If I'm not mistaken, Ganicus bought his prize racing horse from a Manu trader. He might at least be able to point you in the right direction."

"That seems as promising a place to start as any," I said. "Father, what do you think?"

My father looked skeptical. Ganicus Uttara had been a large factor in my brother getting thrown out of so many establishments. At length he nodded. "That seems reasonable."

"I'll send a courier first thing in the morning," Lucius said as he threw back the last of his brandy. "Why is being able so summon this demon such a big deal anyway?"

"Do you jest? Think of the honor it would bring." *Which might give me some say in who I marry...*

"Otter, I understand why *you're* doing it," Lucius said. "I don't get why being able to summon one more demon is so important in the first place. Is the interest purely academic?"

"It's not just 'one more demon'," I said. A glance at my father and Tullias told me they might not fully understand either. I suppose that wasn't too suprising. Few beyond master mages had ever had any dealings with the powerful demons. "Anavayas are substantially more powerful than a normal demon, easily on par with a dragon, and each of them are unique. Setukara can build a bridge or a road with his foot steps. Dra'vi can smelt metal with a glance. Who knows what Shakkar's Anavaya is capable of?"

That explanation seemed to satisfy them and we retired for the evening soon after. Autumn had prepared my old room as though I'd never left. I opened the double glass doors and stepped out on the balcony that overlooked the orchard. The cool night breeze was silk against my face, thick with the heady perfume of the pear trees. I breathed in the sweet fragrance, flush with renewed hope of finally solving my elusive puzzle. Otherwise all my time and effort would be wasted and I'd likely be married off into one of the other Houses. Also, it bothered me to leave a mystery unsolved. I just couldn't do it.

I do not idle well. When I have a goal to work toward, I have the patience of a stalking tiger. When I don't, well, I'm more like a tiger pacing in its cage. Two days of waiting for word from Ganicus was driving me slowly mad. And I, in turn, was driving the rest of the villa slowly mad. After fixing and reinforcing the spells on every magical artifact throughout the house, I was more or less run out of the villa by Tullias.

I hadn't sat astride a horse in some time and figured it would probably a good idea to practice, considering I might need to do quite a bit of ridding in the near future. At the stables, I was delighted to find Precious, the beautiful black and white mare I'd learned to ride on. She whinnied with delight and nuzzled me affectionately, surreptitiously sniffing my bag in search of any pears I might be carrying. My heart swelled. I hadn't realized I'd missed her so.

I had her saddled and went for a long ride through the estate. Precious wasn't very fast but she was sure-footed and good-natured, which was good because I was certainly out of practice. It was nice to just ride and move about with no houseguards on my heels. I took a wide circuit around the estate, avoiding the fields. The sight of House Arga slaves had always made me uneasy and brought up conflicting feelings. I returned to the stables tired and feeling sore but good. Autumn was searching for me with a look of barely contained excitement.

"Lucius received word back from Ganicus," she said as soon as I dismounted. "He said there's a party of Manu traders in Stonehaven for the Equinox Festival."

"What? We must start making preparations immediately. Where's Lucius?"

We found Lucius and my father already speaking on the subject with Koto, my father's captain of the guard. "There you are, Otter," Lucius said. "I can tell by your face you've already heard the news. We'll have to leave before first light to make it to the Causeway."

"We're discussing arrangements now," Father said. "Lucius will go with you to Stonehaven to aid you in contracting a guide. Koto and three of his men will join your houseguards for the duration of the journey."

Eight houseguards to protect me seemed a bit ridiculous. "I don't think I need to deprive you of your capt—"

"I know you're a grown woman," Father said cutting me off, "And a mage besides that, but you've never been out of the Empire before and I'll not have you march off into the wild unknown ill-prepared."

"Sursum is a territory of the Empire, it's hardly—" I started to argue

"No debate. Besides which, Koto served with the Manu in the Ipsum war. He'll be able to provide insight in dealing with them."

I knew when I'd lost a fight. "Of course, Father," I said smiling and facing to Koto. "I'd be happy to have Captain Koto's protection, as well as his insight."

"Don't worry, m'lady. I'll keep ye safe," Koto said with a short bow. He'd been a freeman who earned his citizenship coin as a centurion in the legions before coming into my father's service. Short and solid with grey hair and a neatly trimmed beard, at some point his left eye had been lost in battle earning him a ghastly scar and a magical replacement of smooth white jade to show for it. He reminded me of the rangy cat that slept in the barn when I was a child.

With that settled, we hashed out the remaining details and broke to make preparations. As I stared to walk away, my father caught my arm and pulled me close. "Keep your wits about you and come back to me safe," he whispered.

"Father, I'll be fine. You're acting as if I'm marching off to war."

"I know I'm being silly. I just couldn't bear to lose you like I lost…" Dark clouds rolled across his features and he trailed off unable to finish. It hurt to see how much the loss of my mother still pained him, I stood on my toes and kissed his cheek.

"I'll be back before you even begin to miss me."

"That's a lie," he said with a smile. "I miss you already. Now go, you have much to do in little time."

The next morning saw us on the road well before dawn. Lucius and Autumn both dozed in the carriage but I was far too anxious to sleep. There were no legions stretched around the block this time so the Causeway was much less crowded, though Dirk was no less pale than before. We made our trek through Kardama to another identical Gateroom, save this one was clad in the grey and black of house Uttara.

Stonehaven was the capital of Whitereach, Zura's northern-most state, and it was still cold here. Colder even than it had been in White Harbor. I gazed up at the breath-taking snow-capped mountains towering above and I wrapped my cloak tighter before making my way onto the street with my ridiculous ten person entourage.

"Wasn't Ganicus supposed to meet us here?" I said.

"He'll be here. I'm sure he just lost track of time." Lucius shrugged not looking concerned.

"That sounds like Ganicus," I huffed. "The fastest person in the Empire on a chariot and yet he can't be anywhere on time."

"His wife says exactly the same thing," he chuckled.

"What? Ganicus is *married*?" I said in disbelief.

"Last summer. House Uttara thought it might settle him down a bit."

"Has it?"

"Not that I've noticed."

"So he still…"

"Enjoys the company of many woman? Oh, yes. His wife doesn't seem to mind. Of course, they say she appreciates a feminine touch as well," he said, stroking his goatee.

"Hmm, well I suppose it's a good match then."

After a quarter hour of waiting, I was ready to start walking when a House Uttara carriage pulled up, flanked by houseguards. Before it even came to a stop Ganicus leapt out with the careless grace of a leopard, and swept Lucius up in one of those quick violent embraces that men share. He wore breeches of soft doeskin and a matching doublet covered with an overcoat and ridiculous wide-brimmed hat with one side folded up and two enormous ostrich feathers sticking out, all died the gray and black of his House. The stark Uttara colors suited him well. "Gods, Lucius, don't they have barbers in Summervale?"

"They would weep to cut my lovely locks and I haven't the heart to torture them."

"It's your face their weeping at, Cousin."

"Many weep before the beauty of a perfect work of art," Lucius said dramatically.

I rolled my eyes.

"Ah I see, but how does that explain why women laugh when they see you naked?" Ganicus countered with a grin.

Having no idea how long their banter would go on I cleared my throat loudly.

"Cousin," Ganicus said, removing his hat and dropping into a deep flourishing bow, ostrich feather dragging the ground. It caught me off guard. Even if we were technically cousins, the nobles of differing Houses rarely addressed each other as such. Then again, Ganicus had never cared much for convention. "You've grown as beautiful as the setting sun."

I rolled my eyes again at his melodramatic performance. "Not the rising sun?" I teased.

"I wouldn't know. I'm never awake to see it, except occasionally from the other side," he said smiling with his full lips. Ganicus had one of those faces that straddled the fence between handsome and pretty, set off by sapphire eyes and coarse jet black hair, so unlike the snowy silk shared my most of his house. "Unfortunately, I cannot call you generous."

"Why is that?" I asked waiting for the joke.

"Because you took all the beauty for yourself and left none for poor Lucius," he said with a wry smile.

Lucius drew in a breath, no doubt to come back with some clever retort, but I cut him off. "Perhaps we should be off? Unless the plan is to cross wit in the street for the rest of the day?" Knowing Lucius and Ganicus that might be a real possibility.

"Of course, where are my manners? We'll return to the castle and drink mead while a feast is prepared—"

Lucius must have seen my face because he interjected. "I believe Samara is anxious to meet with this Manu merchant. Perhaps we could attend to that first?"

"As you wish. Let us away," he said with seeming ambivalence, gesturing toward his carriage. He glanced over his shoulder at our entourage. "Think you brought enough guards?" he asked Lucius.

"To protect me from bandits yes, but for protection from the adoring crowds of women I'm constantly beset by, perhaps I'm a bit short."

Gods, this was going to be a long day.

In the carriage there was a pretty blond servant wearing a revealing dress I would have frozen to death in, holding a gilded goblet of mead Ganicus would occasionally reach for. We headed down the grid-like streets of Stonehaven toward the north market, passing their famed hot springs. The city was blocky and squared off, very plain by the standard of the other great cities.

"What do you need a Manu guide for anyway?" Ganicus asked idly.

Judging Ganicus might be less than discreet, I said simply, "I'm working on a project for the Academy and I'm hoping one of the Manu mystics can help me with it."

"Oh," he replied, seeming bored with my answer.

"What can you tell me of them?"

"They breed amazing horses. Once a season or so they come to trade them along with draa."

"*Draa?*"

"It's a cotton fabric they weave that's almost as strong as silk. They sell it mostly to sail makers." He took a long gulp of mead. "They're not bad folk, for tree-dwelling barbarians."

I raised my brows. "Tree dwelling?"

"So I'm told," he shrugged. "Anyway, Darian's a decent fellow. He's even got some Zuran blood. I buy all my horses from him. Shrewd businessman though." He smiled. "I hope you brought plenty of coin."

"Damn," Lucius said, "I was hoping for some backwoods simpleton we could throw a few silver at."

"Let go of that dream," Ganicus chuckled, handing his goblet back to the servant and idly stroking her hair as one might a cat. I would have thought it demeaning but she rather seemed to enjoy it. "I paid him a small fortune for my champion stallion. The horse is worth every copper though."

"He was *brilliant* in Shimmer," Lucius said.

Ganicus brightened. "You should have seen him at Goldmarch. I was down four lengths in the first leg—"

As the boys talked racing, I glanced out the window. The streets were crowded with festival goers. Stonehaven was situated in a valley next to the only pass through the mountains for a hundred miles, so as the pass cleared of snow, thousands made their way to the city to trade or simply revel in the festivities. At the edge of the market we were forced out of the carriage by the thick crowds on the street and continued on foot.

As the guards formed up around us, I asked Koto, "Anything you can tell me about the Manu that might be useful?"

Koto absently scratched the scar beneath his jade eye as he thought. "Aye. They may not be Zuran, but don't think 'em simple. The ones I knew in the war were well-learned and clever."

The air was thick with the smell of food and there were vendors and craftsman of all types while musicians, jugglers, and tumblers plied their trade in hopes of a few coins. We cut our way through the crowd bound toward the northeastern area of the market. Here the air hung heavy with the scent of beasts and dung. Livestock of all types were corralled, being shown, or auctioned off. Cows, goats, sheep, oxen, pigs and yet more exotic fare such as camels and even a few elephants were present.

"There's some of his folk," Ganicus said, gesturing. "They should be able to point us toward Darian."

The man stood with his children selling bolts of undyed fabric. His light brown skin was weathered and his face showed deep lines. His black hair was tied in a thick braid that fell down his back. He wore a tan shirt with carved wooden buttons and matching breeches with boots that came to the knee. His teenaged daughters shared his pallor and clear mahogany eyes. They both wore simple brown dresses with red foxes skillfully embroidered their lapels.

As we approached, he bowed and spoke in the common tongue with a thick but not unpleasant accent. "Good day, m'lords and ladies. Might I interest you in some draa?" I ran the fabric through my fingers. It was nearly as smooth as polished silk and soft as one might think a cloud.

"Not today, I'm looking for Darian," said Ganicus.

"He's set up on the other side of the hippodrome, m'lord."

"Gratitude," Ganicus said.

One of the daughters leaned over and said something to her father in a sing-songy tongue. "Don't be shy. Tell her yourself," said the man, but the girl flushed and shook her head. "She says you have beautiful eyes."

"Thank you," I said and the girl blushed even deeper. *Oh, she and Dirk would be perfect for each other.*

Past the hippodrome there were several temporary corrals and pens set up for horses. We made our way toward a group of about half a dozen Manu. Koto leaned in close. "I recognize them in the coats, m'lady, they're Rangers. They made up the auxiliary light cavalry in the war. Ye'll never see better archers from the saddle."

At a distance, they all looked the similar to the draa trader, if a bit younger. They had matching forest green hooded surcoats with knot-work tooled down the lapels and brown draa shirts and breeches underneath. Twin daggers crossed at their lower backs with a large curved knife almost the size of a short sword on their left hip, and they all carried bows slung over their shoulder.

As we neared, one who had been talking to a customer turned to face us. He was a shade lighter than his companions and his hair was deep wavy chestnut with wooden beads and feather braided in. His face held the same high cheek bones as the others but he sported a short stubbly beard where his companions were clean shaven. The most striking difference were his eyes. Instead of mahogany brown, they were a piercing blue-green with an inner ring of gold. He was actually rather handsome, for a barbarian. He bowed and spoke with hardly any accent, "Well met, m'lord Ganicus. Come to buy another horse?"

Chapter Four
Darian

I almost had the short grouchy farmer sold on a young draft horse when Cayman tapped me on the shoulder and said, "Hey, here comes your best customer." I glanced up to see Ganicus Uttara approach. He was leading a troupe wearing blue and silver. I searched my memory but failed to recall what House that signified, though their eyes told me they were nobles. I nodded to Cayman and turned back to my customer, who was staring into the mouth of the patient gelding.

"Please, forgive me," I said to the farmer. "I have to go tend to another customer, but my friend here will answer any more questions you have." He grumbled something and continued prodding the beast as I turned to give Ganicus all of my attention. Zuran nobles were like infants. When they were happy, they were a joy to know, but when they weren't happy, they made everyone else miserable. And like infants, they required constant attention to *keep* them happy.

I gave the deep formal bow that Zuran nobles expected. "Well met, m'lord Ganicus. Come to buy another horse?"

"Not today. We have other business to discuss," he said. "These are my cousins, Lord Lucius Arga and Initiate Mage Lady Samara Arga."

The young man had lilac eyes, light red hair, and the surefooted gait of a sailor, but it was the woman who caught my eye. She was beautiful. Tall and willowy with rich strawberry hair and fair skin set off by a smattering of freckles across her nose and cheeks. But it was her eyes that caught me. They were the pale, pale blue of arctic ice.

A brown-haired woman followed her. She had the eyes of a noble but the look of a servant, and they trailed a dozen or so guards behind them. Not sure what the protocol was, I gave another deep bow and said, "Well met. I'm Darian Wahya of Vana."

"Well met, Darian," said the lilac-eyed lord. "We'd like to hire your services as a guide."

That took me aback. "I've never acted as a guide before but I'd be willing to discuss it, m'lord. Where do you wish to go?"

The Arga nobles shared a glance before the pretty red-head spoke. "I'd like for you to guide me to a Vija."

What would a mage want with a Vija?

A knot formed in the pit of my stomach. My apprehension must have shown on my face because Lilac Eyes quickly added, "We're willing to pay you fifty gold to guide Lady Samara and see her returned safely."

That was a tidy sum of money, but I wasn't sure the Gura would allow it. Mages had a reputation for trifling with things best left alone. "I'm…not sure I'll be able to do that."

"Please," said the woman. "It's very important to me."

"Sixty gold then," said Lilac Eyes.

"M'lady, what do you seek from the Vija?" I asked, staring into those crystal eyes.

She thought for a moment and said, "Knowledge."

I could hear only truth in her voice. Either she'd found some clever magic that protected her from Azava's gift or she was telling the truth.

"Only knowledge?"

"Yes." Again I could detect no lie.

"Knowledge that will not be used for war or harm?" I asked trying to parse out her intentions.

She considered this for a moment then said simply, "All knowledge may be used for harm, but that is not my goal."

She spoke the truth again. I could think of no other question to ask without risking offense. I fidgeted with the bowstring across my chest as I weighed the decision.

At my hesitation the lord said, "Seventy-five gold and that's as high as I'll go. I'm sure if you're not willing to do it, we can find someone else who will." For that much coin they certainly could. Or simply set out on their own if they could find no Manu to guide them.

"M'lord, you mistake my hesitation. The sum is agreeable," I said, though part of me wondered how much higher he might have gone. "I can guide you to a Vija, but the Gura, the leader of my village, would have to allow it. And even if the Gura allows it, the Vija may still choose not to help."

The Arga nobles shared a look, then she nodded and Lilac Eyes continued. "I understand. If Lady Samara is unable to see the Vija you will still be paid half for your effort."

"That's agreeable," I said.

The pretty mage seemed relieved. "How long will the journey take?"

"If the weather holds, it will take perhaps ten days to reach my village, then a day to resupply, and two or three more to reach the Vija."

"When can we leave?"

"Our caravan will be ready the day after tomorrow. Shall we meet outside the north gate an hour after dawn, two days hence?"

"Very well," she said, seeming satisfied.

"Splendid!" Ganicus said seeming pleased with himself. "Now we can go drink. Farewell, Darian."

"I'll see you two days hence," the woman said.

"Two days hence, m'lady."

She shot one last glance over her shoulder as she departed with her entourage.

Cayman came back over to me having taken the surly farmers money. "Seventy-five gold? You must be touched by Varga. It's the only explanation for how you can peel those tight nobles away from so much coin."

"Did you see the red-haired woman's eyes?"

"You can have her. I'll take the busty auburn-haired one."

"None of us will 'have' either of them. An unhappy noble woman could bring trouble down on all our heads."

"No woman leaves my bed unhappy," he said with a wink.

I shot him an annoyed glance. "No. That's final. Trust me, the last thing you want is to be tasked with keeping a Zuran noble happy."

Chapter Five
Samara

I felt lighter as we made our way through the crowd toward the carriage. Having a definite plan gave me a sense of purpose. After we'd gotten out of earshot, Ganicus slapped Lucius on the back with a chuckle. "I can't believe he got you up to seventy-five gold. Didn't I tell you? All that hesitation was just to drive the price up and you walked right into it." Lucius grumbled an agreement.

"Two days isn't much time to prepare." Lucius said while he absently stroked his goatee, "We'll have to borrow an Arga carriage and some horses. Who do we know that lives in Stonehaven, Otter?"

I wracked my brain. "Great uncle Prater could probably spare a carriage but I doubt he has enough horses."

"Hmm…I guess we'll have to buy them then." Lucius had a far off look and I could see the abacus moving in his head. "We'll just have to draw some more funds from the bank."

"It doesn't make any sense to go buy horses," Ganicus interrupted. "I'll just lend you some of mine."

"That's not necessary—" I started to say when Ganicus cut me off.

"Please, we're cousins. Anyway, now that I've offered, it would be rude to refuse," he said with a smile and nonchalant shrug

I was truly touched by Ganicus's gesture and it made me ashamed to have judged him so harshly in the past. "Thank you, Cousin."

"Pshh," Ganicus waved a dismissive hand. "Now that we're done with that boring nonsense, we can get down to the important business of drinking and foolishness," he said throwing his arm around Lucius.

Upon arriving at the castle, I was introduced to Ganicus's wife Helen, whom I found funny and charming. She was tall and pretty with auburn hair and the amber eyes common to House Vima. She insisted on giving me a tour of the castle while her husband and Lucius were left to find Gods know what mischief.

Castle Uttara could hardly be called beautiful but it was striking, and it had large enclosed garden with exotic animals ranging from large, flightless tropical birds to small deer that hardly came up to my knee. Its best feature by far were the fountains and pools throughout the interior, warming the castle with the beautiful turquoise water of the hot springs bubbling beneath Stonehaven.

The next day was a flurry of activity. Lucius and Harold finished making the arrangements for the journey, then we joined several members of House Uttara on a balcony overlooking the main forum for the Equinox Festival. There was a parade that twisted its way through the streets, bearing a huge marble statue of Azava, God of the sun, wielding a sword in one hand and a golden trumpet in the other.

Once back at the castle I dismissed my guards for the evening, over Koto's protest, so that they could take place in the festivities. House Uttara had prepared a lavish feast and the honey mead Stonehaven was famous for flowed freely. The mead was sweet with light fruit notes and no burn of alcohol whatsoever, a dangerous combination. I went from enjoying the feast to being naked in a huge spring-fed bath with two dozen members of House Uttara and no real understanding as to how I got there. Some distant part of me was aware of Helen's gaze falling heavily upon my naked body and I thought it wise to go to bed before I further embarrassed myself. I had no idea where Autumn was, nor my clothes, but I found a robe and somehow made my way through the labyrinthine castle to my guest quarters before blackness overtook me.

I awoke to Autumn's cheerful singing and a badger trying to claw its way out of my head. "Good morning, Mistress. It's time to wake up."

"Ugh," I managed to reply.

"You must rise if we're to make it on time."

"Hmmm," I whimpered.

"Did you have an enjoyable evening?"

"Yeah, enjoyable," I said rubbing my temple with the heel of my hand. "Where did you go anyway?"

"I was at the festival with Dirk. Don't you remember insisting I leave and enjoy myself?" Autumn asked with a hint of concern.

"I don't remember much of anything. Cursed mead," I said taking an experimental sip of cool water. It seemed like it might stay down. "I don't suppose you've located my dress from last night?" I took a quick inventory. I'd somehow managed to hold on to my citizenship coin, my amulet to Tarka, and my blue jade bangle, so I guess I wasn't *completely* naked in the pool.

"The servants brought your dress up this morning. I'm sure you'll feel better after some breakfast. There serving sausage and poached eggs in the main—"

My stomach roiled and I lost what remained of last night's feast in the chamber pot. Autumn fussed like a mother hen, and with her help I managed to get cleaned up and gathered my things. She even managed to get a little dry toast down me. The only consolation I had was that Lucius looked every bit as bad as I felt.

Ganicus, on the other hand, was bright eyed and whistling. "Glad to see everyone had a good time at the festival," he said with a bright grin.

"Ugh," Lucius managed.

"Thank you for your generous hospitality," I said.

Cursed mead.

"Thank nothing of it, Cousin. Helen informs me she enjoyed your company and would love to have you back any time."

I'll bet.

"I enjoyed meeting her."

Lucius embraced me in a rough hug and said, "Be safe, Otter."

"Don't worry. I'll be fine."

Autumn and I climbed into the waiting carriage. We made our way out of the castle just as the sun peaked over the eastern wall. The carriage was a bit smaller than I was used to but at least it was well insulated. My stomach felt sour again as we bobbed over some loose cobbles. I prayed silently to Kavi, the God of roads, travelers, music, and wine. It seemed appropriate.

Just north of the gate we found a group of perhaps two dozen covered carts not unlike the vardos used by the Dezika, absent the ostentatious coloring. From the window I saw Darian break off from a group of his green-coated comrades and ride to meet us on a beautiful chestnut horse. I could make out only bit of a conversation between him and Harold, who was driving the carriage. A few minutes later Harold appeared in the window. "They're ready to leave, m'lady. We're to join the middle of the column." I nodded an assent and tried to keep down my toast. With that, my houseguards formed up around the carriage on their splendid Uttara horses and we took our place within the caravan.

———————

The Attonitus Pass was once described by a poet as 'the path of the Gods' and has been painted by countless masters because of its stunning beauty. I, however, would have to take their word for it. I spent the trip huddled under blankets, cradling my pounding head and trying not to empty the meager contents of my stomach all over the rocking carriage. Under other circumstances I would have loved to ride alongside and soak up the splendor, but as it was I held my head and tried to ignore the left back wheel squeaking every time it made a full circle. All I know is we went up and up and up, until it felt as though we were not so much taking a pass as just going right over the mountains.

By the Gods it was *cold*. It was hard to imagine that just a few days before I was riding across my father's estate in a summer dress. I considered using magic to warm myself but in my present state, I was pretty sure all I'd manage to do was set the carriage on fire.

We broke for a meal at midday and my stomach had eased enough for me to get some cheese and olives down before we started off again. Eventually we ceased ascending and leveled out. I dozed fitfully on and off until we stopped for the day perhaps an hour before sunset.

As soon as the guards informed me the tent was ready, I wrapped myself up in blankets and dashed from the relative warmth of the carriage into the freezing cold tent. I managed to keep down a bowl of broth, and Autumn and I huddled under the covers together for warmth. I could hear the Manu outside laughing and playing music as I fell asleep.

The next morning, I woke at dawn, refreshed and renewed but still cold. Thankfully the nausea and headache from the previous day had faded. A light coating of snow had dusted the camp overnight and the scene would have been quite serene if not for the wind stampeding down the pass like an elephant.

Not feeling so miserable, the second day's journey was much more pleasant, though no less cold. A thick fog had settled in making the pass dreamlike and ethereal.

At some point we started descending and the air gradually grew warmer. Soon we rolled out of the fog to a breath-taking view of the valley below. We passed below the tree line into a thick alpine forest. The road ran next to a deep gorge with a vibrant cerulean river, flush with snow melt.

We broke for the day a few hours before sunset and set up camp in a large alcove protected from the constant wind. While the camp was set up, the green-coats went to a bubbling mountain stream to return with a bounty of trout and salmon. The Manu had apparently included us in their feast without ever considering otherwise. Spiced with pepper, clove, and just a hint of cinnamon, the fish were delicious.

"Tree-dwelling barbarians they might be," I said to Autumn, "but they can certainly cook."

The next day was lovely. The sun was shining and the air was growing ever warmer as we came out of the mountains. By midday we'd cleared the pass and arrived at Ostium, a city just large enough to hold a legion garrison. The northern wall was huge, easily a hundred feet high, meant to defend the pass against invasion. As we approached the famous Portam gate that led out of Zura, my belly was filled with butterflies. This was the first time I'd ever been outside the Empire. I felt the same sense of excitement and apprehension as I had just before my first kiss.

Outside the gate was a beautiful emerald valley covered in colors. Flowers peppered the rolling hills like a painting, warm with hues of yellow and orange. The morning clouds had burned off and the bright sun shone down on the rolling hills like a blessing from Azava himself, and after two and a half days huddled in the carriage, I was ready to stretch my legs.

"It's a lovely day, I believe I'll ride for a bit," I said.

Autumn perked up. Clearly she'd been hoping I'd suggest that for a while. "I'll have our horses brought up, Mistress," she said, then leaned out the window to talk to one of the guards.

Our horses, which were being led behind the carriage, were saddled and brought up for us. I'd chosen a bay gelding from the ones Gaincus had lent us because he seemed to be the easiest to ride, though he was a tad tall for me.

We rode for a while next to the carriage while we got a feel for our new mounts. Autumn's dapple mare seemed easy enough to handle but my gelding and I were having issues. The slightest tightening of my heels set him to a canter and when I steered the reins he overcompensated. He wasn't listing to me and I was trying too hard. As a result we were mostly confusing and frustrating each other. Pretty much like all of my previous relationships.

"You'll have to use an easier hand on him, m'lady. That horse is Manu-trained," Darian said, appearing next to me seemingly out of nowhere. I tried to steer the bay closer to him but again the gelding overcompensated and we almost ran into his horse. I jerked back the other way and the horse nearly span around.

"Whoa," I said, blowing out a frustrated sigh.

"There's no need to use so much force, m'lady. The horse wants to please you. He's just trying to figure out how," Darian said.

It annoyed me that he just assumed I needed help. "I *have* ridden a horse before. I just need a moment to acquaint myself with this gelding." Part of me realized I was being petty, but that wasn't the part that won out. I was frustrated.

Frustrated that a noble of House Arga, and a mage at that, looked like a child on her first pony, and even more frustrated that I had to be shown how to control the animal by a commoner.

"Of course, m'lady," he said with the same expression Autumn had when I'd tried to re-pin my own hair.

I took a deep breath and cleared my mind the way I did before spell casting. Once I was focused I tried again. I pulled gently on the reins and the horse brought his head around, still more than I wanted but better.

"That's better, m'lady. Now watch me." He held the reigns up so I could see one in each hand. He moved his left rein perhaps a hand span and his chestnut eased toward me. Then he moved his other hand similarly and the beast returned to its original course.

I watched closely and tried to duplicate his movements exactly the way I'd learned the mudras of spellcasting. I eased very, very gently, so gently I'm sure my Precious wouldn't have noticed, but the bay altered course.

"Good, m'lady. You're a fast learner," he said. I couldn't tell if he was really encouraging me or just patronizing me. Probably both. "Now try this." He leaned forward just a bit, without giving the horse heels or any other command and his chestnut increased his pace, alert to the change in his rider's position. Then he leaned back and the horse slowed.

Again I copied his movements exactly and my bay responded the way Darian's had. I flashed him a self-satisfied grin. "As I said, I just needed a moment to acquaint myself. This horse is much more sensitive than the ones I'm used riding."

"That horse has just been taught to pay better attention. And as I said you're a fast learner, m'lady. There's no shame in taking instruction. No one is born knowing everything there is to know about horses." His mouth crept up to form a half-smile. "Except of course a Manu." And with that he galloped off toward the front of the column.

Autumn laughed. "I like him."

I shot her a sideways glance. "You don't find him a bit presumptuous and arrogant?"

"That's what I like about him," she said between giggles.

Autumn and I chatted for a while as we got to know our mounts better. The highway was ancient but well-tended as it wound through lush green foothills dotted by occasional copses of trees. Once we felt fairly comfortable with our mounts, we decided to ride the length of the column, Koto and Dirk trailing behind us like ducklings following their mother.

There were just over two dozen of the vardo-like wagons in the column

spaced out so that there were two horse lengths between them. Bringing up
the rear of the procession were ten of the guards in green surcoats. They gave
a little half bow from the saddle at our approach, as they conversed amongst
themselves in the same sing-songy tongue the draa trader's daughter had used.
Urging our horses to an easy canter on the grassy field just off the highway, we
rode for the front of the procession.

As we passed the front wagon, a hare dashed out of the brush off to the
side. Instantly one of the green-coats, Darian I realized, broke from the group
in pursuit. In terror, the hare dashed to and fro as Darian bore down on it at a
full gallop. Gods, but his chestnut was fast. I wondered absently if it was faster
than the one he'd sold to Ganicus.

Just before the hare made the tall grass, Darian drew an arrow from the
quiver on his back and fired in one quick motion. Then he drew and nocked a
second arrow, which turned out to be unnecessary. The hare was pinned to the
ground by its neck with the first arrow. As Darian casually dismounted to claim
his prize, I glanced back over my shoulder to see Dirk staring mouth agape. I
was no archer, but even I could see that was a difficult shot to make from the
back of a galloping horse.

"Our fearless housegaurd is clearly impressed," Autumn teased.

"I've never seen anything like that," Dirk said amazed.

"Close yer mouth, lad," Koto said, "I told ye they were good."

My body was not used to riding astride and it showed. When we broke for
camp that evening I was sore, tired, and smelling strongly of horse. As I collapsed
into bed after dinner that night, I was greeted by the lullaby of my guards loudly
teaching the Manu drinking songs. "I'm so tired I don't even care," I said to Autumn.

"Oh, I almost forgot. Darian gave me this for you," she said handing me a
small earthen jar.

"What is it?" I asked opening it up. It smelled slightly floral.

"It's a balm to help with the rawness."

I realized I should be thankful for the thoughtful gesture but again his
presumptuousness irked me a bit. Never the less, I slathered the stuff on before
passing out.

The salve did seem to ease the rawness, and the next day I put on long,
thick stockings, hoping it would help. As Autumn and I ate breakfast we
noticed the green-coated Manu behaving peculiarly. They were standing in lines
doing what looked like some sort of synchronized dance.

"What do you suppose that's about?" Autumn asked.

"It's how they practice their fightin'," Koto replied.

After coming to a rest, the group of Manu drew the twin daggers from their lower backs and launched into another of the dance-like performances. It didn't look like any fighting I'd ever seen.

"Well, it's nice to know that if we are attacked by militant mummers we'll be well prepared," I said. Harold laughed so hard he nearly choked on his breakfast.

After the Manu finished the dance with their daggers, they drew the huge knives they carried at their sides and launched into a new series of movements. The wicked blades were bent forward on themselves and looked somewhat like a large metal boomerang with a handle. They seemed unwieldy and impractical.

"Why don't they just use swords?" I wondered aloud.

"They're subjects of an occupied Imperial territory, m'lady," Koto said. "Only legion auxiliaries are allowed to carry swords. 'Sides, in the war I seen 'em lop off a man's head with one swipe o' them kukris." It all seemed silly to me, but Koto's respect for the Manu's prowess was not lost on me.

After breakfast I fed my gelding a few slices of pear which he greedily gobbled up. "Do you have a name?" I asked as he licked the juice from my palm with his hot tongue.

"Komala," Darian said from behind me which caused me jump.

"How do you know?" I asked.

"He told me," Darian said with a sly smile.

"So you talk to horses then?"

"Many people talk to horses. The horses just don't often listen." At my skeptical look he grinned and said, "I sold him to lord Ganicus. His name means gentle." As if to prove it Komala nuzzled Darian as he approached. *Traitor, I'm the one who fed you pears.* "Shall I help you into the saddle?" he asked.

"That's not necessary," I said as I mounted the animal, thankfully with my dignity intact.

Darian merely gave his oddly formal bow and departed.

Autumn and I rode through the morning chatting in good spirits. Farms sprung up regularly on the rolling green hills. Lazy sheep grazed the lush spring grass next to wobbly-legged lambs. Shortly after our midday meal there was a loud crack and the wagons came to an abrupt halt. Koto cast a glance at Dirk who promptly went to investigate.

When Dirk returned, he said, "It seems one of the wagons broke an axle, m'lady. They said it will probably take an hour or so to fix."

I pondered for a moment then said, "Hmm, what say we go take a look?"

Koto looked at me quizzically, scratching the scar under his jade eye. "Are ye sure, m'lady?"

I raised my brows at him. "Captain, you *do* realize that mages do more than simply blow things up?"

"Aye, of course, m'lady. Meant no disrespect," Koto said, inclining his head with a smirk.

Dirk led the way to the wagon in question, which was swarming with Manu trying to unload the cargo. Darian was among those helping and as I dismounted. "Lady Samara, I'm afraid we're going to be a bit delayed."

"Yes, I've heard. I thought I might be able to lend some aid. May I see where it's broken?"

He gave a hint of a smile, one brow raised. "I didn't realize you were a cartwright, m'lady."

I smiled back. "There's a great many things you don't know about me. Now, may I have a look?"

He gave a shrug and gestured toward a man, whom I guessed was the wagon's owner. "Over here, m'lady." He showed me around to the back of the wagon where several men were already crouched beneath. I knelt as carefully as I could, trying not to rip my dress as I slipped underneath. A young man gestured toward the broken axle as though I wouldn't have found it on my own. It was a mess alright, broken diagonally, but it didn't seem to be missing any pieces so I figured I had a fair shot at mending it evenly.

"I'm going to try to fix it," I said to the owner who gave me back a bewildered look. "I'll need everyone off the wagon. And someone should hold the horses in case they spook." The Manu looked at me like I sprouted a second head but they complied.

After everyone was out of the way I took several cleansing breaths and cleared my mind. It was an easy enough spell for me but it had been quite a while since I cast it.

I closed my eyes and focused on my breathing, drawing the energy through my chakras. Then I shaped every aspect of the spell in my mind. Slowly, I began to summon the power. Opening my eyes, I made the appropriate mudras with my hands, which began glowing a soft blue-white. Wispy tendrils of light snaked out of my palms and wrapped themselves around the broken ends of the axle, seeping into the wood and recalling its original pattern. A web of soft light formed between the sundered ends and began to draw them together. Suddenly there was a snap and the light faded to reveal the axle whole.

For a moment there was awestruck silence. Then the Manu around the cart started murmuring and arguing with each other as they jockeyed to see under the wagon. I crawled out from under the wagon and stood up, smoothing my dress. I'd thankfully managed not to rip it or get it too dirty. "It's fixed. Good as new," I said to the owner. He ducked under the wagon with several others to inspect it as though he had to see it with his own eyes.

The owner crawled out and stood with his face tight, seeming conflicted. "Thank you, m'lady. You saved us much trouble." He held his hand up for me to wait as he rummaged around in the back of the wagon for a moment. He returned with a draa scarf of deep burgundy with gold embroidery along the borders. "Please, accept gift."

"That's not necessary," I said. "It was hardly any trouble."

"Please, I insist," he said bearing the scarf toward me.

I surrendered taking the soft fabric. "It's lovely, thank you."

Both he and his son bowed deeply to me then one of the green-coats started barking orders and the crowd dispersed as everyone went about their business. As we rode back to the carriage, I leaned over to Autumn and said, "You'd think they'd never seen magic before."

"From the looks on their faces I'd say most of them haven't," she replied.

"Have they no mages where they come from?" I asked.

"Country folk," Autumn said with a shrug, as if that explained everything.

I ran the soft draa between my fingers. The scarf didn't really match my Arga blue and silver but it was lovely. Examining it I noticed the gold embroidery pattern that ran the boarders was actually tiny wolf paw prints. I wrapped the scarf around my neck luxuriating at its silky embrace.

The story of my magical axle mending spread quickly among the Manu and I saw lots of smiling faces and inquisitive stares. I had meant to ride the whole day but finally in the late afternoon I relented and returned to the carriage. I was tired, my muscles ached, and despite the thick stockings, I was chaffed in some rather sensitive areas. I applied Darian's salve liberally. Wagons I could fix, but unfortunately I had no magic for soreness.

After dinner that evening a small contingent of Manu approached our cooking fire. One of them said, "M'lady, some of traders wanted to show our appreciation for your help today, and were wondering if you and your people would care to join us for a drink?"

I hesitated. Given my recent incident with the Stonehaven mead, that sounded less than appealing. Koto leaned in and spoke softly. "It may give offense if you turn them down."

I was still apprehensive, but this was part of why Koto had come in the first place. I chose a measured response. "We're weary from the day's travels, but we'd be happy to share one drink."

He smiled and gave a short bow. "We'll over by the large fire." Then he and his companions withdrew silently back into the darkness.

The weather was cloudy and so the night was very dark. I don't know how the Manu managed to walk through the blackness without tripping over anything but I didn't trust myself not to fall on my face. I cleared my mind, called my power, and summoned some coldfire. The blue-white flame was about the size of my fist and gave off light slightly better than a torch. I set it to float a few inches above my head before we made our way toward the distant fires.

After the first night of our trip, at my urging, we'd set our tent a bit farther away from the Manu fires, as they tended to sing and play music late into the night. Several dozen Manu sat on blankets around the large fire, and at our approach, some moved to allow our group a place next to them.

One of the Manu started playing a banjo-like instrument and singing while others took up small drums and flutes to accompany him. Everyone soon joined in, singing in their melodic language. Carved wooden cups were filled from a large cask and given to us. The brew smelled strongly of alcohol. I took a tentative sip, and found the liquor was mellow with a strong oak flavor that burned all the way down to my belly.

"What do you think of the whisky, m'lady?" a smiling green-coat asked over the music.

"It's a bit stronger than I'm accustomed to," I said when I could speak again. In the Empire, undiluted spirits were generally considered common fare, fit only for sailors.

His face lit up in a grin. "That means it's good."

As the song ended, I was about to dismiss the coldfire hovering over me when I noticed everyone around me was staring at it with a look of awestruck amazement. Coldfire was one of the simplest spells. Almost every citizen of the Empire, and quite a few freemen, had at least one coldfire lantern, but these people acted like they'd never seen it before.

A boy of perhaps ten worked up the courage to approach me and said, "Aren't you worried it's going to burn your hair, m'lady?"

"No, child, it's not hot. You can touch it if you like," I said. The boy reached out tentatively with his fingertips toward the floating blue flame. Just as he was about to touch it I shouted, "Ba!" and poked him gently in the belly. The boy nearly jumped out his skin and laughter burst out all around. After he recovered, he thrust his hand into the coldfire not wanting to seem cowardly. His eyes widened and he smiled.

Everyone quieted as they watched, until finally someone asked, "What does it feel like?"

"Like caterpillars walking on my hand," he said.

I silently dismissed the coldfire and the boy jumped back afraid he'd done something wrong until he glanced down and saw me barely containing a giggle. Realizing he'd been just been teased again he grinned and said, "Thank you for letting me touch it, m'lady"

"You're welcome, child," I said as another song started up. A man with a lap harp and a clear, bell-like voice sang what sounded like a love song in the Manu tongue and I noticed Autumn surreptitiously holding Dirk's hand.

As the man finished, Darian stood up and began to play a carved wooden flute. The notes he drew from it were mournful and utterly beautiful. Memories of my mother washed over me. Her laugh. Her smell. Her gentle kiss on my forehead. A longing for her gripped me with an intensity I hadn't felt in years. When the song ended, I realized I was crying. For a moment I thought perhaps I'd had too much whisky, then I noticed several other people were crying too, some openly weeping, others shedding silent tears. I began to suspect Darian's flute was the subject of some subtle magic.

As one of the other musicians took up a rousing drinking song, I decided it was probably best if I went to bed. We slipped quietly away to our camp and I fell asleep with Darian's mournful song playing in head and dreams of my mother.

I awoke clear-headed and feeling lighter than I had in days. Unfortunately it turned out that the soreness I'd felt yesterday was mere foreshadowing of the pain to come. As I mounted my bay gelding with a grimace, I bade him give me smooth ride.

Autumn and I chatted idly throughout the morning, our progress slowed only by a herd of cattle in the road, moving with no real sense of urgency. I kept replaying the events of the previous day in my mind. Unsolved puzzles bothered me, especially when I suspected I might be missing a few pieces. I decided to have a talk with Darian.

Autumn and I rode to the front of the procession with Dirk and Koto. The Manu greeted me warmly from their wagons. Apparently my axle-fixing endeavors had thawed them to me.

At my approach, Darian said, "Is everything alright, m'lady?"

"Fine. I thought we might ride together and talk for a while."

"As you wish," he said with a curious look.

I rode next to Darian with Koto on the other side while Autumn fell back behind us, next to Dirk. "Your people have a real taste for music," I said.

"You sound surprised," he replied with a half-smile and a sideways glance.

"You seem to have a rare talent for it."

"Music is important in our culture. My first memory is of my father playing the lute."

"Where do you get your instruments from?"

"We make most of them."

"Really? May I take a look at your flute?"

He seemed puzzled at the request but shrugged, fishing the instrument out of a saddle bag and handing it to me. It was carved from redwood and had intricate, delicate designs worked into it but nothing like the kind used to enchant items. I took a deep breath, summoning my power, and shaping a spell in my mind before releasing it. My vision clouded over, becoming hazy and I knew that to Darian my eyes appeared completely black. I saw intricate threads of magic winding through my bag and jade bangle and a much simpler pattern on my citizenship coin, but nothing on the flute. Not a single thread. I released the spell and blinked a few times until my vision returned to normal. "It's lovely. I especially like the detail work on the ends." I said handing the flute to Darian who glanced at it skeptically.

"I beg your pardon, m'lady, but what did you just do?"

"Nothing," I chuckled. "I was just checking to see if it was enchanted."

His brows came together quizzically. "Why would you think that?"

I thrashed about feebly for something to say, feeling foolish. "Well, last night it seemed...I mean, the song you played..."

Now Darian chuckled. "I assure you, m'lady, there were no magical tricks. My people are merely blessed with a gift for music." I must have had a skeptical look on my face because he added. "I speak truly, m'lady. We don't believe in magic."

It was my turn to stare quizzically. "What do you mean you don't believe in magic?"

"Allow me to clarify. We don't believe in *using* magic."

"No magic at all? Not even coldboxes or firestones?"

"I'm not entirely sure what those things are, but no, we don't use any magic or enchanted items."

"By the Gods, why not?" I asked.

He snickered. "Is it so hard to believe someone would choose not to use enchanted items?"

"Perhaps for someone who never encountered them, but Ganicus told me you trade with the Empire regularly. Your people seem prosperous. Surely you have the money. I find it hard to believe that none of your folk use magic."

"It has nothing to do with money. It's against our Amani."

"Amani? I'm not familiar with that word."

Darian looked down as if in thought. "It's hard to define. Amani is our path of balance, how we maintain the favor of the Gods."

"How does using magic go against this Amani?" I asked not following.

He pursed his lips, seeming to choose his words carefully. "Our elders teach that using magic to impose our will upon the world is an act of hubris. That hubris could lead us away from our Amani, and out of the Gods' favor."

It seemed superstitious and small-minded to me. "Many people all over the world practice magic and use enchanted items. Do you believe all of them out of the favor of the Gods?"

"No, but I would not presume that they live lives of balance either. I make no claim of understanding the will of the Gods, nor would I presume to tell them not to use magic. My people merely choose not to."

I still found what Darian told me hard to believe, but it certainly explained the Manu's reaction to the simple spells I cast. When our conversation was interrupted by another green-coat I noticed with a mild shock that it was a woman. She was dressed just the same as the men except her surcoat was altered slightly to fit her better. As they conversed in their tongue I took a closer look at the other green-coats and noted another woman among them. I also realized the surcoats weren't exactly the same. They had different designs on the back that matched that of their leather and plate bracers.

After the woman rode off I said, "Forgive my ignorance, but what do the green surcoats mean?"

"It marks us as Rangers." At my blank stare he explained, "In Common, the word might be militia. We're tasked with protecting the Manu and guarding Mystewood."

"And do these symbols denote rank?" I asked pointing to the stylized wolf on his back.

"No, our family. This is the symbol of my mother's line. There's no need to mark rank among us as there is within a legion. We all know each other."

"What about your father's house?"

"The Manu are matrilineal," he said, then added with a wink, "You can't always be sure of a child's father, but one always knows who the mother is."

"I suppose you have a point." That was strange by Zuran standards but hardly unheard of. I gave him credit for knowing the word "matrilineal".

Koto chimed in, "If there's no rank, how do ye know who to follow in battle?"

"We decide among us who should lead. Usually the person with the most experience is chosen."

"So what would yer rank be if it was in the legion?" Koto asked.

"Captain, I suppose."

Koto nodded seeming satisfied with that answer. Something else peculiar

I'd noticed made its way to the front of my consciousness. "Do all of the Manu speak both Common and their native tongue?"

"As subjects of the Empire we're required to speak Common, but with each other, we speak our own language. Why do you ask?"

"I've recently come to understand that people holding on to their original language is quite rare, much to my frustration. That's part of the reason I'm seeking the Vija actually."

"The Manu is tongue more expressive, more poetic," he said. "Though we do use the Common script for writing."

"Why?"

"The same reason we use steel for arrow heads and knives. It's more efficient."

I snickered, quoting the philosopher Diocletianus, "The only thing better than inventing something new—"

"—is stealing something new," he finished. I was shocked. Diocletianus was a fairly obscure classical poet, and the only reason I knew of him was because he was required reading at the Academy. It must have shown on my face because Darian said with a wry smile, "You're surprised I've read Diocletianus?"

"No," I lied

He turned to me. "You *are* surprised. You thought me an unlettered barbarian? My people are very scholarly."

I thought perhaps we had different definitions of what was scholarly, but all I said was, "I'm sure you are."

Darian opened his mouth in mock shock. "M'lady is not such a convincing liar." I thought I was a rather good liar actually. When I started to protest he raised a hand and said, "The Manu are seekers of knowledge. When we reach Vana you'll see."

A torrent of giggles drew my attention. I looked back over my shoulder to see Autumn laughing hysterically with Dirk, who was turning a bright red and showing a rare grin. He blushed even deeper when he saw me looking. I just shook my head.

We crested a hill to see walls in the distance. "Is that Metis?" I asked.

"Yes, we have a bit of trading to do so there we'll break for the day and leave in the morning. We'll camp outside the city walls with the wagons and livestock, but there are inns within the city that you might find more comfortable."

We broke with the Rangers then and Autumn and I returned to the carriage. Metis was the first foreign city I'd ever seen, but it had been ruled by the Empire for nearly fifteen hundred years, so it hardly seemed exotic. It was a decent city I suppose, but after spending so much of my life in White Harbor and Zenith, it seemed small and dirty by comparison. The streets were muddy and crowded and the blocky brick buildings lacked character.

We arrived at the Blue Amphora, a decently sized Zuran-style inn, and I was whisked away by an overly enthusiastic elderly inn-keeper to be served wine in the cozy atrium while my guards handled the details and the luggage. After the inn-keeper finally left us, I reclined on the sofa and sighed.

"I don't think I've ever smelled so strongly," I said.

"Clearly you've forgotten the Azuchi incident, Mistress."

I had forgotten about that, actually. I'd summoned a particularly disgusting demon known as an Azuchi for one of my exams and came home reeking of sulfur and rotten meat. "That *was* pretty bad I suppose."

"You suppose? I had to scrub your hair for an hour to get the odor out, and I'm fairly certain the laundry just burned your clothes."

"Speaking of which, let's see if this establishment has a private bath."

Thankfully they did. It had only been a week or so since my last one, but it might as well have been months. It was wonderful. After the bath I collapsed into bed, a proper feather bed with soft linen sheets, with a glow I'd previously only ever had after sex. It occurred to me shortly before the warm velvety darkness claimed me that I would have done very poorly in the legions after all.

I awoke the next morning better rested and less sore than I had been in days. As my entourage rejoined the Manu outside the city Darain said, "Morning, m'lady. It would probably be safer if you stayed near your carriage in the center of the column. The road north of the city into Mystewood isn't as safe as the one we've traveled until now."

"Surely no highwaymen would attack such a well-guarded caravan?"

"Highwaymen no, m'lady, but the Zatru often send raiding parties in early spring," Darian said.

"Zatru?"

His face turned sour. "Brutal people that live in the swamps to the northeast."

"How big 'er them raiding parties?" Koto interjected.

"Rarely larger than fifty," Darian said.

"You've got barely more than two dozen Rangers, you sure that's enough?" Koto asked with an incredulous stare, his white eye gleaming.

"More than enough," Darian said turning to ride off, leaving no room for further debate.

I glanced up at the angry gray skies and decided it might be best if I rode in the carriage anyway. That decision turned out to be a wise one as the skies opened up an hour after we departed. My poor guards looked miserable, drawing their cloaks close to guard against the cold rain. The Manu, on the other, hand hardly seemed to notice. The Rangers simply pulled up the hoods on their surcoats and continued on.

Travel was slowed that day because of the rain. Truth be told, my body appreciated the respite from horseback. We stopped that evening just outside the tree line of a vast forest. The Manu circled their wagons and we made camp in the middle with the horses.

I had just about fallen asleep when Autumn rose, quiet as a barn cat, and slipped out of the tent. I rose quietly myself and peered out of the tent flap just in time to see Autumn leading Dirk by the hand into his tent.

Dirk? Really? Hmm, to each their own. At least she has someone to warm her bed. I crawled back under the covers distinctly aware of how empty and cold my cot was.

Autumn must have snuck in as quietly as she left because when I woke at first light she was back on her cot. The rain had moved on, leaving only a few cotton clouds in the sky, so I decided to ride again. Before we started out for the day I gestured to the nearby tree-line and asked Darian, "Is that Mystewood?"

"The Empire considers it such," he said, "and we patrol it, but it's not our home. The ancient part of the forest where we live is still several days journey. Remember to stay near the carriage, m'lady. We still may encounter a Zatru raiding party and we'll pass near a troublesome verge."

"Really? We've closed all the dangerous verges in Zura," I said with raised brows. "I guess having mages around can be useful sometimes, huh?"

That seemed to annoy him. "As you say," was his only reply as he rode off. I have to admit seeing Darian's feathers finally ruffled was satisfying.

We followed the ancient road into a forest that smelled of pine and cedar. Autumn was positively glowing. "You seem in a good mood this morning," I said.

"I am, Mistress."

"You look quite rested. You must have slept well."

"I slept wonderfully," she replied with remarkable composure. I had figured she would have blushed.

"Mmhmm," I said unable to keep the smile from my face, "I guess Dirk's cot is comfortable." Now she did flush the same color as my draa scarf. "You weren't as quiet as you thought."

"I wasn't the one who had trouble staying quiet. He—"

"I meant you weren't as quiet as you thought when you were *sneaking out.*" We both stared at each other for a moment then burst out in a fit of laughter. When we could breathe again I said, "Dirk? Really?"

"What's wrong with him?" she asked defensively.

"Nothing, he's adorable. I'd have just thought Harold to be more to your taste."

"Harold's married."

"He is? Really?"

"Yes, Mistress," Autumn chuckled.

"Huh. Anyway, Dirk just doesn't seem the type to strike your fancy."

"Well, it's not as though he's proposing marriage or anything," she said. "Do you disapprove because he's a houseguard?"

It might be a bit scandalous if a noble was known to be fooling about with her guards, but Ananda knew it'd hardly be the first time. As a commoner herself, there was no stigma for Autumn, however. "Hardly. I'm just surprised, is all." After a moment I added, "And perhaps a bit jealous. It's been a while since I had a good tumble in the sheets."

"Several of the Manu are quite handsome," she said with a sly grin. "And we're a long way from the gossip mills of White Harbor."

I gave her a cutting glance. "Uh, no."

"You don't find any of them attractive?"

"I find them in need of a bath."

"Perhaps, m'lady is in a mood for something sweet rather than savory?" She made a show of looking around. "I'm sure that lady green-coat would be happy to accommodate…Oww, hey!" she said as I popped her bare leg with the end of the reins.

"One more word, and I'll have you flogged," I said with a smile as I raised my brows, "by Dirk." The dreamy look on her face told me that thought had already crossed her mind.

"Perhaps Darian then?" she asked.

"Definitely not."

"You don't find him handsome?"

"I find him slightly more useful than he is vexing."

"I think he's fetching in a rustic sort of way. You wouldn't kiss those full lips?"

"I'd kiss his horse first."

"He does have a pretty horse. It'd still be the most action you've had in some time." Autumn let loose another squeal as I popped her with the reins again.

Chapter Six
Darian

"She's every bit the spoiled noble I thought she would be," I said. "She wouldn't even get out of her carriage for the first two days. And when she did, it was as if she'd never been on a horse before. I tried to give her a bit of advice and she nearly bit my head off."

"Must have bothered her taking direction from a 'barbarian'," Cayman said. "Still she's pretty handy to have around. That business with the axle was impressive."

"Mmmm, mages," I grumbled. "They're useful until they blow something up."

"That can be useful too, under the right circumstances."

I turned in the saddle to face Cayman. "Well, aren't we feeling philosophical today? At least you've managed to keep your hands off the busty noble."

"I'm not certain she's actually a noble, but it's no matter. Ananda's turned her golden eyes toward the awkward black-haired guard."

"The one who was so bad at dice?"

Cayman smiled. "The very one."

"Hmm, if there's anyone who needs the touch of a woman, it's that one. Maybe now he'll manage a smile every now and then."

"We can only hope it doesn't improve his dice game," Cayman said patting his pouch.

"Truly," I replied with a grin.

"It's not as though you need his coin. You've got seventy-five gold coming to you on top of what you made off the horses."

"Pay equal to the risk I'm taking."

Cayman laughed. "Escorting two beautiful women, with eight guards between them, through friendly territory? Sign me up for that risk any day."

I gave him an annoyed glance. "If either of those women gain a scratch on them, I'm likely to end up nailed to a Zuran cross along the Via Invictus."

"Only you could find fault with such a task, Darian. It's not as though you're guiding her through the gates of Hell. She's a mage. See the aforementioned blow-things-up statement."

"She's also arrogant. Arrogance leads to unnecessary risks."

Cayman gazed at me hard, brows raised.

"Don't say it," I warned.

"You know, now that I think about it you're right. It is a dangerous job, and more profitable than fighting a Varaha by yourself."

I took a halfhearted swing at him with my flute, which he easily avoided, then said, "By the Gods, you're like a bitter old crone. Don't you ever let anything go?"

"Not so far, but I'm still young. It might happen someday."

"I pity whatever woman you finally con into marrying you."

He let out a dramatic sigh saying, "Well, your sister keeps begging me, but I've already told her I'm not ready to settle down."

This time I took a real swing at him with my flute but he was expecting it and narrowly dodged. I heard hooves clopping on stone and looked up to see Sava galloping toward me with another Ranger. She brushed her hood back as she approached and said, "Looks like the extra scouts were a good call. There's a raiding party of three or four dozen Zatru ahead."

"We could beat the bush," said Cayman. "Ride up full force with most of the Rangers and make a show of searching for the swamp-turds."

"That usually scares them off the road. Then we could come back with a bigger force after the caravan's home," Sava offered.

"It would probably work, but there's no telling where they might go before we found them again. They could hit one of the smaller villages," I said, scratching my stubble and weighing the options.

"You could always go fight them all by yourself." Cayman said.

"I was thinking of offering you as a hostage but you'd be worthless to them," I said. "No one would pay your ransom."

"Oh, come now, I'm sure your sister—"

Sava cut him off. "If you two could stop bickering like an old married couple, perhaps we could return to the matter at hand?"

"I trust none of the scouts were noticed?" I said.

Sava stared hard at me with a level gaze. "Of course not."

"Well then," I said glancing down the road trying to remember the terrain, "I think I have an idea that might end their raiding for the season. Do you remember a few years ago outside of Charro?"

Chapter Seven
Samara

The Manu in the caravan seemed tense. They were talking among themselves in quick musical bursts and several of the merchants on the wagons produced bows. I was just about to ask Koto if he knew what was going on when Darian came riding up with several of his fellow green-coats.

"What's the matter?" Koto asked.

"Our scouts found a Zatru raiding party ahead. We're going to go drive them off. There's probably no reason for concern, but Lady Samara would be safer in the carriage."

"Are we stopping the caravan?" Koto asked.

Darian shook his head. "The safest thing is to keep it moving. We'll leave a few Rangers behind as a precaution, but the Zatru will likely just move on. They're looking for easy prey, not a heavily guarded caravan."

Koto said, "He's right, m'lady. Ye should take shelter in the carriage just in case."

Part of me wanted to argue to stay astride my horse and prove I could handle myself. I was a mage after all, but the more reasonable part of me realized they were right. And one glance at Autumn told me she definitely wanted in the carriage. "If that's what you think is best, Captain," I said, then faced Darian. "Irin keep you and your people safe."

He inclined his head at me before taking off toward the front of the column, followed shortly by the rearguard contingent of green-coats.

Once in the carriage Autumn seemed more secure while I felt strangely vulnerable not being in control. There was a noticeable change in my entourage. They were well-trained guards of House Arga and every one of them had served in the legions, but there had been an easiness about them on the road up to this point. It was gone now. In its place was a sharpness I'd rarely witnessed. As Dirk loaded his crossbow I caught a glimpse of what Autumn must see in him. Gone was the awkward shy boy, and in his place a soldier whose duty it was to keep us safe. All my life houseguards had been present in the background, glorified servants who drove carriages, and carried bags, and held doors. For the first time I appreciated the fact that my guards were there for one real purpose: to protect me, to sacrifice their life for me if necessary.

As Autumn huddled in the middle of the carriage nervously fidgeting, I moved restlessly from one window to the other, searching the tree line where I spotted a half dozen or so green-coats spaced out along the column in alert vigil. In some places, cedars crowded the road making it impossible to see more than a few feet. In others pines made room for each other so that a legion could have marched easily through them.

After about an hour of tense waiting and nothing happening, I began to relax and I settled back into my seat. Darian was probably right. The green-coats would drive off the Zatru before they ever laid eyes on the caravan. I had to admit part of me was relieved, but part of me was disappointed as well. I'd never been near a real battle of any sort and it would have made a great story to tell in White Harbor.

A cry rang out from one of the green-coats on the left side of the column that then echoed down the rest of the caravan. I flung myself across the carriage to the window. Among the roomy pines there was a thick copse of cedars about a hundred yards off the road. Perhaps two score of the Zatru broke through the cedars and charged toward the caravan, letting loose echoing war cries.

They were as terrifying and savage has my childhood idea of barbarians. Clad in skins and furs, some only in a loin cloth, their faces and bodies were painted various shades of green and brown. Some wielded crude axes or hammers and carried small wooden shields. Others carried spears and hollow tubes that must have been blow guns. Still others carried a small wooden block with a handle, loaded with an object that looked like a cross between a spear and an arrow. Something danced at the edge of my vision between the caravan and the approaching horde but the bloodcurdling battle cry of the savages drew my attention from it.

The Zatru must have eluded Darian's green-coats somehow and there were only a half dozen guarding the wagons, not counting my houseguards. The merchants in the caravan could hold them off for a time but they weren't soldiers. We were going to be overrun. I had to find a way to buy time for Darian's force come to our aid. Judging by the sweeping line of barbarians I had only enough time to cast one or two spells. I might be able to do some damage to them, but I certainly couldn't take out all forty warriors spread out among the pines. However, I might be able to give the caravan a measure of protection, at least against the spears and blow guns.

I drew in a deep breath, gathered my power, and began shaping the spell in my mind. I released the spell, gesturing with a mudra just off the road. A wall of icy wind with the strength of a hurricane stampeded down the length of the column beside the highway. I figured it would be enough to turn any spear, or certainly any blow dart, and it might give the savages pause before they ran headlong into the freezing torrent. I could also maintain that spell with relative ease while I cast others. We were about to see what a bolt of lightning would do for their morale. If that didn't work I'd have to resort to using the jade bangle, which I was loathe to do.

The raiding party was about fifty yards out. Just as I was about to start shaping the spell a hail of arrows came out of nowhere, literally nowhere, to cut into the front line of the raiders. From the space that danced at the edge of my vision earlier I noticed a ripple, like the air above a fire. Then as if a veil had been lifted, the green-coats were suddenly there, spurring their horses toward the Zatru. I blinked hard several times to make sure my eyes weren't lying to me. There was magic that could cloak a person in invisibility, but it was very difficult to do. The green-coats formed a large V driving the raiders back the way they came.

The bulk of the Zatru who were still standing ran for the thick cedars where the horses would have difficulty following, but about a half dozen charged the green-coats. It was madness. They came at the Manu fearlessly, shrieking like wild beasts, and were cut down as such. One was trampled, three felled by arrows, one lost his head to a wicked kukri. One actually managed to drag one of the green-coats off his horse before the Manu recovered and cut his throat with one of his twin daggers. It was brutal. It was violent. It was fast.

The green-coats chased the remaining Zatru, herding them back into the thick cedars. The Manu fired a few more arrows but they were clearly intended merely to discourage further fight as most either grazed or missed the target entirely. I sat in my carriage stunned at what I had witnessed.

I realized Koto was talking to me. I could barely hear him over the wind so I released the spell, letting it dissipate.

"Are ye alright, m'lady?" Koto asked.

"Of course," I replied. What a stupid question. "I was in the carriage, why wouldn't I be alright?"

He scratched the scar under his jade eye, compassion in his gruff features.

"It can be hard seein' death the first time. It's never like ye think it will be."

I could think of nothing to say to that. He was right. I'd seen a murderer hanged once but that was different. Very different. I cast my gaze back toward place where such violence had been only a moment before. "Have my horse brought up."

"What for, m'lady?"

"Because I'm going out there."

"By the Gods, why?"

"I need to see."

"Lady Samara, it's not safe."

"Captain, get my horse."

Koto glanced toward Harold for support who wisely kept silent. "There's no need fer ye to see that, m'lady."

"*Captain Koto*," I shouted. "I am going out there. Do you wish to accompany me?" I met his white jade gaze without flinching.

He stared back at me with an expression I had trouble reading. After a long moment he bowed his head and said merely, "Aye, m'lady."

Autumn was shivering like a plucked chicken, eyes shining with unshed tears. "Mistress…" she started.

"Stay in the carriage, Autumn."

"If you…if you need me…" she stammered.

"Stay in the carriage. That's an order," I said touching her cheek briefly. As I exited the carriage I said, "Dirk, please get Autumn something to drink and tend to her. She's a bit shaken up."

I mounted my horse and proceeded toward the battlefield with my houseguards in tight formation. The last of the Zatru were struggling to get to cover whether on their own or with help. What remained were fourteen of the raiders who were either dead or too injured to move.

As I arrived the Manu were tending to their wounded, minor injuries for both riders and horses, and trying to determine if any of the Zatru could be saved. One of the raiders was being bandaged and, from the string of what I'm assuming were curses, he seemed like he would probably pull through. The only other one I saw moving wasn't going to. He laid splayed out with half a dozen arrows his chest. One of the green-coats was holding his head up and giving him water. Blood covered his nose and mouth and between gulps of water he'd give a weak cough that sent a spray of tiny blood droplets onto his caretaker's coat. The Manu tending him talked evenly in his musical tongue and the man stammered a reply in a guttural language. Finally the raider's raspy breathing grew ragged and then ceased all together. I wondered if a legionnaire would have shown similar kindness to a dying enemy.

I looked away, glancing at the other dead. I noticed with shock that one of the Zatru who had charged the green-coats was a boy of no more than fourteen. He'd died with a look of disbelief, while clutching his bleeding throat. I thought about the lightning I'd almost loosed upon the charging Zatru. This boy could just as easily have been lying here blackened and twisted by my hand.

"Lady Samara?" I heard someone call in a gentle tone. I glanced up to see Darian with a look of concern in his eyes and I realized it wasn't the first time he called my name.

"Why?" I asked.

"It's their way," he shrugged. "Their people survive by raiding."

"No, I...I mean why did this boy charge you when most of his people retreated?"

Darian looked down for a long moment. "A Zatru boy doesn't reach manhood until he's killed a Manu, or taken one as a hostage to be ransomed back to their family."

"I...that's terrible."

Darian shrugged. "The world is full of brutal people, m'lady." He dismounted and knelt to close the boy's eyes.

"You were right."

He looked up on confusion.

"You had more than enough to handle them."

A nod was his only response.

The shock of the whole ordeal was beginning to wear off and I felt my wits returning to me. Suddenly something occurred to me. "You used the caravan to lure them here didn't you?"

"Yes. If we just drove them off they might have sacked one of the smaller settlements before we could come back with a larger force. This way, they'll likely return home and hopefully stay gone for the season."

"Or go raid villages outside of Mystewood."

Darian shrugged. "Can't save the world, m'lady."

"What are you going to do with the injured one?"

"That's for the Gura to decide, but he'll probably be traded for Manu prisoners." A bitter scowl crossed his face. "He'll receive better treatment at our hands than one of us would receive at the hands of the Zatru." The green-coats started to mount up and head back toward the caravan leaving the dead behind.

"Are you just going to leave them for the crows?" I asked, slightly horrified.

"Their people will be back for their bodies as soon as we move on. Now, m'lady, we really must go."

I turned my horse about and my guards started to close ranks around me when something that had been nagging at the back of my consciousness came crashing to the front. "Wait," I said as Darain started barking orders in Manu, "How in the name of the Gods did you do it?"

"Do what, m'lady?" Darian said looking utterly perplexed.

"What do you think? How did you hide yourselves?"

"That explanation will have to wait, right now we need to—"

"You told me your people use no magic," I said.

He blew out an exasperated sigh. "I promise I will give you an explanation you will find satisfactory later, but right now we need to rejoin the caravan. Now please, return to your carriage."

"M'lady—" Koto started.

I held up a hand to silence him and said, "Very well." I glanced one last time at the carnage before returning with my guards to the caravan.

I stared out the window of the carriage, watching the merchants joke and laugh. It was odd how quickly everything went back to normal. After Autumn calmed her nerves with the help of some wine, she passed out in the carriage. I spent the time in silence pondering what I'd seen. I kept mulling over how the Manu were able to hide themselves without magic, assuming of course, Darian was telling the truth. Another possibility occurred to me. Perhaps the Manu somehow were able to use a small amount magic innately without the need for training, as dragons did. *That* idea was intriguing enough to merit further research.

I kept waiting for Darian to come back and give me my explanation but he never did, at least not by the time we stopped to make camp. I tried to busy myself by practicing spells and reading but mostly I just huffed and paced around the tent.

"Mistress," Autumn started and I figured she was going to chide me for impatience but all she said was, "I'm sorry."

I gave her a quizzical look. "For sneaking about with Dirk? I certainly don't care who you roll around in the covers with. He probably wouldn't have been *my* first choice but—"

"No mistress, I…I mean for how I acted earlier in the carriage. I shouldn't have fallen apart like that."

"Autumn, you got scared when we were charged by angry savages. That's hardly something to apologize for."

"You didn't," she noted.

"I can throw lightning and summon demons, you braid hair and draw baths. Anyway I would have been scared if they'd made it to the carriage," I said, placing a kiss on her forehead. "Now that's enough of this. Your sullenness is getting in the way of my anxiousness."

"Alright, Mistress," she said drawing a deep breath and composing herself.

"Perhaps some wine will help calm both our nerves."

"I'm afraid we're running quite low."

"Oh my," I gasped covering my mouth dramatically. "Tragedy."

"We could see if the Manu would share their whisky?"

I felt my nose wrinkle. "I doubt I'll become that desperate."

"Lady Samara," one of the houseguards said from the door of the tent, "Darian's here to see you."

"Finally," I said. "Send him in please."

Darian entered and gave a tired bow. There was a tightness in his shoulders. "First, let me say thank you for your aid, m'lady. They told me you used your magic to protect the caravan before we sprang our trap."

I waived my hand dismissively. "It was nothing. I was part of the caravan too."

"Still, thank you."

"You're welcome. Now about my satisfactory answer..?"

He chuckled. "M'lady is like a wolf hounding a wounded elk." I heard Autumn snicker from the corner of the tent where she's started mending the seam of a gown.

"I don't like it when there's something I don't understand," I said, my eyes narrowing. "*Or* when I've been lied to."

"I've spoken no lies."

"Then how did you hide from the Zatru?"

He took a deep breath and blew it out running his fingers through his long hair. Finally he spoke. "A gift from the Gods."

For a long moment I just stared at him incredulously. "You call that a satisfactory answer? Do you think I—"

"Close your eyes, m'lady," he said, then added, "Please. And you as well, Lady Autumn." Autumn, who beamed at being called "lady", glanced over at me then shrugged and closed her eyes. I followed suit and closed my eyes as well, quickly becoming frustrated with the whole absurd conversation.

After a few moments I said, "Can I open my eyes now? Darian?" I opened my eyes and looked around the tent spotting only Autumn sitting in the corner with her sewing, eyes still closed. "Darian?" I said again and Autumn opened her eyes looking around the room. *I swear if he walked out of the tent when my eyes were closed...*

And then he was there standing next to me. "I'm right here, m'lady. No need to shout," he said with a wry grin. Autumn and I both jumped.

"Do it again. With me *watching* this time," I said.

He shrugged. "As you wish."

I stared intently at him. After a moment he simply faded from view and Autumn let out an excited gasp. Where he had been standing just moments before, I could spot the same heat-ripple shimmer as I'd seen earlier by the side of the road. If I watched closely I could follow the vaguely humanoid ripple move across the room and reappear next to the tent flap. My innate magic theory was seeming more plausible. If it was true it had far reaching implications. What if others could learn to cast magic as such?

"That's amazing," Autumn squealed.

"Amazing indeed," I said. "One more time, please."

"M'lady mistakes me for a circus performer."

"Humor me."

He huffed a resigned sigh.

"Just a moment," I said taking a breath and casting a quick spell. The world took on a hazy glaze and I glanced down to see the threads of magic woven through my jade bangle. I turned my now black eyes to Darian. "Please proceed."

Darian again disappeared from view and I could see only the hazy outline. A few curious sparks flashed across his shimmery silhouette every so often, only to disappear like a firefly in the night. I didn't exactly know what that meant, but there were certainly no gossamer threads of magic stretched across him. I was at once disappointed and more intrigued.

"Satisfied?" asked the hazy form.

"Yes," I said dismissing the spell and blinking my vision clear.

"It's as I said, m'lady," Darian spoke, reappearing. "We use no magic, merely a gift from the God Tarka to our people."

"How do you do it? What does it feel like?"

He rubbed his stubbly beard and glanced down in contemplation like that was the first time he'd ever been asked that question. After a few moments he went over to a bowl of fruit and snatched up a large plum. "Hold your hand out like this," he said extending his arm straight out to the side palm up.

I did as he instructed and he sat the plump round fruit in my hand. I waited for him to explain further and when he didn't, I said, "It...feels like holding a plum?"

He rolled his eyes. "When it's the only thing you have to concentrate on, it's easy. Now walk around the room." I did as instructed, leaving my arm out. It was a bit of a challenge to keep the plum in the flat of my palm. "Now imagine trying to do that and ride a horse, or sight down a bow. It's almost impossible to do a complicated task and maintain it. And eventually you begin to tire." As if on cue, my shoulder started to burn with the effort. I tossed the plum back to him and he effortlessly plucked it out of the air.

"Do all the Manu have this ability?"

"Yes, m'lady. But it's like swimming, or climbing, or anything else. It comes more naturally to some than others. Though any who wish to join the Rangers must demonstrate a real skill at it."

I was baffled. I'd never seen anything like it in all my nineteen years. Perhaps it was as he said and his people were favored by the Gods after all. "Fascinating," was all I could say.

I had about a thousand more questions to ask, but Darian said, "If that settles your curiosity, m'lady, this day has left me quite exhausted and I long for my bed."

He did look tired, or at least tired of answering my questions. "My curiosity is never settled but you've done as you said you would. Thank you for indulging me."

"I would expect nothing less form a devotee of Tarka, m'lady," he said, giving a formal bow and exiting the tent.

Though his answers had just led to more questions, my curiosity was somewhat sated and I realized I was exhausted as well. I went to sleep with thoughts of Gods and magic, and the shocked face of a dead boy swimming in my head.

———————————

The next day was far less eventful. Despite Darian's warning that we were passing a troublesome verge, we saw no twisted monstrous beasts or hungry Fae. I did see my first redwood, however. It was massive, towering at least a hundred feet above the neighboring pines, and I was informed by one of the traders that it was a small specimen. As we moved deeper into the Mystewood the giant trees became more and more common, and thick lush ferns replaced much of the undergrowth. Darian rode up with a broad leaf from one such fern that was light green and shot through with deep violet veins.

"Most of the brush is safe for the horses to graze but keep them away from this," he said holding up the fern leaf for my entourage to see.

"Poisonous, eh?" Koto asked.

"No, but it makes the horses aggressive and hard to manage. And it's addictive."

"Thanks for the warning," Harold said.

"One other thing," Darian said. "It's against our law to harm the redwoods. They are sacred to us."

Harold laughed. "I don't imagine that'll be too much of a problem. I don't even know how someone would go about felling one of those monsters."

"What about your flute and the little carvings I've seen among the Manu?" I asked.

"We harvest only what has naturally fallen," he said, as though it should be obvious.

The farther we traveled into Mystewood the larger, more splendid, and more numerous the redwoods became until we passed an old weathered statue of a woman with tree trunk legs, bark-like skin, and hair of nettles. I figured she must be a Manu representation of Suravani. There was writing at the base of the statue but it was far too faded to make out.

After we passed the statue the road changed. No longer was it the straight Zuran road it had been. It bent and curved around the ancient titans. By the time we made camp for the evening we were utterly surrounded by the giant trees. The Manu were different as well. Happier, more at ease. They seemed in their element, just as I would be walking the streets of White Harbor. I sat on a moss-covered stone while dinner was being prepared, staring up into the canopy formed by the giants, where a constant light fog played among the treetops.

Mystewood indeed.

———————

The next day was uneventful, serene even. A few of the wagons broke from the caravans as we crossed other roads, taking a couple of the green-coats with them, but most continued on with the column. That evening Autumn and I bathed in the clearest stream I'd ever seen, while handful of river otters chased each other nearby, leading me to thoughts of Lucius.

The following morning was the tenth day of our travels and Darian assured me we'd reach Vana before nightfall. Late in the afternoon I noticed a herd of wild horses off the road happily grazing on moss and ferns.

When I pointed them out, Darian smiled and said, "Those horses aren't wild."

I looked at them again not seeing any fences or herder watching over them, but a few of them did have Manu markings. "How do you keep them from wandering off?"

"We ask them not to," he said. As often was the case I couldn't tell if he was telling the truth or just teasing me.

"Do you ask the sheep to shear themselves as well?"

"We do, but they have a hard time holding the scissors," he said with his wry grin.

The road curved around a particularly large tree and as we came out of the bend I caught my first glimpse of a Manu home. Ganicus had mentioned that they lived in trees but of course I'd had no concept of redwoods at the time. I'd pictured the small tree huts that some nobles used as blinds for hunting. The reality was as different as it was stunning.

The Manu homes circled the enormous redwoods like some great tree fungus. Far from the rustic craftsmanship I'd envisioned, they were elegantly and meticulously constructed. Each individual home seemed to be two stories with a gently sloping roof, and was complete with windows and terraces. There were as many as five or six to a tree, one stacked atop the other.

I'd been caught so off guard I'd forgotten to look unimpressed. Darian glanced at me with a self-satisfied grin saying, "Not bad, huh?"

"Not bad I suppose," I said, a wry smile spreading across my lips. "For barbarians, of course."

"Of course, m'lady," he said with a snicker.

A couple of young boys who'd been wrestling around on the ground finally noticed us and ran off yelling in their musical tongue, eager to be the first ones to tell of the returning traders. Happy shouts and cheers arose as people came running to greet the caravan at the edge of town.

"Welcome to Vana, m'lady."

It was unlike any place I'd ever seen. A spider's web of rope bridges stretched overhead between the circular homes and the road snaked through the giants while the constant mist drifted amidst the treetops. Unlike Zuran cities, which were usually laid out on a grid, the roads slithered through the trees making it difficult to tell what direction we were heading or how large Vana actually was.

A hitching post in front of a shop caught my eye. The top of it was intricately carved to look like the head of an eagle, and the one next to it was in the shape of an open hand. The pole bearing a sign had figures carved into it, one on top of another. Looking around I noticed that there were similar workings *everywhere*. All the everyday items were carved into other things rendering them a unique piece of art. Even the walls were engraved with scenes, from the mythic to the mundane. Glancing up I noticed that the sloping roof of one of the Manu homes had its shingles cut to look like the scales of a dragon, while another had the shingles arranged to form the face of a man, and still another into the shape of a howling wolf. Now that my eye was open to it, anywhere I looked there was another piece of art waiting to be discovered.

I saw signs on many of the ground level structures and realized that they must be shops. Cobblers, apothecaries, and tanners advertised their wares in front of their shops while children ran alongside the caravan as it wound its way deeper into the interior of Vana. A few of the ground-level shops extended between two or three trees creating a space between them for livestock and forges and such.

As we crossed a large wooden bridge over the river that bisected Vana, I saw naked children and adults alike bathing and playing unselfconsciously in the slow, gurgling waters. On the other side of the bridge there was an empty cart parked in front of a shop. As we passed it, Autumn let out a gasp and I followed her gaze to see a panther sleeping curled up in the cart, looking to all the world like a large house cat.

"Ah," Darian said tapping his head as though he'd just remembered something. "I believe there's something I neglected to mention. Many of us keep animal companions that you are probably are not accustomed to seeing around people. They aren't dangerous…that is, they won't harm you, but they're not exactly what a Zuran would consider *tame* either. My advice would be to ignore them and they will ignore you."

My entourage and I exchanged skeptical looks while the panther looked up as the noisy caravan passed. It merely yawned and curled up in a tighter ball before falling back asleep.

"We'll break from the caravan up ahead and I'll lead you to the Imperial district," said Darian.

We turned from the main road and took a meandering path that loosely followed the river. The Imperial district turned out to be a small group of maybe a dozen buildings arranged together. Amongst the buildings was a branch of the Imperial bank, a small inn, a general store, and a few modest homes. The squat Zuran-style structures seemed rather out of place amidst the towering redwood houses of the Manu, but it was comforting to know I wouldn't be sleeping a hundred feet up in the air. I had a wee problem with heights.

"I have to finish my obligations with the caravan," Darian said.

"Don't we need to go speak to the Gura?" I asked.

"Tomorrow. I'll meet you here after breakfast."

Eager as I was to be off to see the Vija, I must say I wasn't too heartbroken. I was travel-weary and more than ready for a hot bath and a soft bed. "After breakfast then," I said.

Darian bowed from the saddle before heading back down the road.

The inn was acceptable if a bit small. A middle-aged Zuran couple greeted us with smiles and lots of bowing. "Welcome, Lady of House Arga," the inn keeper's plump wife said with a smile plastered to her face. "It's been quite some time since we've had noble guests here. If you need *anything*, please don't hesitate to ask."

"Thank you," I said. "If you could direct me towards a bath I would be most grateful."

The woman beamed. "We happen to have the only Imperial style bath in two hundred miles, m'lady. I'll have it prepared at once."

I daresay the woman overdid it a bit. The inset granite tub had rose petals floating in the steaming floral scented water with a large assortment of oils and soaps. I'd have been happy with a barrel of hot water and lye soap. Ten days on the road had apparently lowered my standards quite a bit.

After Autumn and I finished luxuriating in the bath, we retired to our suite and donned clean clothes. It seemed my party were the only guests and we had our pick of rooms, which were nothing special. They did have a tasteful blending of Zuran and Manu style, though. Every conceivable surface had a carving or engraving upon it. We went to take a meal at the inn's large attached dining hall. Considering we were the only ones with rooms I expected it to be empty or nearly so, but to my surprise it was full, even overfull. There were easily two score crowded shoulder to shoulder, both Zuran and Manu.

The inn keeper led us to a reserved table and his plump wife served us. "You certainly are busy this evening," I said.

"It's like this all the time, m'lady. We serve the only Zuran cuisine in Vana," she beamed.

After a delicious meal of lamb and potatoes I asked the woman, "Would you mind talking with me? I have a few questions."

She vibrated with excitement and looked as if her head might explode. Apparently they didn't get very many Zuran nobles in Mystewood. "Of course, m'lady. What would you like to know?"

"Do you like it here in Vana?"

"Oh yes, it's quite peaceful."

"What do you think about the Manu?"

"They're good folk mostly, for uncoined," the woman said using the slang for freeman or foreigners. She looked round conspiratorially to make sure no one was listening before adding, "Even if they are a bit uninhibited."

Zurans weren't usually considered prude and the Manu of the caravan didn't strike me as particularly wild. I thought maybe she was referring to the people I'd seen bathing in the river, but Zurans really didn't have much of a problem with nudity. All but the richest citizens and freemen used public bath houses with large communal pools. "What do you mean?"

The woman looked around again then lowered her voice. "It's just that they're not that discriminating about who they share their beds with. Not that I'm being judgmental, mind you."

"How so?" Autumn asked.

The woman dropped her voice even lower. "Marriage doesn't mean anything to these barbarians. They'll roll in the covers with whomever they want, whenever they want. And it's not just men and women. Men with other men, women with other women, whole groups of 'em together." She shook her head in disapproval. "You'd think they'd have jealous husbands gettin' in all sort of fights, but that hardly happens. It's as normal as rain to them," she sighed then said with a shrug, "Barbarians."

Autumn shot a guilty look at me, fighting to suppress a giggle and echoed, "Barbarians."

The woman simply nodded her head, and raised her voice back to normal as she said, "Other than that though they're honest, hard workin' folk."

"What do you know about the Gura?"

"Elian? He's a good leader. Goes out of his way to keep the Zurans who live here happy."

That was promising at least. "Thank you for tolerating all my questions," I said, rising from the table.

"It was no trouble, m'lady. We don't get very many nobles through here," the woman said with her rosy-cheeked grin. I thought she might swoon from excitement.

Autumn and I walked into the courtyard to take in the cool night air. The silvery light of the waxing moon drifting through the misty tree tops was the only illumination. I wondered how the Manu got about at night with no street lamps. So much about them seemed odd. I wondered distantly if all foreigners were so strange. There had been quite a few students from outside the Empire at the Academy and none of them seemed as alien as the Manu.

The soft Zuran bed was a welcome relief for my back. I was awoken at dawn the next day by bells ringing lazily in the distance. Autumn was nowhere to be found, so either she'd risen early or snuck off to Dirk's room and fallen asleep there. The courtyard was quiet and serene so I performed my mediation and hatha stretching there. Autumn found me eventually with a guilty smile that told where she'd been.

As many of the Manu as there were for dinner I was surprised to see none at breakfast. When I commented on it the inn keeper, who'd been so quiet I was beginning to think he was a mute, spoke up. "They all go to the Alaya in the morning."

"The whole village?" I said.

He nodded.

"What is the Alaya?"

He thought about that for a long moment. "It's hard to say, m'lady. It's a civic building but it's also a school, a library, and a temple."

"So why does the whole town go there every morning?"

He shrugged.

I waited for him to continue but he didn't. It was like he and his wife shared a daily pool of words between them and she used the lion's share. He was more than a little frustrating. Just then another frustrating man I was acquainted with walked in.

"Good morning, Lady Samara," said Darian, "Are you ready to be off?"

"Quite ready. I'll just have our horses saddled," I said.

"That won't be necessary. We'll just be heading to the Alaya, and it's a short walk."

"Very well. Lead the way," I said.

My entourage set out, absent Harold and another guard who were tasked with replenishing our supplies. Walking through the streets of Vana was no less amazing than it had been the day before. The Manu going about their daily chores stared at us with open curiosity as we passed. I looked for more strange animals among them and was a bit disappointed when I saw only common cats and dogs.

We followed the gently flowing river for about a quarter hour when a building came into view. I suppose I was expecting something like the tree homes but this structure was massive. At least five stories tall, it was a perfect hexagon, roughly the size of the Great Amphitheater in White Harbor. Rather than clear the trees that were present, the great structure was simply built around them and several could be seen rising above it, bearing more of those circular homes. People scurried in and out of the building's many entrances like bees from a hive

"Impressive, mmm?" Darian said, adding straight faced, "For barbarians, of course."

"It has a certain charm," I admitted.

We followed Darian through a tall arch that led into a huge interior courtyard containing one of the ancient redwoods reaching skyward into the misty abyss.

"Wait here, m'lady," Darian said. "It would be best if I go speak to the Gura first."

"Whatever you think," I said.

He bowed and to my surprise walked right into an opening in the tree that I realized must be a doorway. I glanced inside after him to see what I would have called a spiral staircase save there were no stairs, only smooth sloping redwood.

"Alright, that is rather impressive," I admitted to no one in particular.

We waited for a few minutes as my stomach did its best to work itself into further knots and I noticed Autumn was craning to see what was going on in the far corner of the courtyard. A group of children was gathered listening raptly to what could easily have been the oldest man I'd ever seen. Bent with age, knobby fingers gripped heavily on his staff, his leathery skin was wrinkled like a prune left out in the sun and all that was left of his hair was a few white wisps. He was dressed in red and green robes of fine draa with a blanket draped over his bowed shoulders.

My curiosity was piqued and anything was better than waiting around, agonizing over whether we'd made a ten day journey for nothing. "Let's go listen," I said to Autumn.

As we grew closer, I could see the old man stood with his back to a half circle of carved redwood statues of the Gods, facing a herd of children. Though he was bent with age his eyes were bright and clear as he spoke in Common with his musical Manu accent, "…Ten beings that would later become known as the Gods came together and created three distinct Realms: Acala, Eather, and Heaven."

It was a story I'd heard countless times, yet I found myself listening mesmerized, drawn in by the man's melodic voice. His ancient eyes twinkled as he continued. "Acala they created to be stable, and be governed by fixed rules. Eather they created to be malleable and fluid, but was attached to Acala to give it stability. At last they needed a place that could accommodate their vast and powerful forms. And so they created Heaven, which constantly shapes itself to their wishes and acts as a bulwark between the Gods and the other Realms, lest their powerful presence accidentally destroy that which they lovingly created."

Faintly I realized that Autumn and the houseguards were as invested in the old man's words as I was, which a distant part of my mind realized was a bit odd. My thoughts drifted back to Darian's performance with his flute.

"Over countless eons they shaped and changed the realms," the old man continued, "until at last they were happy with what they'd made. Upon our world, the Gods created an abundance of life, including humans and dragons. In Eather, they made the mercurial Fae, as well as the Elementals to help keep the forces of the Realms in balance. In Heaven, the Gods created the Devas, who could bear their powerful presence and act as their servants in all of the Realms.

"Eventually the Gods' creations drew the attention of other beings similar to the Gods, yet different. These beings, the Rajasa, became envious of what the Gods had created. The Rajasa existed in an alien Realm known as Kardama, and it seems they were unable to create a place that could remain stable without their constant attention. They wished to use Acala and Eather as their canvas, but the Gods denied the Rajasa because their nature would corrupt the Realms with their chaotic presence. The Rajasa decided that, being similar to the Gods, they could simply take what they wanted. They opened a portal to come through with the creatures they had created. The Rajasa, however, had misjudged."

The old man paused for effect, looking out at the sea of attentive faces hanging on his words, "The Gods fought back. They attacked the Rajasa, striking one of them down. The death of that titanic elder was enough to destroy Kardama. Many of the Rajasa's creations chose to abandon them, becoming the beings you know as the Forsaken."

"However, the God Rocana looked forward and realized there was no way to strike down the remaining Rajasa without destroying Acala and Eather with them, so they devised another plan. The God Varga constructed a new Realm, similar to Heaven, but in addition to protecting the other planes from the power of the Rajasa, it would act as a prison to contain them. This new Realm he named Hell.

"The Gods then offered the Rajasa a choice: exile to Hell, or destruction. The Rajasa, becoming aware for the first time that they could die, became afraid and surrendered. The Rajasa accepted their cage but chafed at it, waiting for the moment they could escape and enact vengeance on the Gods, and at last take for themselves the Realms they so coveted."

Now a few of the children had fearful looks upon their faces. The old man's smile returned, "But don't worry, children. The Rajasas' prison is flawless. It has held them for thousands of years. Now," he said turning to the statues behind him, "let us pray."

In the Empire, statues of the Gods were almost always carved from marble and tended to be at least twice the height of a man. The Manu statues were life-sized and carved from their sacred redwood. So finely wrought were they that I expected them to step down from their dais at any moment. The overall effect was a much more intimate portrayal of the Gods.

"Azava," the old man said, lifting his voice to the statue standing resplendent with a trumpet in one hand and a sword in the other. "Lord of the sun. God of virtue, honor, justice, and truth, we pray to you. We ask that you continue to light the path of the just."

He turned to the next statue, which stood upon an anvil, and wielded a hammer in one hand and a chisel in the other. "Vastuvit. The Great Maker, God of forging, crafting, and building, we pray to you. We ask that you guide our hands to create wonders worthy of your greatness."

He turned to the statue of a woman in a flowing gown with a crescent moon upon her forehead, her arms outstretched, and said, "Ananda. Mistress of the moon, Goddess of love, healing, compassion, and pleasure, we pray to you. We ask that you soothe our pains, and open our hearts."

He turned next to a form I recognized very well. "Tarka. Lord of dragons, God of knowledge, learning, and reason, we pray to you," I noted with some annoyance he left magic off the list. "We ask that you open our minds to learning and leave us ever hungry for knowledge." That was an invocation I'd never heard before. I rather liked it.

He turned to a figure seated with legs crossed and hands folded in his lap staring to the heavens. "Rocana. Lord of the stars, God of time, fate, and the night sky, we pray to you. We ask that you help us find peace and understand the great mystery."

He turned next to what must have been a statue of Suravani, but she was as I'd never seen her depicted. Elegant antlers still graced her head but feathery wings stretched out from her back and one of her hands was that of an eagle's claw while the other was that of a lion. She wore a long dress made of leaves while dainty cloven hooves poked out from underneath the bottom hem. The old man cleared his throat and spoke again. "Suravani. Mistress of Nature, Goddess of seasons, storms, and all that walks, swims, flies, and grows, we pray to you. We ask that you help us walk in balance with all your creations."

He turned to the statue of a man with a pan flute in one hand and a cup of wine in the other, bearing a look of joyous abandon. "Kavi. Master of journeys, God of wine, music, and roads, we pray to you. We ask that you keep our feet firmly and safely upon the long road."

He turned to the image of a man with a scale in one hand a parchment in the other. "Varga. Lord of law, God of commerce, cities, walls, and gates, we pray to you. We ask that you guide us always toward order and prosperity."

He turned toward the image of a woman clad in leathers wielding a flail in each hand. "Arati. Mistress of darkness, Goddess of suffering, redemption, growth, and death, we pray to you. We ask that you help us to always find the lesson inherent in suffering."

He turned stiffly to the last statue. This one, too, differed substantially from the Zuran version who was usually clad in legion armor. Here he was dressed as one of the Rangers. "Irin. Lord of war, God of strength, conflict, and battle, we pray to you. We ask that you grant us the strength to defeat our enemies both within and without."

He turned back to the children, "Now, how many of the Devas can you children name, hmmm?"

My dreamlike reverie broke as the children all shouted out answers at once, sounding quite a bit like a gaggle of geese. I hoped that when the day came for me to teach at the Academy, I was assigned to the older children. I had no idea how people dealt with the noise of the younger ones.

"Lady Samara."

I turned to see Darian approaching with another Manu. He was a big man, broad of both shoulder and chest, with a crooked, flattened nose that had clearly been broken several times. He was perhaps sixty, and had the lines of his life etched deeply upon his face. He was garbed in red draa with a yellow embroidered sash that I guessed was the symbol of his office and wore his long black hair unbound.

"M'lady, this is Gura Elian," Darian said.

"Lady of House Arga, it is a pleasure to meet you," the large man said bowing deeply.

"Likewise, Gura Elian," I said.

He glanced around at my entourage, "I would invite you to my chamber for refreshments but I fear it would be rather crowded. Shall we take the air instead?"

"As you wish," I said. He led us down a corridor to another of the courtyards that hosted another lumbering giant. This courtyard though, was a garden bearing the first early buds of spring. Morning songbirds sang happily as a pair of squirrels chased each other haphazardly around the redwood.

"Are your accommodations adequate?" the Gura asked. "We have homes among the upper branches for visiting dignitaries. I'd be happy to offer it to you for your stay."

Just the thought of being that high made me tense up. "That's very gracious of you Gura, but my accommodations are quite adequate."

He seemed conflicted for a moment, as though he wasn't sure he'd fulfilled the requisite amount of small talk, but finally he continued. "Darian has told me you wish to meet with one of the *Vija*."

"That's correct," I said preparing myself for the coming question.

"If I might ask, m'lady," he said, as his gaze focused on me intently. "Why?"

I'd rehearsed my answer several times, which was good because now my throat was dry and my heart was pounding. "I have an ancient book written in a language that appears to be lost. As a devotee of Tarka, it is my wish to preserve the knowledge locked within the text. My hope is that the Vija can aid me in this."

"Do you have any idea as to the contents of this book?" A sharp intellect stared back at me through those mahogany eyes.

"I have some idea. We believe it was written by an ancient mage, but until it's translated we won't be able to authenticate it," I said, which was technically the truth. I just left out the part about it being used to summon demons.

Finally, after a lifetime he said,

"Alright, Lady Samara, I'm inclined to grant your request."

I blew out a breath I didn't realize I'd been holding. "Thank you, Gura Elain."

"Provided," he continued, "that you show proper respect, and if the Vija commands you to leave, you will do so."

"Agreed," I said my heart swelling with another hurdle cleared.

"I was hoping you might be able to lend your wisdom toward selecting a proper tribute," Darian interjected.

We discussed this at some length with Koto asking questions and taking notes. Finally Gura Elian bid us farewell and we left to procure the needed tribute. I'd been imagining gold or livestock or some such, but the things we were after were all very ordinary: herbs, spices, bolts of draa, and a few bags of salt. Along with a donkey to carry our gifts, this was apparently the going rate to procure the services of a Vija. I realized with irony I'd spent far more getting an audience with Master Tertias.

We discussed final preparations over dinner at the Inn that evening.

"There's no road, so you'll have to leave the carriage behind," Darian was saying. I was glad I'd taken the opportunity to get myself reacquainted with the back of a horse.

"Aye. Can you show me where we're goin'?" Koto said producing an old legion-issued map.

Darian studied the map for a moment before putting his finger on a fork in the river. "Near there. It'll take us about two and a half days, if the weather cooperates."

"What're ye talkin' about, lad? If the map's right it'll hardly take us more than a day."

Darian shook his head. "We have to go this way," he said tracing his finger along the river then making a wide arc before returning to it.

"Why?" Koto asked, turning his head so he had a better view with his good eye.

"There's a verge with a Fae encampment right here," Darian said tapping right in the middle of the arc he'd traced.

My entourage and I all exchanged looks. "How is it ye've got a Fae encampment at yer doorstep?" Koto said.

Darian smirked at Koto's obvious discomfort. "We have an old agreement with the sidhe that rules there. As long as we don't enter the verge, we won't have any problems."

"Two and a half days it is," Koto said shaking his head.

Chapter Eight
Darian

"Is she pretty?" my sister Nia asked as she helped me repack my things.

"Yes, but all Zuran nobles are."

She looked at me incredulously. She took after our father's classic Manu features, not sharing the wavy hair and slightly lighter skin of our mother. "They can't all be pretty."

"All the ones I've seen have been."

"How many have you seen?"

"I don't know. It's not as though I have a checklist. Maybe two dozen I can remember? And they were all attractive."

"The men too?"

"Not that I was paying particular attention, but yes."

"Hm. No wonder you like going there to trade. I'll have to make an excuse to go with you next time then," she said with a smirk. "How long will you be gone anyway? Mother wants you to take her to the springs in Jarpa."

The idea of the hot spring water on my back sounded wonderful. I'd only gotten to sleep in my own bed for two days in the last month. "I should only be a few days. Tell Mother I'll take her when I get back," I said, tying my pack shut and throwing it over my shoulder.

"May Kavi see you safely on your journey," she said, kissing me on the cheek. "And Varga see you returned with a purse full of Zuran gold."

I departed, stopping only to give a simple offering at the Alaya before making my way to the squat little Imperial inn. The Zurans were waiting outside, ready to go when I arrived. Samara seemed to be chomping at the bit more than her horse was.

We headed out of town and followed the river for about half the day before breaking off and starting our wide circuit around the outside of the verge. We made good time despite the path we were on being little more than a game trail. Luckily the good weather held. I could only imagine how Samara would handle being rained on. All in all, she acquitted herself rather well, though I did note that as soon as her guards finished putting up her ridiculously large tent, she disappeared into it before the sun had even fallen behind the horizon, while her guards and I sat around dicing and drinking.

About an hour later, Autumn slithered quietly out of their tent and took the dark haired guard by the hand, leading him off into another tent to some good-natured cheering from his fellows.

"Lucky bugger," one of the guards said.

"Can I ask you a question?" I said to the Harold, the pleasant blond guard.

"It's a bit late for that I'd say," he snickered.

"It may be a bit impolitic."

"Do I seem the political type to you?" he asked, draining his wine cup.

"How do you heel to them all day?"

"It's good money." Harold said with a grin. "And Lady Samara's not bad. She's got a kind heart."

I tried to imagine myself following her around all day, driving carriages and opening doors. I failed.

Harold got up to refill his cup from a wineskin and asked, "Want some?"

"No, thank you," I said.

"Your pallet's too refined for our wine, huh?" Harold said with a chuckle filling his cup.

"It's just so weak. It's like drinking juice," I said, which earned me a round of jeers.

"Here, try this. The green-coats I served with liked it alright," Koto said pulling the stopper out of a metal flask and pouring some into my cup. It was light green and smelled vaguely like licorice. I took a tentative sip. It had a sweet floral flavor with a pleasant burn.

"Not bad. What is it?"

"It's called absinthe. They give it to ye in the legions to purify water, though that's not the purpose it's normally put to," he said with a guffaw.

"You fought in the Ipsum war?"

"Aye," he said.

"I lost some family in that war."

"Lot o' people did. I just lost an eye," he said, taking a pull from the flask.

"S'alright though, they let me keep the axe they dug out o' my face," he said gesturing to the scar. "And they gave me a fancy magical eye, so I figure I made out better than most."

"What's it like?" I asked, "The magical eye, I mean."

"Lad, at my age, I see better through this here jade eye than m' real one," he said tapping the white eye, which caused me to blink involuntarily. "Just can't see color out o' it. Everything's shades of gray."

"I find that's how life truly is anyway," I said. "Shades of gray that is."

"Too true, lad."

"Don't you ever unstring that thing?" Harold asked pointing to the composite bow at my feet.

"It doesn't shoot very well when it's unstrung," I said, which got me a round of laughs.

"If you leave a bow strung all the time it loses tension," he said.

"Not Manu bows. The only time you need to unstring it is when it gets wet, and that's only until it dries."

"How do you manage that?"

"Superior craftsmanship," I said, draining my cup and heading off to bed.

The next morning I witnessed Samara doing a series of stretches and poses as she often did in the morning and she caught me watching. "It helps me focus my energy for spell casting," she said. I must have had a skeptical look because she said, "It's certainly no stranger than the dancing around that you do in the morning."

"The movements keep me in practice for fighting."

"So do mine," she said with a smile.

I didn't see how, but then she was a mage. Mages did strange things.

We struck camp and continued skirting the edge of the verge seeing no one but a couple of hunters carrying a stag a between them. The women chatted happily amongst themselves while Koto and I talked of his time in the war. By midafternoon, we found the Green River and again followed the muddy bank on its winding course through the forest. We camped that evening near a small waterfall so the women could bathe easily. I valiantly fought off the urge to call Tarka's gift around me and go watch them.

I was awoken in the middle of the night, by what I couldn't say exactly. Something was just wrong. I felt as though I was being watched. The two guards who stood sentry chatted quietly and the horses, which were a far better indicator of danger, dozed easily. There were panthers, wolves, and bears in these woods, but none of them would approach a fire and all would draw the attention of the horses. Still I felt a tingling between my shoulders.

I took care to slip out of camp silently. Tarka's gift may have hidden me from sight, but it did nothing for noise. The dark cloudy night was to my advantage as Arati's gift illuminated the forest to my eyes. I moved a distance away and just listened. Nothing more than the normal nocturnal sounds of the forest. I made a wide slow circuit around the camp taking my time to be thorough and remain as quiet as possible. Eventually I found a spot about a hundred yards out from camp where the ferns had been trampled down. I looked around for tracks or droppings but found none. I searched the trees for some indication but the forest gave up no further clues.

Something had been watching us from here, but it could have been anything from a bear to a deer. I made another circuit around the camp but found nothing else out of place. Finally, I returned to my bed roll and went back to sleep. I made another round in the morning but found nothing new.

When I mentioned my findings to Koto he said, "Don't think it was them Zatru, do ye?"

I shook my head. "Doubtful. They rarely travel through this part of Mystewood. And the horses would have noticed them."

"Any idea what it was then?"

I shrugged. "Probably just a curious beast."

"Well, we'll keep our eyes open." He looked around for a moment then lowered his voice and said, "Probably best not to scare the women over nothing."

"Whatever you think, Captain," I said.

We followed our course along the river until we came to a meadow I recognized just before mid-day. "Hold, we'll set up camp here, "I said. "The branch in the river is just up ahead."

"Are we stopping?" Samara asked.

I nodded. "We're not far from the Vija. You should probably take only a few men so you don't seem threatening."

The guards started to bristle at that but Samara held up her hand silencing them. "Do you think two would be alright?"

"Yes, but I'd have them take off their armor so they seem more like escorts than professional soldiers. The rest of your men can go ahead and set up camp. There's no telling when we'll be back."

"Very well. Koto, I'll take you and Harold."

"Aye, m'lady," Koto said dismounting and starting to work off his chainmail.

"Shall I accompany you, Mistress?" Autumn asked.

"No, you stay here," Samara said, glancing pointedly over at Dirk, "and take your leisure when camp is set up."

"Yes, Mistress," Autumn said blushing.

A thought occurred to me. "Take your rest for a moment, m'lady, I'll go scout for a good place to cross the river." She looked like she wanted to argue but apparently decided against it. Instead she just nodded at me and dismounted.

I knew the area fairly well, having come here with my mother several times, and I made my way to a shallow, clear area of the river. I returned to the group a half hour later with a pair of decently-sized salmon.

"Ah, 'scouting', huh?" Harold said upon seeing the fish.

"They're an offering," I said.

"You don't think that's enough tribute for the Vija?" Samara asked, pointing to the laden donkey.

I smiled. "It's not for the Vija."

Chapter Nine
Samara

I followed Darian to the river with Harold, Koto, and the donkey in tow, along with a bubbly feeling of both dread and excitement. Darian led us past the fork in the river to a slow-moving area to cross. The muddy water was deceptively deep. "Do you think we might find a shallower place to cross?" I asked as the water lapped at my feet.

"Not for several miles, m'lady. You do realize that horses can swim?" Darian said with his little half-smirk.

I cast a baleful glare at him as I hiked my dress up as high as I dared. At least I was wearing stockings. The water was cold as it hit my knees but the horses didn't seem to mind. There was no trail on the other side but the woods were relatively open. Darian led us on a winding journey through the trees for about a half hour until we came upon a camp. There were lines strung up with laundry hanging, racks stretched with curing animal hides, a fire pit with a spit above it and a large cauldron, all next to a redwood that appeared to be partially hollowed out. I looked farther up the tree but either it didn't have one of the round Manu homes or it was so high as to be lost in the canopy.

"This is it," Darian announced.

My heart leapt, I searched around but didn't see any sign of anyone. "Where's the Vija?"

Darian shrugged. "Not here," he said, as he dismounted. "Be sure and tie your horses securely, in case they spook."

I obeyed his ominous command. "When will the Vija return?"

He shrugged again taking a seat on a seat on one of the pine stumps that served as seats around the fire pit. "Hopefully today."

I groaned and flopped down on one of the other stumps to remove my waterlogged stockings. The smell of herbs wafted in the air and I could see dried plants hanging inside the hollowed tree. I craned my neck to see if maybe the Vija was hiding in there.

"Patience, m'lady," said Darian.

I sighed again. Patience was not my strong suit, and at that moment I was a twisted ball of nerves. I closed my eyes and did some of my breathing exercises which helped. I thought about everything that had led me to this place in the middle of nowhere, the chain of events and clues that had me setting on this stump in the woods getting eaten by mosquitoes. I wondered if Master Carter had undergone something similar in seeking his Vija.

I sat there on my stump, imagining scenarios about Master Carter's adventures in Mystewood, when a warm breeze blew my hair and tickled the back of my neck. It felt wonderful after the cold wind that had been blowing all day. I reached back to scratch my neck when another warm breeze washed over me feeling unusually moist, then stopped suddenly. One of the horses whinnied loudly and I glanced up to see what was the matter.

Koto was sitting off to my left but Harold had taken a seat across from me next to Darian. Harold just stared at me, white faced, eyes as big as saucers. Eventually he stammered, "M-m'lady..." Just then a shadow grew over me.

Darian finally looked up from picking dirt out from under his nails and said, "Don't startle, m'lady." Then he looked above me and said slowly, "*It's alright, Yona. They're friends.*"

I turned ever so slowly to see a furry mountain towering over me. The grizzly bear that had just been sniffing me stared down at me from a height of a thousand feet, or maybe it was more like twelve, but in that moment it felt like a thousand. Some distant part of me realized I should probably move but I was utterly paralyzed. Darian calmly picked up one of the salmon at his feet and tossed it to the massive creature, who snapped it out of the air eagerly. The bear then sat down holding the fish between its massive claws and, grabbing with its maw, skinned it in one fluid motion. Then it settled down to feast on the fat.

Some small part of my brain noted idly the strange leather straps on the bear. I finally regained my composure enough to stagger slowly across to Darian. The enormous beast hardly seemed to notice us as it gnawed happily on its meal. Darian moved over to calm our mounts, especially the donkey, which was baying obnoxiously. A few words from in his musical tongue gentled them and he retook his seat before tossing the second salmon to the bear just as it finished the first.

"Kadeshdae, child," said a melodic voice behind Darian. "I hope you brought some fish to share with the humans as well."

"Kadeshdae, Vija Saptarsi. I didn't, though it's a situation easily remedied. I was fairly sure the humans wouldn't decide to eat me if they were hungry."

For some reason I expected the Vija to be a wrinkled old man like the priest at the Alaya, painted head to toe and bearing necklaces of bone. What I saw instead was a striking Manu woman. She was tall and well-muscled with strong cheek bones and long black hair unbound, save for a pair of braids at her temples. She was barefoot and wore only a simple shift of brown draa and a carved redwood Rocana medallion. Her age was difficult to tell. She could have been anywhere from thirty to fifty. Her face was lightly lined but her eyes possessed years far beyond her body. She had both a wildness and a calmness about her, moving with the easy grace of a stalking crane.

Darian rose to stand before her. Vija Saptarsi stood nearly a hand span taller than Darian, who was not short. Speaking in his native language, he closed his hands together in a prayer position and raised them just above his head, then dropped them to his heart, then knelt down before her to touch her feet.

As Darian was kneeling, she reached down and cupped his face with her hand, gently raising his head to stare in his eyes in a way that was somehow both maternal and intimate. Her features softened with compassion as she murmured softly to him in their shared tongue. His eyes shimmered with unshed tears as he muttered some response, rising with his back to us.

After he had regained his composure, he turned back to her and said in Common, "Vija this is Initiate mage Samara of House Arga. She has traveled all the way from Zura to petition you for guidance."

Wishing Darian had prepared me better on proper protocol, I approached her. "I humbly offer tribute and request your aid," I said, gesturing to the donkey. Then I did as Darian had, folding my hands in prayer and raising them above my head, then bringing them to my heart, before kneeling down to touch her feet. As she had with Darian the Vija gently cupped my chin with a rough calloused hand, tilting my head back to meet her eyes.

My brother had once described swimming in the open ocean and how small he felt staring down into the deep blue abyss. That's the only comparison I have. Her mahogany eyes held the vastness of the night sky in them and I felt as if her gaze penetrated me, though there was no sense of intrusion. The core of my being was simply naked and laid bare to her. I felt small. I felt vulnerable. I felt humble.

I'm not sure how long we stayed like that, staring into each other's eyes. It could have been a minute or an hour. Finally, the corners of her mouth edged up in the barest hint of a smile and she said simply, "Aye." My heart leapt. As I rose to stand she added, "But first Darian's going to go gather some more fish for dinner."

"As you wish," Darian said with a bow and a good-natured smile. He mounted his horse and rode back toward the river.

"You can put the offerings over there," the Vija said to Koto indicating the hollow tree, "though you may keep the donkey. I have no need for it." The Vija moved over to the bear that was now diligently licking its claws and gave a quick scratch behind its ears. I could see now the leather harness held on some sort of modified saddle.

Koto and Herald watched the bear wearily as they unloaded the donkey but the enormous beast merely sat back on its bottom, idly scratching its side with a hind claw, and watched them dispassionately. After a few moments, it flopped down and stretched out next to the fire pit, ready for a nap. Apparently bears snore.

"Come. You can help me prepare," the Vija said, abruptly walking off toward the tree.

"Oh…er, alright," I stammered, rushing to catch up.

I assumed the Vija meant for me to help her prepare for a ritual or something, but I quickly realized she meant for me to help her prepare for dinner. Now I wished I'd brought Autumn. "I'm not that handy in the kitchen, but I'll help however I can," I said. And by that of course I meant I'd never cooked before. I had servants for that.

The Vija said nothing and simply handed me a well-used knife and a bag of small potatoes. If she noticed my amateurish dicing job, she was either too polite to say anything or simply assumed it was the Zuran style. She handed me some more vegetables to chop before scooping them all in a large pot and setting it over the fire.

Darian eventually returned with a bounty of fish, throwing a few more to Yona for good measure, before spitting the rest over the fire. He set down on a stump and removed his water-logged moccasins to dry. After the bear finished the fish it ambled over and sniffed Darian as if trying to make sure he didn't have any more food. Darian was calm and patient while the shaggy giant investigated him. Finally the bear leaned forward and rubbed its enormous head against him, nuzzling him with enough force to knock him off his stump. He picked himself up and started petting the huge beast as it continued to nuzzle on him like a large, deadly housecat.

The bear was shedding its winter coat and patches of fur stuck out haphazardly. Gently, Darian started pulling out the errant tufts. At first the bear grumbled in protest but finally it just laid down at his feet and let him go about it.

Dinner was fish in a thick stew. We ate quietly with a grizzly lazing mere yards away. I stared at this surreal scene and realized how quickly we accept strange things as normal.

"So you would like for me to aid you in translating your book?" the Vija said out of nowhere

"Uh…yes, Vija," I stammered. As far as I knew no one had mentioned the book. I'll admit that was impressive.

"What do you know of Lord Rocana's purview?" she asked.

The abruptness of her question caught me off guard. "Rocana is the God of time, fate, and the night sky."

"Aye. Rocana tends the threads of fate that connect everything. He sees every possible future, and in this, he is the wisest of the Gods," she stated mater-of-factly. "Did Darian tell you of Rocana's gift to our people?"

I shook my head. He'd mentioned a gift from Tarka but nothing about Rocana.

"He shared a small sliver of his insight with the Manu," she explained, "granting us the vision to see the connection between things, and thus what is most likely to occur."

I was somewhat skeptical but seeing Darian disappear and reappear in front of my eyes certainly opened me up to the possibility. I wondered if the other Gods had granted the Manu any gifts. "So the Manu can see the future?"

She shook her head. "Only what is likely, but the Manu learned long ago not to seek the gift because of the danger."

"Why? What danger?" I asked in shock. If I had such a gift I'd use it constantly.

The Vija didn't answer. Instead she got up from her stump and went into her tree to return a moment later with an egg in her hand. She walked over to me and held the egg out at arm's length. "I'm going to drop this," she announced.

I stared dumbfounded at her for about a second before she dropped it. I shot my hand forward to catch the egg, thinking it to be some kind of test. I managed to catch it but spilled my stew all over the ground in the process. I held the egg up triumphantly not understanding the point.

"Why did you do that?" the Vija asked.

"Because you told me to," I said.

"I only told you I was going to drop the egg. You assumed I wanted you to catch it. Perhaps I was disposing of it because it had gone bad? Perhaps I wanted to feed it to Yona? And look, now you've spilled your food just to catch a silly egg." I was beginning to understand her point. "Rocana's gift is dangerous because we're just humans. We lack the perspective needed to understand the visions of the future we see. Only those who spend years focused on controlling the power, and interpreting what is seen, have any hope of using it safely."

"Like the Vija?" I said, catching on.

"Aye," she said flashing me one of her almost-smiles.

"So…the average Manu doesn't use Rocana's gift at all?"

"The wise ones don't," she said. "Though sometimes it manifests spontaneously. Maybe just before one would be struck by a snake? Or walk across a rotten plank on a bridge?"

It's a good thing I wasn't Manu. For me, having that kind of power and not being able to use it would be torture.

"Perhaps I can see a connection to your book that will allow it to be translated. There is no certainty, but I will try."

"That's all I ask, Vija."

She nodded and said, "I will ask one thing of you."

"Name it."

"I ask that you swear to the Gods that you use any information you gain wisely."

"By the ten Gods, I swear it."

"Very well then," she said, walking off toward her hollow redwood. "We'll go when the stars watch over us."

Now I understood why Master Carter suggested come here before any further action. Hopefully Vija Saptarsi could point me right where I needed to go to translate the book. Visions of being the youngest Adept Mage in the Academy's history and bringing glory to House Arga once again filled my head. I was roused from my reverie by an enormous bear head between my legs, licking stew off my feet. I thought about gently trying to extract myself but decided to simply leave it alone as long as it didn't get rough. When the bear finished cleaning up the spilled stew, it wondered off into the woods to forage or do whatever bears do.

"Good fortune for both of us, huh?" Darian said. "You get your answer and I get full pay."

"I don't have any answer yet," I pointed out. "Why didn't you tell me about Rocana's gift when we were discussing Tarka's?"

Darian walked over to a spot of thick grass and flopped down, stretching out. "We're guarded about what we tell outsiders, m'lady. I was hesitant to tell you about Tarka's gift, but if I'm not mistaken you would have just hounded me day and night until I finally relented."

"You're not mistaken," I said wiping the bear slobber off my leg. "Did the Gods grant your people any other gifts?"

"Indeed, m'lady," he said pulling his hood down over his eyes. "We're blessed with very good looks. Now I suggest you get some rest before tonight."

Taking a nap was probably a fine idea, but I was far too excited to sleep. I spent the time going over my books and pondering all that Vija had said, while my guards polished their weapons. Sunset cast long shadows across the camp as Yona came back from its wanderings to flop down next to Darian with a thud.

The temperature cooled quickly and though the air smelled of distant rain it was a clear, calm night. The stars added their twinkly illumination to Ananda's silvery beams. Vija Saptarsi emerged from her tree with a thickly-stuffed pack on her back. I noted with little surprise that she hardly reacted to the coldfire I'd summoned. "It is time," she said.

Darian stretched and gained his feet as the Vija walked past him and drew herself onto the saddle on Yona's back. "Leave the horses here, but be sure to bring your book," she said.

I patted my endless bag more to reassure myself than any other reason. The shadows were deep beneath the redwoods and my guards squeezed close to my coldfire, though I noted Vija Saptarsi and Darian easily managed by only the moonlight piercing the canopy.

After half an hour we broke through the trees to see a series of rocky bluffs. The Vija led us up to a stack of large boulders, and climbed gracefully off her ursine mount. "There's not enough room for everyone. Your escorts will have to wait here," she said and turned to face the houseguards adding, "She will come to no harm. You have my word."

"It's alright," I said.

"As ye wish, m'lady," Koto said with a resigned sigh. He was proving far easier to train than I'd figured he'd would.

Darian and I followed the Vija as she squeezed through a narrow opening between the rocks. We stepped into a small cave formed by the boulders. It was maybe ten strides across with a fire-pit in the middle. The walls of the cave were black from the smoke of countless fires and there was an opening to the sky. I looked through it to see stars twinkling down upon us.

The Vija gestured for us to sit around the pit as she pulled wood from her pack and kindled a small fire. Once the fire was going she took a seat and gazed skyward through the opening. "Lord Rocana," she said in the Refined tongue spoken by priests and devotees, "hear my prayer and guide me in the use of your gift." She reached into her pack again and withdrew several long braids of what looked like dried grass and pitched them into the fire. "The smoke will allow you to see as I see," she said, as the fire began to billow a pleasant sweet-smelling gray smoke. Vija Saptarsi extended her hand toward me. "The book."

I gently withdrew the Sarga Paza from my bag and handed it to her. The Vija cradled it gingerly in her lap as she cast her eyes toward stars with a distant unfixed expression. With her gaze still skyward, she reached down and opened the book unerringly to the page with the mysterious diagram. The smoke swirled and churned as it began to take on noticeable shapes. I found myself gasping as the smoke poured itself into the form of a young mage, sitting in front of a table with two open books as he painstakingly wrote in one of them.

"That's the mage who copied the book," I said with a shock of recognition.

The Vija said nothing, her gaze serene and distant. The smoke shifted to form the image of the original book being pulled from the rubble. Just as the image solidified it shifted again to that of a man wearing a jeweled turban bearing the book under his arm.

"Do you recognize him as well?" Darian asked.

I squinted at the swirling image. "I don't think so."

The Vija sounded far away. "We are witnessing the distant past."

"He's talking to someone," Darian said.

The smoky image panned back, revealing a massive bulky figure I'd never seen before. The creature was easily twice the height of the man standing next to him, with huge leathery wings sprouting from its shoulders and backward legs ending in cloven hooves. Its head bore sweeping horns and a bestial maw filled with sharp teeth, while great clawed hands gestured as it talked to the man. It was difficult to make out in the smoky image but the demon seemed to have skin liked cracked stone and a hazy aura about him. I'd seen images of every Anaviya, but I'd never seen this creature, which led me to the most likely conclusion.

"That's Shakkar the Wise," I said, mouth agape.

"What?" said Darian.

The image changed again. The demon was now trapped in a circle and raging against it inside the ruins of a vast cathedral. A surge went through me as I noted the diagrams of the circle matched the mystery one from the book. I'd been right! But something about the image was out of place.

"I recognize those columns. That's the ruins of Vizipa," I said, noting the famous structure. "That doesn't make any sense. It was only destroyed a few hundred years ago. When are we seeing?"

The Vija still gazed at the stars, and her voice sounded far off when she responded, "Now. What you are looking at is happening as we speak."

"What? That's not possible," I said. "There must be some mistake. That demon hasn't been seen on this Realm for three thousand years."

"There is no mistake, child. We are watching the present," the Vija said with certainty.

I watched the demons rage play out as it gave up and slumped down in the center of the circle. "Well…can you see how it got there?"

The image softened and blurred, taking on a series of half-formed shapes. For a brief moment, the smoke congealed into what looked like an Eastern-style tower topped with a minaret. Vija Saptarsi's eyes snapped open, her serene features replaced by a look of shock and horror.

The smoke swirled violently forming a new image. Robed figures stood in a wide ring chanting, performing some kind of ritual with the rising sun behind them. In the center between them, a rift began to open. It was similar to the kind a mage could open between Acala and Eather while on a verge. When the rift was large enough to fill the space between them, demons began to flood out of it. They came in the hundreds, then in the thousands.

"They're opening a gate to Hell," I gasped. "But a gate directly between our Realms shouldn't even be possible…"

"Vija, what are we seeing?!" shouted Darian.

"The future," the Vija said between in quick shallow breaths and visibly straining.

"When?" I asked.

The scene before us sped up. Demons continued to flow out of the gate as the sun rose higher in the sky. Finally as the sun crossed the horizon again, the rift shrank and closed as the stars became visible in the sky. "The Autumnal Equinox," she said.

"That's less than six months away," Darian said.

"There are millions of them," I said reaching out to touch the roiling mass of tiny smoky demons.

My mind raced as I sought to put the pieces together. The walls between the Realms were the thinnest during the equinox, but it still shouldn't be possible to open a rift. It would, at the very least, take mages on both sides holding a portal like that open. "How is this connected to the book?" I asked.

Sweat beaded on the Vija's forehead as she gazed at the stars. The smoke roiled and flowed, returning to the present-day image of the demon in his circular prison. Her voice was strained when she spoke. "This event appears to be tied to the creature trapped in the circle." The smoke churned violently as the images cycled quickly in reverse ending with the mage copying the book again. "And the book is definitely connected to the demon."

"Where does it happen?" Darian asked with a look of panicked determination. "We know *when* the ritual happens. If we know *where* it happens we can kill the robed men, or at least disrupt their task."

The Vija's composure began to slip as she shook visibly. The images cycled quickly forward again returning to the open rift. The image strained and shook, seemingly twisting on itself and dispersing only to reform with slight differences such as mountains or a river in the background. Vija Saptarsi shook her head quickly, eyes shining with unshed tears. "It doesn't matter. Seeking them out will only cause them to move their ritual elsewhere."

"There *must* be something that can be done," I said. "Millions of unbound demons flowing into the world would be catastrophic."

Tears flowed freely down the Vija's face as she stared skyward grimacing in pain. The smoke flowed and churned like an amorphous beating heart before finally forming into the image of a woman standing in the ruined cathedral before the imprisoned demon. It looked like she was dismissing the circle holding the Anaviya.

"Samara, that's *you*," Darian said reaching into the smoky image to point out my endless bag. He was right. The woman before me was garbed in strange clothes but it was definitely me.

"Surely there's another way?" I pleaded. "Vija, there's got to be another way to stop this."

The image shimmered and blurred several times before returning to me standing before the demon. Finally the Vija had reached her breaking point, collapsing back in exhaustion and pain, the image devolving into an unrecognizable puff of gray smoke as it wafted to the sky. Darian threw himself to catch her, and then cradled her against him as sobs wracked her body.

I sat dumfounded by what I'd just seen. Thoughts crackled through my head like lightning between clouds of a thunderstorm. There was no way the fate of millions, maybe even the world, rested in the hands of one Initiate mage. Surely she must be mistaken. After a moment Vija Saptarsi's weeping abated and she regained enough control to set up by herself, though she was still shaky. Darian handed her a water skin from her bag and she drank deeply.

"Vija, are you sure of what you saw?" I asked. To me my voice sounded like that of a little girl asking her father if he was sure her mother wasn't coming back.

A look of profound sadness and compassion crossed her face. "Aye, child. I'm sure."

"But…you said Rocana's gift only let you see what is likely to happen. How likely are the events you saw?" I asked plaintively.

"As likely as the egg would have been to hit the ground if you hadn't caught it."

"Maybe when you've recovered you can look again? P-perhaps there's something you missed?"

She shook her head. "No, nothing was missed. I'm sorry to lay this burden upon you."

It felt as if the ground shook beneath me. Vija Saptarsi then turned and spoke to Darian in the Manu tongue. Whatever she said to him left him looking stricken. Suddenly it seemed there wasn't enough air in the cave. I stumbled back out of the entrance and fell on my knees in the cold dirt trying to catch my breath.

Koto startled at seeing me. "M'lady, are ye alright?"

I was a long way from alright. I knelt there hyperventilating, trying to get my breathing under control. At length when I regained my breath I said, "Something bad is coming. We must return to warn the Empire with haste."

Darian emerged from the cave with Vija Saptarisi leaning heavily on him. Yona appeared immediately, nuzzling her gently with a concerned look. She murmured to the bear in Manu, who knelt so she could mount with ease.

"Did that witch do somethin' bad to ye, m'lady?" Koto said with a tone of concern.

"Yes," I said drawing myself up. "She showed me the future."

The light from the open tent flap woke me from my uneasy slumber. We'd gotten back to camp well after midnight and I'd slept fitfully, plagued by dreams of portals and demons. I glanced up to see Autumn entering the tent with a bundle of clothes under her arm. The outside world looked gray and foggy.

"Sorry to wake you, Mistress. There's no need to rise just yet. The houseguards have barely woken."

"What about Darian? We need to be off soon."

"He went down to the river. Try and get some more rest, Mistress. I'll wake you for breakfast."

"Alright," I said laying back down as Autumn busied herself packing the tent.

I had just dozed back to sleep when I heard a series of clicks in quick succession followed by cries of pain. My eyes snapped open and I thought maybe I'd dreamed the noise until I saw Autumn's panicked face.

"What was that?" Autumn said in a barely audible whisper.

I shook my head violently and pressed a finger to my mouth to silence her. Panic welled up inside me making it hard to breathe. With an effort of will I bottled it up and pushed it aside. I slipped out of bed and crept over with

Autumn to the tent flap, easing it open just enough for us to see out.

The horses bayed and whinnied in alarm. A thick fog, accompanied by a drizzling rain, had moved in overnight limiting visibility to a couple dozen feet. All I could see was my houseguards splayed out on the ground or kneeling, clutching at the shafts of the crossbow bolts protruding out of them. They hadn't even put their armor on yet. Then men emerged from the fog of the meadow. They were sharp men, clad in leather armor, bearing either crossbows or long swords and round knobby shields. All except for one. One was clad in robes of scarlet damask bearing strange tattooed symbols the color of tarnished copper on his brow and his throat.

Autumn and I huddled together, shivering and trying to keep quiet as nearly a score of men walked out of the fog toward the injured houseguards. One of men said in Common, "I don't see the women."

The one with the tattoos answered in a lilting accent. "Finish off the guards and search the tents." The men split into two groups. The one led by the tattooed man moved to search the tents and the other moved toward the wounded guards.

Most of the Arga houseguards were too wounded to move but Koto had managed to draw his sword and used it has a crutch to stand. "Come and get some, ye cowardly cunts," he said in a wheezy breath.

Two of the leathered men strode forward with easy confidence and one of them lunged forward with a strong thrust going for the quick kill. With a burst of unforeseen speed Koto parried the blade with his gladius and kicked the knobby shield to the side, bringing his fast short blade back around with a blur across the man's gut. He looked down with shock and disbelief as he tripped over his own bowels before falling hard to the ground. Koto then turned to the other soldier with a bloody smile and said, "Yer turn, lad."

Another series of those horrible clicks sent a half dozen more bolts slamming into Koto and still he wouldn't fall, only sinking to his knees and feebly managed to hold on to his gladius. He said something weakly as the man he just threatened kicked his sword out of his hand. Koto spit blood in the man's face just before his head was struck from his shoulders.

Autumn started to make a noise but I thrust my hand over her mouth to silence her. We had to keep our senses and act quickly or we were both about to die. My head was a bee hive of wildly buzzing thoughts. I couldn't kill them all, but maybe I could cast a spell that would confuse them long enough to escape into the woods. In this fog we might be able to make it to Vija Saptarsi, who would surely know what to do.

We watched with horror filled eyes as the leather clad men started searching the tents and putting put my poor wounded houseguards to the sword. The only consolation was that most of them were too far gone to notice. Dirk wasn't though. He rolled over on his back and started dragging himself away, and saying, "Please no. D-don't d-do this." One of the armored men strode forward without the slightest hesitation or remorse, ready to put his sword through Dirk's heart.

I felt Autumn tense a split second before she shrugged off my grasp and broke from the tent screaming, "Dirk, no!" In that moment all reason fled. I saw in her gold eyes only terror for the man she loved. Autumn ran up to the leather-clad man from behind and grabbed his sword hand with both of hers out of pure reflex. The man probably had a hundred pounds on her, but Autumn held on to that hand with all her might and he couldn't gain the leverage to get free of her. Finally he twisted and slammed the edge of his shield into her face, sending her falling limply to the ground. He turned dispassionately back to his previous task of putting his steel through Dirk's chest. The light faded from his eyes, fixed on Autumn crumpled on the ground next to him, feebly reaching for her hand.

"I got her over here," the man said as he flung Dirks blood off his blade.

The tattooed man answered, "That one has brown hair. The Ally said the one we're looking for is a red-head. Finish her off and keep searching."

Rage, deep and all-encompassing, welled up inside of me and pushed the fear aside. Normally one wished for a calm mind when spell casting, but I let my rage focus me. I put all of my pain and terror and anger into the spell as I drew the power and shaped it with my will.

Dirk's murderer turned to raise his blade toward Autumn's prone, unmoving form. It was the last thing he ever did. Lightning split the air between my outstretched hands and my leather-clad target. His head exploded from the force of the power coursing through him and blew his armor off his body, sending smoking pieces of leather in all directions.

Few have stood next to a lightning strike and yet live to tell, but the thunder is deafening. My spell protected me form the ear-splitting noise but the soldiers stood dumbfounded clutching their ringing ears. All except for the tattooed man in the red robes. He cast about looking for the source of the spellcasting.

"There she is," he said, pointing at me. Though no one heard him, he had a group of nine soldiers who were searching the tents with him and they followed his finger to see me. The tattooed man's hands started to glow as he shaped a spell of his own. Unfortunately for them, I'd already begun casting again the moment after I'd loosed the lightning. They had no chance of escape.

As my hands formed the final mudras, a gout of flame a dragon would have been envious of erupted from between them. The soldiers had maybe a second to scream before the cone of flame washed over them stealing the air from their lungs to fuel my vicious inferno. I released the spell, seeing the destruction I'd wrought as twisted black forms crumpled to the ground and canvas flew free of blackened tent posts.

I was torn from my trance by another chorus of clicks as the tent flap bucked wildly and my breath was stolen from me. I looked down to see a shaft protruding from my belly and another from my thigh. A distant analytical part of my brain noted they must have had time to reload the crossbows.

I reached down in disbelief to touch the shaft protruding just below and to the right of my navel. As if touching it finally made it real, pain sprung from my wounds, erupting through my body. I sank slowly to my knees, reality coming into focus even as my vision blurred with tears. I was about to die. "I'm sorry, Autumn…I tried," I whispered hoarsely.

A torrent of emotions rushed through me. Anger, fear, longing, but mostly sadness. I was sad for my houseguards, for Autumn, for my brothers and my father, who'd already lost so much. Sad for the people who would suffer if the portal opened. But mostly I was sad for me. Sad I'd never fall in love, or get married, or have children. Sad I'd never learn any more magic or be honored by my house. And as strange and unimportant as it seems, sad I'd never solve the mystery of Shakkar's demon.

I slumped down on my side laying my head against a half full pack of clothes and thought of Darian. Autumn said he'd gone down to the river. Maybe he'd heard the thunderbolt and escaped. Surely there's no way the soldiers would find him in the forest. He was resourceful and tenacious, hopefully he could find a way to warn the Empire. The Vija had said I was the only chance of stopping the portal, but then she hadn't seen this coming. Maybe she was wrong about that, as well. Finally, I felt annoyance that my last thoughts were about Darian.

The pain slowly faded as warm, velvety darkness enveloped me. Apparently Arati had decided I'd suffered enough, learned enough, and grown enough to take my pain away. *Thank you,* I prayed. Most people were scared of the Mistress of Darkness, but in her embrace all I felt was safe. If this was death, maybe it wasn't so bad.

I just hoped I would see my mother again on the other side.

Chapter Ten
Darian

The thick soupy fog that often appeared at this time of year crept its way through the forest just before dawn, and had brought with it a gentle misting rain. The dour weather suited my mood as I picked my way through the moss-covered trees toward the river. Smoky visions haunted me, robbing me of sleep until dawn found me.

How had I gotten involved in this mess? I should have simply told the troublesome Zurans I wouldn't be their guide. I made my mind up that when this was over, I was done with nobles, no matter how much they paid for horses.

I was so wrapped up in my thoughts that I almost missed the tracks. Perfect fresh horse tracks, no more than an hour old, scored the earth. They most likely belonged to Manu going to see the Vija, but as I bent down to examine them, I noted they bore the imprint of Zuran-style horse shoes. They weren't ours, so what were Zuran horses doing this far into the Mystewood? My thoughts went to the trampled plants I'd seen the other night. We were being stalked.

In that moment, it was as though the light of all the stars in the sky flashed before my eyes as Rocana's gift flooded my senses. I saw myself standing over Samara as she lie in a pool of blood. As fast as it came, the vision was gone, leaving me staggered for a moment as my wits returned.

Vija Saptarsi's words echoed in my ears from the night before as Samara fled the cave. "Without your aid, she will never complete her task," she'd said to me with compassion in her eyes. "I'm sorry to add weight to an already overburdened heart."

I yanked my bow from my shoulder and fled back toward the camp, heedless of any other concern. There was no way I was going to let another woman under my protection slip from this world. And if Samara died, she condemned millions more to the same fate before an army of demons.

I tore back through the forest, scanning the trees for any sign of our faceless pursuers. The fog made it impossible to see farther than a dozen strides in front of me. I heard the sounds of panicked horses before I saw anything. The tents had been arranged near the tree line with Samara's in the middle. I drew Tarka's gift around me as I cleared one of the tents on the far end.

The camp was in chaos. Nearly twenty leather-armored men were spread about the camp. Samara's guards lay dead or dying, scattered amongst them like cord wood.

I was nearly blinded and deafened by a lightning strike as one of the men simply exploded. I was stunned for moment and I realized I'd dropped Tarka's gift. I pulled it around me once again and my vision cleared just in time to see half the soldiers immolated in a burst of flame. The heat stung my face from clear across the camp.

Samara.

Seven soldiers remained, three of them armed with crossbows. After a moment of shock at what they'd just witnessed, they turned their crossbows on Samara's tent. I quickly drew an arrow and fired taking one of them in the chest, but there was no time to stop the other two. A hand closed around my heart as the tent flap whipped and bucked from the impact of their crossbow bolts.

Whatever else happened today these men were all going to die.

I released another arrow at one of the remaining crossbowmen, the effort causing me to drop Tarka's gift. Only luck saved the man as he turned at the last instant. He took the arrow in his leather pauldren instead of his neck. One of the men took note of me pointing and shouting.

I moved behind one of the redwoods calling Tarka's gift back around me as I came out the other side with an arrow drawn. The men bearing the shields were closing on my position, leaving the crossbowmen who were still reloading vulnerable. I took the one who'd been spared by his pauldron in the eye.

As the swordsmen saw me become visible in front of them, one of them shouted, "Another mage! Take 'em down, quick!" The swordsmen rushed in, bearing their shields aloft giving me time for only one more arrow before they closed on me, so I took the only shot I had. One of them howled as my arrow slipped beneath his shield, catching him in the thigh and bringing him down hard.

The other three were upon me, forcing me to toss my bow aside and draw my kukri. My options were limited. I had to finish this fast to have any chance of saving Samara and there was still one remaining crossbowman. If the men had confronted me using legion tactics and faced me as a phalanx, I might have been forced to retreat and try another plan, but they chose to break apart and attempt to surround me. That, I could work with.

A man with a ghastly scar that pulled his lip up chose to engage me while the other two worked their way around to encircle me. He wielded a longsword like he knew what he was doing but he was clearly no expert. He swung a couple of tight slashes using the reach of his sword to try and position me as he wanted. I parried lightly with the side of my heavy kukri and I gave ground. He betrayed his intention to send a hard thrust to my belly when he set his shield and followed it up with slow footwork. I shot forward and to the left of his thrust, catching his blade in the bend of my kukri and let it slide up his blade. I eased my dagger out of its sheath with my left hand. My knife bit through his leather armor, searching for his kidney.

I had no time to press my advantage as a man with a red beard charged in from my left. I continued with my circular momentum, putting my left shoulder to Scar Lip's right. I spun and yanked my dagger free, ending with my back to his, robbing Red Beard of his target. My safety was short-lived though, as I saw the crossbowman aiming down his sights at me. I continued circling around, putting Scar Lip between us as I squared off against his allies.

Red Beard and his friend, a tall man with bright green eyes, came at me more warily. They closed on me slowly, working together as I struggled to keep the grimacing Scar Lip between me and the crossbow. They attacked together with a series of conservative thrusts and chops, trying to slip something past my defense. I parried and dodged, then sent a few slashes of my own to keep them at bay. If I gave up too much ground I'd be digging a crossbow bolt out of my back.

Finally Green Eyes came forward with a hard slash that I knew would leave him overextended. I fell into a low crouch, letting his steel pass harmlessly over my head, then popped up, slashing hard. Green Eyes managed to get his shield in the way but was forced to retreat quickly. Red Beard came in for my unguarded back exactly as I hoped. I twisted, letting the thrust pass within a finger's width of me, and took the man's sword hand off at the wrist. He stared in disbelief at his missing hand for an instant before I took his head.

Thrown into a rage at the death of his friend, Green Eyes came at me wildly with a barrage of swings. I gave ground, waiting for an opening. Just as I was about to strike, however, I heard a click and immediately fell to the ground. I could feel a crossbow bolt pass through my hair as I dropped. Scar Lip had caught on to my game, taking a knee to let his friend have a shot at me.

Green Eyes had me at a strong disadvantage and he knew it. He pressed me hard. I didn't have time to dodge his attack but I managed to get a plate-backed bracer between my head and his sword. The impact sent a numbing shock through my arm and I barely managed to hold on to my dagger. I took the only escape I had, rolling back toward Scar Lip, which I realized immediately could prove a fatal decision.

Despite his grievous wound, he moved forward with a burst of speed to slash at my vulnerable back before I'd recovered. There was nothing I could do except hope his first attack didn't kill me outright, so I braced for injury. His blade fell short.

He looked down in surprise to see a hand around his ankle. Harold held fast despite the bolts protruding from his chest, which bought me enough time to gain my feet. Scar Lip turned back in frustration and opened Harold's throat. Still the brave houseguard held on. It was Harold who killed him, not me. I was just the instrument of his death.

Wounded, his foot trapped, Scar Lip could do nothing but stare at me with hate-filled eyes as I batted his sword away and struck. He brought his shield up to cover his head so I took him across the belly. He dropped his shield and my kukri split his skull like a melon.

Green Eyes came at me again so I dove over Scar Lip's corpse and rolled to my feet putting his body between us. The crossbowman had his head down as he reloaded his weapon so I seized the moment. I threw my dagger end-over-end to catch him in the neck just below his ear. I turned to face Green Eyes and calmly removed my other dagger as he surveyed the scene with a new sense of perspective. All of his allies were dead or dying and now he faced me alone. He looked around for a chance to escape.

That wasn't going to happen.

I came at him with a flurry of powerful attacks, using my heavy blade to slap his sword aside when he tried to use his reach against me. He gave ground before my barrage, stumbling over a root, and I pressed my advantage, seeking to split his head as I'd done his friend. Somehow he managed to get his shield in the way, and my kukri split it nearly in half. I tried to withdraw my blade and finish the job but it was stuck. Green Eyes knew it, too. He shouldered forward, slamming his shield into me with all of his weight.

I rolled back as he came at me with a series of blows and he tripped over the same root again, giving me an opportunity to gain some distance. Green Eyes regained his balance and tossed aside his broken shield. I was facing him with only a dagger and he smiled wickedly at me. "Got you now, you bastard," he growled.

"Do you?" I said, calling upon Irin's gift to take the edge off the exhaustion and the pain in my arm. I shifted the dagger to my right hand, and gave ground freely against his aggressive flurry. I looked for an opening until finally he gave me one, thrusting hard when he thought I was off balance. I stepped, in sliding his blade harmlessly down my dented bracer.

"Clever savag-" was all he got out before my dagger found his throat. As he fell to the ground, I looked around, searching for any who were still a threat. The one with the arrow through his thigh had hobbled over to reclaim one of the fallen crossbows and was in the process of loading it.

I moved behind the tree, calling Tarka's gift around me once more, and found my discarded bow. I stepped back to see the man searching for me frantically and calling out for any remaining allies. I ended his search with another arrow, this time finding his heart.

Seeing no one else moving in the camp, I let go of both Tarka and Irin's gifts. Weariness and pain washed over me in a hot wave. The light drizzle had grown into rain, choking out the remaining fire from Samara's inferno and washing the blood downhill in small crimson streams. "Thank you for the help, my friend," I said, as I knelt and closed Harold's wide blue eyes.

I crossed the camp, stepping over the corpses of friend and foe alike to reach Samara's tent, terrified of what I would find. It was just as I had seen before with Rocana's gift. Samara lay unmoving crumpled on her side with bolts in her belly and thigh.

"Samara? Can you hear me?" I asked, kneeling in a pool of her blood. I laid my hand lightly on her chest to see if I could feel her breathing. Her eyelids fluttered briefly and she gave a weak cough. I blew out a relieved breath. "Thank all the Gods. I'm going to have to move you so I can get a better look at your wounds."

She gave no response but when I gently rolled her to her side, a weak moan escaped her lips. The bolt in her abdomen went all the way through, poking out her back as I had suspected, and the one in her leg had thankfully missed the big veins and arteries, but she'd still lost a lot of blood.

I heard a noise from outside and someone moving about. I realized I still hadn't reclaimed my missing weapons so I took up my one remaining dagger and called Tarka's gift around me before slipping outside. It was Autumn. She was clutching Dirk's body against her and rocking back and forth as she wept. She looked like she'd taken a hard blow to the head. Her left eye was swollen shut and blood trickled out of her nose, staining the front of her dress.

"Thank the Gods again. Autumn? How bad are you hurt? Can you walk?" She continued to rock, holding Dirk clutched against her. "Autumn, please I need your help." When I got no response from her again, I knelt next to her and put my hand on her shoulder, giving her a gentle shake. Her gold eye opened wide with terror for a moment before she focused on me, recognition slowly dawning.

"D-Darian? I don't know what to do. He's…he's…" she said looking back to Dirk.

"There's nothing you can do for him, Autumn. He's gone. But if you can walk, I need your help with Samara."

"Samara?"

"Yes, she's hurt."

"She…she's hurt?"

"Hurt badly, and we must act with haste if we're going to save her."

She nodded rapidly and looked back at Dirk one last time, kissing him gently on the forehead before setting him down and shakily gaining her feet. She looked around and noticed the carnage of the camp for the first time. "Wh…what happened? Are they all dead?"

"Yes."

"Are you sure?"

"Yes. Now come on," I said, losing patience.

"How?"

"Samara killed most of them and I cleaned up what was left. Now come on. There's no time to explain more." There very well could be others out there but we didn't have time to deal with that if we were going to help Samara.

When we got into the tent, Autumn lost her fragile composure again. "Oh, no. No, no, no. Mistress, can you hear me? Mistress?" she said, turning Samara's face to hers.

"Autumn," I said, "I need you to find something to cut up that we can use as bandages."

Autumn continued to cradle Samara's head. "Mistress, please say something. You have to say something!" Maybe she'd been hit harder in the head than I realized.

"Autumn, I need you to listen to me."

"Please, Mistress just say someth—" I gave her a swift slap across her face, not with enough force to hurt her but with enough to get her attention.

"Do you wish for your mistress to die?" I shouted.

She stared back at me with one watery gold eye. "N-no. Of course not."

"Then you need to do exactly what I say. No arguments. Do you understand?"

She blinked a few times, clarity returning, and said, "Yes, I understand. What do you need me to do?"

"Good," I said blowing out a sigh. "I need you to cut up some blankets or something into long strips to use as bandages. Alright?" I said, holding my dagger out to her by the blade.

"Alright," she said, nodding vigorously as her hand closed around the knife's handle. She worked quickly while I gingerly moved Samara to the cot to make it easier to keep pressure on her wounds while I worked on her.

Autumn presented me with several long strips and said, "What now?"

"Fold a couple of them up to make pads," I said. "We've got to remove the arrow so I can close the wound."

"Do you need a needle and thread?"

I shook my head. "That wouldn't work for this type of injury anyway."

"What then?"

"Just trust me," I said. "The first thing I have to do is break off the ends so I can push it through cleanly. Just be ready to hand me the pads when I ask for them."

Autumn looked pale as a lily but she nodded. "I'm ready."

I stood over the cot with Samara lying on her side beneath me as I gripped both sides of the bolt. "You may have to hold her if she fights." Autumn nodded and sat down on the cot. I took a breath to steady myself, and then in quick succession broke off first the head then the fletching.

Samara let out a sharp cry and fluttering lids revealed pale arctic eyes staring up at me. "S'not s'post to hurt," she mumbled.

I let out a short laugh, despite myself. "How is getting shot with a crossbow supposed to feel then?" I asked

"S'not what ah meant," she slurred.

Tears streamed down Autumn's cheeks as she said, "It's good to hear you speak, Mistress."

Samara turned to gaze at Autumn through heavy eyelids. "Autumn? M'srry. Tried t'save you."

"You did save me, Mistress."

Samara's brows crinkled infinitesimally in confusion. "Then why'r you here?"

Autumn looked at me with questioning eyes. "She's just confused from the blood loss. Let me see those pads," I said. She passed me the pads and I positioned them just below the wound on both sides. "Alright, hold her tight." Autumn leaned over Samara's shoulder gripping her snuggly. "I'm afraid this is going to hurt, m'lady."

"What'r you do....Ah!" Samara cried out clenching her eyes shut as I pushed the shaft through in one fluid motion, quickly putting the pads over the wounds as the bleeding started freely flowing again. Pale eyes stared at me with recognition. "D...Darian? That hurt. Why'd you do that?"

"Apologies, m'lady, I had no choice," I said the glanced over at Autumn.

"I'm going to close the wound now, it may take several minutes and I need to concentrate." Autumn nodded again and took Samara's hand.

I took a deep breath, pushing all the pain and fear and panic out of my mind. It wasn't so much a question of calling Ananda's gift as it was creating a space for it. Like an upside down wine bottle, the cork simply had to be removed. I gazed down at Samara lying helpless beneath me and let my compassion and concern for her wash over me. I felt Ananda's love and mercy flowing in through the chakra at the top of my head and filling me until I overflowed. My hands glowed with soft silvery moonlight as Ananda's mercy flowed into Samara's broken body.

Some of the tension eased out of her form and she sighed, her eyelids fluttering shut. "Mmm, tha' feels good. You c'n keep doin' that."

I kept it up, letting Ananda's mercy permeate the wound, until I sensed a change in the flow. I released my concentration, letting the gift slowly fade. I gingerly moved the blood soaked pad to see the wound. It had sealed up nicely, leaving only fresh new pink flesh.

Autumn gasped. "By the Gods! How?"

"An explanation will have to wait. Now help me do the same with her thigh wound."

Autumn nodded with wide eyes as I wrapped the pads in place with the strips of the makeshift bandages. The other wound was much easier to deal with. It was shallow, having gone in at an angle, and Samara slept through the whole procedure, only wincing when I pushed the shaft through.

"What now?" Autumn asked as I finished tying the bandage around the wounded leg.

"The wounds are closed but she can't stay here. She's going to need more healing."

"Can't you do it?" Autumn asked.

I shook my head, wiping my bloody hands on the remnants of the blanket. "She needs someone more talented with Ananda's gift."

"*More* talented?" Autumn said. "Her wound looks like it's been healing for days."

"I'm considered weak by Manu standards," I said shaking my head. "Besides, she's going to need an herbalist. Ananda's gift works wonders for trauma but it's less effective against infection. And if the wound to her belly nicked her bowel, she could be septic in a matter of hours."

Autumn gripped her mistress's hand tighter. "So what do we do?"

I blew out a deep breath, running my fingers through my hair. "I'm going to go get Vija Saptarsi, she should know what to do. Just stay with Samara and try to keep her comfortable. I shouldn't be gone for much longer than an hour."

"Just…just please come back. Don't leave us here." Fear was naked in her gold eye.

I didn't know Autumn very well but I pulled her in to a tight embrace and whispered into her ear, "I'll be back. I swear to all the Gods."

She took a ragged breath and squeezed me hard. "You'd better. May Kavi keep you safe."

As we pulled apart I reached down and brush Samara's cheek as she slept before turning and striding out. I walked through the carnage of the camp and collected my missing blades before going to saddle my horse. Just before I mounted a thought occurred to me. I picked up a crossbow and loaded it, bringing it to Autumn in the tent.

"Here take this," I said.

"I've never used one. Wh-what do I do?"

"Hope you don't need it. But if anyone other than me or the Vija walks through that door, point it at them and pull the trigger."

Autumn looked shaky but she took the crossbow without any protest. I left, mounting my horse and pulling my hood up against the rain. I made a wide circle around camp and easily found our attackers' horses just a few hundred yards away. There were no further signs that any of the leather-clad strangers yet stirred, so I gave Tavas my heels and sent him back the direction we'd come from just hours earlier.

I arrived at the Vija's camp to find it empty. I figured she would still be asleep, given the strenuous events of the night before but she was nowhere to be found. "Vija Saptarsi," I called. No response. "Vija Saptarsi, please, I need your help!" I called even louder.

She'd moved her laundry and the curing hides in the hollow of the tree and I saw clear bear tracks leading away to the north. She was gone. I thought about going after her. Yona would be easy to track, but for all I knew, Vija Saptarsi had left hours ago. I went into the tree and riffled through her herbs but saw nothing to treat infection. With a curse of frustration, I jumped back on Tavas and fled back to Autumn and Samara.

Thankfully the camp was just as I had left it. "Autumn, it's me," I made sure to call out before I entered the tent. Being slain by a spooked hand maiden would be an awfully bad way for a warrior to die.

"Did you find the Vija?" Autumn asked, sounding both panicked and relieved.

"No, she was gone," I said noting Samara's flushed cheeks as she slept. I knelt down putting my hand on her brow. She was already warm with fever.

"So what do we do?"

"We're going to take Samara back to my village."

"Won't it be bad for her to ride in her condition?"

"She doesn't have a choice."

"So what? We just throw her on a horse and ride two-and-a-half days back the way we came?"

I shook my head, "Samara doesn't have that long." When Autumn looked stricken I added, "But we can make it back to my village by nightfall."

"How?" she asked.

I met her panicked eye evenly and said simply, "By going straight through the Fae encampment."

Autumn saddled her horse and got together what we needed in relatively short order while I tended to Samara again. Together we carefully cut off what was left Samara's nightgown and wrapped her in a thick robe, and my leather surcoat to give her some protection from the rain. Sweat beaded on her flushed forehead as I gently picked her up and carried her outside.

I approached Tavas and said, "*Kneel down my friend*," relying on Suravani's gift to help him understand. Tavas's nostrils flared as he sniffed Samara once before laying down on his belly. With Autumn's aid, I mounted with Samara in front of me side-saddle leaning against my chest. I tied a long strip of the ruined blanket around both of us for some extra stability. "*Tavas, up*," I commanded. As he rose Samara winced at being jostled before relaxing again.

"Are you ready?" I asked.

"Yes," Autumn said, mounting her horse with Samara's bag. I changed position in the saddle a bit and leaned Samara's head against my shoulder. When I looked up I saw Autumn gazing back over the smoldering corpse-strewn hell that used to be our camp, her eye falling on Dirk's still form.

"We'll send someone back for them," I said. Autumn opened her mouth to reply then closed it and simply nodded as a tear slid down her cheek. She had no words. I, too, glanced over the fallen houseguards one last time. I hadn't known them very long, but I'd liked them. They certainly didn't deserve their fate.

We made our way to the river in silence and traveled along its banks for a few hours. By midday the rain had ceased and the sun burned through the clouds, giving the illusion of a serene, peaceful day. A few times Samara grew restless, murmuring and moaning in her fevered sleep. I called Ananda's gift to soothe her, as best I could on horseback. Despite my efforts, I could tell her fever was worsening.

As we neared the verge, conflict grew in me. I thought about sending Autumn along the path we'd taken before, but she was a woman of cities and palaces, not of the wild. I was afraid she'd get lost or make a decision that would get her killed in her ignorance. I finally decided she'd be better off staying with us, despite the threats we were about to face.

"What do you know of the Fae?" I asked, my voice piercing the relative silence of the forest.

She looked as though the question had caught her off guard. "Not that much. Just what I learned in school I suppose. I know that they're from Eather, they're dangerous, and they live in verges."

"All true," I said nodding. "You're going to have to try to stay calm. The Fae feed on emotions."

"What emotions?" she asked.

"It's different depending on the Fae. Some feed on greed or fear, others feed on anger or sadness. You've got to do your best to stay calm."

"I-I'll try."

"Try hard. If we're very lucky, we may make it through without them noticing us. Or they might choose to ignore us."

"Couldn't you just turn invisible and pass through? Then you could come back and get me when Samara's safe." It wasn't a bad idea, but it wouldn't work.

"Even if I wasn't exhausted I couldn't keep Tarka's gift around all of us for very long. And it wouldn't matter either way. The Fae don't need to see in order to find us. It would probably just make them angry." She shuddered at that as I continued. "This is important. If we do encounter the Fae, follow my lead and *do not talk*. No matter what. Do you understand?"

"Yes, I understand."

"However," I said continuing, "if I am attacked, or if I use the phrase 'diplomatic solution', you will immediately turn and spur your horse to the river, then follow it back to my village. Don't hold back and don't look back."

"I...I couldn't leave you and Samara," she said, aghast. I thought in that moment she might be the most loyal person I'd ever met.

"You *can* and you *will*. Someone has to stop the robed men from opening that portal, and that can't happen if no one knows it's coming," I said.

"Y-you're right. What...do you think my chances of making it would be?" she asked. I simply shook my head. She took a deep breath to steady herself and said, "Well, let's hope it doesn't come to that then."

"Let's hope," I echoed.

"What are you going to do if they do find us?"

"Treat with them," I said simply.

"Darian?"

"Yes?"

"In case I don't get to say it later. Thank you."

I stared back over my shoulder at Autumn's swollen and battered face and said, "You're welcome, Lady Autumn." She smiled a little at that.

I felt my skin prickle and noticed the forest around us was suddenly different. "Better start controlling those emotions now. We're at the verge." Autumn took a few deep breaths, obviously trying to get her feelings under control.

A verge was a weak spot between our Realm and Eather. They sprung up seemingly at random, some lasting weeks, others lasting millennia, and they were dangerous even under the best circumstances. Some of Eather's mercurial wildness bled over into our Realm, often driving the things in the verge mad, or twisting them into monstrous abominations, as was the case with the Varaha of the Black Creek verge. Elementals and the Fae could use these weak spots to easily pass back and forth between our Realms, causing them to be prime real estate. To make things even more interesting, the undead sometimes congregated at verges. Everything from mostly harmless, insubstantial shades, to bone-gnawing ghouls loitered there.

In this particular verge we only had to worry about the Fae, which was like saying, in this particular cave we only have to worry about the bears. It wasn't much of a comfort. The Fae were addicted to feeding on human emotions. In many places they constantly raided villages and settlements for victims. However, my people had a long-standing agreement with this particular enclave. As long as they stayed inside the verge, we stayed out of it, and they agreed to keep it free of other troublesome creatures. Neither side was anxious to breach that agreement, but that wouldn't necessarily protect us. I'd seen what was left of a Zatru prisoner that escaped and fled into the verge. When the Fae were done with him he didn't care enough not to soil his clothes, much less eat.

I didn't notice any Fae milling about as we entered their domain but I did notice some subtle differences in the forest. Vines slithered under their own volition, like snakes climbing the trees, while bees the size of sparrows buzzed about. Squirrels stopped chasing each other and simply watched us pass with a scrutinizing gaze, chattering back and forth as if discussing how strange and out of place we seemed to them.

Autumn and I spoke only in hushed whispers as we traveled down the muddy river banks going as quickly as we could while keeping Samara relatively comfortable. She burned with fever now, quietly murmuring incomprehensibly to herself. I did what I could for her, while at the same time, trying to keep my mind empty and my emotions calm. I maintained a sharp vigil as we followed the river for several hours, seeing nothing of note but the small strange oddities of the verge. When we were no more than an hour away from the far edge of the verge, hope began to rise in me that we might indeed make it through without being noticed. That was probably how they found us.

Movement drew my attention to the tree limbs that hung over the river. A creature dangled forty or so feet above the water, either believing itself hidden or just not caring if it was seen. It could have been mistaken for a child at a glance…but only at a glance.

Oversized, clawed feet gripped the branch as the goblin dangled bat-like, gangly arms crossed over its chest as it watched me. A tan doublet and breeches covered ruddy brown skin. His brown hair was shot through with white stripes and shaved on the sides, highlighting the large fox-like ears that jutted out from his head. Once he noticed me watching him, his smile grew impossibly wide, showing off a mouthful of long, needle-like teeth. Scuttling noises farther up in the branches told me he wasn't alone.

I whispered to Autumn, "Don't startle, but we've been spotted."

"Where?" she asked, searching around frantically.

"Up in the trees," I whispered, "Remember to stay calm. They may just let us pass."

As Autumn made an effort to control her breathing I noted three more goblins, indistinguishable from the first, skittering among the tree branches like squirrels.

"Where are you going in such a hurry?" asked a raspy voice in the airy Eatherial tongue from behind us. I turned my horse about to see a form emerging from the water. Tight black leather covered the alabaster skin of the lithe male Fae who stepped onto the riverbank. Instead of hair, a mess of slippery black octopus tentacles writhed and squirmed about his head, hiding half his face. The one eye I could see was like a large black pearl weeping tears of tarry jet. Obsidian lips parted in a mocking smile to show perfect ivory teeth. A shining silver owl broach was pinned to what I would have called a corset had it been worn by a woman. Even with a head full of squirming tentacles he was beautiful, but it was the detached alien beauty of the expensive porcelain dolls sold in Stonehaven.

"We seek but to pass through," I said.

The fae's nostrils flared as he tilted back his tentacled head and sucked in a deep breath. "Ahhhh, but you smell of such delicious despair. Especially you," he said turning his opalescent eye toward Autumn. When she visibly shuddered the corner of his mouth curved up in a cruel smile that held no trace of humanity.

I'd never met one if his kind before but I'd read about them at the Alaya. He was a sluagh. "Measure your tone when speaking to the lady unless you wish to be pulling my iron out of your body," I said, putting as much conviction into my words as I could manage. The one thing the Fae truly feared was iron.

The sluagh's black eye moved as it looked up and around indicating the goblins that surrounded us. "You don't seem to be in much of a position to make threats." He glided forward with the languid grace of a cat.

They were clearly not planning to let us pass, so I moved on to the backup plan. Bluff, bluff, bluff, and bluff some more. "If I were you," I said, "I wouldn't come any closer."

"Why is that? Are you going to throw the red-head at me?" he asked, still oozing forward.

"If you take another step, this mage is likely to cook you with a bolt of lightning," I said, gesturing with my head toward Autumn. "I've heard that your kind are tough, but I wonder how long it would take you to recover from that. The last man's head exploded." Autumn cast a confused look my way and I gave her an almost imperceptible nod. *Just go with it*, I willed her.

"Would you break the treaty between our people so easily?" he said, but I noted he did halt his approach.

I laughed mockingly. "Does she look like a Manu? She's a mage of the Empire. She could fry you and eat you with a side of butter in front of your friends and it wouldn't violate the treaty. But since you brought it up, if harm comes to any of us I imagine the Rangers will wipe out all of your kind by the end of the week."

The sluagh shook his head, sending his tentacles swaying. "All you humans look the same to me. You entered the verge, so I could feed upon you until you willingly cut your own throat to escape, and it wouldn't violate the treaty."

It was my turn to smile wickedly. "Do you think my kin would see it that way? We allow you to stay here in our forest because the arrangement is convenient for us. They would happily put iron through the heart of every bloody faerie in this verge if it was no longer so."

Now he looked unsure. "So I'm just supposed to let you walk out of our territory? I don't think—"

"Clearly thinking is your problem," I interrupted. "I'm obviously talking to the wrong faerie. Take me to the Owl Queen so that I might parlay with someone of real authority. Unless of course the two of you would like to settle this disagreement amongst yourselves?" Autumn took the cue beautifully, gesturing at the sluagh and making the same movements with her hands that Samara did during spell casting.

Tentacles twisted violently. The sluagh obviously seethed with anger at being talked down to by a mere human. However, it appeared as though he wasn't too interested in having it out with a mage, either. "As you wish," he spat. I could hear goblins snickering in the trees above us. "Follow me." He turned and stalked bonelessly off into the woods.

I wiped the sweat from Samara's brow and adjusted her a bit more comfortably before following. Autumn shot me a worried glance but said nothing as the beautiful, terrible creature led us deeper into the verge. The goblins followed as well, attracting more of their kin. Some skittered among the tree limbs while others ran along the ground with the awkwardness of a youth caught between childhood and adolescence. They were indistinguishable from one another as they watched us with predatory eyes and sharp smiles. Every now and then our guide would cast a baleful opalescent glance over his shoulder at us, but he maintained his dour silence as his tarry black tears dripped to the forest floor.

Once we arrived at the heart of the verge, I had to check myself to keep from just staring in awe. Zuran-style homes hung suspended in the air attached to the redwoods like birdhouses in a twisted mockery of a Manu village. Some dangled from branches that obviously couldn't support them, while others seem simply glued to the tree trunks with no visible support.

A multitude of Fae congregated around us or watched from their suspended homes. Some I recognized from books or stories. There were painfully beautiful nymphs and dryads with bark-like skin or ivy hair who could have been mistaken for aspects of Suravani. A huge, tusked ogre with curving ram's horns and jaundiced-yellow skin effortlessly held a pine log over his shoulder as a club. Redcaps, with their jutting shark-like teeth and dripping crimson hats watched us with barely contained looks of hunger, while tiny, brightly colored pixies buzzed to and fro between us. There were a dozen or so other types of Fae I couldn't name. Some seemed to be odd mixtures of human and animal, while others were utterly alien.

The Sluagh led us to the center of a rough replica of a Zuran forum, where huge carved owls of white marble stared down on us from atop matching columns. A horde of Fae crowded around the edge of the paved forum to watch. The sluagh raised his face to the white marble villa that filled the space between two of the great redwoods about fifty feet above the forum. "My queen, we have guests who wish to parlay," he spat with a scowl.

A pair of twins emerged from the villa identical in every way, save they were negative images of one another. They were both clad in armor obviously modeled off the lorica segmenta worn by the legions, though the edges came to long, wicked points. Instead of the gladius and legion-standard shield, they each wielded a small buckler and long thin blade similar to a rapier. One set seemed crafted from alabaster and the other from obsidian. The one in white had a long thick braid as black as the sluagh's eye, while his twin's was as white as new snow. The thin, graceful ears that jutted from the oversized cutaways in their helmets identified them as sidhe. They moved in unison, one a dark reflection of the other.

Behind the twins flowed another sidhe, this one a tall woman. She wore a high-collared cape made entirely of owl feathers over an elaborate tawny gown that fell to her feet. The straight blond hair that framed her angular face was interspersed with the same feathers as her cape and her graceful fingers ended in raptor claws. A line of feathers dangled from her elegantly-pointed ears, and the yellow eyes of a horned owl stared down on us from her strikingly beautiful and utterly inhuman features. "Well," she said in thick rolling Eatherial, "let's see what our guests have to say."

The twins stepped from the villa falling the five stories to land as effortlessly as though they'd just hopped over a log. Now that they were before me, I could see the crest of their helmets were made of feathers. The Owl Queen followed them, gliding to the ground like a feather on the breeze, landing soundlessly behind the other two. The moment she stood before me, her power washed over me like a wave, making me want to bow and kowtow before her. I fought it off but it was difficult even to look her in the eye.

I had to clear my throat twice before I could speak. "Thank you for granting us an audience, Queen. I am Darian Wahya, Ranger of Vana, and this is Autumn Arga, mage of the Empire of Zura," I said, inclining my head toward Autumn and bowing as best I could from the saddle while holding Samara. Autumn played her part perfectly, despite the fact I could only assume she was feeling the same compulsion to submit as me.

"Well met, Darian Wahya. I am the Owl Queen, sovereign of this enclave," she said as half a dozen goblins came forward bearing a throne aloft to set down behind her. It was metal, but it gave the appearance of being woven together with sticks, like a bird's nest. She perched regally upon it and directed her piercing yellow eyes at me. "I'm told you wish to parlay?"

"Yes, Queen," I said, forcing myself to meet her gaze through an effort of will.

"Well, then by all means. Parlay."

"We wish to treat with you for safe passage, your Majesty."

"Hmm," she said, tapping one talon upon her lips. "I am disinclined to grant your request."

My mind raced as I swallowed the ball of dread in my stomach. "Why is that?"

"I'm insulted that you thought you could sneak through my domain and escape my notice," she said, reaching out with one talon to tease the sluagh's tentacles.

"With all due respect, your Majesty, that's incorrect. We had every intention of seeking an audience with you. We simply didn't know where do go. This sluagh was very helpful in directing us to your court," I said, glancing over to watch his tentacles writhe in anger.

"Even so, I am under no obligation to grant you an audience or treat with you, per our agreement. I could decide to feed you to my people right now for your arrogance."

"Perhaps you're right," I said looking around at the Fae crowding the outside of the forum, "but I don't imagine my comrades will see it that way. If we don't arrive home, they'll come in here looking for us. And if they find us in a less than ideal condition, they will decide the agreement between our people doesn't work for them anymore."

"You're probably right. They would be quite angry," the Owl Queen said idly picking at her feathered collar. "If anyone knew you were here."

I swallowed the knot in my stomach. For my plan to work, she had to believe my friends knew where I was. "I assure you my people know where I am," I said, thinking about the Vija and willing myself to believe it. If the Owl Queen was reading my emotions it would hopefully be enough to deceive her. "I would have been a fool to come here otherwise."

A cruel smile spread on her thin lips. "You're no fool, just desperate. You had no choice but to come through my territory to save that woman. No, I think the only people who know you're here are standing before me."

I had one advantage…Azava's gift. It told me that she wasn't sure enough for that statement to register as true. There are those who say the Fae can't lie. That's nothing more than a faerie tale, but they can't lie to a Manu.

We were about to find out which one of us was a better card player. "Care to bet all your people's lives on it?"

A hushed silence fell over the crowd. The sidhe stared down her nose, scrutinizing me, and I felt the gravity of that gaze bearing me down but I managed to stand fast. After an eternity under those harsh eyes, her thin lips broke into a genuine smile. "Well then. Let us treat."

I had to work hard to let the breath I'd been holding out slowly.

"You wish for safe passage for your party. What do I get in return?" she asked.

I'd finally convinced the devil to deal with me, and now I had to dangle something she wanted. A fresh sense of dread welled up in me. All Fae fed on emotions, and the sidhe were the most feared. They fed on our desires, our hopes and dreams. Take that away and what's left?

"A dream willingly given," I said.

Now the Owl Queen stared at me, lust clear in her heavy-lidded eyes. "Mmm, alright, human. But all of you have trespassed in my territory. I deserve a dream for each transgression, though I don't think your red-headed friend has very much left to give."

I steeled myself for what I was about to do. "Agreed," I said. Autumn's calm broke and I saw panic on her face. "But you take them all from me. And I get to decide what you feed on."

"Five of your dreams for safe passage? I suppose that agreeable."

"Perhaps your Majesty needs help counting?" I said, "There are only three of us."

"Your horses trespassed as well. Or did you wish to leave them here? They aren't suitable for feeding, but I'm sure we can find a use for them."

"Don't get greedy. Three dreams for safe passage."

"Five."

"Three," I said again.

She let out a piercing laugh reminiscent of an owl shriek, "Very well then. Three."

"We have an agreement then? Three dreams of my choice for safe passage?"

"We have an agreement," she said. *Truth.* She planned on honoring her word.

"Very well, your highness," I said, "*Tavas lay down.*" The horse knelt down and I dismounted with Samara in my arms. "Autumn, can you take her?"

Autumn hopped off her horse and came over to me as I sat Samara down against one of the columns. "You don't have to do this," she whispered frantically. "I'll give up one of my dreams."

"No arguments, remember? Try to get Samara to take some water."

"How do you know she won't just betray you and take everything?"

"I just know," I said, taking Autumn's swollen face in my hand. "This is the only way we all make it out of here." I wiped away one of her tears with my thumb. "It'll be alright," I said, with a reassuring smile. In that moment, I was glad she wasn't a Manu. I wasn't sure my words were true. "Just tend to your mistress." Autumn nodded, tears still streaming down her cheek.

I turned and stood before the Owl Queen's throne. I knew the only currency I had to trade with the sidhe were my dreams, so I'd been prepared for this from the moment I knew we were going have to enter the verge. I just didn't expect to have to give up three.

"Kneel," the Owl Queen commanded. Her power flowed out in waves making it easy to comply. I knelt before the throne and the twin sidhe warriors towered over me on either side. Without warning, the Queen reached out and took my head firmly with both hands and leaned in close.

"Choose your dreams wisely," she whispered, the feather's from her cape tickling my chin. "If you offer one that's not satisfying, you'll owe me another."

"Let's get this over with," I said.

Her lips parted and she forced her mouth roughly against mine. Any similarity to a kiss ended there. I felt her reaching into me with her power, searching like a hungry badger digging for a root. The first dream I gave her was also one of my oldest. A vision of me wearing the torc of the elder council rose in my inner sight. My family stood around me with pride in their eyes as my every word commanded the respect of my people. As soon as the image was clear in my mind, the sidhe's power became a void pulling at the dream. Trying to hold on to it would have been like holding up a boulder, so I let go. The dream was sucked out of me, leaving behind only an aching, raw emptiness.

The Owl Queen pulled back and languidly swallowed like she was eating a juicy peach, her eyes rolling back in her head. "That one had a nice age to it," she said, licking her lips. The twins look on with naked jealousy in their eyes. She gave me no respite roughly shoving her mouth back over mine.

The dream hurt as I called it forth. It hurt like it was covered in barbs. I formed an image of me holding an infant in my arms. The baby was just like the son that was taken from me, but he was hale and happy, giggling as he stared up at me with eyes just like mine. As soon as the image solidified, it was torn away from me, consumed by the waiting abyss.

The sidhe's grip on my head was vice-like and she quivered with orgasmic pleasure. Her head fell back as she savored the flavor. "That one had some spice to it," she purred. It felt as though I'd just had my liver sucked out through my mouth. I didn't know if I could take another feeding.

She pulled me onto the throne with her as her mouth closed over mine one last time. The last dream I gave her was dark. I'd barely acknowledged it myself. I reached deep into a nearly-hidden part of my consciousness to bring it forth. The image formed was of me dying in battle, and in doing so I was reunited with the family I lost. Sitana threw her arms around me, pulling me tight and kissing me with her fierce passion. Swiftly and cruelly, the Owl Queen took that dream as well. Her tight grip released and I collapsed before her throne.

"Mmm...bittersweet like chocolate," the Owl Queen said. She grabbed the sidhe in alabaster armor pulling him in for a fierce, lingering, kiss. When she released him he licked his lips like he was savoring the after-taste of the dreams she'd taken.

"Decadent," he said.

The sidhe in obsidian said, "Don't be greedy," and grabbed his twin, pulling him into a probing kiss.

They may have continued to discuss how wonderful my dreams were but I didn't hear it. I curled into a ball gripping myself on the hard stone of the forum. I felt used. I felt dirty. I felt violated. I felt empty. So great was my emptiness I feared I might just collapse in on myself.

Hopelessness was an anchor around my neck dragging me down into the inky depths of despair. I was so weary, though, I hardly cared. I hurt. My arm ached, my heart ached, my soul ached. Some distant part of me whispered that I needed to get up. If I didn't Samara was going to die. Millions were going to die. It hardly seemed to matter.

A curtain of auburn hair fell over me, smelling of lilacs. "Darian, you've got to get up," Autumn said.

"C-can't."

"You can and you will," she said, throwing my words back at me.

"Just go. Take Samara and go." I said.

"I will. But you're coming with me," she said, throwing my left arm over her shoulder and trying to pull me to my feet.

I grunted as fiery pain burned through my injured forearm.

The Owl Queen laughed. "It seems I might have taken all he had."

In that moment, despite the hopelessness, the emptiness, and the pain, I knew she was wrong...because I was *angry*. Stubbornness, pure and simple, drove me on in that moment. I called Irin's gift to numb the pain and weariness. As the God of war's gift blossomed in me, it met that stubbornness and kindled into a righteous fire. I was a Ranger of the Manu. I would *not* cower before this faerie.

I stood before her throne under my own strength and said, "Hardly."

"Oh, good. There are still a few embers left in the fire." She gestured to the sluagh. "Alistaire will see you safely out of my domain as promised."

Alistaire's tentacles slithered and writhed as he glowered at her but he merely said, "Of course, my queen."

I turned and walk away with Autumn. As I gently picked up Samara, the Owl Queen said, "Do come back and see us again, Darian Wahya. You're welcome to join us any time," she licked thin lips as her yellow eyes closed in pleasure, "For dinner."

———————————

Alistaire and a cohort of goblins escorted us out of the verge, stopping just at the edge. I adjusted Samara against me as I turned my mount about. She shivered in my arms despite burning with fever.

"Fare well, human," the sluagh said, giving a courtly bow. "You played a good game. We'll see if your cleverness saves you when next we meet."

"There won't be a next time," I said.

His only response was to blow a kiss at me, his opalescent eyes still wet with tarry tears. He gave Autumn a dainty wave before he turned and strode off. I gazed at the verge on last time issuing a silent prayer of thanks to the Gods that I was finally out of it, despite the cost. We found the river and resumed our course toward the village.

Like all of our gifts, Irin's took concentration, which was slowly siphoning away what strength I had left, so when we put some distance between us and the Fae I released it. Pain and weariness hit me like a palpable force. My encounter with the Fae had utterly drained my strength. That combined with the fact that I hadn't really slept in a day and a half meant that the only thing keeping me going was sheer stubbornness.

Autumn noticed me grimacing and asked, "Are you alright?"

"No, not really. I'm exhausted."

Her gold iris searched over me. "Was it the Fae? Did they...I mean, are you...?"

"I don't know. But it doesn't matter right now. We have to get Samara to a healer, and we wasted a lot of time with those cursed faeries."

Autumn said nothing, only reached out and squeezed my arm. We continued on in silence, the breathing of our horses and Samara's occasional murmurs mixing with the noise of the woods.

The sun waned, casting long shadows through the trees. My weariness grew and my eye lids felt as though they had heavy stones attached to them. I dozed off in the saddle, nearly falling off my horse with Samara. When I jerked awake, I griped Tavas hard with my legs sending him to a gallop. I slowed back down looking around to get my bearings.

"Is something wrong?" Autumn said looking around for danger.

"No. Yes. Sort of. Do you remember those ferns I told you not to let you horse eat?"

"The ones with the purple veins?"

"Right. See if you can find one."

She hopped off her horse and started searching. After a few moments, she located one. "Is this it?"

I nodded, "Let me have it." She handed it to me and I started stripping out the veins. When I had them all rolled in a violet ball I popped it in my mouth. It was bitter with a heavy acrid taste.

"I thought you said it was addictive?"

"Very," I said. After just a moment my mouth started to burn. Immediately I felt more alert and my heart started beating faster. "Now, let's see if we can make it to Vana before this wears off and I'm in worse shape than before."

We pressed hard as the sun grew dimmer behind the trees. Soon night consumed the Mystewood. I led Autumn's horse when it grew too dim for her to see. After an eternity, I saw riders off in the distance. They gave the warbling whistle the Rangers used identify each other and I gave the whistle back that signified we were in danger. A score of Rangers came riding up at a full gallop with Cayman leading them.

As they drew near Cayman called out, "Darian? What happened? Where are the guards?"

"We were ambushed. The guards were all killed. And there's more, but it'll have to wait. Samara's been wounded badly and she's burning with fever. We need to get her to Gambi immediately."

Sava came forward and said, "I'll take her, my horse is fresh."

I wanted to argue, but it made too much sense and I just didn't have the strength. She eased her horse up next to mine and I slipped off the strip of fabric that held Samara to me and handed her gently to Sava. "Tell them she's had penetrating wounds to the belly and thigh that were closed with Ananda's gift."

"I understand. You can let go, I've got her," she said, settling Samara against her.

I brushed one of Samara's red locks off her flushed cheek. "Go with Kavi's speed."

Sava turned and rode off into the darkness with several of the rangers following her. Now that we'd made it, exhaustion returned in full force and I slumped forward in the saddle.

"Are you hurt, too?" Cayman asked. "You look like you just got shat out by a dragon."

"He was fed on by a sidhe," said Autumn.

"What? By the Gods, those bloody fairies broke the treaty?" he said, his face a mixture of hatred and pity.

"No. I mean, yes. I was fed on but they didn't break the treaty." A wave of nausea washed over me. "Look, I'll explain later. Let's get back to the village before I pass out."

"I guess you were right."

"About what?" I said, giving Cayman a puzzled look.

"It wasn't worth the seventy-five gold."

Chapter Eleven
Samara

I had no idea where I was. Memories of hazy, half-forgotten dreams danced at the edge of my consciousness but told me nothing of my surroundings. All I knew was that I was comfortable, I was warm, there was some rhythmic sound… and something tickled my nose.

I opened my eyes. Moon light streaming through the windows and a lone flickering mundane lamp across the room was the only illumination. All I could see was a red blur with a black nose and whiskers directly in front of me. The whiskers were doing the tickling. I was lying on my side so I moved my head back to get a better look at the purring red lump in front of me. The creature was slightly larger than a house cat. It had a long, fluffy, ringed tail and a white face with red around the eyes sliding in a line down its cheeks like a tear streak. It looked like the love child of a fox and a raccoon.

Where am I?

My furry bedmate opened its eyes at my stirring. It yawned and rolled over on its back stretching out to its full length, and reaching out to touch my shoulder with one hand-like paw before closing its eyes and resuming its trilling purr.

Clearly I've gone mad.

I started to sit up to get a better look at my surroundings but a sharp pain in my belly halted me. I reached under the soft draa blankets to find that I was naked except for a robe and bandages across my belly and thigh. I stretched out my leg to find that it hurt too, though not as much as I feared. Grimacing through the pain, I sat up in bed. I was terribly weak and my throat was dry as a bone. I searched around the smallish room to find my red friend and I weren't alone.

A pretty Manu woman set in a chair across from me. She was immensely pregnant and had a piece of embroidered draa laying across her protruding belly, her head lulled to the side in sleep. I looked around noticing the telltale engraving decorating the room. Was I in Vana?

How did I get here?

I tried to speak but I was dreadfully parched. I swallowed painfully a few times and cleared my throat, still my voice came out as a horse whisper. "May I have some water please?" The woman stirred but didn't wake so I cleared my throat and tried again, my voice a bit stronger. "May I have some water?"

The woman's brown eyes popped open. She looked around wildly for a moment and mumbled, "Mmm, must have dozed off."

I tried third time, "May I have some water please?"

"Oh, you're awake," the woman said, delighted. "That's wonderful! Yes, of course, you can have some water." She set her embroidery on the table and waddled over to fill a small wooden cup from a carved ewer. "Go easy or you won't be able to keep it down," she said, putting the cup in my hand.

I took a few tentative sips that soothed my aching throat but also awakened my thirst. I followed the woman's advice however, and sipped slowly. When I finished, she took the cup from me and I cleared my throat again, finding it easier to speak now. "Thank you," I said.

"You're welcome," she said beaming a wide smile. "We were afraid we were going to lose you for a while."

"Am I in Vana?"

"Aye."

"What happened to me? How did I get here?"

"You were attacked out in the woods. Darian and your friend Autumn brought you here for healing." Vague memories were starting to come back. I remembered leather-armored men in the camp. I'd been shot with a crossbow. Autumn was on the ground...

"Autumn is here too? She's alright?"

She nodded, "Her and Darian have hardly left your side."

"Where are they?"

"In the next room, asleep. It's the middle of the night. Shall I wake them?"

"No, let them sleep. Wait, it's the middle of the night? How long have I been asleep?" I asked.

"Five days."

"F-five days?"

"You were badly wounded, m'lady, and half-mad with fever." I lay back in bed suddenly sleepy again. "How's the pain? I can give you some milk of the poppy."

My pain actually wasn't that bad surprisingly. "No, it's not too bad. I'm just tired. Are you the healer?"

"No, just her neighbor. I help her a bit and look in on her patients every now and again." The red furry thing settled back in next to me. "I think Panya likes you," she said with a chuckle.

"What is it?"

"A firefox. Have you never seen one before?" she asked incredulously.

I shook my head.

"They're native to these woods. Many Manu keep them because they hunt tree rats. When they're not slothful layabouts that is," she said poking Panya in the belly, which he didn't seem to mind.

"We call those squirrels."

"I beg your pardon, m'lady?"

"Tree rats. We call them squirrels."

"No, m'lady. Tree rats are large brown nuisances that eat all your food stores."

"Like I said."

She laughed. "Are all Zurans as funny as you?"

"I'm in a class by myself." My eyes grew heavy as I talked. "What's your name?"

She smiled as she tucked my blanket over me. "Pushpa."

"Thank you, Pushpa," I said before I drifted back to sleep.

When next I woke it was to a full bladder and a very welcome face. "Autumn?"

"Mistress," Autumn shouted as she hopped up and ran over, grabbing me in a long tight embrace. When she finally released me, she said, "You have no idea how good it is to see you awake. Are you in pain?"

"Just my bladder. Help me get to the chamber pot." My abdomen was still tender but motivated by my urgent need, I dealt with it. It hurt to stand on my left leg and I was shaky but with Autumn's help I managed.

Once I was back in bed Autumn asked, "Better, mistress?"

"Much." My mind was clearing and I was starting to separate my memories from the vivid fever dreams. The horror of our camp site near the fork in the river came back to me. "When that man hit you and you went down I thought...I thought..."

Autumn squeezed my hand. "I've thought the same thing about you a few times during the last few days."

"Did anybody else...?"

She opened her mouth to speak but nothing came out. Finally she just shook her head.

"Oh, no. Dirk and...and Harold, he...he was married. And Koto..." I could barely breathe. It was as if a hand gripped my heart. They'd died protecting me, all of them. Suddenly everything felt hazy and surreal, like remembering a strange dream just after waking, and my pain faded to a distant numbness. I could tell Autumn was holding back tears, trying to be strong for me. On top of everything else, she'd lost a lover. I didn't even know how to begin to comfort her. I reached up and touched her face where she had the remnants of a black eye. "Are you alright?"

She put her fingers over mine. "It's nothing compared to what happened to you and Darian."

"Darian was hurt as well?"

Something crossed Autumn's face that was difficult to read. "Yes, but he managed to save both of us."

"He killed all of those men?"

"The ones that were left. Apparently you did quite a bit of damage." The memory returned and the smell of burning flesh filled my nostrils. I almost lost what little was in my stomach. "Oh, and I sent a courier to your father to inform him of what happened."

"Ugh, you shouldn't have done that. He'll be worried half to death." I winced, imagining my father's reaction.

"Mistress, we weren't sure you were going to make it," she said reasonably.

"Well, next time make sure I'm dead before you send my father a...wait, did you say a courier? Vana has a courier?"

"The bank has one on staff."

"Oh, I suppose that makes sense."

Autumn patted my hand. "I'll go get the healer. She'll want to see you now that you're awake."

She left the room and returned with a small gaggle of Manu. A short, middle-aged woman with an air of authority smiled and spoke to me. "It's nice to finally see your pretty eyes, child."

Something was familiar about her. She was pretty for her age, and had a short pixie-cut hair and high cheek bones. Her skin was a half a shade lighter than the average Manu and she had blue-green eyes with a familiar inner ring of gold. "You're Darian's mother, aren't you?"

Her rich, warm smile was genuine. "Yes, child. I'm Gambi and this is my daughter, Nia, and my apprentice, Rigg." The girl looked perhaps thirty and had her mother's look but with the darker complexion and rich brown eyes common to the Manu. The boy was around sixteen and rail-thin with a shy smile. "Now, let's have a look at you," said Gambi.

She took my pulse and asked me a series of questions obviously meant to test my memory and mental ability. Seemingly satisfied she removed my bandages to examine my wounds. I braced myself for what the grievous injury might look like but all I saw was fresh a fresh pink scar. "I thought I was only unconscious for five days?"

"That's correct," the short woman said.

"This wound looks like it's been healing for months."

"That's because of Ananda's gift." I must have given her an incredulous look because she said, "You'll see. We were about to do another healing." Gambi put her hands over my belly wound and Rigg put his hands over the one on my leg. Nia went around to the other side of the bed and put one hand on the crown of my head and the other on my brow. After a moment their hands started feeling warm and glowed with soft silver light.

The warmth seeped into me, which triggered a half forgotten memory of Darian doing the same thing. *So I was right. The Manu were gifted by other Gods.*

As Gambi and Rigg poured silver light in my wounds, Nia worked her way down my body, covering all my chakras. There were no words to describe the healing. My pain eased and I was permeated with a feeling of…love? Mercy? Compassion? It felt like them all rolled into one. I was transported back to being held as a child in my mother's arms. Overwhelmed, at some point I started crying. They weren't tears of pain or sorrow. They were just tears.

"Are you alright, child? Is there pain?" Gambi asked when they were finished.

"No," I said wiping away my tears. "I'm just…I've never experienced that before."

"You've experienced it quite a few times over the last several days, you just don't remember it," she said with a compassionate smile. "I'll be right back with some medicine to take." She was gone for several minutes while Rigg smeared something that smelled minty on my wounds and redressed them. When she returned she bore a small cup of cloudy black fluid and a cup of water. "Here you go. Drink this all down."

The inky fluid had a dubious smell to it. "What is it?"

"Extract from the Propolis plant."

I took a deep breath and swallowed.

It. Was. *Horrid.*

I almost retched. Somehow I managed to swallow it and keep it down, chasing it with a full cup of water. "That…was the most vile substance I've ever put in my mouth."

"Yes, well that 'vile substance' saved your life. It's what killed the infection and the fever," said Gambi. "Rest now and regain your strength. I'll be back in a few hours with some more medicine and another healing."

"I have to take *more?*"

She chuckled. "Yes child, I'm afraid so." With that the Manu left the room, leaving me alone with Autumn.

We chatted while she helped me take a passable bed bath with a rag and hot water, though after days of fever I still felt a bit gritty. An hour or so later there was a knock on the door and Darian entered carrying a tray bearing a bowl of cereal and a small chunk of bread.

"Lady Samara," he said, inclining his head. "How are you feeling?"

A warm sense of gratitude washed over me. "Reasonably fair. I hear I have you to thank for that."

"You took care of most of the attackers, I just mopped up a bit," he said setting down the tray.

"And healed me, and carried me back to the village for treatment."

"Just doing the job you hired me for, m'lady. Your brother did specify I return you safely," he said, giving his little half smile.

He was as vexing as ever. "I'd say you went a bit above the call of duty. Autumn told me you were wounded." His eyes met Autumn's and something passed between them. I couldn't quite put my finger on it, but there was something in his eyes. He seemed different. "Are you feeling better now?" I asked. I couldn't help but feel guilty. He never would have been at that camp if not for me.

"I am…still recovering, m'lady. But I'll be alright eventually."

"Well, in any case thank you. I'd be dead if not for you."

"The Vija told me that without my aid you wouldn't succeed in your task." *Huh. She was right about that.*

I blew out a sigh. "By the Gods, can't you just let me say thank you?"

He bowed with his half-grin. "You're quite welcome, m'lady. But it wasn't as though I had another course of action," he said continuing. "If you had perished you wouldn't be able to stop the gate from opening. Millions would have followed you to the grave."

That stung. I couldn't say why, but it did. I guess it was flattering when I thought he went through so much just to rescue me. I knew I was being childish but my eyes started to well up with tears. No doubt it was just a result of the trauma I'd been through. I pushed the feelings down, discreetly wiped my eyes, and busied myself with eating.

I was expecting the usual spicy Manu fare, but the cereal was practically flavorless. "It's kind of bland," I complained.

"You'll need to eat that for a few days to give your bowels a chance to recover."

"Lovely," I said swallowing the tasteless mush. After I'd finished eating, I was given a rich, creamy tea that settled and warmed my belly. As I set the cup down, something occurred to me. "What of my houseguards? I-I'd like to see their,' I hesitated, "remains returned to their families."

Darian nodded with sympathy in his eyes, "I've already arranged it. We sent a party to retrieve them as soon as we arrived in Vana. They should be back today or tomorrow."

"Thank you."

"They were good men."

"Yes, they were."

Darian simply nodded again as he collected my tray. "Let me know if you need anything, I'm just in the next room. I'll be back later with dinner and some more medicine."

"Ugh, you make me eat bland mush to ease my bowels, but that vile medicine is alright?"

He glanced back over his shoulder as he left the room. "I'm sure complaining about it will make it taste better, m'lady." The door closed before I could get a retort in.

So vexing.

The rest of the day was filled with sleeping, mush, and more disgusting medicine, though at least they gave me a sweet roll to banish the horrible aftertaste. I have to admit by the end of the day I was feeling stronger and more clear-headed. The next day was more of the same until Darian showed up around midday wearing a dour expression.

"The party returned, m'lady," he said.

"Did they find my guards?"

He nodded, "And the horses. They brought the bodies of our attackers and their animals as well. I've just been to see them." It was obvious he was troubled.

"And?"

He took a deep breath. "Many of the bodies were too burned to recover anything from, but the leather armor they wore had an eagle on it that may be the symbol for a mercenary group."

I'd spent some time over the last day pondering what had happened so that was hardly surprising. "That tracks. Mercenaries in the Empire aren't allowed to wear metal armor. What else?"

"All their horses are from Stonehaven, which means they likely followed us from there—"

"Wait," I interrupted. "How are you so sure their horses are from Stonehaven?"

"Their shoes all bear the mark of the same Stonehaven smith."

"Oh." That was pretty clever. I was fairly impressed he'd thought to check that, but horses were his business.

"As I was saying," he continued, "they likely followed us from Stonehaven but they didn't come through Vana." Anticipating my next question he said, "I asked around. They would have been noticed. Now, they had no dogs or other tracking animals. So how did they find us?"

"Me," I said. "They were after me. I heard them say they were looking for a red-head."

He nodded, not seeming surprised by that revelation. "There were several Vijas we could have gone too, and none of their locations are common knowledge to anyone but the Manu…"

"So how did they know where I'd be?" I said finishing the thought.

"Exactly," he said. "They would have had a very difficult time tracking without knowing where we were going."

I had already pondered that. "One of them was a mage. It is possible to view a location remotely with magic but not people, so it would be *extremely* difficult to track someone that way."

This obviously was news to him. "They had a mage with them? Did you recognize him?"

"No, I definitely had never seen him before but he was the one giving the orders. I think it was one of the robed men from the Vija's vision."

"Was he one of the one's you burned?"

"Yes, he was." the words came out dripping with venom. He'd ordered the death of my men.

I could see the gears turning behind Darian's eyes as he digested this new information. "That adds some perspective…"

He was holding something back. "What else?" I asked. When he hesitated I said, "Out with it."

"I found this in one of their saddle bags," he said as he reached into his pouch and produced velvet purse, dumping its contents on the bed. A pile of shiny new Imperial platinum pieces glimmered on the cream draa sheets.

"By Varga," I whispered.

"This was an assassination," Darian said. "And someone paid well for it."

I did a quick tally. "There's easily a thousand gold worth of platinum here."

He nodded saying, "And add to it the money they already spent buying supplies and horses."

My mind was racing, "This had to have been planned while I was in Stonehaven."

"I'd wager before."

"What makes you say that?"

"Why did they have to buy twenty horses in Stonehaven?"

Darian clearly thought the answer was obvious but I had no clue which was annoying. "Why?" I shrugged.

"The same reason why you needed horses there, m'lady."

"They came across the Causeway," I said, my head spinning. "This doesn't make any sense. Someone in bed with one of these robed men planned my murder before I ever left?"

"Do you remember anything else about the one you saw other than the fact he was a mage?" Darian asked.

Much of that fight was hazy but I concentrated and fought through the blur. "Yes, he was foreign. He talked with a lilting accent. And he said something about an ally." Darkness crossed Darian's face. "What?"

"He must be talking about a noble." I was struck by the certainty in his voice.

"You don't know that," I said. In answer he grabbed a handful of coins and dropped them clanking onto the pile for emphasis. "It could be from a rich merchant. Or maybe someone not even from Zura. Imperial coin is used all over the world."

"A merchant would pay with precious stones," he said holding a piece. "This coin is freshly minted, there's not a scratch on it. Only a Zuran noble would have so much Imperial platinum. I'm telling you, m'lady, I've sold a lot of horses."

It was as though the house shook beneath me. If Darian was right then a noble, probably someone I knew, had paid for my death. I felt sick to my stomach. Thoughts blew through my head like leaves in a thunderstorm. "The book. It has to be someone who knew what was in the Sarga Paza."

"How many people knew?" he asked.

"Not very many. I didn't want anyone to beat me to the translation. And most of the people who did know are mages at the college or members of House Arga."

"Well then," said Darian collecting the coins back into the velvet purse. "I think we should assume for the moment that this 'ally' is someone from that pool of people."

The world felt like it was closing in around me. I wouldn't have thought it possible for the situation to get more complicated. "When can we leave?" I asked.

"As soon as my mother says you're well enough to travel, m'lady. Gura Elian has already offered his full support to us." I nodded, feeling very tired all of a sudden. "M'lady," Darian said looking at me with earnest blue-green eyes. "Be very careful of whom within the Empire you place your trust."

My strength increased steadily over the next two days with the regiment of healings, bland food, and foul-tasting medicine. I grew steady enough on my feet to walk around, with some discomfort, leaning heavily on Autumn or Darian. It was at that time I learned two facts to which I was previously unaware. First, I was in Darian's home. Second, it was nearly a hundred feet up a tree. When I first glanced out the window I nearly fainted. As one might expect in a home that was built around the trunk of a tree, in every room one "wall" was the bark of the redwood, and another was always facing the outside and tended to have large windows. There was no place I could go to escape the view.

On the fifth day after I woke, I was allowed to eat small servings of real food. At first it was just chicken broth with vegetables, but after nearly a week of flavorless mush it was a welcome change. I begged Gambi to let me go to the Zuran inn to take a real bath and finally she relented.

Darian presented me with a carved redwood cane to aid me. When I took it I realized with a shock the head of the cane was carved to look like the eagle of House Arga. He must have carved it for me based on the image on my citizenship coin. I was touched by the thoughtful gift.

The interior of the great redwood contained a carved ramp spiraling upward through the heart of the tree, which was how the Manu ascended to their arboreal domains. I was embarrassed when Darian had to carry me down because of my injured led, even though I realized he'd hauled me miles to get me back to the village. We used my Arga carriage to transport us to the Inn where Autumn and I luxuriated for an hour in the hot bath, while the inn keeper's wife lamented about how horrible our ordeal was.

The next morning while I was walking about the house, with Pushpa's aid, trying to regain the strength in my leg, I came across what seemed to be a small shrine. Sitting on a low table was a carved redwood bust of a woman with fresh flowers laid about it. She was beautiful. Her hair was held back in an elaborate braid and the right corner of her mouth tilted up in a mischievous grin. So masterly rendered was it I could have easily believed it was a woman covered in red paint rather than carved from a block of wood.

"Is this a depiction of Ananda?" I asked.

Pushpa's face fell a bit as her mouth formed into a sad smile. "No, m'lady. That's Sitana, Darian's wife. She passed away the winter before last."

"Oh, I didn't know he was married."

Pushpa nodded, "She made him work for it, too."

"She did?"

Pushpa glanced around to make sure we were alone. Darian had gone out earlier and Autumn was still asleep. "Darian could have had any woman he wanted, and he *did* have quite a few, but Sitana wouldn't have anything to do with him."

"Really?"

"Aye. And as with any man, that only made him want her more." We giggled together. "But it was more than that. Sita had a fire in her, and Darian was attracted to it like a moth." Pushpa reached out lovingly patting the statue's cheek.

"Were you friends?"

"Aye," she said, nodding. "And I was quite jealous of the attention she was getting from Darian." She glanced around conspiratorially again and said, "Have you ever *been* with him?"

I felt my cheeks flushing despite myself. "Uh…no."

"You should. He's quite talented," Pushpa said with a half-lidded gaze and I felt my face grow even warmer. "But anyway, Sita would have none of it. It didn't matter how charming or handsome he was, she said he was too arrogant."

I was starting to like Sitana. "So what happened?"

"She tortured him," came a voice from behind us, "until she decided he'd showed enough humility."

We both turned, sharing matching guilty expressions, but it was just Nia bearing my afternoon dose of medicine. I breathed a sigh of relief until I saw what followed her. The largest wolf I'd ever seen glided behind her through the door. It was easily two hundred pounds and as beautiful as it was terrifying. A sleek gray and black coat carried highlights of white and tan. Intense amber eyes bored into me out of his perfectly symmetrical mask while his nose twitched, testing my scent. It was the first time I'd stared into something's eyes as it tried to determine whether or not I was food.

Nia followed my gaze, "It's alright. He won't bother you." She glanced back over her shoulder, "*Simber, go lay down.*" The huge wolf rubbed his side against her hip then ambled over and flopped down with a thud on one of Darian's thick rugs. The wolf continued to watch me from where he laid, which probably would have been more disconcerting if I hadn't had a grizzly licking soup off my feet the week before. My life had become very surreal, very quickly.

"He's beautiful," I said.

"He knows it, too," said Nia. As if in response, the beast rolled over on his back exposing his belly to be rubbed. She handed the vile medicine to me and bent down to accommodate him. The wolf closed his mouth in bliss as his back foot thumped against the wall in rapid succession.

I chugged the cloudy liquid and chased it with a swig of water and the sweet roll. It was just as horrible as the first time, despite Darian's assurances it would get easier to take.

Pushpa continued, "Darian wrote songs for Sita, showered her with exotic gifts—"

"And even gave her a particularly expensive horse if memory serves," Nia interjected.

Pushpa nodded. "But none of it moved her. Sitana had a wild spirit and no desire for a man to take care of her or tell her what to do. It was only after she was sure Darian had no intention of 'taming' her that she finally relented."

"She was a beautiful soul. I was proud to call her sister," Nia said smiling at Pushpa. I looked at the statue again feeling an odd sense of mourning for someone I'd even met.

Nia gazed up form where she scratched the wolf's belly and chewed her lip. After a moment she said, "Can I ask you a question, m'lady?"

"What is it?"

"My brother said all Zuran nobles have eyes like you and Autumn. Is that true?"

"Yes."

"Do...you use magic to make them that way?"

"Sort of." I considered how to answer that question. "Long ago a mage of one of the great Houses was distrustful of his wife and sought a way to be sure his heirs did indeed belong to him. Our unusual eyes are a result of that," I said, keeping my answer deliberately vague.

"Well, they're lovely," Nia said. "Darian was fortunate enough to get mother's eyes and I've always been jealous." She stood up and stretched. "Alright, I have more patients to see. I'll be back later with your next dose."

"Wonderful," I said. At least if I died I wouldn't have to suffer through any more of that disgusting concoction.

"*Come on, Simber,*" Nia said, slipping out the door. The wolf lazily gained his feet and padded out behind her in no particular hurry.

My strength continued to grow over the next two days and soon I was able to walk with a cane unassisted and with only moderate discomfort. I thought I might be ready to leave, but Gambi said I couldn't travel for a few more days. I was beginning to feel antsy. Eventually, Darian suggested I might enjoy seeing the library at the Alaya and I agreed. I was ready for anything to distract my mind from recent events and the dark, uncertain future.

I'd become somewhat of a connoisseur of libraries in my research, so I wasn't expecting much. I was shocked, however, by the Manu library. The thing was massive, taking up perhaps half the space of the Alaya. It was divided into an enormous honeycomb of interconnected rooms that stretched several stories tall. Each room was dedicated to a single subject, with tables and a common area where discussions were had. There were an astounding number of books and scrolls with subjects ranging from geometry, to magic, to flower arrangement. And it was surprisingly crowded. Manu young and old, women and men, stretched throughout the labyrinth. Some were teaching lessons to children, some were doing research, while others were clearly reading only for pleasure.

"I told you we were a scholarly people," Darian said, reading my face with a smug smile.

"*All* these people can read?" I said gesturing around at the vast number of Manu. Literacy rates this high outside Zura were unheard of. Even some regions inside of Zura…

"There wouldn't be much point in being in a library if they weren't able to."

"Well…"

"Come on, you can say it."

I let out a deep sigh. This was going to hurt. "You were right, this is fairly impressive."

Darian made a show of cleaning out his ears. "What was that?"

"If you missed it the first time, then fortune frowned on you," I said. "Because you're never going to hear it again."

"Isn't that the truth," Autumn said with a chuckle.

I've been in quite a few libraries, including Victory Hall in Emeraldhue, which was said to be the largest in the world, and even for me the Manu library was a bit confusing at first. I'd set out to do some research that might aid me in the coming task, but I was struck by the sheer diversity of the place. Most libraries tended to focus on one particular subject while this one seemed to do just the opposite. I sat down in a comfortable Manu chair with the arms carved in the likeness of beautiful cobras and lost myself.

I'd collected books on history, geography and, one of my old staples from the academy, "Girard's Theory of the Realms". After a few hours of research that pretty much confirmed everything I already thought, I set out to track down Autumn. I found her in the poetry room surrounded by a small fort of books and scrolls, one of which I noticed idly contained the works of Diocletianus.

"Mistress, you should read this Manu poetry. Some of it's actually quite good," Autumn said when she noticed me.

"Perhaps later. Do you remember that foreign geometry instructor I had when I was twelve or thirteen?"

"The short one with the limp?"

"That's the one. Do you recall where he was from?"

Autumn squinted and chewed her lower lip as she stared intently off in the distance. "I think he was from Rastraka, but I'm not entirely sure. Why?"

"The robed man that was looking for me at the...the camp," I said, swallowing a sudden surge of grief and panic. "He had an accent somewhat similar. I'm trying to place it."

"Do you think it'll help?"

"It's a place to start," I shrugged. "I'll know more when we get back to White Harbor." Autumn's face sank a bit. "What's the matter? I figured you'd be happy to be home."

"I will be. It's just...there are people who are trying to kill us there. At least here, I feel safe."

"Me," I corrected her. "People are trying to kill me."

"That didn't make any difference for the houseguards."

That hit me like a fist to the gut. Tears welled up in my eyes.

Compassion softened Autumn's features. "Mistress, it's not your fault. I didn't mean it that way. All I'm saying is whomever is responsible doesn't seem too particular about who they hurt to get to you."

"But the houseguards would still be alive if they hadn't been with me."

"And I wouldn't be alive if you hadn't saved me with your magic." She took my hand, "Samara, it's not your fault."

I embraced Autumn right there in the middle of the poetry room. It was her calling me by my first name that got me. She never did that. Autumn started crying, and I held her until she regained her composure. I hurt as well, but no tears came. In a way, the events of the past few weeks still didn't feel real.

The next day I decided it was time for me to stop feeling sorry for myself and try to get back into my routine. I hadn't performed any spell casting since my injury. Though it came naturally to me, the practice of magic was difficult and dangerous. Seekers, those wishing to be trained as mages, spent months and sometimes even years preparing the mind and body for the rigors of working one's will upon the world, before ever learning the simplest spells. I figured I had to start somewhere.

I sat in the middle of the bed with Panya purring happily beside me and tried to cross my legs. My left thigh was stiff. It ached and protested when I tied to arrange myself in seated-lotus, so I settle for half-lotus instead. I sat with one leg folded under the other and straightened my back, breathing through the pain. When it receded to a tolerable ache, I folded my hands in my lap, closed my eyes to narrow slits, and relaxed.

After a few cleansing breaths, my body relaxed and the discomfort faded from my notice. I focused on my breathing, being mindful only of the sensation of the air moving in and out of my nostrils. After a time I sat, peaceful and relaxed with my mind silent. Meditation was more or less the only time my noisy head was ever quiet.

Once I was peaceful and focused, I ran through the series of breathing exercises used to direct the flow of energy through my body. I'd done it many, many times and it came back to me easily. When I was finished, I opened my eyes to the realization Panya had crawled into my lap. I set the lazy red bundle aside and stretched out my left leg. It spasmed painfully for a moment but then relaxed.

I stood up off the bed and went about clearing a space to perform hatha stretches. That was a different thing entirely. Some of the stretches were challenging to do even when uninjured. My muscles were tight, my balance was off, and both my wounds complained. I fell over several times and was forced to release stretches early that I'd done easily for years. It was frustrating and it was hard, but at least my injured, tight body was an enemy I could confront, unlike smoky robed men and demons bound in circles half a world away.

The last stretch was difficult. Sweat drenched me and I was shaky as I lifted my left leg in the air with my right leg straight, my right hand on the ground and my left hand reaching for the ceiling. Just as I reached full extension a noise behind me caused me to lose my balance and fall unceremoniously on my rear.

"Well, child," Gambi said, "I think perhaps you're well enough to travel after all."

Chapter Twelve
Darian

"And you're sure you have to go? What will your presence accomplish?" Nia said as she carefully folded my clean clothes and slipped them into my pack.

"I told you, Vija Saptarsi said she'd fail in her task without my aid."

"You *did* save her once already. Perhaps the Vija's prophecy has already been fulfilled?"

"Perhaps," I said with a shrug, "Care to wager the fate of millions upon it?"

"No, I suppose not," she huffed. "Is Uncle Rav taking care of your horses?"

"Yes," I said chuckling bit. He'd been married to our mother for nearly a decade and still my sister called him Uncle Rav. "Though I expect your son to help out as well." My nephew Cade loved the horses. I'd been teaching him how to ride and train them since he could walk.

"I couldn't keep him away if I tried." She rose and handed me the pack.

I took a deep breath and prepared myself. "There is one more thing we need to talk about. I told Rav if he's received no word from me after a year he's to sell half the herd and give the money to Mother. The other half's to go to Cade, as well as my house."

"Darian, that's not necessary."

"I have no wife or children—"

"That's not what I meant," she interrupted. "I mean, you'll return."

"I hope so," I said drawing her into an embrace. "But I'm being practical. It would be naïve not to realize this will be dangerous."

"If you didn't want to take Mother to Jarpa, there's easier ways to get out of it."

"Damn," I said with a smirk as I took a step back and resettled my pack. "I wish you'd told me that sooner." She chuckled as Simber came over and leaned against me. I reached down and scratched him just in front of his tail. His ears went back and his eyes were half closed in bliss.

My mother found me in my home packing the last of my things and presented me with a small bag of medicinal herbs for the journey. The Zurans had gone to the inn for a bath and Panya lay curled up on the bed that Samara had been using.

"I fear Panya may like Samara more than you," my mother said as she scratched the plump firefox behind the ears.

"Looks that way. He's been her constant companion since she arrived. Though I fear their relationship might have been strained when he left the dead tree rat on her pillow as a gift," I chuckled. "She screamed like she found a viper in the sheets."

"That's not funny," my mother said. I stopped my packing and just stared with brows raised. Finally she said, "Alright, it's a little funny. Don't forget to pack some warmer clothes just in case."

I smiled back over my shoulder. "Yes, mother."

"And some sandals."

"Uh huh."

"And a sewing kit."

"Mother, I have traveled before. Hell, Rav and I went all the way to Maula to trade horses with the Imazighen."

"Oh, and don't forget your grandfather's cloak, it may come in handy."

"Already packed," I said turning to face her. "You are aware I'm a Ranger, yes?"

"I *had* heard that somewhere," she said rising to her full five feet. "You are aware that I'm your mother and I could still take you over my knee should the need arise?"

"I have no doubt," I said, suppressing a chuckle.

She went over and smoothed out the sheets on the bed where she'd sat down. "Samara's recovering nicely".

I smirked. "She had a good healer I'm told."

"What about you?" she asked, looking up at me with the eyes full of concern. I slumped a bit. I'd been hoping to avoid the conversation.

"Not as well," I said truthfully. There was no point lying to a Manu.

My mother crossed over, patting me on the chest. "You'll form new dreams in time. It's part of life."

"That's a worry for another day," I said. "Making sure Samara keeps that portal from opening is all that matters right now."

"Some men strive for greatness, my son, and some have it thrust upon them."

"I don't know about great, but I'm certainly too stubborn to step aside."

"You get that from your father," she said. "And your strength as well. But you get your cleverness from me. I've no doubt the combination will see you through." She smiled as though as some inner joke. "I've noticed Samara lacks neither cleverness nor stubbornness either. She has a fire in her, that one. She reminds me of Sitana."

At the mention of my wife's name, a fresh wave of grief washed over me, brought to the surface by my pain at the hands of the sidhe. My mother saw it cross my face. Mothers know their sons.

"Would Sita wish to see you suffering so? You have to find a way to move on, my child."

"I'm trying," I said simply. It was the only thing I could say that wasn't a lie.

Unburdened by a long stream of wagons and buoyed by good weather, we traveled much faster than we had on the journey from Stonehaven. Twenty Rangers protected the Arga carriage and the single covered Manu wagon that bore the bodies of the fallen houseguards, though we were troubled by neither Varaha, nor Zatru, nor assassins. As we passed out of Mystewood I glanced back at my ancestral home and wondered when I'd see it again.

The evening after we left Mystewood Samara came to my fire and eased herself to the ground next to me, leaning heavily on her cane. "Alright," she said. "Out with it."

I cast a confused glance at her over my bowl of stew. "Out with what, m'lady?"

"What are the other gifts?"

I stared blankly back at her.

She huffed out a sigh. "Don't be obtuse. I know about Tarka, Rocona and Ananda's gifts to your people. It stands to reason the other Gods bestowed theirs as well."

I'd been expecting this conversation actually as soon as Samara could talk, but since she hadn't brought it up, I thought maybe she'd let it go. I should have known better. "Alright, I'll tell you if you promise to keep it in confidence."

"Agreed. It's likely no one would believe me anyway. May I take notes?" she asked. When I nodded she reached into her bag and pulled out a book, a quill, and a small inkwell.

I set my bowl of stew down and scratched my stubble. "You're correct. All the Gods have bestowed a gift upon the Manu. Vija Saptarsi explained Rocana's gift and you already know Tarka's gift allows us to hide ourselves, and Ananda's allows us to heal." She nodded scribbling with her quill. "Azava's gift allows us to tell if someone is speaking the falsely."

Her eyes widened. "Can I test it?"

I sighed, "If you must."

She tapped her chin for a moment with her eyes half closed before a smile formed on her lips. "I, Samara Arga, was born on my father's estate in Summervale."

I nodded. "True."

"That one was easy," she smiled. "I've never fallen off a horse."

"True," I said, a bit impressed.

"The first boy I kissed was named Claude."

"Lie," I said, shaking my head.

"When I was young, I had a cat named Mittens my mother wouldn't let in the house."

"Lie."

She scribbled in her book. "Can you tell which part of the statement was false?"

"No," I said. "Just that it wasn't true."

Her eyes narrowed. "There are five-thousand, two-hundred, thirty-seven students enrolled in the Imperial Academy of Magic this term."

I could hear neither truth nor lie in her voice. "You don't know how many students there are."

She smiled widely and scribbled in her book some more. "How did you know?"

"The gift doesn't let me check facts. It only tells me if you believe what you're saying."

"Fascinating," she said with more scribbling. "When I was eight my brother cut my hair while I was sleeping."

"True. Are we going to do this all night or can we move on?"

"Alright, alright. What about Suravani?"

"Her gift allows us to communicate with beasts," I said.

"Like the horses you 'ask not to run off' outside Vana?" she asked. When I nodded she said, "Do animals just speak to you?"

"No, it's not as though I hear a voice. I just sort of understand what they mean. And I assume it's the same for them."

"What about Vastuvit?"

I took another bite of my rapidly cooling stew and said, "Vastuvit's gift allows us to craft things with some small shadow of his greatness."

"Like your bows and the all the carvings in the village?"

"Yes. It's also how we make draa," I said, grabbing my sleeve for emphasis.

Her brows went up as she continued to write. "Kavi?"

I chewed on my lip thinking of a way to explain it. "It's basically the same as Vastuvit's only with music."

Recognition dawned in her eyes. "That's why I thought your flute was enchanted."

I nodded. "Arati's gift is fairly straightforward. It allows us to see in the dark."

Again I saw recognition in her eyes. "And Irin?"

"His gift allows us to ignore pain and exhaustion for a short time, but it takes concentration and it's draining."

She blew on the ink to dry it before turning the page. "I guess that leaves Varga?"

I chewed my lip. "Varga's gift is a bit hard to explain. It lets us gauge rough equivalency between things." She drew a breath and I could see the question in her crystal eyes. "Put simply it gives us a general idea if a trade is favorable. I can't explain it better."

She was quiet for a few moments, allowing me to take a few bites of my almost-cold stew then before asking, "All Manu have these gifts?"

"Yes, but it's as I said when we spoke before: some people have more talent with one gift or find another challenging, just as some people are naturally stronger swimmers than others. Now, may I finish my stew before it gets cold?"

"I suppose," she said with a smirk. "But don't think I'm done with my questions."

"M'lady, I don't think you're ever done with questions," I said going back to my stew.

The next day as we passed the turn off that led toward Metis, Samara called me over.

"Are we not stopping here?" she asked.

"I hadn't planned on it. We have all the supplies we need."

"If those mercenaries really did follow us from Stonehaven, there's a good chance they stopped here."

"And maybe we can learn something?"

"Exactly."

I was annoyed with myself I hadn't considered that. A few hours of questions in Metis turned up several people who remembered seeing the eagle symbol from the armor about five days after we passed through on our way to Mystewood, though no one remembered a tattooed man with a foreign accent, so we took that to mean it was likely he hired the men within the Empire. Eventually we found some women in a brothel who had been paid with Imperial platinum. It wasn't as much as information as we hoped for, but it was something.

We returned to the road with the rest of the Rangers and continued our journey southward.

"So, they left Stonehaven five days after us," Samara said.

I shook my head. "I think we have to assume it was more like seven days. Absent wagons, the mercenaries would have gained quite a bit on us, especially through the pass."

"Alright, so a week then. It still gives us a timetable."

I shrugged. "It's more than we knew when we came here."

The next two days went by quickly and without incident. With aid Samara even mounted her horse and rode for a bit, getting her body used to it again. As we crested a hill near the border of Zura we saw a huge contingent of Arga houseguard on the road directly before us and they did not look friendly. Their hostility was apparent and some of the men around me started reaching for their bows. I called out to the Rangers in the language of our people, "Whatever happens *do not* fight them!"

A man near the front of the Arga procession yelled, "There he is!" It was Lucius. "Darian Wahya, you are under arrest by order of House Arga."

I sighed. I might wind up on a Zuran cross after all.

Chapter Thirteen
Samara

I'd nodded off, lulled to sleep by the rhythmic rocking of the carriage, when shouting voices roused me from my light slumber. We were stopped and, for one terrifying moment, fear welled up in the pit of my stomach. I thought I was back in my tent by the fork in the river before realization caught up with me. I was about to ask Autumn what was going on but her wide eyes told me that she didn't know either. I glanced out the window to try to see what was going on. Were we under attack?

I could see a few of the Rangers right outside the window. None of them had their bows in hand but their bodies were tight with tension.

"What happened to my sister?" a voice shouted. Lucius? It sounded like him but we were still several days' travel from Stonehaven.

"She's alright, m'lord. Give me a chance to explain," said Darian's calm voice.

"Where is she?" screamed Lucius.

Cayman's face appeared in the other window. "Uh, m'lady? You might want to come out here. Now."

I flailed about looking for my cane in a panic, and when I found it I struggled with the door latch. When it came open I nearly fell out of the carriage but managed to catch myself on the door frame. I looked up, surprised to see a score of Arga houseguards on the road before us.

Darian had ridden a few horse lengths ahead of his fellow rangers and was only a half dozen yards from the Arga procession. I spotted a man in noble armor pacing hotly toward him. It was Lucius.

"M'lord," Darian said holding up his hand and speaking in soothing tones one would use with a spooked horse. "Just calm down and let—"

"Don't you 'm'lord' me! I *will not* calm down," Lucius said, a fury the likes of which I'd never seen burning in his lilac eyes. He reached up and grabbed Darian by the front of his surcoat and yanked him off his mount, slamming him down hard on the road.

"Lucius," I cried, but in his maddened state he didn't hear me. I was afraid. Afraid Darian might hurt Lucius, afraid Lucius might hurt him, afraid to what that fight might cause between the houseguards and the Rangers.

"Where is Samara?" Lucius screamed again. Darian was wheezing like he had the wind knocked out of him. Both Darian's people and Lucien's were eyeing each other with intense uncertainty. I saw hands easing towards bows.

"Lucius, stop! I'm right here! *I'm alright,*" I shouted. Still he didn't hear me.

Lucius drew his gladius, putting the point under Darian's chin. "Where... is...my...*sister?*" he said enunciating each word.

Someone was about to get hurt, probably a bunch of someones. "Oh, enough of this." I hadn't cast magic since being attacked by the river and I would have liked to ease back into it, but it didn't seem as though I would be allowed that opportunity.

I started calling the power, putting all of my desperation and fear into the spell. Pale blue light shimmered off my hands as I made the mudras of spellcasting. I shaped the magic in my mind as I released the spell with a shout. A powerful gust of wind burst from between my outstretched hands, similar to what I'd summoned by the road when the Zatru rushed us, but much more focused. It slammed into my brother with the force of a charging ram, tearing his sword from his grasp and knocking him from his feet. Several horses spooked, both Arga and Manu. As their riders tried to regain control of their animals I hobbled forward as fast as my healing leg would let me.

"Are you alright?" I asked as I reached Darian's supine form.

He coughed as he massaged his low back. "Never...better." he said with a grin.

I'd never met a more vexing man. Though at the moment my brother was competing for that honor.

"Otter?" Lucius said gaining his feat.

"Oh, now you see m—"

I was interrupted as Lucius crushed me against him in a fierce hug.

"Are you alright? Autumn's letter said you were hurt."

"I was but I'm alright now. Thanks mostly to the man you were just holding a sword to," I said, pointing to Darian, who had gained is feet and was in the process of reclaiming the arrows that had been slung from his quiver.

"Samara," my father, who had been at the rear of the procession, broke though the houseguards. It'd been years since the last time he'd left Summervale. He hopped off his horse and scooped me up in an embrace that left my feet dangling. "I wasn't sure I'd ever hold you again."

"Sorry to have worried you so," I said into his shoulder.

He set me down gently. "*This* is what I was worried about. Even with all those houseguards and your magic, the moment you set foot outside of Zura I almost lose you to bandits—"

"Father, they weren't bandits" I interrupted, "They were assassins. And they followed me from Stonehaven."

"What?" my father and brother said together.

"And there's more, but first," I looked around at the houseguards and the Rangers who were still very tense. "By the Gods, tell the guards to stand down. The Manu gave me aid and protection when I was hurt. They are definitely *not* the enemy."

They both looked skeptical but Father raised his hand and said, "At ease, men." Crossbows lowered and hands moved away from sword hilts, and in turn the tension eased out of the Manu as well.

Darian, having reclaimed his horse, approached cautiously and said, "Perhaps we should camp here for tonight? You have much to discuss with your family."

"He's right. I'm weary from traveling and we do have much to discuss," I said before anyone else could speak.

"Of course, Daughter," my father said, though Lucius stared at Darian with open distrust.

The Manu made their camp some hundred yards away from the Zuran group in order to help diffuse the tension. I sat in my father's large tent with a full belly and a cup of wine. I told Father and Lucius everything, including what we'd learned in Metis, and I showed them the platinum coins and the symbol Darian had cut from one of the dead assassin's armor. Autumn confirmed what I said and added a few details from the time I was mad with fever.

When I finished, Father and Lucius looked at each other, uncertainty clear in their gaze. "Are you sure this seer is for real?"

I nodded. "Master Carter can vouch for the Vija. Also, I never mentioned the demon I was looking for, and she showed me the robed men in the smoke before they attacked."

"Maybe it's an elaborate deception?" Lucius said.

"To what end?" asked Father as he tapped his lips.

"Perhaps the Manu are in league with the robed men?" Lucius replied.

"That's ridiculous," I said. "They healed me, gave me shelter, and an armed escort back to Stonehaven. If they're trying to kill me they're doing a bad job of it."

"Maybe it was strictly a financial arrangement," Lucius pressed. "You said yourself that finding you in the woods would have been nearly impossible. I just find it hard to believe that Darian managed to survive unscathed and dispatch your attackers when all of your houseguards were killed."

"That *is* suspect," Father said.

"Darian was down at the river when we were ambushed at the camp. He came back after I'd already killed half of them with magic."

Lucius's brows went up. "Rather convenient, isn't it?"

Autumn spoke up. "M'lords, I can vouch for Darian. He gave Samara care that surely saved her life and led me out of the wilderness while carrying her. If not for him, we would have both died."

"All of which cost him nothing," Lucius spat. "That doesn't prove anything. Perhaps he merely saw an opportunity for a greater payoff."

Autumn grew tense. "It cost him dearly, m'lord."

"What do you mean?" my father asked.

"The only way to get lady Samara to a healer was to pass through a Fae encampment." Autumn swallowed audibly before continuing. "In exchange for safe passage, Darian allowed a sidhe to feed on him."

"What?" the Arga men said in unison.

"I saw it with my own eyes."

The realization dawned on me. "That's what you meant when you said he was wounded."

She nodded. "He asked me not to say anything, but you must understand what he gave up, m'lords."

A pang of sympathy shot through me. I felt horribly guilty about being angry with him before. Lucius was silent. At length my father said, "No one would allow themselves to be fed on by a sidhe for any amount of money. I think we must assume this Manu's intentions are pure for the moment." That was my father, ever practical.

"Agreed," said Lucius, his bluster gone.

"So I suppose the question is, what do we do now?" Father mused.

I took a deep breath and blew it out, trying to clear my mind of the business with Darian and the sidhe. "I suppose we get back to White Harbor and inform the Emperor of what we know," I said.

"There's still someone trying to kill you, Otter," Lucius said. "If your theory is correct and there's a noble involved they're likely to try again, especially if their plan is in danger."

I shrugged. "We're careful and we take it one step at a time. What else can we do?"

"I don't like it," said Father.

"Neither do I, but what other option we have?"

We all looked around at each other. No one had an answer to that question.

The next morning as camp was being struck, Lucius, Father, and I approached Darian. "I'm told we have you to thank for my daughter's safe return," Father said, offering a regal bow. "I wish to offer my deepest thanks on behalf of myself and House Arga."

Darian returned bow and said, "You're welcome, m'lord."

Lucius cleared his throat and spoke with some difficulty. "I...wish to apologize for my behavior yesterday. I let my temper run away—"

"No harm done, m'lord," Darian said, tossing him a small brown bag.

"What is this?" Lucius asked.

"The seventy five gold you paid me, m'lord. You specified I return lady Samara safely. She was injured, therefore I cannot accept your payment."

Lucius just stared at the Manu, his mouth agape. "You clearly acted beyond what was asked of you. You deserve payment for that," he said, tossing the purse back to Darian.

"I'm sorry, m'lord. I cannot. I failed to complete the terms of our agreement, and I fear that if I accept your payment, I would be risking Varga's displeasure." Darian tossed the bag back to Lucius.

Lucius stared at if for a moment and I could see the cogs turning behind his lilac eyes. "Then allow me to give you a small gift as recompense for my actions yesterday," he said, again tossing the bag back to Darian.

Darian snatched the bag out of the air and said, "You were simply overcome by your feelings for your sister, as is understandable. I bear you no ill will for your actions, however I don't wish to insult you, so I will accept your gift."

He'd come up with a way for everyone to save face and still get paid. In that moment I looked at Darian and thought he might have a bright future in politics.

There was some discussion that the Manu might accompany us the rest of the way to Stonehaven but it was ultimately decided that the Rangers would return to Mystewood, minus Darian, leaving my safety and the bodies of our fallen comrades in the hands of House Arga.

Autumn and I bid farewell to the Rangers and thanked them for watching over us. In return we received deep bows and warm smiles. Darian went to speak with them in their native tongue and the concern and respect the Rangers felt for him was apparent. As they were getting ready to depart he and Cayman locked arms and had an intense earnest conversation... until Cayman said something that made Darian take a swing at him with his flute. He barely ducked it and rode off, braids bouncing as he laughed.

We split with the Manu and took again to the road. My father and Lucius rode with me in the carriage and discussed further the events of the previous weeks and what would be the best course of action moving forward. It was nice merely to be in their presence again.

By midmorning we could see the tall walls of Ostium but as we approached I noted that something was different. The large Portam gates that had been open before were now closed, and the number of legionnaires guarding it had tripled. A long line of wagons and travelers stretched out before us seeking entrance. Each one was being checked by the guards, which of course caused a significant wait for those farther back.

"Why are the gates closed?" I asked.

"I don't know. They were open when we passed through yesterday," Lucius said.

"I fear I may know the answer," Father said with a grim expression. "The legions only take those precautions when the Empire is at war."

We moved swiftly through the pass, encountering neither raiders nor assassins. Though still cold, it was notably warmer than it had been just a few weeks before, though the wind was no less intense. As we ascended we moved into a cloud bank that brought back eerie half-memories of the foggy morning we were attacked, leaving me jumpy and irritable. I gazed out the window into the gray seeing imagined forms just past the edge of my vision, and tensed at every sharp noise expecting it to be followed by a chorus of terrible clicks.

As we descended from the mountains on the last day of our voyage, Father climbed in the carriage with me wearing the same expression as when he told me Koto would be accompanying me. "Do you still believe your attackers followed you across the Causeway?"

The question caught me a bit off guard. "Based on what we know, it seems likely."

"Then you will stay as Ganicus's guest in Castle Uttara while Lucius and I go to

Imperia."

My jaw dropped, "But Father—"

"The men who made the attempt on your life either followed you from Imperia or Zenith, therefore you will remain in Stonehaven, where you will be safe."

"I need to speak with the Academy and the Noble Council. I'm the only one who fully understands what's going on—"

"You may write as many letters as you wish," Father interrupted, "and I'll make sure they're delivered. Once your attackers' plan is no longer a secret, they'll have less reason to come after you again. And perhaps we'll be able to locate the noble who's responsible, if indeed there is one."

"Father, they must hear it from my lips—"

"I've made my decision. That's final."

"I know you're worried, but—"

"Final," my father said, his deep purple eyes narrowing. I wanted to argue, but I knew there was no point. He reached across the carriage and cupped my face. "This isn't the time to be taking unnecessary risks." His eyes softened. "I almost lost you once already."

I laid my hand over his. "I know you just want to protect me, Father, but I'm a grown woman, a mage. I understand what—"

"You're my daughter no matter how old you are. You'll stay where I know you'll be safe until I can make better arrangements. Understood?"

I sighed, "Yes."

"Promise?"

I thought about it for a moment. "I promise I'll take whatever action is prudent to stay safe, under the given circumstances."

My father pursed his lips and for a moment I wasn't sure he was going to accept that. Finally he smiled, "Are you sure you're a devotee of Tarka and not Varga?"

"Just trying to make a promise I can keep," I said. "I do have to say I'm surprised you trust Ganicus that much."

"Ganicus Uttara may be many things," Father said, his expression hinting that he could name quite a few, and none of them would be particularly positive, "but he's not a traitor. And I have a hard time imagining a group of mercenaries storming Castle Uttara to get to you."

"Not without a legion of soldiers," I conceded.

We arrived at Stonehaven after dark. The heavy gates were already locked for the evening but our noble coins granted us passage. It was strange seeing the legionnaires at the gate so on guard. The last time the Empire was at war I was a small girl and I remembered very little of it.

House Uttara must have had a runner at the gate watching for us because by the time we arrived at the castle there was a group waiting just inside the walls to greet us. Helen I recognized and Ganicus was easy to spot, looking as flashy as one could wearing only gray and black. All the rest were strangers save one.

With her high cheekbones, snow white hair, and slate gray eyes she stood a paragon of her House. Projecting a commanding presence despite her average height, the lines etched across her face were graceful, and if I didn't know her age to be near sixty, I would have shaved two decades off of the estimate. Lusandra Luminara Uttara had ascended to a place few women attained, Prefect. The Prefect of each House governed their state and enforced the rules enacted by the Senate and the Emperor. The only other position even close in rank was the High Councilor, who served on the Noble Council. One member of each House served on the council and their job was to advise the Emperor and vote yea or nay on new laws, as with my great-uncle Decias.

As I eased out of the carriage Prefect Lusandra greeted me. "Lady Samara, I'm glad to see you well. I'd heard you were injured." Her face was that of a lifetime politician, giving nothing away.

"Thank you for your concern, Prefect," I bowed, grimacing through the stiffness. "I'm recovering slowly. I am, however, rather tired from the journey," I added the last part hoping to get out of some tiresome dinner where I recounted my story again.

"Of course you are," she crooned with sympathy in her voice as her slate eyes drank in every detail. "We have a suite of rooms set aside for you. Ganicus will show you to them."

"Thank you, Prefect," I stiffly bowed again.

Autumn and I were led off by Ganicus and Helen with a trio of Arga houseguards. When we were out of earshot Ganicus spoke quietly, "I'm glad you're safe, Cousin. Clearly Darian was a poor choice—"

"On the contrary, I'd be dead if not for him." I squeezed his hand. "And I'm touched by your concern."

We were led to a lavish chamber, easily thrice the size of the one I'd stayed in before, with a private attached bath.

Autumn dipped her hand in the hot, spring-fed tub. "Well, Mistress, let it never be said House Uttara doesn't know how to treat a guest."

"That's no jest. This must be the room the High Councilor stays in when he visits. Have you ever been in a room with a private bath?"

"Clearly you tease, Mistress."

Bathed and fed, with Autumn as my impromptu scribe, I set about writing letters. I first composed a lengthy letter to Master Carter explaining everything, from a detailed recount of the smoky cave, to my theories about a noble being involved somehow. Next, I authored a much more formal and compact version for the Masters of the Academy and the Emperor's Archmage. When that was finished, I wrote three identical documents that summarized much of the technical arcane jargon. One letter was for the Senate, one for the Noble Council, and the last was for the Emperor. As I pressed my magical House seal to the wax of the note bound for Emperor Pullo, I noted again how surreal my life had become.

I blew out a sigh and stretched my back, which was especially sore where the crossbow bolt had been pushed through, and stared up into the harsh light of the coldfire. It was well past midnight but I had a few more letters that needed writing. I dipped my quill into the ink, smoothed out the thick vellum, and started writing a letter to Harold's wife, whom I didn't even know existed until a few weeks ago.

I didn't really know what to say, but it was important to me that she know how highly I thought of him, how grateful I was for his service and his sacrifice. Words flowed from the quill, filling up the smooth parchment, but when I read them they seemed hollow. What was I supposed to say? Nothing would make his death any easier. I thought back to all the trite, clichéd things people had said to me after my mother died. Though I'd meant everything I'd said in the letter, my words looked just the same as theirs had. Tears blurred the ink as the eagle of my House, the House he'd given his life for, sealed my words.

I wrote a similar letter to Dirk's parents, whom Autumn informed me lived on my father's estate, and then a series of generic letters for the other guards who'd died. Somehow the fact I hardly knew them made it worse. I lay down on the enormous cloud-like feather bed as a mixture of grief and apprehension settled in my belly, until my weariness became enough to drag me into a dreamless black abyss.

---

he nervousness built up in my chest making it hard to breathe. It'd been two days since Father and Lucius had gone across the Causeway and there'd been no word from them. Having bamboo shoots jammed under my fingernails would have been less torture than the waiting. I'd very swiftly run out of things to occupy my mind and so fear, speculation, and uncertainty had taken root. To make it worse, my houseguards had orders that at least two of them were to accompany me everywhere I went. Rather than making me feel safe, it made me feel claustrophobic.

"I noticed the castle had a training arena for horses. Perhaps you would enjoy riding a bit?" Darian finally prompted.

I couldn't think of anything better to do and I was going to suffocate if I stayed in the castle any longer. "Why not? Perhaps you're right," I sighed.

I followed him to the stables, houseguards hovering close behind. Darian saddled our horses and I let him help me onto Komala. Azava's light beamed down from the clear sky kissing my skin with warmth. It seemed that spring had finally gotten a grip on Stonehaven. I nudged Komala into a canter and watched with humor as the guards jogged to keep up.

The large, open-air arena was actually for hosting tournaments and games rather than training as Darian thought, though I supposed it would work for that function. Long bleachers bordered the loose dirt with a series of hurdles and obstacles set up in a gauntlet for the horses to navigate. Without warning, Darian's horse bolted away and sailed over one of the jumps. I though perhaps something had spooked it until I saw the grin he cast over his shoulder.

"Show off," I said.

In response, he spurred his horse through the rest of the gauntlet, dashing between barrels and leaping over hurdles. Both he and his horse were breathing hard as they pranced back toward me when they were done.

"How was it?" I asked.

"A bit on the easy side," he said with a shrug.

I glanced over at the first hurdle he cleared and had an impulse. "I want to learn how to jump. Will you show me?"

His eyes narrowed skeptically. "Are you sure you feel up to it?"

The muscles around the wounded areas were still tight and I was a bit wobbly on my left leg, but since I'd resumed my hatha stretching even that was fading. "I'm up for it."

"Are you sure they won't object?" he said, nodding toward the houseguards.

"They're my watchers, not my keepers," I said, not entirely sure it was true.

"As you wish then." He went over and moved the hurdle bar to a lower rung. "Alright, m'lady, let the horse have his head and give him heels just before the jump, then keep your heels down and lean forward. The horse'll know what to do. Be sure to hold on tight with your legs and don't cut his reins hard to either side on the landing. Understand?"

"I think so."

"Good, now watch me a few times first." He nudged his horse to an easy gallop rather than the lightning speed of his first run and it was easier to see what he was doing. I watched intently as his horse made the jump easily and effortlessly. Not for the first time I wondered how much that beast was worth. He came around he started to say, "Now this time notice—" when I spurred Komala forward into a gallop and was rewarded with Darian's shock wide eyes as I passed him.

My excitement built as I neared the hurdle. I let him have his head and gave him heels just as Darian had said. I leaned forward and hugged his neck as Komala leaped effortlessly over the bar. My wounds stung a bit as we landed but the rush of the experience dampened it so that I hardly noticed. I heard clapping and turned around to see.

Ganicus was watching from the bleachers. "Not bad, Cousin, but you need to keep your heels lower." He hopped down onto the freshly churned dirt making his way toward us. "You breed good horses, Darian. That can't be argued."

I patted the bay gelding on the neck. "He's not bad. I might invest in one."

"Pft, that bay's better for you than he ever was for me. You can have him," Ganicus snorted.

"What? Ganicus, I can't. It's too much."

"He's a gift. I insist. Now if you turn him down, you'll be denying hospitality and incur Kavi's wrath," he said with a smug smile.

"Does that mean you're in the market for a new horse, m'lord," Darian said with a grin.

"Only if it's that chestnut stud you're riding," Ganicus purred with a predatory smile.

Darian's grin faded. "I'm sorry, m'lord. He's not for sale."

"Oh, come now. There's a price for everything. I'll give you a hundred gold for him."

I felt my eyes widen. That was a high price for a horse. "I…I'm sorry, m'lord, I can't," Darian stammered. "But I have another that's just as good for—"

Ganicus's sapphire eyes glittered. "I want that one. Two hundred gold."

"Again, m'lord, I'm sorry—"

"Three hundred."

Darian swallowed audibly, sweat beading on his brow. I'd have thought Ganicus was just teasing him if I couldn't see the look on his face. Ganicus Uttara had to have the best, whether it was women, wine, or horses.

Darian cleared his throat. "That's a very generous offer, m'lord, but I can't sell this horse for any amount of money. He has deep meaning to me."

Ganicus hesitated, and I thought he might press the offer, but instead he said, "Very well. But you have to sell me one of his colts then."

Darian blew out a sigh. "That I can do."

"Well, now that you're done torturing the commoners," I said, "have you heard anything yet?"

"No, but your father took the Causeway to Zenith today."

"He probably went to talk to the Prefect…wait, what? If there's been no word, how do you know that?"

"I checked the Causeway record," he stated matter-of-factly. At my blank stare he said, "A record is kept of every party that crosses the Causeway. Any noble can go down there and review it."

I'd either forgotten that little tidbit or I never knew it. A few things clicked into place. "Cousin, care to take a trip with me to the Gate?"

———————

Autumn was waiting for me as we returned. "Did you learn anything, Mistress?"

"A little." I sighed. "Mostly we just confirmed what we already suspected. Some freeman named Cyril paid for twenty to pass from Imperia to Stonehaven six days after we left."

"That's something," Autumn said.

Darian said, "The Gate record is likely how they knew Samara had traveled to Stonehaven." His brows raised as he cut a glance at me. "And that can only be accessed by nobles."

"Or military officers," I countered, but I acknowledged that it did lend even more credence to his theory that the man who hired the mercenaries was a noble.

Shortly after we returned to the castle, Lucius arrived in the atrium with a familiar and very welcome face. "Master Carter," I exclaimed, putting the straightened fingers of my right hand against the flattened palm of my left looking like a crooked "T" and I gave him the bow used only between mages.

He returned the bow and his eyes went to the cane. Worry knit his brow.

"I'm fine, Master." His genuine concern warmed my belly like a sip of Manu whisky. "As it turns out, you were right about the Vija."

"So I've heard," he said, turning to face Darian. "And you must the Ranger who aided her. *Kadeshdae.*"

Darian's eyes widened a moment before he bowed saying, "Kadeshdae, Master Carter."

"Thank you for saving my protégé. I've got quite a lot of time invested in this one. It would have been an awful bother to have to train another." He had a wry half-grin not dissimilar to Darian's, and it was no less vexing.

"Of course, m'lord," Darian said stifling a chuckle with obvious effort.

"Don't 'm'lord' me, son. I'm just a citizen."

Darian inclined his head. "As you wish."

Master Carter's soothing presence was already beginning to relax me. Then my eyes found Lucius's face. He'd never been able to hide anything from me. "What is it?" I asked.

"Not here," Lucius said.

I glanced over toward Ganicus. He nodded and led the way to one of the castle's studies. The five of us sat in overstuffed chairs arranged in a rough semicircle.

"What happened?" I asked. The ball of tension in my core threatened to rip its way out through my chest.

"It didn't go well," Lucius said, staring at me gravely. "Father delivered your letters himself, then he convinced Uncle Decias to call a joint meeting of the Noble Council and the Senate."

"And?" I prompted.

"They don't trust that the prophecy is true."

Master Carter interjected, "I testified as to the abilities of the Vija but the Academy was also unconvinced."

"Didn't they think it was worth at least looking into?" I said, my blood rising.

"Vizipa is located in the heart of Moravar, with whom Zura is at war. If the Empire sent an envoy they would think it was a trick," Lucius said.

"We're at war of over a couple of rocks in the ocean that *no one cares about*," I shouted. "*Millions* will die if this gate is opened!"

Master Carter shook his head and in his soothing voice said, "We're at war with an expansionist power. One that's sunk quite a few of our ships, by the way. Many people think war is *justified*, especially in the Senate."

I dug my fingers into my hair messing up Autumn's expert braidwork. "And while we fight this justified war, an army of demons is about walk out of Hell and into our Realm. *Ugh*, I knew I should have come with you."

Master Carter shook his head. "It wouldn't have made a difference. I told the Council of my experience with the Vija but they were still skeptical. It would take a mage in both Acala and Hell to open a portal—"

"I know that, Master. I'm not an idiot. But that's what the Vija saw."

"The leaders of the Academy decided there wasn't enough evidence to recommend to the Emperor that we take resources away from the war effort."

It seemed there suddenly wasn't enough air in the room. I rested my face in my hands and took a few deep breaths to calm myself down. "This is madness."

"I'm sorry, Otter."

"What did the Emperor say?" I asked looking up.

Lucius shrugged. "The Emperor's away fighting the war. A message was sent to him and we've yet to hear a reply. But with the Academy, the Senate, and the Noble Council all advising against it..." he trailed off.

"There's very little chance the Emperor will do anything," I finished.

"Maybe once the war is over..."

"Lucius, we have five months. What war between two powerful countries ever ended in five months?" Frustration gripped my chest and I felt tears welling up in my eyes. Gods, but sometimes I was envious of men. They never cried in these situations.

Master Carter laid his hand on top of mine. "There are those at the Academy and among the Senate who agree with you, or at least think it's worth looking into."

"A lot of good that support is doing us," I said wiping at my misty eyes.

"So that's it?" Darian frowned, his brows coming together. "The most powerful Empire in the history of the world won't lift a finger to stop what might be the worst disaster since the Dragon War?" He shook his head in disbelief. "If that gate opens there will be more dead bodies than sand on the beaches of White Harbor."

"No one in this room is questioning the truth of what you're saying," Master Carter said soothingly, "But the ones who wield the power don't believe Samara's story. And unfortunately by the time they realize she is right, it'll be too late. So the question becomes...what do we do now?"

All our eyes danced back and forth between each other. No one knew what to say. A moment of clarity crystallized in my mind, leading me to a terrifying conclusion. "We're on our own."

"What are you saying, Otter?"

"The one thing we know is that to stop this gate from opening, I have to get to Shakkar's demon at Vizipa."

Lucius shook his head. "Father's never going allow it."

I shrugged, steeling myself for what I was about to suggest. "Father doesn't have to know. I'll take a small, fast ship to Moravar. I can be there in just a few weeks."

"Otter, we're at war. There's a blockade at the Palankar. No civilian ships are even *allowed* in the Vizaya Sea. Not to mention that what your suggesting madness."

"Lucius, I have to get there by some means."

"What are you suggesting? Round up as many houseguards as you can and march there? As I said, it's *madness*. And you'd never make it out of Zura without Father finding out and putting a stop to it."

"Even if you made it to Moravar, the king wouldn't let you anywhere near Vizipa," Master Carter interjected.

"I-I could fly a white flag, try to talk to them. If I explain the situation—"

"You'd be taken prisoner at best. At worst…" Master Carter shook his head.

"But it's the *truth*," I shouted. Even to my ears it sounded naive.

"Otter, the mages at the Academy don't even believe you. What makes you think total strangers, whose country is at war with ours, will think you're telling the truth?"

"A small group on horseback dressed as civilians might pass to Vizipa unnoticed," Darian said.

I considered that carefully, examining all the angles. It was a terrifying prospect, but… "That could work."

"You can't be serious about this?" Lucius shouted.

"What do you expect me to do?" I shot back.

"You promised Father you'd stay safe."

That made me angry. "Lucius, I'm not *safe* here anymore than anyone else is. You think that horde of demons is going to spare me when they get here?"

"M'lord, they're correct," Master Carter said. "What other alternative is there?"

"This is insane. There has to be another way," said Lucius.

"And what would you suggest?" asked Master Carter.

My brother dug both hands into his hair. He was quiet for a long time, struggle clear on his face. "You're right," he said finally. "How do we go about this?"

"Lucius, you don't have to come—" I started.

"If you think I'm going to let you out of my sight again, you *are* mad."

"I think all of you are mad," said Ganicus breaking his silence. His full lips crept up into a smile. "But it's far better to be mad than boring. How can I help?"

I smiled. "Bless you, Cousin. We'll need to borrow horses again."

"Done. What else?" Ganicus asked leaning forward.

"We'll need food and supplies for the journey." My mind was running like a wild colt. "And maps I suppose."

Lucius said, "We'll need armor that can be hidden under clothes. How many guards should we take?"

Darian scratched his stubble. "No more than six I would say. You'll need to choose men who won't seem as if they're soldiers."

Lucius shook his head. "We're putting the cart before the horse. The moment you disappear with half a dozen houseguards Father will turn the country inside out looking for you."

"I actually have an idea about how to keep Father from realizing I'm gone," I smiled, pleased with my own cleverness. "For a time at least. We'll have to get out of the Empire quickly and obviously we can't take the Causeway."

Master Carter spoke up, "I could send you a couple hundred miles with transportation magic but it won't get you past the wards at the border. You'll have hard time crossing out of the country with the increased patrols."

"I have something in mind for that," Darian said, his blue-green eyes twinkling. "If m'lord Ganicus would be generous enough to lend me some paint and a few able bodies?"

"Of course," Ganicus said with a smirk. "Now I'm intrigued."

"We'll have to act quickly," Lucius said. "We have maybe two days until Father returns from Stonehaven. And there's another problem. I don't know how to gather the funds we'll need without drawing the attention of House Arga."

"That's not an issue," Darian said, as he jingled the coins in his pouch. "The men who attacked us have graciously offered to fund our expedition."

Lucius rubbed his forehead. "We'll need forged papers."

"I can handle that," Ganicus said, which was unsurprising.

"Can you get ahold of one of the blanks they use for citizenship coins?" I asked. Forging one of the magical coins was going to be substantially harder than a few papers.

"No, House Uttara has nothing to do with that. The Imperial Registry handles it," he said.

I nodded. "I'll figure something out."

Master Carter said, "I'll see if I can make contact, discretely, with anyone in Moravar who might be able to aid you. I should have at least one or two former students there. I'll also create something that will allow us to stay in contact."

Lucius said, "Father went to speak with the Prefect, but he could be back at any time. I can probably stall him for a couple of days without raising suspicion."

"I guess we'd better get to it then," I said. As mad and terrifying as the task before me seemed, I was calmer and more focused than I had been in days. Having a plan and something to do always crystallized my thoughts. I just tried not to think about how dangerous the road before me was.

"Well, m'lady, what do you think?" Darian asked.

Much like staring at the sun, it was rather hard to look directly at his creation. He'd painted the covered Manu wagon an eye-piercing mix of yellow, orange, and green with purple accents. "I think it's hideous."

"But?" he asked brows raised.

I sighed. "But it does look like a Dezika vardo."

He leaned back and crossed his arms beaming his vexing smile.

"If you're waiting for me to tell you how clever you are, it's not going to happen," I said glaring at him. "But the wagon will suffice."

"There's no need to say it out loud, m'lady. The look in your eyes tells me everything I need to know," he said with a bow.

I rolled the eyes in question as Lucius walked into the courtyard with a letter in his hand. "What is it?" I asked.

Lucius held up the paper shaking his head. "Word from the Emperor. It's as we suspected. He's not going to pull resources away from the war effort or…" His eyes rested on the wagon. "That's your plan? I thought the idea was *not* to draw attention to ourselves?"

Darian merely smiled. "We don't have to remain unseen, m'lord, just unnoticed. The beasts with the best camouflage may hide in plain sight."

He shook his head and looked back at me. "Father's making arrangements for a contingent of houseguards to escort you to Zenith. I told him the hot springs were easing your wounds, which should buy us a couple of days."

"How are you going to explain your absence?"

"I'll tell him I'm taking a group of guards to go run down a lead on your attackers. Hopefully we'll be out of the country by the time he figures out I'm missing."

"Have you picked out the guards yet?" I asked.

"Yes. Ganicus is having them fitted for some sleeveless mail shirts right now. He also procured some plain clothes and weapons without a house seal on them." He glanced over at Darian. "You and I will need to be fitted for armor as well."

"I beg your pardon, m'lord, but that's not necessary."

"It's necessary because I say it is," Lucius spat back with a frown.

"I've never worn metal armor before—" Darian started before Lucius cut him off.

"Well here's a perfect opportunity for you to learn."

"As you wish," Darian said, bowing.

Lucius glanced back to the impromptu vardo, and huffed out a sigh before he stomped off.

Apparently there was at least one person Darian couldn't charm. "He'll warm to you eventually," I said.

He shrugged. "You can be the ripest, sweetest peach in the world, but not everyone likes peaches."

With another eye roll, I left him to find Autumn and complete my part of the preparations. I came upon her in our suite packing a riding satchel. "What are you doing?"

"Packing, mistress."

"I can see that. Where are you going?"

"Well obviously, I'm going with you."

Her matter-of-fact statement caught me off guard. "Autumn, listen…"

"Mistress, I'm not letting you do this alone."

"Autumn, I'm touched, truly touched, that you're willing to come with me but—"

"I know it will be dangerous but—"

I grabbed her by the shoulders. "Autumn, you can't come with me because I have another task for you. One that's every bit as dangerous as mine. Perhaps even more so."

"What?" she asked tilting her head to the side with brows drawn.

"Would you say you know me better than anyone else?"

"Without a doubt."

"Then you're the only person who has a chance at pulling it off."

———————

I stood scrutinizing my own reflection, save there was no mirror. I glanced back over my shoulder to see bevy of wide-eyed stares, all except Master Carter who simply beamed a look of pride. I put my arm around my identical twin and said, "Well?"

Lucius, Ganicus, and Darian stared slack jawed. Finally Lucius said, "It's amazing, Otter. Say something, Autumn."

Autumn smiled out of my mouth and asked in my voice, "What would you like to hear, m'lord?"

"Uncanny," Ganicus said.

Lucius shook his head, "Remember no more 'm'lords' or someone will get suspicious."

Master Carter shed bright red light on the room as he went through the mudras of spellcasting. As his eyes turned black he crossed the room and walked around Autumn, assessing my work. "It's a passable illusion. Anchoring the spell to the jade bangle was inspired. If a mage scrutinizes it they won't realize it's not yours."

"As long as they don't look too hard, anyway," I said, tapping the bangle that was a copy of mine, save for the engraving. "I'm more worried about the citizenship coin. I didn't have time to forge one so I just put a spell on mine to make it work for Autumn. It's pretty weak, though. Go ahead and give it a try."

Autumn cleared her throat and said slowly, "Samara Arga." The coin fluttered a few times then shed its warm golden glow on the room.

"It'll have to do," I said with a shrug. "Careful with the hair I have braided through the chain, if that comes off it won't work for you. And remember if you take the bangle off you'll look like, well, you."

"I understand, Mistress," she said in my voice, which of course I'd never heard out of someone else's mouth. It sounded strange to my ears.

I handed her the cane Darian had carved for me. "Walk around a bit."

Autumn took the cane and walked around the study, imitating my mild limp.

"It's pretty convincing," said Ganicus.

"Let's just hope it's convincing enough to fool her own father, or this will be a very short journey," said Darian.

Master Carter blinked away his black eyes and handed me a plain silver mirror gently aglow with magical writing engraved around the edge. "This is the best I could do on short notice. We'll be able to send messages through these, though they can be no longer than a minute or so." He held up his copy of the mirror for emphasis. "The face will tarnish over when you have a message waiting."

I studied the mirror, amazed he'd been able to make such a pair of items in a day. Hopefully I lived long enough to match his skill at magic. "This is perfect."

"I'll alert you to any new developments," he said.

"The horses and supplies are ready," said Ganicus.

"What about the maps?" asked Lucius.

"Ah, I almost forgot." Ganicus said searching through a rucksack and handing a rolled up doe skin to Lucius.

Lucius unrolled the skin on a gray stone table in the middle of the room. It contained a two by three foot map of the known world. "Where's the rest? We need to be able make out the roads."

"Oh, ye of little faith. Just make a circle with your finger around the area you want to see."

Lucius made a circle on the map around Stonehaven, which was but a tiny dot, and the image faded only to be replaced by a map of the area around Stonehaven showing all the major rivers and roads. He made another circle bringing up an even more detailed map of the indicated area. "How do I return to the original map?"

"Just roll it back up," Ganicus said.

"This is marvelous," Lucius said, rolling it up before uncurling again it to see the original map.

I circled an area on the map in the northeastern corner of Zura near the border with Abhamatra. I tapped a fairly recognizable area where the Deer River formed an oxbow lake. "Can your magic get us this far, Master?"

Master Carter squinted over the map. "I believe so."

"If we can get over the border, the journey shouldn't be too difficult until we get to Moravar," I said as I traced the spider web that ran between the towns and cities.

Darian frowned. "Assuming we don't encounter any more of the red-robed mages along the way."

"Well, if Autumn's disguise manages to fool my father it should work for them as well," I said. A pang of guilt shot through me at leaving her in my place when someone was trying to kill me, but we weren't exactly flush with other options.

"I'd feel better about our plan if it didn't rely so heavily on luck," said Lucius.

"As would I, but there's not much we can do about it. We'll just have to hope the Gods favor us," I said with a shrug.

Ganicus snorted. "Right, because they've favored you so strongly up to this point."

"We're still alive. That's something," Darian said.

"I guess that's it, we'll leave just after dawn," said Lucius.

We broke then and I retreated to my chamber to take a long, soaking bath, not knowing when my next opportunity to do so would be. Autumn doffed her bangle so she again looked like herself and joined me. As she washed my red locks, she said, "I shudder to think what your hair will look like without me to do it."

"At least my amateurish attempt will lend some authenticity to the ruse that I'm a commoner," I said. We both laughed.

After a moment she said, "I'm scared mistress."

I faced her. "Don't do anything risky and you'll be fine. Just stay near the guards and—"

"Not for me...well, I mean I'm scared for me too, but I meant I'm scared for you."

"I'm scared too. But what other choice do I have?"

"I wish I had your courage, Mistress."

"You're taking a huge risk as well," I said, staring into her gold eyes. "And you don't need to call me mistress all the time."

Her brows came together as though she didn't understand. "What would I call you then?"

"Samara," I said with a chuckle. "That is my name."

"Samara..." she smiled shyly. "It sounds strange out of my lips."

After we'd dried ourselves from the bath, I put a letter in her hand addressed to my father with the magical House seal on it. "If my father discovers our ruse, give him this. It says I ordered you to impersonate me, and it's witnessed by Lucius and Ganicus."

Autumn looked down at the letter. "I don't imagine he'll be very happy."

"No, I don't imagine so either. What are you going to say as to why my trusty handmaiden is missing?"

Autumn shrugged. "Nothing."

"Father's clever. He'll notice you're not there."

"Nobles don't notice a servant's absence unless they're late with their wine. Oh, he might realize after a week or two and I'll just say 'Autumn's taking a well-deserved break after the excitement in Mystewood' or something like that."

"I'm definitely going to notice your absence."

She grinned mischievously and said, "You will every time you see your hair in the mirror."

I covered my mouth in mock indignation and threw a pillow at her.

As I lay in bed later that night, I feared I might not be able sleep, but the next thing I knew Autumn was shaking me awake. When I opened my eyes, she was wearing one of my dresses.

"It's time to wake up, Mistress."

It felt like I'd just closed my eyes. "Really?"

"Yes," she chuckled.

I stretched out the tightness in my leg and dressed in clothes that weren't mine, consisting of a flowing black skirt with an ivory peasant top and a burgundy bodice. It'd been a while since I'd worn a bodice and, despite the absence of boning, as Autumn laced me up I was beginning to remember why that was. I favored loose clothing and the tight constrictive garment was less than pleasant.

"I'll be happy when I can be rid of this thing," I said.

"There are women who wear them every day," she said tying the laces into a neat bow.

"Cleary not women who ride. Or breathe. Or eat," I said adjusting my breasts a bit. Uncomfortable though it may be I was happy with what it did to my bust.

I sat down at a bureau with a large mirror and went about spellcasting. The illusion spell was simpler and less complicated than Autumn's, though it wouldn't last as long. I used the women I'd met in Vana for inspiration, blackening my hair and darkening my skin to match their copper shade and hide my freckles. Most importantly I changed my eyes to match the mahogany hue of the Manu. I tied a scarf over my hair to finish off my disguise off.

"What do you think?" I asked.

"It's convincing," Autumn said, running her eyes back and forth over me. "If I didn't look closely at you I could easily mistake you for a Dezika."

"That's the idea." As I picked up my endless bag, the only luggage I was bringing, and slid on my riding boots. I handed Autumn the eagle cane Darian had carved and took up a plain one. "Alright, let's be off."

Autumn slid on the bangle that gave her my visage. We left the suite as different women than we'd entered and made our way out of the castle. The vast, clean stable was free of servants, as Ganicus had assured us it would be, containing only our clandestine little group.

Master Carter and Lucius were already there, as well as Ganicus and our plain clothed houseguards. I searched about for Darian for a moment before I realized I'd mistaken him for one of the guards. His disguise was nearly as impressive as mine, though less magical. He'd shaven his stubbly beard and his hair, absent its normal feathers and beads, was tied back with brown ribbon in a neat queue. He wore baggy black pants with a red sash and a purple shirt. Under the circumstances, he looked quite a bit more Zuran than me.

He smiled when his eyes found me and he said, "We've traded places."

"So it would seem," I chuckled.

"We're ready to go," said Lucius.

"Alright," I said. I turned and looked at Autumn who promptly wrapped me up in a tight embrace. We'd never been apart from each other for more than a couple weeks since we were children. There was nothing more to say so I just hugged her tight, fighting the urge to cry. As we broke the embrace she opened her mouth to say something but nothing came out. I mouthed the words "Me too."

Ganicus and Lucius clashed in a rough embrace and Ganicus said, "I'd come with you if my absence wouldn't bring suspicion. Do try not to die. You know how I hate having to make new friends."

"You have other friends?" Lucius quipped.

Ganicus shrugged. "Sycophants, friends, what's the difference?"

"Tell Helen not to worry. I know she'll miss me but I'll be back soon,"

Lucius said with a grin.

"I'm sure she will miss you. She does enjoy the company of women," Ganicus shot back, returning the smile.

I rolled my eyes and went over to Master Carter. "Thank you for all your help, Master."

"I'm going to tell you the same thing I did last time I sent you away. 'That which is worth seeking is rarely easy to find'. Though I hope this time you'll return home in better shape."

"Gratitude," I said.

Autumn crossed over to Darian and gave him a kiss in the cheek. "Stay safe Ranger Darian."

He bowed to her. "And you as well, Lady Autumn."

"Let's mount up," barked Lucius. He and the guards mounted their Uttara horses while Darian and I climbed onto the wagon.

"Come together as closely as possible," ordered Master Carter, motioning with his hands. The men crowded around the wagon in the tight quarters of the stable.

"It's important that you keep a tight rein on your horses and stay still. It could be dangerous to move around while I'm working the spell, and it will take several moments."

As Master Carter began his spellcasting, a bubble of crimson light formed around our group. The light deepened and the air began to feel thick as it did on a nexus. The bubble of energy grew so deep we couldn't see out and the pressure made my ears feel like they needed to pop.

"If I survive this they'd better make me and Adept," I said to no one in particular.

Chapter Fourteen
Darian

The sphere of light around us became brighter and brighter, until I had to shut my eyes against it. I felt as though there was a rock sitting on my chest as the pressure around me grew. Finally the crimson energy that surrounded us began dissipate into an ocean of tiny red fireflies before flickering out completely.

A quick glance showed me everyone had made it. We were in a lightly-wooded meadow that was filled with bright spring grass and some very confused sheep.

"Well at least we made it here with all our—" Lucius started.

"Shhh," Samara interrupted him putting her fingers to her lips. She pointed to a tree about twenty yards away where a long-limbed shepherd boy was sleeping.

"He certainly missed a show," I whispered, setting my bow between us in easy reach. After taking a moment to get my bearings, I pointed south. If Master Carter had set us down mostly on target, we ought to be able to find the river and figure out where we were from there.

The ground was relatively open and clear, easy enough for the wagon to cross. The houseguards fell into formation around the wagon as they had around Samara's carriage. "That's not going to work," I said. "You look too much like soldiers. Try to seem less, I don't know, less organized. Like we're all just traveling together."

The captain was a large man named Oenus with a shaved head and skin the color of Manu eyes. He glowered, seeming unhappy at receiving orders from me. He looked over to Lucius and said, "M'lord?"

"He's right," said Lucius. "We'll ride in front. It looks more natural. And no more 'm'lords', either."

"Aye, m'l…" said Oenus, making a face like he was swallowing a lemon whole, "Lucius."

After traveling a couple of miles, we found the oxbow lake and gained our bearings using the map. We set out on one of the smaller roads that roughly paralleled the highway, and encountered only a few people, mostly farmers who gave us no notice. There was hardly any wind and by mid-morning, it had grown quite hot. The chain mail chafed against my collar bone through the thin under-shirt. Just after noon, we crested a hill that looked down over flat, green pasture land, and off in the distance, I could just make out the slow muddy Intrepid River that denoted the border between Zura and Abhamatra. From our vantage we could see mounted legionnaires patrolling along the banks. We'd grudging come to the consensus that the safest place to leave the Empire was the highway.

At my urging we waited until sundown just before the night watch took over to try to slip across the border, figuring the guards would be less apt to want to check us after a long day on the job. As the western sky began to grow pink with the sun's descent, we unsaddled the horses and tied them to a lead-line. Lucius and the guards crammed into the makeshift vardo with their horses' tack. It was a bit cramped but everyone fit.

As we pulled onto the highway, Samara leaned over and in a whisper asked, "You can pull this off right?"

"I can't believe you would ask such a silly question," I said in my best Dezika accent.

"That's actually pretty convincing," she said sounding mildly impressed.

"We trade with the 'Zik's regularly. They breed great draft horses."

"It always comes back to horses with you."

"What can I say? Remember your name is Ylsa Petulengro, and I'm your husband, Luca."

"Why can't I be your sister?"

"Because…because the story just works better if you're my wife. Just follow my lead and don't volunteer any information."

"Yes, *husband*," she huffed.

We pulled onto the highway and I could see the bridge off in the distance with a small line of travelers at the checkpoint. We waited for a quarter hour while bored-looking legionnaires inspected cargo and collected tolls.

A pair of soldiers in freshly polished lorica approached the cart. "Good evening," I said cheerfully.

"Papers or coin," he said in a monotone.

I handed him the freshly pressed papers Ganicus and given us and realized they looked a bit too perfect. I should have crinkled and folded them a bit first but it was too late now.

"State your business…" he squinted at the paper, "Luca Pet…Petulengro?"

"My wife and I were trading horses," I said while Samara beamed a lovely smile at him.

"It'll be five silver and one copper each for the horses."

"Of course," I said fishing the coins out of my pouch. Just as I was handing the money over, there was a thump from the back of the wagon. Someone must have dropped something. A shock of fear shot through me but I fought hard to keep it out of my face. I risked a glance at Samara and saw she'd gone pale.

The soldiers looked to the wagon then back to me. "Do you mind if we check your wagon?" he said, his tone making it clear it wasn't really a question.

"Go right ahead," I said my mind racing, "but I must apologize in advance for the smell. My boy Nicu has the runs from all the rich Zuran food."

The legionnaires shared a glance and the first one said, "No, that's alright. I, uh, wouldn't want to disturb the boy if he's not feeling well. Go on through."

It took all my effort not to breathe out a sigh of relief. "Gratitude."

He waved us past him and we made our way onto the large sturdy bridge. Samara let out the breath she was holding. "That was way too close. Fast thinking back there."

"If a foolish idea works, it isn't foolish," I said.

We soon came to a little town that had built up on the other side of the bridge and a short man in chain mail glanced at our papers half-heartedly and waved us on. After we'd gotten a few miles outside of town we turned down a side road and Samara opened up the door into the wagon. "Alright, I think we're safe," she said. "Who made the noise?"

"Sorry, m'lady, I knocked over one of the saddles," said one of the houseguards, sounding sheepish.

"Don't be so careless, that almost sunk us. And stop saying 'm'lady'."

"Aye, sorry," the man said.

"Finally. I'm ready to get out of this wagon," Lucius said.

"I'd like to put a little more distance between us and the Empire first," I said.

"But it's hot back here."

"File a complaint," said Samara, shutting the door.

We continued on for a few more hours, long after dark. Finally, I pulled off the road to a spot where a fire pit had been set up by previous travelers and we camped for the evening. The next morning I noticed one of the horses had thrown a shoe. When I showed Lucius he said, "We were planning on stopping in Cargov anyway. We'll just find a smith there."

The main highway was busy with spring trade. We had to stop and pay two tolls, but with all the traffic came anonymity, and the guards hardly looked at us longer than it took to collect our money. We came to Cargov about an hour before sunset. It was an open trade town of perhaps a thousand people with no walls, thatched roofs, and narrow cobblestone streets.

I turned to Lucius. "I'll take the horse to get shod and meet you at the inn."

Lucius nodded and I reclaimed my bow before switching places with the guard whose horse bore the missing shoe. The blacksmith was about to close shop for the day but was happy to have one more customer. I had to haggle with him a bit to get him to a fair price. It's not that we didn't have the money, but if we started throwing too much coin around it might call unwelcome attention.

The sun was hanging low over the squat buildings by the time I found the decently-sized inn with an attached stable. I turned my steed over to a short young man, who was already brushing out our other mounts, and made my way inside where everyone was waiting for me.

"How long does it take to shoe a horse?" Samara whined. "I'm star-ving."

I smirked and said, "Apologies, my lovely wife," which earned me a glower from both Argas.

Lucius said, "The inn keeper said there's a tavern down the road that's decent."

"By all means lead the way," I said, with a grin orchestrated to annoy Samara. It seemed to work.

Lucius led the way down the wide cobbled streets as shops were finishing their business for the day and young men were beginning their drinking. As we rounded the corner the tavern came into view and judging by the noise bleeding out, it was a fairly popular place. My eye caught a broken wooden sign blowing in the light spring breeze that might have once advertised an apothecary. As starlight filled my vision I saw myself lying under that sign, helpless as men approached me with swords drawn. I blinked rapidly trying to clear my vision while Rocana's gift faded and yelled, "Ambush!" as I jerked my bow clear and reached for an arrow.

Lucius and the guards reacted quickly, drawing their swords and forming up around Samara, who was still blinking in confusion. "Where?" asked Lucius with a gladius in each hand. He didn't have to wait long for his answer. Men rushed out of the alley on either side of the shop with the broken sign. My arrow took the first one I saw in the chest. It struck me as odd that they weren't wearing any armor. I drew and aimed at the next one when something hit me from behind, tearing my bow from my grasp and pinning my legs together and my arms to my side.

I fell like a tree, hitting my face on the cobbles. I jerked and fought, trying to wiggle out of whatever had me wrapped up, but the harder I fought the tighter it held me. I rolled on my side and looked down expecting to see bolos or something similar but what I saw instead looked like a single gossamer thread wound around me. "Damn mages," I cursed as the sounds of battle erupted around me.

I called Tarka's gift as I wiggled and pushed off with my legs like a drunken caterpillar, trying to get out of the way of the fighting, until my shoulder hit something hard. It was the neglected apothecary shop.

I looked back to see the men who ambushed us engaged with the Arga siblings and their houseguards. These men were different from the mercenaries who attacked us before. Those men had uniform armor, well-maintained weapons, and the bearings of soldiers. These men lacked all of that. Clad in dirty clothes, they wielded rusty swords and daggers and lacked any real coordination.

Pale blue light drew my eyes to Samara who was in the midst of spell casting, focused intently on something in the distance. I followed her gaze past the men attacking us to a sickly green light. A man wearing red robes, with a tattoo of tarnished copper on his brow, was casting a spell as well.

A thunderclap split the air taking with it all sound, save a dull ringing in my ears, as Samara loosed a blinding flash of lightning at the tattooed man. A translucent, shimmery hemisphere like a soap bubble formed in front of the man, and Samara's lightning deflected off of it onto one of the nearby buildings setting its thatched roof ablaze.

I had to escape these cursed bindings fast. I inched up to the shop's steps trying to use its lip to catch one of the crossed daggers at my low back. It was hard to do while maintaining Tarka's gift with a battle raging around me. Finally I managed to slip one of the blades free. I rolled over, grasped the hilt and angled the blade to slice the gossamer threads entangling me. The steel passed right through the shimmering thread with no result. In shock I tried again. It was as though the thread that bound me simply didn't exist to my knife. I rolled over on my back and cried out in frustration at the broken sign swaying above me.

Chapter Fifteen
Samara

As we left the inn and turned down the wide cobbled streets, my mind drifted toward thoughts of roasted lamb, followed by a hot bath and a warm feather bed. What I was probably going to find was greasy hash, a tepid bucket of water, and a hard pallet, hopefully without too many bugs. I was hungry, tired, hurting and Darian was being his usual irritating self.

As I visualized myself soaking in the hot springs of Stonehaven with Autumn washing my hair, Darian cried, "Ambush!"

Terror gripped my heart yanking me back to our camp by the fork in the river. Fear paralyzed me as Lucius and the guards drew their blades. Armed men ran at us out of the alley between the buildings on my right. I heard the twang of Darian's bowstring and snapped my head around to see men coming out of the alley we just passed, the first of whom fell to his knees gripping the arrow in his chest. The two groups were moving to encircle us. We were trapped.

A shimmering bolt blurred by me and struck Darian, tearing his bow away and slamming him to the ground wrapped in the magical binding that was the first evocation spell I'd learned. My head jerked back the direction the casting had come from, as sickly green light faded from the hands of another red robed man with a tarnished copper tattoo on his brow. He stood twenty yards behind the armed men with a smile that seemed to stretch too wide.

Anger coursed through my body, purging my fear and banishing the paralysis that held me. I started to dismiss the spell on Darian but he must have called Tarka's gift, because when I looked back I couldn't see him. I had to deal with the mage quickly. I cleared my mind and began to summon power as my guards formed a defensive circle around me.

I fought to keep my focus as our enemies fell upon us. A quick flurry from Lucius's twin swords dropped one man and forced the others around him back a few steps. He'd always had a gift for sword-play. I shaped the spell, drawing in all of my desperation and anger before gesturing at the red-robed form and releasing it.

Lightning thundered toward the other mage in the blink of an eye…and deflected harmlessly off the magic shield he'd raised only an instant before. A building farther down the street shook with the impact of the bolt and flames sprung up its thatched roof. The robed man's smile grew impossibly wide as he began flicking his fingers in the mudras of another spell, his shield still hovering in place.

Having all served in the military alongside battle mages, Lucius and the guards hardly reacted to the lightning, but our attackers recoiled or stood stunned, buying us a crucial moment. I could summon a shield to protect myself from whatever the tattooed was casting just as he had, but my allies would still be vulnerable. If he was skilled enough to maintain a shield while casting, he could pick them off one by one. Hell, if he didn't care about his allies, he could try and get everyone at once. So I did what I should have done by the fork in the river, what I would have done if I'd been thinking clearly. I took my jade bangle off and threw it on the ground in front of Lucius.

"Bahiskuticara!" I cried in Eatherial. "I call you forth to me. Bahiskuticara, again I call for you to enter my Realm. Bahiskuticara, thrice I ask you stand before me. Come and fulfill your bargain." I glanced up at the robed man bathed in green light from his casting and added, "Now!"

The engraving on the bracelet began glowing as the air above bulged like the surface of the ocean just before a whale breaches. A crack rang through the air, not unlike the thunder a moment before, as the wall that separated our Realm and Eather parted for an instant. The ground shook with the weight of the massive Elemental that now stood before me.

Thrice the height of a man, he appeared roughhewn from granite, as if molded by a child. His upper half was vaguely humanoid save his arms ended in claws reminiscent of a lobster's, while two more human-like arms sprouted just below them. His lower half ended in four stony, crab-like legs.

"*I have come as agreed,*" Bahiskuticara said with a strange echo. "*What is thy bidding, mage?*"

"I need your protection. These men are trying to harm me and my allies," I spit out as quickly as I could.

Quartz eyes glowed with soft white light as he asked, "*Do I have your leave to kill them?"*

"Yes!" I shouted.

In that moment a spray of glass shards sprang forward from the tattooed man's outstretched hands. The wicked razors streamed across the distance striking friend and foe alike, though Bahiskuticara's bulk shielded us from the worst of it. I crouched down and threw my hands up over my face, but as the glass shattered and ricocheted, I was stung by a deep cut on my right cheek and several along my arms.

The elemental turned his granite head towards the robed mage, unphased by the barrage of shards, and said, *"I will start with that one."* He turned and moved with deceptive speed, trampling right over two of the unlucky attackers who were rolling around on the ground clutching at the glass in their backs.

Any thoughts the tattooed mage had of casting another spell were short lived as Bahiskuticara bore down on him with the speed of an avalanche. The man's arms twisted and stretched, elongating like an ape's, his too-wide smile still plastered on his face. The Elemental reached him and took a swipe with one huge stone claw. The mage ducked and rolled as quickly and easily as a monkey, his robe trailing behind him. Bahiskuticara turned and brought both his claws down together trying to hammer his opponent, but again the man was too fast and merely hopped through rocky crab legs. The impact of the stony claws shook the ground.

I covered my ears as Bahiskuticara threw back his head and loosed a scream that sounded like two boulders slamming together. The Elemental tried to turn and snap the mage up with his claws but he managed to stay between the pillar-like legs. The man rolled out behind Bahiskuticara and hopped up on the elemental's massive back as easily as child jumping on a bed. I'd never seen a human move like that; he had to be using some sort of magic, though I hadn't seen him cast the spell.

The Elemental flailed about in a circle and tried to snap behind him but the man held fast and avoided being caught by the deadly pincers. Finally one of Bahiskuticara's humanoid arms reached back and seized the mage by the leg, yanking him around to the waiting claws. The robed mage furiously made mudras to cast a spell, but it was too late. There was a sickening crunch as the granite claw closed around the mage's torso. The lower half hit the ground first, scattering entrails as it fell. As upper half hit the ground the elongated arms still moved about, feebly trying to drag what was left away, though the mage's head lulled to the side limply. Bahiskuticara gave the body one last slam with his giant claw to be sure. The arms stopped moving.

Glowing quartz eyes turned back to the remainder of the men who ambushed us. Those who could flee, did. It didn't save them. Bahiskuticara chased them down with the speed of a charging bull, then leapt the last ten yards as easily as hopping over a puddle, landing on one of the unfortunate men. The Elemental fell upon the men mercilessly, smashing or tearing them to pieces.

I glanced down to see a few small shards of glass sticking out of my arm. Lucius looked about the same, but several of the guards were bleeding pretty badly. Luckily, everyone was on their feet. I still couldn't see Darian, which probably meant he was hale enough to use Tarka's gift.

The Elemental finished with the men who had run and, in his zeal to complete our contract, turned his attention to those who were too wounded to flee.

"Bahiskuticara, there's no need to kill them," I yelled. To my horror he reached down and smashed one of the wounded men to a pulp. Specific. You need to be specific with Elementals.

"Don't kill anyone else."

Without hesitating, he reached down and snipped a leg off one of the wounded men.

I cried in frustration. "I command thee to stop."

Bahiskuticara paused just before he was about to take the man's other leg off, "*But I must fulfill our contract. They cannot harm you if they have no limbs.*"

"I hold our contract fulfilled," I said.

Bahiskuticara turned to face me crossing both sets of arms and bowed. "*You willingly relinquish thy token?*"

"I do," I said, picking up the softly glowing bangle and crossing over to him.

He reached out with one massive claw to pluck it out of my hand gingerly. "*So be it.*" The air around his massive stone form began to bulge and deflect and with a pop he was gone.

My eyes fell over the gruesome scene. Fifteen men lay dead or nearly so, though thankfully none were ours. The fire from my deflected lightning had spread to two other roofs. My eyes were drawn to one of the men trampled by my Elemental. He wasn't even recognizable as human, just a flattened, oozing pile of meat. I tasted bile and bent over, emptying the meager contents of my stomach onto the ground.

"By the Gods," said Darian, who was now visible by the steps of the building.

I wiped my mouth with a shaky hand as I gained my feet and looked over to Lucius. "Is everyone alright?"

Lucius winced as he pulled a piece of glass out of his elbow. "More or less. Those men weren't too skilled, and the glass couldn't get through the chain shirt.

But we need to get out of here."

"Ri-right," I said walking on wobbly legs over to Darian, who was still thoroughly entangled. The spell would wear off eventually now that there was no one sustaining it, but we didn't have that kind of time. "Hold still. I'm going to get rid of that binding." I drew a deep breath as I formed a spell that would unravel the magic holding him. Pale blue light washed over Darian and the gossamer thread dissolved.

"Gratitude," Darian said, rubbing his arms as he got his feet under him.

Commotion drew my attention down the street. Townsfolk were scrambling to put out the fire that had now spread to a fourth building. "I-I have to do something," I said.

"Samara, the town guards will be here any moment," Lucius said.

"But it was my lightning that caused it. Maybe I could use my magic to—"

"A few buildings may burn down but no one's going to die. We have to leave now while they're distracted by the fire," he said.

"He's right, we need to go," Darian said, reclaiming his bow.

I glanced back at the fire, feeling sick again. "A-alright."

The fire behind us cast a warm glow on the street as we fled back toward the inn.

"Hold a moment," Darian said, as we passed the mangled, bisected remains of the mage. "I want to see what he carried."

As Darian searched the lower half of the body, entrails splayed out like the tentacles of a jelly fish, my eyes were drawn to the upper half. His arms had returned to their original size, though one of them had been crushed, and his mouth was still fixed in its too-wide grin as though he were wearing a mask. Seen up close the marking I thought was a tattoo was scarred and raised, like a brand that had tarnished coppery-green as it healed. He also had a different symbol on his throat and the top of his bald head.

As Darian returned, pouch in hand, I said, "Cut his shirt open."

He knelt and complied with no question, opening the man's shirt with his dagger as easily as skinning a rabbit. Another tarnished brand marked the center of his chest. "Roll him over," I said.

"Otter, we need to go."

"This might be important, Lucius." I looked at Darian, "Do it."

Darian rolled the grisly mess over and I could see two more symbols on the back of his head and neck. "Do I need to cut off the rest of this?" he asked, holding a handful of what remained of the robe and shirt.

"No, I've seen enough. Let's go."

We fled over the cobbles and back to the inn just long enough for the men to grab their rucksacks before heading to the stables for our horses.

"What about the wagon?" asked Oenus.

"Leave it," Darian said. "It'll just slow us down."

The guards loaded the supplies from the wagon onto the horses with military efficiency. When they were finished, we mounted up and made a hasty exit out of town, the orange glow of the fire competing with the last warm rays of the setting sun. We rode until the darkness forced us to stop, then we dismounted and led our horses until Darian found us a game trail that cut off the main road. Finally, we stopped and made camp near a trickling creek.

One of the guards made a fire while Lucius doled out some of our dry rations and Darian went about treating our wounds. We'd been lucky. The worst of it was a deep gash on one of the guard's legs and rather large piece of glass stuck in another's shoulder. Darian solicitously picked the glass out of our wounds and closed them with Ananda's gift.

The wound on my cheek had bled quite a lot and I'm sure it looked ghastly. "Do you think it'll scar?" I asked as Darian put his hand over the wound. The warm silvery light felt like distilled love, as it eased my pain.

"I doubt it. If it was my mother or Nia healing you I'd say certainly not, but you're stuck with me."

I grinned. "I suppose I will try to make do."

"Stop smiling."

"Sorry."

"Why don't you just do that every time?" he asked as he wiped the dried blood away with a wet rag.

"What?"

"Summon that giant stone, crab-man…thing?"

I chuckled tiredly at his description. "It's a one-time thing. You have to make an agreement with the Elemental beforehand, which is dangerous, time consuming, and expensive."

"Too bad," he said, slathering some ointment on the wound. "We'll give it another healing tomorrow."

"What about you? Are you hurt?"

"Just my pride." He frowned rubbing his arms and said, "And few welts from that magical thread and a bloody nose."

With my wounds tended, my belly no longer empty, and the danger behind us, my mind was running like a wild horse. "What the Hell happened back there?"

"That's a good question," said Lucius. "They knew we exactly where we would be."

"It was like that in Mystewood," I said. "The thugs were different though."

Darian nodded. "These definitely weren't mercenaries. No armor, no tactics, poor weapons. They were probably just local muscle who had a few coins tossed their way. That mage definitely didn't have any qualms about hurting them."

"It's a good thing you spotted that ambush," one of the guards said to Darian, "or it could've gone the other way."

"How'd you do that by the way?" Lucius asked. "I didn't see anything. And I was looking for trouble."

"Rocana's gift," Darian said.

Lucius scrunched his brows up. "What?"

"Remember I told you about the Vija's power? All Manu possess a small bit of it," I said.

"How convenient," Lucius said. "And how fortunate for you that mage just bound you, rather than raining glass on you."

I ground my teeth in frustration. "Stop it, Lucius. Darian didn't have anything to do with what happened back there. And I don't think that mage was very skilled anyway. All of his spells were novice level."

"Lucius is right though," said Darian. "They did know right where we were going to be."

"Someone must have seen through Autumn's disguise," I said, pulling Master Carter's mirror out of my bag to make sure I hadn't missed a message. The face wasn't tarnished.

Lucius shook his head. "Even if they saw through her disguise immediately, *and* took the Causeway, they would have been hard pressed to beat us here."

"Someone who was with us at Castle Uttara must have tipped them off," Darian said, "It's the only way—"

"I've known Ganicus my whole life. He'd never betray me!" Lucius shouted.

Darian put his hands up in surrender. "I'm not saying it was Ganicus. A servant maybe?"

"Perhaps," Lucius conceded.

"Or maybe this man was already here before we ever left," I said. "Lucius, pull out the map." He fished the skin out of his bag and handed it over. I summoned some coldfire and unrolled the map on the ground before me. I focused it down to the area between Zura and Moravar, tracing the road we took. "This is the most straightforward logical route. If they were worried about someone from the Empire going to Vizipa, they could have simply left our robed friend in Carvog just in case. Hell, for all we know they could be all along the highway."

"So much for all the careful forethought and deception," said Lucius.

"The first casualty of battle is usually the plan." Darian said.

A thought that had been swimming beneath the surface popped into my head. "Let's have a look in that mage's pouch."

Darian retrieved it from his saddle bag and handed it to me. The belt was tacky with dried blood and other things I didn't want to think about. Inside was a folded up piece of thick vellum with lines of squiggly foreign writing, and a money purse. I opened up the money purse and dumped a pile of freshly minted Imperial platinum into my hand.

Darian snorted. "That looks familiar. What does the paper say?"

"I don't recognize the script."

"Great," Lucius said. "Another strange language for her to try and translate."

"Funny," I replied with a glower. "So what do we do?"

Lucius winced as he knelt down next to me and studied the map. "Since we don't know for certain, we have to assume your theory's correct, Otter. If that's the case, they're expecting us to travel east to Madhayma, right? So then we head north through Zarani, and Kandali, then follow the Blood river south east through Kazil. We can enter through Upari, they'll be less likely to expect that. We'll try to stay off the main highways."

"It'll take longer," I said.

"A lot longer," echoed Darian.

"It doesn't matter how quickly we can get there if we're not in one piece."

"Fair enough," I said, feeling suddenly exhausted.

"I suppose it's a matter of choosing the lesser evil."

"Precisely. Besides, we should still arrive weeks ahead of the equinox." Lucius said, focusing the map further down on the area where we were.

I yawned, my eyes growing heavy. "Let's hope so."

The next morning I rinsed myself off in the little creek and tried to wash the blood out of my blouse to mixed effect. I decided it was a lost cause and put on a new one. While Darian was giving another healing to the guards with the worst injuries, I retrieved the mirror and sent a message to Master Carter summarizing what had happened and our change in plan. Almost immediately the face tarnished over and I received his message.

"You're getting rather good at surviving ambushes, young mage," said Master Carter's image. "Let us hope you don't have to put those skills to any further use. Autumn returned with your father back to his estate yesterday, and as far as I know, the ruse hasn't been discovered, though I shall investigate further. Keep your wits about you and stay safe. *Nir palam kil paykiratu.*"

We stuck mostly to trails and back roads throughout the morning, wary that guards from Carvog might be looking for us to answer for the previous day's chaos. By mid-afternoon however, absent any sign of pursuit, we turned down a dirt road that cut through the heart of the thick pecan forest. The day was warm, the weather was fair, and we encountered no red-robed men. By the time we made camp however, I was again chafed and sore from my hours astride. All the gains I'd made getting my body used to the saddle were lost to the days I'd spent laid out and injured, so it was back to Darian's ointment.

The next morning I woke to dull grey clouds overhead. A spring storm opened up the skies drenching us with a cold soaking rain. Everyone else pulled their cloaks up and continued on like it was nothing. I, however, was miserable. I was drenched, cold, stiff, and my tender bits hurt. I definitely would not have done well in the legions.

"Why the sour face?" Lucius said seemingly oblivious to the rain. "I thought otters were supposed to like the water."

"This otter would be happier with a hot bath."

Darian said, "I've been meaning to ask why he calls you Otter?"

My lips pulled up into a grin. "You want to tell him, brother, or shall I?"

Lucius heaved a dramatic sigh. "It gives you such pleasure to tell the story. I wouldn't deprive you of it."

My mouth turned up in a smirk. "I'd always been the stronger swimmer between us, but the year we turned eleven, Lucius spent the summer with our mother's kin on the west coast, just outside of Shimmer." I edged my horse to the side so I could see Lucius's face. His expressions were the best part of telling the story. "Lucius had spent nearly every day swimming with his cousins in the ocean, so when he got back to the estate he proclaimed himself to be the fastest swimmer. I, of course, disagreed with him. So he challenged me to a contest across the pond and back twice. Now, he was sure he was going to beat me, so he told all of the kids who lived on the estate to come watch. When we showed up there was at *least* a score—"

"It wasn't a score. It was a dozen a most," Lucius interrupted.

I looked back to Darian and rolled my eyes. "It was at least a score. So when we got to the pond, he even gave a little speech to the kids who had assembled about how badly he was going to beat me, how it wasn't even going to be a contest…and he was right about the latter. I was finishing my second lap before he was even done with his first one."

"That is *not* true! I was maybe half a lap behind you."

I raised my brows at Darian. "It was a full lap. So now, not only had he lost to a girl after all his boasting, there were twenty witnesses who he had to see every day."

"A dozen witnesses," Lucius said with a sullen pout.

"It was twenty. So what does he say to them? It wasn't a fair contest because he forgot that I'm half otter."

"I stand by my statement," Lucius said smugly.

"So he's called me Otter ever since."

Darian laughed. "Did you ever best her at swimming?"

Lucius cut his eyes over to me. "I never tried again. A man's pride can only take so much."

"I understand," Darian said. "I, too, was humbled by a woman, and the experience stuck with me as well."

I noticed for the first time Darian's cloak was of a style that went out of fashion before I was born. Instead of having a clasp, the fabric folded over itself to make the hood. "Where did you find that cloak?"

He pinched the waterlogged fabric. "It was my grandfather's. He was Zuran."

Ganicus had already told us as much, but I'd forgotten. I was going to ask him about it, but we came to an abrupt pause at a fork in the small muddy road so Lucius could check the map. "We'll go to the left. It looks like it'll be less traveled."

"Does it have a bridge?" asked Darian.

Lucius squinted and focused the map down. "Doesn't say on the map."

"Perhaps we should go the other way? If there's not a bridge, the road may be washed out," Darian said.

Lucius shook his head. "It's not worth the risk. We'll go to the left."

Darian shrugged. "Whatever you think."

We slogged down the left-hand road and the rain picked up. After some three hours, we came to a low point in the road that was at least six feet under a fast moving stream.

"Lovely," I said.

"We could try to cross—" Oenus started

"No," Lucius said. "It's too dangerous. We'll have to go back to the fork." He looked at Darian, "Not a word."

The Manu wisely said nothing.

We lost half a day doubling back to the fork, which, combined with rain and mud, added up to a long miserable day with very little forward progress made. I climbed into my tiny tent that night soaked to the bone. There wasn't even enough space to adequately dry my clothes so I just set them aside, content at least to be dry for the moment. That was when it came to my attention my wretched little tent had a leak.

The next day it stopped raining, but the storm left the air stale and muggy. The only people we saw were farmers carting their crops to market and the occasional shepherd. Mosquitoes and flies descended on me in an obnoxious buzzing cloud. Apparently my fair skin is a real delicacy to mosquitoes, as they hardly bothered anyone else.

After half a morning of my slapping and cursing Darian disappeared into the trees, emerging a quarter hour later rubbing some pungent, greenish substance between his hands. "Here, rub this on your skin."

I stared at the stinky mash that looked like Darian had already chewed up. "What is it?"

"Does it matter if it stops the bugs from biting?"

Reluctantly, I took the tacky substance and smeared it over my arms and neck. The sharp, acrid smell bit at my nose but it did seem to discourage the bugs.

When we stopped to set up camp that evening, Darian said, "I'm going to head back to that town we went around a few miles back. Are we low on any supplies?"

"We definitely need some more grain for the horses. We're running a bit low on salt too," said Oenus.

"That should be easy enough," Darian said.

"What are you going back there for?" I asked.

His mouth slowly curved up in his half grin. "To find a she-wolf."

———————————

Despite my weariness, I tossed and turned on my bedroll, unable to find sleep. I longed for my nice soft bed, or at the very least the cot I'd used on the trip to Mystewood. My mind simply wouldn't quiet. I was worried about the red-robed men, worried about Autumn, worried about what my father would think of me, and irked by Darian going into town to find a whore. So what if he was horny? He could tough it out like the rest of us. Eventually, I decided maybe some wine would help me sleep.

I crawled out of my tent and began rummaging through the bags for a wineskin. "Is everything alright?" the guard who was standing sentry asked.

"I'm fine, just having trouble sleeping. I'm hoping a little wine will aid me," I said, retrieving the wineskin and plopping down by the embers of the fire.

"I always find it does," Darian said dropping Tarka's gift and startling the poor guard. "Though I'm not sure how that watered-down Zuran stuff will help."

So vexing. "Did you find a whore?"

"Several," he said with a wink, hopping off his horse.

I rolled my eyes. "Several, huh?"

He began unloading the supplies he'd bought. "Remember where most of the information we gathered in Metis came from?"

Realization dawned on me. "The brothel."

He nodded. "They get plenty chatty for a few coins. Remind me never to tell any of my dark secrets to a prostitute."

"I never do," I said dryly. "So?"

"No one knew anything about the tattooed mages, nor any mercenaries or strange travelers, so hopefully that means there aren't any more surprises waiting for us this direction."

I took a long pull from the wineskin. "Well, that's something."

"I also managed to get a local map."

"You do remember that we have a map of practically the whole world?"

"This map has something your map doesn't have."

"Pray tell?"

"Bridges," he said as he unsaddled his horse.

"Hmm, I have to admit that would be useful."

"Local maps often have hazards marked on them as well, like verges, or places frequented by bandits and such."

"All right, I get it."

He sat down next to me. "I also found a money changer and got some gems and local coin."

"Why? Imperial currency's accepted everywhere."

"What if someone's following us? Remember how easy it was to track? I'm not keen on leaving a trail of shiny platinum breadcrumbs."

It irked me that I hadn't thought of that. "Anything else?"

He shook his head. "Mind if I have a drink?"

"I thought your standards were too high for our 'watered-down' wine?"

"Any port in a storm."

"Fine," I said handing the wineskin over. He took a swig. "Well? How does it taste?"

Darian looked down, considering it for a moment. "Like disappointment."

The next ten days went smoothly. We stuck mainly to the back roads and the weather was mostly fair as the land shifted from densely packed pecan forest to low, rocky hills. Darian hunted to supplement our food stores, bringing back mostly rabbits and fish, but he took down a boar and some fowl as well. There were several opportunities to hunt deer or larger game but, absent our wagon, we couldn't carry the meat with us and he refused to kill something and let it go to waste. Eventually we decided it was worth the risk to try some of the smaller towns to renew our supplies and, thankfully, we didn't encounter any trouble.

One morning, I awoke with an urgent need to empty my bladder and I left my tent in such a hurry I forgot my cane. I discovered, much to my elation, that I didn't need it any more. It seemed like we had finally hit a patch of good fortune.

I should have known better.

Chapter Sixteen
Darian

"Darian, I need some more of your stinky bug-plant. They're starting to bite again," Samara complained.

"I'll keep an eye out for some," I said as I finished tending a gash on one of the horses from a mesquite thorn. We'd stopped for the day in the early afternoon to give everyone, man and beast alike, a chance to rest. "Let me take a look at your cheek."

She stopped combing the massive tangle in her hair she'd been picking at for the last half hour and tilted her face up toward me. She'd let the illusion spell lapse so for the moment she'd regained her natural skin and hair tone. I ran my fingers over the spot where she'd been cut and felt only her creamy skin. "Not a trace. You heal well."

"With a bit of Manu help, anyway," she said.

"It's a good thing," I said standing up. "Because you sure have a knack for getting hurt."

"Only since I met you. Before that my worst injuries were skinned knees or jammed fingers. It's Lucius who's always getting hurt. Falling out of trees, being bucked off horses—"

"It's called being adventurous," Lucius said from where he reclined against a shady oak.

"It's called being clumsy," Samara said. "Not to mention all the fights you and Ganicus got mixed up in."

"At least I never set the garden on fire."

"That was one time!"

I sighed. "I'm going to see if I can find some 'stinky bug-plant' for Samara, and maybe some dinner as well." The twins were so involved in their banter they hardly noticed when I left, and most of the guards were passed out in the shade enjoying their well-deserved break.

We'd placed our camp off the road in the shadow of rocky bluff. I was winding my way around looking for the plant when some movement caught my attention farther up the hill. A medium sized boar was snorting at the ground heedless of me. I called Tarka's gift to hide myself and slipped cautiously up the slope. The pig couldn't see me, but they have keen noses and if he smelled me he'd spook. I took my time, moving quietly and staying down wind. It wasn't easy. The breeze changed direction several times and I had to move in a wide circle to remain undetected, ending up near the top of the rocky hill.

Just as I moved to draw my arrow back and take the shot I heard voices. At first I dismissed it as one of my group, concentrating on the shot, but then I realized it was coming from the wrong side of the hill. I lowered my bow and eased up to the summit to see down the other side.

"Bloody Hell," I whispered.

In the valley below was a dozen armed men bearing the black head wrappings of the Turaggin, a fierce, brutal people from the frozen land to the far north and east, known for producing fierce soldiers and even fiercer mercenaries. They were well armed and armored, riding strong, heavy war horses. With them rode not one, but two of the tattooed mages.

They were still too far away for me to understand what they were saying, but I could hear the mages barking orders. One of them gestured to the southwest of the bluff, which was the opposite direction we had taken, and the group began moving that way. I glanced down the slope and tried to gauge how long it would take them to make it to our camp. Five, maybe ten minutes.

I hopped from boulder to boulder and skipped my way down the rocks with all thoughts of a pork dinner forgotten. I crashed into camp at a full run, tripping over one of the saddles in the process.

"What? Did you spook a bear?" asked Lucius.

"There's a dozen or so Turaggin making their way around the bluff right now!"

"Turaggin?" Samara said in horror.

"Yes," I said grabbing my saddle and throwing it on Tavas. "And they've got *two* of our tattooed friends with them." At that the houseguards jumped up and began scurrying about.

"I don't like those odds," said Lucius.

Hastily strapping on my packs, I said, "Nor do I."

"What do we do?" asked Samara.

"All of you are going to double back the way we came and take the highway north. They're riding heavy war horses and you'll easily outpace them on Manu mounts. I am going to go engage them and buy you time."

"Darian, that's stupid. What, are you going to kill a dozen armed men and two mages by yourself?" Samara asked with wide eyes.

"I don't have to kill them, just lead 'em in the wrong direction."

"That's a horrible plan. Maybe we could—"

I lost my temper and yelled, "Samara, there's no time! They'll be here in minutes." I grabbed her roughly by the shoulders and spun her around shoving her to her horse, which one of the guards was saddling.

I hopped up on my own mount and said, "I'll meet you at the Tsava ferry at sundown two days hence. If I'm not there go without me."

Lucius nodded. "I hope to see you there."

I span my horse around when I heard Samara say, "Darian—"

I gave Tavas heels and tore out of the camp. I don't know what she was going to say, but I didn't have time to hear it.

I cut through the grove at a full gallop trusting Tavas to keep his footing. If there's one thing a Manu horse knows it's how to avoid roots. I slowed down at a promontory that would act as a blind corner off to my left, it would be as good an ambush point as any. There was a sizable oak off to the right. I figured they'd have to pass between it and the promontory and I could use the hard wood for a bit of cover. I checked my escape path and it was clear enough, no deadfall or anything, but there were plenty of rocks. That suited me fine. Let the big war horses try and chase me through it. I drew a deep breath to calm myself then called Tarka's gift to me and waited.

I didn't have to wait long.

The mercenaries came around the bluff in a loose double line with the mages near the middle. I'd never really met any Turaggin, just seen a few in a tavern once, but these men were the image of their fierce reputation. Soldiers are often fearful or resigned before a battle, while most mercenaries are stoic. These men looked excited, ready for a fight. They were killers.

Full beards and long braids fell out from beneath their head wrappings. They carried all manner of weapons from axes and shields, to lance, sword, and crossbow. One saber even bore glowing writing down the blade that was a telltale sign of an enchanted weapon. I knew from experience, however, that the truly dangerous enemies were the ones in red robes, they were my targets. If I could kill both of them maybe the Turaggin would decide it wasn't worth fighting us.

At this distance I could see that one of the mages was a woman. That surprised me, though I don't know why. I drew back and aimed for the other one, waiting for a perfect shot. To their credit, the Turaggin were alert. One of them checked behind the promontory and another, who was scanning the woods, looked right at me. They weren't used to fighting Manu, however. I waited until I had a nice clear shot at the mage and loosed my arrow.

It was his lucky day. He turned to say something to one of the Turaggin at that moment and the arrow missed him by a finger's width, hitting the man he was talking to and taking off his ear. I knew I only had one more shot, as the Turaggin were already starting to react. I drew back and released another arrow at the robed man.

The tattooed mage unhinged his jaw like a snake eating a mouse, and a long pink tongue like a rat's tail shot out and snatched the arrow out of the air in front of his face.

Having no time to digest what I just saw, I turned and spurred Tavas away as the Turaggin bore down on me.

Well, at least my plan worked. They were chasing me.

At a full gallop my horse soared over the rocks, zig-zagging through the trees as easily as he did in Mystewood. I stole a glance over my shoulder as we splashed through a shallow creek. Their heavy mounts had been slowed by the terrain but none had stumbled or fallen. I'd say this for the Turaggin, they were decent horsemen.

I changed directions several times, taking hard turns and doing my best to keep the trees between us. Unfortunately I hadn't had the opportunity to scout my route so I had no real idea where I was going. I just knew it was away from Samara. By the time I realized I'd entered a narrow valley between the bluffs it was too late to do anything about it.

I emerged from the canyon onto a sprawling expanse of rolling, rocky grassland as far as I could see. There were no trees or large rocks for cover, nor was there anywhere to hide and call Tarka's gift. I turned to my left, keeping the steep cliff face to my left shoulder. Hopefully I could find a way back into the trees and lose them.

After a couple hundred yards, I glanced back to see all the bad guys had followed me. Apparently they thought I'd lead them back to the rest of my party. I was quickly outpacing the Turaggin with their big war horses, already out of archery range, but the snake-jawed mage had pulled out ahead of them on a smaller, faster horse.

I felt the heat of the lightning bolt before I heard the thunder as it arched past me, striking the side of the cliff and sending a shower of pebbles flying.

Tavas spooked and broke to the right, but I yanked hard on the reigns pulling him back on course. "*You have to trust me my friend.*"

I drew an arrow and twisted in the saddle trying to judge the wind and the distance to the man chasing me. His fingers were already going through their rhythmic movements casting sickly green light. I noted with shock and disgust he held the reins with his long whip-like tongue. I loosed my arrow at the top of the gallop, and it flew true until the tongue again flicked out and batted it away.

I hated what I was about to do, but I was out of options. "Sorry about this," I said as I loosed another arrow, this time at the tattooed man's horse. The beast screamed as it tumbled, sending the mage vaulting from his saddle. The instant he struck the ground, green electricity arched across his body and he let a blood-curdling, inhuman cry that reminded me vaguely of a Varaha.

I turned my attention in front of me again, focused on outrunning my remaining pursuers. I continued to gain ground on them as I followed the curve of the cliff to my left and, after the longest five minutes of my life, found a dry creek bed that led back into the trees. Out of sight, I found a spot to rest between two large boulders and called Tarka's gift around us. I wasn't well hidden, but I hoped if someone did look this way the hazy rippling of Tarka's gift would be lost in the gray stones.

When the Turaggin did come around the bend, it was at a canter and there were only four of them. I guessed they weren't sure if I'd turned down the creek bed, so they only sent a few men. They came so close to my hiding place that I was sure they would hear Tavas, who was still breathing hard, but they passed right by me.

I waited until Tavas and I both caught our breath before slipping down the creek myself. I moved carefully with Tarka's gift still cloaking us, but I didn't encounter anyone. I came to an area I recognized and made my way back to the spot we'd set up camp. A few blankets and a cooking pot had been left behind in their haste. I collected them, not knowing if the mages might have some manner of using them against us.

Consulting my map, I set out on a different route than I figured my Arga companions would have taken. It was a less direct and slower than the highway, but alone I traveled faster, making up the time. I didn't notice anyone following me but I did some counter-tracking just to be sure.

Tension crawled into by back and stayed there. After the first day on my own, I was reasonably sure they weren't following me, though that did nothing to ease my mind. Since my Dezika disguise obviously wasn't helping me, I let my hair down and donned my surcoat and draa clothes, though I did keep the chain shirt. I worried about Samara and questioned my decision to separate from the group, but I really couldn't see any other option at the time. Besides, it was done so there wasn't any point agonizing over my decision.

That realization didn't help either.

There was another thing that was bothering me. We'd been attacked twice since we left the Empire. Samara could be right about the tattooed mage lying in wait for us in Cargov, but the ones with the Turaggin were clearly tracking us. How? They didn't seem to have dogs and tracking us on the highway would be really tricky. Samara had said that it would be impractical to track someone using magic, but that was looking more and more plausible.

The second day, I had to push hard to make it to Tsava before sundown. The docks were packed with merchants unloading barges and people waiting on the last ferry across the muddy river, which made finding anyone difficult. I had to dismount and lead Tavas though the throngs of people. I was worried my companions might not have made it, or else had been forced to take an earlier ferry, until I saw Samara waving to me frantically. She'd put up her magical disguise again so I almost missed her.

"Darian," she said as she leapt up and wrapped her arms around me fiercely.

I hugged her back saying, "It's alright, I'm fi—" but my words were cut short by a sharp slap.

"*Idiot,*" she said, her eyes shimmering with unshed tears. "Don't you *ever* do that again."

You're welcome," I said, spitting blood onto the dock. She was deceptively strong for someone so slight.

"By the Gods, you're vexing," she said, surreptitiously wiping her eyes.

"It's true what they say," Lucius said gripping me by the arm and pulling me hard thumping embrace. "Kavi does watch over fools."

"Apparently," I said as the houseguards slapped me on the back and punched me in the shoulder. Zuran gratitude was painful. "Did the Turaggin pursue you?"

Lucius nodded. "We caught sight of them once from a distance but we lost them. What happened? Did you manage to kill any of them?"

"I don't think so. I wounded one of the Turaggin, and one of the mages took a hard fall off his horse." I smiled. "With some assistance."

"Hard enough to kill him?" Samara asked.

"I don't know but he was in the middle of casting a spell when he went down and green lightning went everywhere."

Samara's brows went up. "He might be dead then, depending how much energy he'd built up. Spell backlash can be lethal."

"We can hope. Mostly I just led them on a long chase."

Samara frowned. "Next time you're thinking about abandoning me and running off by yourself, don't. Remember, Vija Saptarsi said I'd fail without you."

It was my turn to frown. "I remember very well what the Vija said. It's not like we were lousy with other options." The bell for the ferry rang ending any further debate.

The ferry was a barge perhaps forty yards long by twenty wide. Two ropes stretched across the water attached to a large, hand-operated wench that pulled the vessel along. The aft quarter had stalls for the horses with half-doors that latched in case they spooked. When Uncle Rav and I were coming back across the Anhu Straight from Maula we'd been caught a squall that pitched the vessel about pretty fiercely. Since then Tavas had been wary of boats, so I decided to stay in the back and try to keep him calm.

As the ferry lurched forward, I cast one last glance back at the docks and mouthed a silent prayer to the Gods that we'd lost our pursuers. Not that very many of my prayers had been answered.

Chapter Seventeen

Samara

It might not have been so bad if it wasn't such a windy day, but it howled like a ghost out of the north, sending the boat pitching and rocking against its mooring line. I probably wouldn't have been so bothered if I wasn't drained by constant worry over the last two days, about Darian, about the tattooed mages, about our mission.

In my head I knew the boat was safe. This ferry made the trip a dozen times a day, wind or no, but that knowledge clearly hadn't made it down to my belly, which squirmed like I'd swallowed a live eel. The ship lurched as the crew started wenching us across with the crank. I cast one last look across the dark, churning water. It was maybe seven hundred yards to the other side. How long could that take?

Forever, that's how long.

I turned to face the solid wall of stables and tried to keep my breathing even. Darian stood with his back to the half-door of the stall. If his chestnut was bothered by boats he didn't show it, the horse stood with his head resting over his master's shoulder, eyes half closed as Darian stroked his long face and crooned to him gently in Manu. The beast looked to be doing substantially better than me.

I went over to the stall next to him and gripped tightly to the door where my bay gelding was. Komala munched at his oats not seeming to mind the ferry at all, happily ignorant of the knowledge that if this boat sank, likely only a handful would survive.

"You alright? You're shaking," Darian said.

I hated it when my body betrayed me. "I share your horse's distrust of boats."

"I thought you swam like an otter?" He said giving his half-grin, which under the circumstances was even more annoying than usual.

"I'm not afraid of drowning. I'm afraid of sinking."

Darian just stared at me, brows raised.

"It doesn't have to make sense," I said turning my back to him, still gripping the top of the stall door. Dark thoughts crept into my mind. I couldn't help but wonder how my mother felt as her ship was breaking up beneath her. She'd been a strong swimmer too.

Darian put his hand on my shoulder and I jerked away. "I'm *fine*," I said irritably. I didn't need anyone's pity and I was still angry with him for causing me to worry about him for two days. I fixed my glance down on the deck and focused on my breathing.

Strangely the tension in my chest eased almost immediately. I felt lighter and less scared, as if my mother were standing beside me. I stared at the deck, took deep breaths and tried to keep my mind empty. Suddenly we came to a stop. I thought for a moment there was something wrong, that maybe the wench broke, but then I realized we'd reached the other side. I'd made it without throwing up, or having a breakdown, or anything.

I looked to the side to see Darian's hand about an inch from my shoulder, silver light fading. "What are you doing?"

"I thought Ananda's gift might help," he said taking a step back.

"You didn't even ask me!"

"I…No, but you just seemed—"

"You can't…I mean, you don't just…" I trailed off, unable to articulate what was wrong. I closed my eyes and took a deep breath. I knew Darian was just trying to help, but this fear was something I needed conquer on my own. His assumption that I couldn't handle myself irked me, just as it had when he'd assumed I needed help with Komala when I'd first tried to ride him. I was too tired and emotionally raw to have this conversation. "Never mind. Let's just go."

"Right…sorry."

As we led our horses off the ferry, Darian turned to Lucius and asked, "What's the plan?"

"Since that's the last ferry of the day, I figure it's safe enough to stay in town tonight," Lucius said.

"Assuming there's not already another group waiting for us," I said.

"We'll stay vigilant and leave in the morning before the ferry's first run," Lucius said with a shrug.

A hot meal and a real bed sounded too good to argue against. "Alright, lead the way."

We settled on a little two-story wooden inn that was behind a brewery, off the main streets. The smell of brewer's yeast was overpowering, but I was too worn out to care. We stabled our animals, paid for our rooms, and headed to a tavern on the corner. I was jumpy on the walk given what happened the last time we tried to stay in a town, but the only trouble we encountered were a couple of drunks who were having a loud argument in the middle of the street.

The Blue Badger was dark, crowded, and loud. At least we managed to find a table in the far corner, away from the band belting out drinking songs. Despite the noise I was so tired I could hardly keep my eyes open, that is until food was set in front of me. After three days of dry rations, the hearty vegetable stew with bits of lamb was ambrosia. I don't know if it actually tasted good or not, but I know I inhaled the whole bowl and got seconds. They even had mulled wine. It wasn't good as Zuran wine—in fact, had I been at home I probably would have turned my nose up at it—but I drank cup after cup.

"Darian," Lucius said after he finished his stew, "what you did the other day…thank you."

"You're welcome," Darian said between bites.

Lucius ran his hands through his hair, which had gotten even longer since we'd left the Empire. "I've been suspicious of you this whole time and you've given me no cause to be. I should have listened to Otter, but this whole business with the Vija, and demons, and Samara getting hurt…" Lucius refilled both their cups before raising his, "Anyway, I trust you now."

Darian looked down into his cup and for a moment and said, "Buy me a real drink to replace this watered-down swill and we'll call it even."

Lucius was quiet for a moment then he burst out laughing and slapped the table. "It's a deal. I'm starting to like you, Manu."

"A few of you Zurans are alright," he said with a half-grin.

———————————

My bed was a lumpy, rough, little straw-stuffed mattress, and it felt *heavenly*. If it harbored any bugs I was asleep before I noticed them. The next morning, I stumbled out of the inn to see our horses saddled and ready to go in the predawn darkness. I started to pull myself into the saddle when Lucius handed me a fresh piece of warm buttered bread and said, "Hold for a moment. We're waiting on Darian."

"Where is he?"

"He said he had to run an errand."

"Typical," I huffed, chewing on my bread.

After a quarter hour Darian materialized into view, dropping Tarka's gift with a grin that said he was pleased with his own cleverness. "We should probably be on our way."

I cocked my head. "What did you do?"

"Me?" he said with his mouth open in mock indignation, "I did nothing."

"Mmmhmm…"

Darian leaned in conspiratorially, "But the word is that someone cut the mooring line to the ferry. Ought to take most of the day to string another one."

"We probably *should* get out of here then," Lucius said grinning. "We're making quite a mess of the towns we visit."

I made a show of sighing. "I can't take you boys anywhere."

Changing directions, we headed southeast, hoping throw our pursuers off the trail. Despite everything, I felt better than I had in days, now that the worry over Darian was gone. The next two days we pushed hard, traveling until after dark every night and rising before dawn every morning. We turned off on a less-used highway that had fallen into disrepair. The frequent, large potholes made it problematic for wagons, so there were far fewer people on it. Eventually, we relaxed our pace, even taking a whole day by a charming little lake to rest and recover. I received a message from Master Carter saying my father had realized Lucius was missing, but as far as he knew Autumn's deception was still holding.

Five days passed as the weather grew hotter and the landscape became arid and rocky. Flowing water was shallower and less frequent. There were long tracts of nothing but rocks, prairie grass, and small scrubby copses of trees. Despite my best efforts to find a way to remain covered and stay relatively cool, I got one the worst sunburn of my life. Darian was out of salve, but he cut a long, thick leaf off a pointy plant and smeared its slimy green blood all over me. That, combined with Ananda's gift, made the pain tolerable.

We were able to buy supplies at a few small towns, after approaching cautiously, while Darian managed to scrounge up a new local map. We came across a group that might have been highwaymen, but they shied away after we got close, likely due to the prevalence of weapons and lack of apparent valuables.

"When this business is over with, I'm going to spend a whole month filled with nothing but drinking and whoring," Lucius said to me as we rode next to each other.

"So pretty much the same as your whole term at university," I said.

"More or less, absent any pretense of learning or accountability."

I shot him a wry grin. "As I said."

"My, my, aren't we cheeky today."

"Perhaps delirium has finally set in? Or more likely sunstroke."

"You had more brains than you needed anyway."

"Hardly," I said, throwing my arms out wide to indicate my present state of being. "Here I am."

"What does that say about me? I let you me convince me."

"Obviously it says you spent too much time drinking and whoring rather than going to class."

One of the guards cut in, "Begging your pardon, Lucius, but look at that."

The houseguard turned his back on the slope we'd been climbing and pointed to the valley we'd been in most of the day. Squinting my eyes, I could barely make out a hazy dust cloud and a group of riders.

"Do you recon it's…" the guard trailed off.

"Aww, come on," groaned Lucius.

"I see two red robes among those turbans. Looks like I didn't kill Snake-Jaw after all," Darian said with a frown.

"Bastards can track," Lucius said with a snarl.

Darian drew a breath as if to say something but then just blew it out, shaking his head.

"Come on, let's put some distance between us," Lucius said.

When we cleared the ridge we rode hard for about an hour before coming to a crossroads. Lucius and Darian pulled out their respective maps and deliberated before deciding to turn left, taking the road north. I hadn't thought it possible, but the new road was rougher and more dilapidated than the one we'd turned off. It looked like it could have been built when the Empire ruled this land a thousand years ago. As the road twisted and turned between jagged rocky cliffs, I kept looking back over my shoulder expecting to see our pursuers at any moment.

We turned a hard corner to see a chasm gape before us, easily thirty yards wide, with nothing but a rope suspension bridge stretching across it.

"Oh, now the Gods are simply tormenting us," I said.

Lucius cast a baleful glance at Darian. "This is where your map took us?"

"It only showed that there was a bridge here, not what kind of bridge," Darian said.

"Lovely," Lucius said peering down the sheer cliff face to the shallow, rocky river below.

"I'm not going across that thing," I said. "We'll have to find another way."

"We can't," Lucius said. "Not unless we plan on fighting our way there. The only other bridge for a hundred miles is on the road we just turned off of."

I glanced back at the rope and plank bridge that was maybe five feet wide and said, "I don't even trust that thing to hold *my* weight, much less the weight of a horse."

"Only one way to know." Darian dismounted and walked over to hold the guide ropes that also acted as handrails.

"Careful," I blurted out.

He stepped tentatively out on the planks. The bridge hardly moved. Slowly, carefully, he walked across the bridge, gripping the hand ropes and testing each plank. The bridge swayed a bit as he made it to the middle, but not so much as I would have thought. Once on the other side he waved to us, then went back to the middle. I jerked involuntarily as he jumped several times, then deliberately tried to make it sway to minimal effect. When he returned he said, "It's sturdy, and far better tended than the road. I think it'll hold the horses."

"This is such a horrible plan," I said.

"No doubt," said Darian. "But we're not exactly spoiled for options at the moment."

"If we're going to do this we'd better do it now," Lucius said looking back down the road. "No telling when our 'friends' might show up."

"Everyone else should go across on foot, then I'll lead the horses across one by one in case I was wrong about the bridge," Darian said.

"I'll stay back and help you," said a blond houseguard named Marcus.

I didn't like that idea, but then again I didn't really like anything about this plan. After a moment's hesitation I dismounted and edged toward the bridge. Darian walked up to me and gestured to the draa scarf in my hair, "May I borrow this?" he asked.

I slid the crimson scarf out and held it out for him, but when he tried to take it I didn't let go. "You'd better give it back when you're done with it."

He smiled. A full smile, not one of his half-smiles. "I will."

"Promise?"

"I promise."

I let go of the scarf, "I'll hold you to that."

Darian walked over to his horse and tied the scarf across the chestnut's eyes as a blindfold. I moved to stand in front of the bridge next to Lucius and the other houseguards.

Lucius gestured across and I shook my head. "Uh-uh, you first."

He blew out an exasperated sigh and strode confidently across the bridge. When he got to the other side he shouted back across, "It's nothing. Just don't look down."

I closed my eyes and focused on my breathing for a moment. *Don't look down. Right. Also don't throw up, or pass out.*

I gripped the hand-ropes tightly and tried to look only at the boards before me and not let my gaze focus on the frothy, rocky river below. I stepped out on the bridge which, thankfully, did feel fairly sturdy beneath my feet, and started across. Thanks to my years of meditation and spellcasting, I was able to maintain my focus on the boards in front of me and keep my thought from wondering. That is, until right about the middle.

A strong gust picked up, blowing my hair about me and sent the bridge swaying. I startled and looked down. A wave of vertigo washed over me as I stared down into the expanse. I squeezed my eyes shut, concentrating on the rope in my hands and the planks beneath my boots. This time I did wish Darian was standing behind me with Ananda's gift. After an eternity the swaying eased and I remembered how to breathe again.

"You alright, Otter?"

"Just peachy," I said as I opened my eyes and firmly focused on the wood before me. About a thousand years later, I made it to the other side. As my feet once again reached terra firma I blew out a long sigh.

"See? Not so bad," Lucius said with a smile.

I somehow resisted the urge to slap him.

The rest of the houseguards followed me across single file. Only one of them seemed to have anywhere near as much trouble as me. When the last guard stepped off the bridge, Darian led his stud gingerly out onto the planks. The horse hardly hesitated, trusting his master to lead him to safety. Ropes strained and boards groaned as the bridge swayed more than it had before, but it held. Darian led his chestnut across in probably less time than it'd taken me.

"*Good job my friend,*" Darian said as he untied the scarf and handed the reigns over. The horse turned to nuzzle him, as if asking what all the fuss was about.

"Well, that's promising," said Lucius.

"Let's not break out the good whiskey just yet," Darian said before striding back across to get the next animal.

Not all of the horses were so easy to convince, however. Some of them took quite a bit more persuading after feeling the wood swaying beneath their hooves. One silky black mare in particular fought and pulled, trying to get back on stable ground. Darian managed to get the beast across, crooning softly to her in Manu as he had on the boat, but the process was time consuming. Darian was three quarters of the way back across the bridge to collect the last horse, and the guard holding her, when Lucius shouted, "*Look out!*"

Marcus had enough time to turn and reach for his sword before the Turaggin ax split his skull.

I screamed, "Darian, *run!*"

Darian hesitated for but a moment before turning and sprinting back across the bridge. Arrows chased after him but, for a blessing, another gust of wind picked up sending them off course.

My eyes fell upon a tattooed mage with a hideously distended jaw and long whip-like tongue shaping a spell, his gaze focused on Darian's fleeing form. From the pale green light, it looked like he'd get his spell off before Darian made it to the other side.

I cleared my mind and began shaping my own spell. It was one that I'd never tried to cast on someone else, let alone a moving target, and it had to be done fast. On a good day, with a chance to concentrate and take my time, I was fairly sure I could do it. This wasn't any of those things. The chance of me screwing it up and the spell backlashing were pretty high. But I had to try. I performed the mudras, giving the spell power and releasing it.

A light blue translucent hemisphere appeared behind Darian an instant before the air was split with thunder. Snake-Jaw's lightning struck the newly formed shield and deflected off of it just as mine had in Cargov, striking the bridge. Wood exploded and flames leapt up the ropes behind Darian, but they held. He was only a few strides from the end and it looked as though he might make it.

Then there was a loud snap and the bridge fell apart.

Darian disappeared from my sight.

Something broke inside of me and I went numb. It was as if all the sound had been sucked out of the world. I was distantly aware of Lucius shouting beside me, but I heard nothing. Across the chasm the Snake-Jaw stared at me through the swirling translucent shield and shook with laughter.

The bastard thought that his shield would protect him from my wrath. He was wrong.

I began shaping my own lightning spell. It was different than it had been with the man standing over Autumn at the fork in the river. There was no fury. No hot, seething hatred. There was nothing. And from that nothingness a calm, clear thought crystallized. I was going to murder this man. I was going to murder all of them.

The female mage had her shield up as well, but the lightning wasn't aimed at her. It was aimed at the oak tree on the ridge fifty feet above them. Their shields might protect them from my magic, but they offered no respite from the fiery maelstrom of burning wood that rained down upon them as my thunder echoed down the canyon. As men screamed in pain and horses spooked, I just stared.

I felt nothing.

Chapter Eighteen
Darian

I barely registered the strange tingly feeling that washed over me before I felt an intense heat at my back and heard another bloody ear-splitting clap of thunder as the bridge shook. I never stopped running. Then the world fell out from beneath me.

Instinctively, I grabbed the hand ropes as I fell. There were plenty of rope bridges in Vana and I'd spent most of my life in the trees. I'd be damned if I was going to die from a fall.

Pain lanced through my knuckles and my right cheek as I slammed against the wooden slats, and the brutal impact against the cliff face nearly jarred me loose. I gritted my teeth and called Irin's gift to me, fading my pain and freeing my mind to focus on my predicament. Through blurry eyes I could see there was just enough space between the slats to slip my fingers in, but they were wet with sweat and blood so I'd have to be careful.

Tentatively, I let go of the rope and grabbed the makeshift ladder with my right hand, then my left. I was able to wedge the tips of my soft boots between the slats to give me a toe-purchase to start my ascent. I felt utterly vulnerable on the cliff face, but I forced myself to go slowly and methodically. Another thunderclap rang out from above and the shock of surprise caused me to lose my footing. I flailed, holding on with only my fingertips for a moment before my feet found purchase again.

As my head cleared the top of the bridge, I could see Samara's face staring across the gap. Her gaze was distant, her face empty and pale, void of expression. "You alright?" I called. She gave no response, looking like Autumn had after Dirk had been struck down. "Samara? Are you hurt?"

Finally she looked down. "Da-Darian?" Tears streamed down her face as she fell to her knees.

"Are you hurt?" I asked.

"N-no."

"Good, because I could use some help."

She gave a little chuckle despite the fact she was still crying. She reached down and grabbed my shoulder with both of her hands. A moment later, Lucius was there with a few guards and they dragged me up and over the side. Black circles danced at the edge of my vision as Samara slapped me again, then threw her arms around me in a crushing embrace.

"Alright, you can't slap me every time I survive something—" I said into her hair.

"The Hell I can't! Maybe eventually you'll learn," she said, wiping her eyes.

"Take a look at that," Lucius said, pointing back across the chasm.

Samara and I disengaged and turn to look. Thick black smoke obscured much of the scene, but what we could make out was chaos. Horses screamed and panicked trying to get away from the fire. One of the Turaggin tried desperately to slap out the flames on his ally, while another rolled on the ground and screamed in utter agony as he was being immolated. Out of this madness the female mage calmly strode to the edge of the chasm and cast off her robes to stand naked across from us, save for her translucent magical shield.

"What is she doing?" Lucius asked.

Samara shook her head. "No idea."

I could see through the shimmering hemisphere the woman had seven of the tarnished copper tattoo-brands in a line down her body. She threw her head back and raised her arms, her mouth open in a silent cry. Bulges appeared and then started moving as if something was crawling around under her skin. A shiny, copper wasp, perhaps as long as my finger, flew out of her open mouth. Then another flew out from between her legs.

"What the..?" Lucius said.

As if a dam suddenly gave way, a buzzing cloud burst from the tattooed woman. Most streamed from her mouth and genitals, but a few crawled right out of her skin. A swarm of glittery death surged across the chasm toward us.

"Samara," I cried, but she was already in the throes of spell casting. She swung one of her glowing hands before her and an icy wind came howling down the chasm, sweeping away the wasps in its path and cutting off the seething, writhing, mass on the other side.

"We need to get out of here," said Lucius.

We jumped on our horses and thundered down the gravely road, again leaving fire and death in our wake.

───────────

"What the Hell…No…What the bloody Hell was that back there?" Lucius took a long pull from one of the few remaining wineskins before continuing. "I've never seen a spell like that."

We thought it best not to build a fire, which left only twinkling starlight for illumination as we sat in a rough circle, sweat soaked and exhausted, munching on hard, flavorless biscuits.

Samara shook her head chewing on her lip, "It wasn't magic."

One of the guards who was shivering despite the heat said, "Begging your pardon, m'lady, but I saw a wasp crawl out of that woman's…" he glanced over at Samara, "…nether-lips. Seems to me like magic had something to do with it."

Samara sighed and rolled her eyes. "I realize I'm a lady of House Arga, but you can say vagina in front of me." Samara grabbed the wineskin and took a long draw from it herself. "It wasn't magic. At least, not magic the way lightning or coldfire is."

"What then?" Lucius prompted.

"I think it has something to do with their tattoos. Did you notice where they are?" Samara reached up and touched the top of her head, then moved down between her brows, then her throat, then between her breasts, then her navel, then her waist, then a few finger widths farther down.

"Their chakras," I said.

Samara's nodded. "That's right. At first I thought they were just normal tattoos, but when we searched the one in Cargov it looked more like a brand that had scarred over. I think those mages have been, I don't know…changed somehow."

"I thought there were spells that could be used to shape the body?" Lucius said.

"There are, but those spells are permanent, at least until you use another spell to change it back. The long-armed mage who fought my Elemental went back to normal after he died. More to the point, there's no magic that I've ever heard of that does what that woman back there did."

My tired mind struggled to grasp what Samara was saying. "What could do something like that?"

"Remember the Vija's vision? Remember how I said there would have to be mages in both Realms to hold the portal open?"

My mind made the leap. "You can't be serious?"

Lucius looked back and forth between us with a frown. "Obviously I'm missing something."

"You think the Rajasa made the brand?" I said, mouth agape.

"The Rajasa, or a very powerful demon," Samara answered.

"Otter, is that even possible?" Lucius asked.

"I have no idea. But we know some of the tattooed mages have to be on the other side to open the portal—"

Lucius cut her off. "But I thought Hell was a perfect prison?"

Samara craned her head toward her brother raising her brows, "It is a perfect prison for the *Rajasa*. That doesn't mean other things can't pass through under the right circumstances. How did you think we summon demons?"

Lucius's eyes narrowed. "So what, that woman just waltzed in to Hell and asked for a tattoo that would let her puke wasps?"

"Look, I don't know. It's just a theory. But in addition to Waspgina, the mage in Cargov grew monkey arms and the guy back there has a three-yard-long tongue. I'd bet my spellbook the mage who ambushed us in Mystewood would have done something equally as disgusting if I'd given him the chance. *Something* must have made them the way they are."

We sat in silence for a time. It seemed no one knew what to say. Oenus finally cleared his throat and said, "I just wish we could give Marcus a proper burial."

"As ash returns to the earth, and fire ascends to the heavens, his body will find its way to Suravani's embrace, and his spirit will find its way to whatever awaits beyond," I said.

"They're behind us again," I said as I slowed my horse to match the twins' pace.

"Of course they are," Lucius said. It'd been four days since the battle at the bridge and we'd been pushing hard to stay ahead of them. "How many are there? I suppose it's too much to hope Otter's flaming tree got most of them."

"I counted ten including the mages," I said, feeling my lips curl into a smile. "Though several of them were bandaged or missing hair."

"By the Gods, they have to be some of the best trackers on the continent," Lucius said with a snarl.

"Especially since they don't have dogs," I said.

Samara's eyes opened wide like something had just occurred to her. "Maybe the tattooed mages have a hound's nose or something."

Lucius narrowed his eyes at her like he was trying to decide if she was teasing.

Samara shrugged. "If they can grow monkey arms, why not?"

"That would actually make a lot of sense," I said.

"How far back were they?" Lucius asked opening the enchanted map.

"Three, maybe four miles."

Lucius studied his map. "I suppose we could turn north-northeast again, try and loose them in these woods," he said running his finger over an area with a bunch of trees.

I consulted my local version as well. "This map says there's a large verge there."

"Damn. I guess we could head for these mountains just to the south of the woods. Hopefully we can stay ahead of them, or maybe even lose them all together."

"It's as good a plan as any," I said as he handed the map back.

Mountains was a generous term for them. It looked like Suravani had just dumped handfuls of coral-colored granite boulders into large piles and filled the space between them with thick prairie grass and spindly, scrubby trees. For two days, we'd followed the old pockmarked road, pushing late into the evening and starting before the first rays of Azava's light graced the sky, and still we couldn't keep a lead of more than a few miles on our pursuers. It seemed they were as determined as we were. The heavy Turaggin war horses had quite a lot of stamina for such big creatures. I'd have to see about acquiring some to breed for draft animals…if I survived this endevor.

It was only by luck that we hadn't had any real problem with any of the horses. Actually, the horses seemed to be doing better than I was. I was dirty, bone-weary, and I hadn't had a hot meal in more days than I cared to think about. If that's how rough I felt, I could only imagine how Samara was doing. She'd kept her complaining to a minimum since the bridge, which I had greatly appreciated.

I didn't know how many more days' worth of biscuits and jerky we had left, but I knew I was sick of eating it. The tall grass however was providing ample cover for small game and the loud footfall of the horses on the road was giving them plenty of warning. "I'm going to go scout ahead for a bit, maybe scare up some real food in the process."

Samara perked up. "That sound like a great idea. Maybe a quail? Oh, or a nice fat boar?"

I raised an eyebrow. "I'm not taking requests. It's more likely to be a marmot, or porcupine, or maybe a snake."

Her eyes narrowed. "Alright, now I know you're joking."

"You've never had snake?" I licked my lips. "It tastes like chewy chicken."

"I think you're probably lying, but I'm hungry enough to find out."

I winked at her. "I'll make sure you get the heart and liver. They're the best part."

I rode down the road for a while, giving Tavas his head and letting him stretch his legs. I could tell this journey was taking a toll on him. He'd always been lean and muscular, but now I could see every rib.

We were on the leeward side of one of the taller mountains and I broke off from the road near a group of tall flowers the color of sunset. There were several cacti with unripened fruit, but they bore beautiful yellow flowers. I let go of my aches and discomfort, and just took in the sight of the land around me. It seemed unsullied by man's greed and ambition. There's wasn't nearly enough tall trees for my liking, but the untamed beauty of the land flowed through me.

I could tell Tavas smelled water, so I let him follow his nose to a small pond at the base of the mountain. As he drank I saw a small flock of gray and tan fowl that looked somewhat like chickens. I called Tarka's gift around us, eased two arrows out of my quiver and placed one in my mouth. I drew back and fired, then yanked the arrow out of my mouth and fired again. The flock startled and ran off to reveal two plump birds that had volunteered to join us for dinner.

I hopped down to claim my prize, but just as I remounted something danced at the edge of my consciousness. It sounded like the low calls horses make to one another. With Tarka's gift pulled around me again, I hugged the base of the mountain toward the noise. It was probably just a wild horse or another group of travelers. Most likely I was just being paranoid. I rounded the corner to see five Turaggin with Snake-Jaw laying in ambush.

I slipped quietly down the path I'd just taken until I was out of earshot, and then I let out a full gallop back to the group.

"What is it?" Samara said at my approach.

"Snake-Jaw and half the Turaggin are waiting in ambush about a mile up the road."

Lucius spat. "Son of a monkey-raping *whore!*"

"Where is the other half?" Samara said.

"I don't know, but if I had to guess I'd say they were still following us."

"No doubt driving us into the ambush. How'd they even get in front of us?" said Lucius.

I shook my head. "That's a mystery to contemplate later. What do we do now?"

Lucius said, "The maps show south is impassable, and we're blocked by enemies to the east and west. I guess the only way to go is north."

"That'll take us into the verge," Samara said.

"You have a better idea?" said Lucius.

Samara huffed and shook her head.

"Yeah, me either," said Lucius. "Darian?"

"Nothing comes to mind." I said.

"North it is then," he said with a frown.

We put our left shoulders to the sinking sun and broke from the old weathered road.

The thin scrubby trees turned out to be rather thorny. We were moving between two mountains through a thick patch of the stabby bastards. There were no cleared paths, but I managed to find a game trial that allowed us to ride single file. Even so there were a few places where we had to dismount and lead the horses or else get a face full of thorns. Needless to say, our pace had been slower since leaving the road but we hoped that meant our stalkers had as well, considering we hadn't seen them in almost a full day.

"You think we'll make it out of the mountains before nightfall?" Lucius asked.

"It depends on how rough the terrain is, but based on the maps I imagine so," I said.

"I wonder what kind of forest we'll be going into?" Lucius mused.

"It has to be better than the thorny wasteland we're in," Samara said.

"Not if it's a verge, it's doesn't," I pointed out.

"You say that, but I swear, if I get my hair caught in one more…" Samara trailed off her gazed fixed in the trees above us. Then I saw it. A single copper wasp. As if it knew we had spotted it, the infernal little thing took off, disappearing into the canopy.

"Move," I said, "Now."

We spurred out horses to a canter, which was all we could manage on the trail, and even so I caught a few sharp branches. We could hear crashing in the distance, they were only a few hundred yards behind us. Finally, the trees thinned and we were able let our horses go at a full gallop.

Our fast, sure-footed Manu mounts tore at the ground, putting distance between us and our enemies. If we could just avoid any further ambushes, we could stay one step ahead of them. It was only when we cleared the trees I realized I was wrong. We'd already made our fatal mistake. The valley before us was vast, several miles wide and long, but it was a bowl, completely surrounded by mountains.

"Bugger me," Lucius said.

Samara looked back behind us. "What do we do?"

My mind was racing, trying to find a solution. "We push forward. Try to…try to find a good place to ambush them. With Tarka's gift and your magic, maybe we can lure them into a trap?"

Samara took a deep breath. "Maybe we can make that work? If we—"

"No," Lucius said, his tone calm and sure. "You and Darian are going to hide while the boys and I lead them off."

"Lucius, that's mad," Samara protested. "We shouldn't split up. Look maybe we can—"

"No, Otter," he said shaking his head. "All they have to do to is get you and it's all over. The two of you can head up that creek over there. It should hide your scent and Darian can use his gift to hide you." He turned to face me with earnest lilac eyes. "It'll work on both of you, right?"

I hesitated, "For a time."

Lucius turned back to his twin. "The boys and I will lead them off on a merry chase."

"Lucius, stop." Samara's crystal eyes welled with tears. "We…we can fight them."

"If they get you, they win."

"Lucius…"

"Otter, *this is* the smart play."

Samara shook her head as tears fell from her eyes. "You came with me so you could look out for me, remember?"

"Otter, this is me looking out for you. We don't have time to argue. Darian will get you to Vizipa and keep you safe." Lucius turned his lilac eyes toward me. "He's proven pretty good at that so far."

"I love you." Samara threw her arms around him as best she could from the saddle. "You idiot. You'd better not die on me."

He squeezed her. "Back at you, Otter."

Lucius pushed her away with a shaky hand and turned to me. "You'll need this," he said, handing me the map. "You want one of the pack horses?"

"I doubt I could hide us all," I said, shaking my head.

"Right. Darian," Lucius reached out and clasped my arm. "Take care of her."

His hand shook, but his gaze was steady and intense. "I will." He released my arm and I turned my horse about. "I'll see you at the end of all this."

He gave the barest hint of a smile just before he turned to ride off and said, "Or beyond it."

Chapter Nineteen
Samara

We splashed down the muddy creek as the sound of my brother and the houseguards thundering away echoed off the mountains. My head told me my brother's reasoning was sound, but there was a tightness in my chest that told me this was wrong, that we should have stayed together. As usual, when my head and heart disagreed, it was my soul that suffered.

There was a grassy clearing just off the bank about twenty yards up from where we'd turned down the creek. Darian craned his head, listening. "This'll have to do, hop down."

I stepped down on the squishy damp grass as Darian looked his horse in the eye and said, "*Lay down.*" The horse complied immediately, lying all the way down on his side. I could now hear the steady drumming hoof beats of Turaggin horses.

"Darian…"

"I know," he said, taking the reins from me and issuing the same command to Komala, directing the gelding with his hands to lay down with his back to Darian's chestnut. "Get down between them."

I wedged down in the space between the two horses on my back in the soggy grass. Without warning or preamble, Darian straddled my waist and put one hand on each of the horses.

"Um…"

"Quiet," he snapped.

He closed his eyes and I felt a strange sensation, like feathers being gently dragged over my skin. The world around me stayed the same, but I could see Darian and the horses only in muted colors, and there was a distorted haziness a finger-width or so above their skin. Darian looked as a statue above me, rhythmically rising and falling with my breathing, his face a mask of concentration.

The sound of horses grew louder. Already sweat beaded on Darian's forehead and crow's feet spider-webbed out from the corner of his tightly shut eyes. I could feel the staccato beat of the horses' hooves through the ground at my back, and then I heard splashing. They'd made it to the creek.

I could hear the water sloshing a mere stone's throw away.

Then they stopped.

Terror rose in my throat. I could hear men talking back and forth in a guttural language. Maybe our trick hadn't fooled them? Maybe they'd found us after all? One of their horses whinnied and Komala started to give low response but he quieted when I reached over to pet his neck and whispered, "Shhh."

He hadn't been very loud but still I mouthed a silent prayer that our pursuers hadn't heard it. Sweat dripped off of Darian's face forming a puddle on my chest and he started shaking. I didn't know how much longer he could hold it.

Finally, I heard our pursuers gallop off in the direction Lucius had gone and I let out a breath I hadn't realized I'd been holding. They must have just been watering their horses. I looked up at Darian, red-faced with a vein bulging out at his forehead, now shuddering violently.

"I think they're gone," I whispered. When he didn't respond I reached up and touched his cheek. "Darian?"

He let go of Tarka's gift and collapsed on top of me in a sweaty pile, gasping for breath. Anyone walking by at that moment would have definitely thought we'd been up to a different activity. I gave him a moment to catch his breath before I asked in a quiet voice, "You alright?"

He rubbed his head, "I could use a drink."

"You and me both."

He straightened his arms slowly pushing himself up on shaky legs.

We got the horses up and mounted. He turned to go back down the creek the direction we'd come from. "Shouldn't we go this way?" I asked.

He shook his head, then grimaced like he regretted it. "They're going to be looking for us eventually. We'll reverse our course. Whether they're following us by tracks or scent, it should throw them off."

The idea of heading toward our pursuers terrified me but I just nodded. We did as he said, retracing the path we'd taken only moments before. He kept looking back over his shoulder to be sure we weren't being followed, which of course made me do the same thing every time. I jumped at every little sound in the woods and my eyes constantly flitted around, hyper-alert for the glint of one of those devilish wasps. We pushed on as quickly as we dared in the thick foliage, stopping only to water the horses at a shallow pond.

A thick gray curtain of clouds was drawn ominously across the sky, echoing my mood. As twilight faded, Darian took my reins and led us on into the inky blackness. The cold hand of terror gripped my heart as I heard thunder echoing off the mountains from the direction we'd come.

"Lucius," I said.

I could barely make out Darian's silhouette as he looked back. "Don't let your mind torture you. That thunder could be Suravani's."

"Or it could belong to the tattooed mages."

"You don't know that."

Fury welled up inside of me. "Don't."

"Lucius is as clever, and nearly as stubborn as you. If anyone could find a way through the mountains or outwit—"

"Stop," I spat. "Just stop. You're not helping. I know what their odds are, I don't need you to patronize me."

"Look, we need to keep our thoughts on our situation, and we can't do that if we're worried about—"

"Talking isn't going to stop me from worrying about my brother, so you might as well save your breath," I shouted. By the time I finished I was shaking.

"Alright. Keep your voice down," Darian said in hushed tones.

Thankfully he got the idea and stopped trying to console me, and merely led our horses silently in the starless night. We continued for hours. Despite my worry, I found myself nodding off in the saddle, only to jerk violently awake as my head drifted forward. When our horses' hooves clicked upon the battered old road, Darian turned us to the west.

"Wait, shouldn't we be going the other way?" I asked.

"No. If they can't find our trail they'll assume we took the road east. We'll double back and turn south of mountains." He sounded as weary as I felt.

We traveled on for several more hours before Darian finally led us off the road to a spot behind a rocky outcropping we'd camped at a few days before. As I slid off Komala I nearly collapsed from exhaustion. My wounds hurt. My head hurt. My heart hurt. I had no tent or even a bedroll, all that had been on the pack horses. I flopped down on a thick spot of grass, wrapped my cloak around me, and used my endless bag for a pillow. I was asleep the moment my eyes closed. For a small blessing at least I didn't dream.

When Darian shook me awake it was still dark. "It's time to go."

I groaned as I gained my feet and rubbed at the kink in my back. My belly grumbled loudly, but we didn't have any food. That was also on the pack horses.

"It's not much of a town," I said as I looked across the river at the dozen little buildings nestled around a mill with a lazy waterwheel.

"We can look for another one if it's not up to your standards," Darian said with an annoyed glance.

"And they say Manu aren't known for their sense of humor."

"Hopefully they'll at least have a blacksmith and a general store."

"As long as there's a hot meal somewhere, I couldn't care less about anything else," I said rubbing my belly. They only thing I'd had in the last two days was a handful of pecans and a couple of wild persimmons. We'd pushed so hard that Darian hadn't had time to hunt, much less build a fire.

"A tent and a proper bed-roll would be nice too. It's only luck we haven't been rained on," he said.

"Oh yes, we've certainly been overburdened with luck. Remind me to make an offering of thanks."

"We haven't seen any see any Turaggin, or women with wasps crawling out of their twat, so I suppose that's something."

I giggled at that despite myself. We crossed the little arched stone bridge and passed a corral with a flock of fat sheep, happily grazing the lush summer grass and I had an utterly irrational burst of jealousy. I was jealous of sheep. Clearly I was going mad.

There was a broad-chested middle-aged man who was missing an eye, filling up a horse trough in front of one of the buildings. A quick conversation with him revealed where the general store and the blacksmith were. Apparently the inn burned down over the previous winter, but the man said there was a woman up the road who rented out her extra room.

I gave Darian my best doe eyes. He sighed, "Go on, and get settled in. I'll handle this," he said handing me a few of the local coins.

"You're a gentleman and a scholar," I said hopping off Komala and making my way down the road.

"Yeah, yeah," Darian said, fighting a grin.

The wooden house was painted blue with a meticulously tended garden in the front. A thick broad-shouldered woman with ruddy cheeks answered the door, and after a brief conversation and a scrutinizing look, she took my money and showed me to our room for the evening.

The room was small but not tiny, and a far cry better than my recent sleeping arrangements. The bed wasn't large but we would both fit if we slept on our sides. Maybe I could convince Darian to sleep in the floor…

There was a sloshing sound and a boy of ten or so with the same ruddy cheeks as his mother carried a bucket of water in into the room and set it next to a stool in the corner with a bar of soap, a few rags, and rough towels.

"Gratitude," I said picking one of the coins out at random and handing it to him.

The boy's eyes got wide as an owl's. "Thank you, thank you, miss," he said as he ran off. I shook my head as I slid the small bolt on the door. There was no telling how much I just gave him.

The water was cold and the soap was coarse. Once upon a time that would have bothered me quite a bit. I scrubbed, and scrubbed, and scrubbed at the dirt that was engrained into my skin until I was nearly raw, but I finally managed to get reasonably clean.

As I dried off, I pulled Master Carter's mirror out and stared at my image. It was depressing. If I'd been thin before, I was waifish now. Every rib was visible and my hip bones stuck out. I looked like some starving slum peasant, begging for a crust of bread. I hadn't been able to wash clothes in nearly two weeks, but I put on the least-dirty dress, then set down on the bed and started combing out my hair.

I was nearly done when Darian came through the door, his hands full of supplies.

"Took you a while. Did you get everything we needed?" I asked.

"Most of it," Darian said, setting down the bags. "We'll just have to travel light, but at least now we have a tent. The blacksmith was a bit confused when I asked for the horses to be re-shod, but he was more than happy to take my money." He glanced about the room. "That's not a very big bed."

"I noticed that too. I was wondering if maybe—"

"Nope."

I rested my hands on my hips. "You don't even know what I was going to say."

"You were about to try and convince me to give up the bed."

"No, I wasn't."

"Lie."

Damn it. Azava's gift was annoying. "Come on. I'm a lady."

"Concerned about your reputation now are you?" he asked raising an eyebrow. "Not going to happen."

"I'll pay you."

"You can't afford me," he said with a smirk. "Now, see if you can find the porter to get me a fresh bucket of water."

"Yes, *husband*," I pouted, collecting the bucket. "A true gentleman would let me have the bed."

"Well, that's settled then," he said.

I sighed and went find the boy who'd brought me the bucket and towels.

The woman was pleasant at dinner. We chatted over a delicious creamy chicken soup with fresh baked bread. I ate far past the point of being full and well into the realm of misery. Her four young children peered at us over their bowls with the unashamed curiosity of youth.

She was explaining to us how her husband shipped timber down-river when something dawned on me. "When does your husband return?" I asked.

Her thick eyebrows drew together. "Should be back before noon tomorrow. Why?"

Darian and I shared a glance and he said, "How big is his boat?"

"This be it," Captain Bjorn said, pointing from the bow of his barge to the hard bend in the river up ahead. "The bank be sandy. We can pull right up to it."

"Easy enough," Darian said, pulling on his boots. "Thank you for your hospitality."

"Been a slow season," he said, flashing a broad grin that was missing more than a few teeth. "Happy to have a little extra coin."

Darian went back to saddle the horses. His chestnut and I had both been a bit skittish in the beginning, but the wide barge and slow waters had made for a smooth journey, and we'd both calmed down soon enough. Actually, I'd been far more worried about Lucius than the boat.

"Gratitude again," Darian said as we led our mounts on to the loose sand.

"Gods keep ya safe," Bjorn said as he and the only other crew member pushed off the bank with long poles.

"Let's look for a place to camp near the river," Darian said.

"We're not pressing on?" I asked. "There's still hours of light left."

He shook his head. "I want to let the horses graze. Besides we made up a week's worth of travel in two days on the water. It's a shame the river couldn't take us farther."

"I'm *plenty* happy to be back on solid ground," I said, and Darian's chestnut snorted in seeming agreement.

"At least we've finally shaken the Turaggin and the damned tattooed mages. There's no way they can find us over the water. And even if they could, we reshod the horses so they don't know what our tracks look like."

"You say that, but every time we think we've lost them they show up right behind us."

"Not this time. Though once they realize they've lost us, they'll likely try to get ahead of us again and set up another ambush."

"All I'm saying is we underestimated their tracking skill before." I smirked. "Maybe it's time to admit they're just better than you."

His brow went up. "We'll see."

We found a flat little clearing about twenty yards from the water. Darian unsaddled and unpacked the horses then let them graze. He took a long drink from his water skin and said, "I'm going to go hunt. Do you think you can manage to set up the tent and start a fire?"

I gave him a level stare. "I'm a mage of the Academy."

"So…that's a yes?"

I crossed my arms and said, "You're about to find out just how good I am at making fire." He chuckled and melted off into the trees.

I've bound demons and Elementals into my service, I've made wondrous enchanted items, and I've worked my will upon the fabric of creation, but that wretched little tent wouldn't stay up. It was as if I was missing some integral piece. I almost quit out of sheer frustration, but I'd be damned if I was going to give Darian the satisfaction. Eventually I managed to get the thing to stay up. Thankfully the fire was an easy thing. I gathered up some wood and lit it with a simple spell.

When I was done I flopped down exhausted on my bedroll, mopping my sweat-soaked face on the blanket. I'd been lying down for maybe a minute when I heard Darian approaching from the river. I threw the blanket over me and closed my eyes, forcing myself to breath evenly.

"Samara?" Darian said setting down a string of fish.

I didn't answer, just stirred a bit under the blanket.

"Samara?"

"Hmm?" I yawned and made a show of stretching. "Oh good, you're back. I'm famished."

He glanced around our little camp. "I see you didn't have any trouble."

"You were gone so long I decided to take a nap," I said.

"Sorry to disturb your beauty sleep," he said with an annoyed frown.

"I'll forgive you this once," I replied, suppressing a smile.

Darian cooked the fish in the small iron skillet he bought at the general store. I was deciding whether or not to go bathe in the river when Darian pulled out a needle and began sewing on a button that had popped off his surcoat. "Do you know how to hem?" I asked. "One of my skirts is a bit too long."

He heaved a long, labored sigh. "Clearly, I'm the wife in this relationship."

"You do have better child-bearing hips than me."

"I know what I'm going to sew shut with this needle."

"Psh, it's hardly the first time I've heard that threat."

"Somehow that doesn't surprise me."

Over the next two weeks we covered a lot of ground as we found our rhythm and settled into a routine without any sign of our pursuers. We would rise with the sun and do our exercises, eat the leftovers from the night before and be off. We'd stop around noon for a meal of dry rations and to give the horses a break, then get moving again. An hour or two before sundown we would find a place to camp. Darian would tend to the horses and hunt, while I made the fire and put up the tent, which got easier with practice, thankfully. After the meal we would wash up and go to bed. Some nights Darian would play his flute.

As frustrating as he could be, I had to admit Darian was a good traveling companion. The little tent was cramped with the both of us in it, but at least it didn't leak. Darian would sleep crossways at my feet next to the tent flap so he could keep an ear on the horses. He was a light sleeper, which was a comfort to me, though sometimes he did snore. It wasn't too loud but it was constant and grating. I would try to get to sleep before him, usually no chore after a long day of riding, but every now and then he would fall asleep first. In the beginning I'd wake him up gently, but after a while I progressed to simply kicking him in the shoulder.

We avoided main roads and towns as much as possible, figuring them to be the most likely place for an ambush, and traded with the local farms for the things we needed. Some of the farmers we dealt with were friendly and welcoming but several were suspicious, or even openly hostile toward us. I couldn't decide if they treated all outsiders that way, or if it was because of our Dezika guise. I wondered how often I acted that way.

I thought about many things I'd never really considered before, like how bloody tedious most things were. Washing clothes, cleaning dishes, gutting fish, all the little things I never had to do because I'd been born a noble. Things I'd never even noticed being done before, unless of course they were done wrong. I thought back to every time I'd griped at a servant because my food wasn't warm enough or my dress had wrinkles. Honestly, when I thought about it, I was mildly surprised the servants didn't suffocate us all in our sleep.

I mopped the sweat off my brow. The thick canopy of the lowland forest shielded us from the worst of the Azava's burning light, but the humidity was stifling and the air was utterly stagnant. I watched as Darian hung his quiver and bow from his saddle and stripped off his coat, chainmail, and draa shirt. It wasn't the first time I'd seen him shirtless but my eyes lingered on his sweat-soaked form. He wasn't bulky, but every corded muscle was visible, and veins snaked up his arm under the skin.

"That's hardly fair," I said.

"You're welcome to take your shirt off as well, I don't mind," he said. He didn't need to look back, I could hear the smirk in his voice.

"How considerate of you," I said dryly.

"It's not as if I haven't already seen your bare chest," he said.

I didn't consider myself either prudish or shy, but at the thought of him treating my wounds I felt my cheeks flush despite myself. "House Arga frowns upon its ladies riding about half naked in public."

Now he did turn back to face me. "I can't imagine why."

"Do Manu women regularly walk around topless?"

"If it grows hot enough, absolutely."

"And you would be alright with your sister doing that?"

"Why not?" he shrugged.

"You're not afraid some man might lose control and take her?"

He scoffed. "You mean rape her? For merely being shirtless? In my village a man who did that would quickly find himself lacking the needed equipment to do so again."

"A just punishment in my mind," I said.

"I don't understand what all the fuss is about. Don't you Zurans bathe together in big pools?"

"Yes, but it's not the same."

"How so?"

I blew out a deep breath thinking how to explain. "House Arga has an image of modesty to maintain."

He moved to look down the path behind me, then making a show of looking forward, then around. "I don't see any member of House Arga around. Who's here to judge you?"

"Darian Wahya," I said with narrowed eyes and crossed arms. "If I didn't know better I'd think you were just trying to see my breasts again."

He smiled, "Why, I just want you to be comfortabl—"

"Lie," I said.

"Oh, so you have Azava's gift now?"

"No, just a woman's talent for seeing through men's schemes," I said swatting at my arm and splattering a particularly fat mosquito.

He merely chuckled and turned to face forward again spreading his arms and saying, "Ahhh, this is so much better. I may take my boots off and roll my pants up as well."

"You're evil," I said to his sweat-covered back.

That evening after dinner, while Darian was tending to the horses, I noticed the mirror had tarnished. My teacher's visage faded into view replacing mine. I didn't know if it was simply the strange sensation of his face staring back at me from the mirror, but I'd swear he had more gray in his beard, and the crow's feet that pulled at the corner of his eyes had deepened.

"Greetings. I have a small bit of good news. I managed to reach one of my former students in Moravar who is willing to help you return to the Empire once you've completed your task. I'll pause while you get parchment." I quickly shuffled through my endless bag for a loose sheaf of paper and a small piece of charcoal. As I flattened the parchment against my saddle the message continued, "Her name is Shara Stavek, and she has an enchanting business in the west district of Sivat along the north bank of the Brown River. When you meet her you'll need to say the phrase, 'I was hoping to pick up a Vesuvian tea kettle for my aunt,' to which she should reply, 'I have one in blue'. Please approach her discretely."

Master Carter sighed and shifted in his chair. "I've heard nothing regarding Lucius other than your father's offering a sizeable reward for information leading to his whereabouts." He paused to rub his temple like he had a headache. "Autumn wrote me to say that the ruse is still working, though she fears your father may be growing suspicious. That's all I have for you. Stay strong and trust your instincts. May the Gods watch over you both."

I finished scribbling the information down and sent a quick response, saying simply, "By the Gods get some sleep. You look awful."

I stuck the parchment under the cover of one of my journals and walked over to Darian, who was diligently cleaning one of Komala's hooves. "I think we should take the day off tomorrow and rest, the horses could use a break."

"Not to mention the humans," I said. The thought of spending a day *not* riding a horse brought me an irrational amount of joy.

"You're not going soft on me now, are you?" he said looking up from the hoof with his half grin.

"In my defense, I was never hard," I said with a shrug.

I woke up just before dawn, as my body had grown used to, but promptly rolled over and fell back asleep until nearly noon. It was *glorious*.

"Well, look who's finally awake," Darian said when I did rise. He was bare-chested, reclining against a tree sharpening one of his knives, as the rest of his clothes dried in the sun a few yards away.

"You already washed clothes? I was hoping you would do mine too."

He raised his eyebrows. "Something wrong with your hands?"

"No, but you're so much better at it than I am," I said batting my lashes at him.

"Nice try."

"It was worth a shot," I said with a shrug. "Is there any food?"

"Fresh trout," he said.

"You couldn't find anything else?"

He ran his finger gently across the edge of the blade, testing it. "If you don't like my trout your welcome to go hunting for yourself."

"Sorry, it's just that I've never eaten so much fish in my life."

"Better than stale bread, or tough, over-salted jerky."

"Can't argue that, and you're certainly a better cook than I am."

"In that I actually cook?"

I swallowed a flaky bite, then fanned my mouth because it was a bit too hot. "Exactly. What would I do without you?"

"Probably starve."

"Most likely. Can you imagine me hunting? I suppose I could shoot lightning at a deer or something?"

"You could always try nagging them to death."

"You know if this whole horse trader thing ever falls through, you'll have a bright future as a court jester." I blew on the fish to cool it and took another bite. "I just wish we had some spices. I got used to Manu cooking."

"We'll be close to Casca in a week or so, maybe we can find something at the market?"

"Oh, and some cheese. I'd do anything for a nice, creamy wheel of goat cheese," I said imagining it melting in my mouth.

One eyebrow shot up and a broad grin spread across his face. "Anything?"

I shook my head as I set the pan down next to the fire. "Men."

I meditated and took my time with hatha stretching, banishing some of the stiffness from all the time spent on horseback, then took up my endless bag and said, "I'm going to go bathe and wash clothes."

"You can clean out the skillet and fill the water skins while you're down there," he said, blowing the steel dust off his whetstone.

I huffed and grumbled, but I picked up the skillet and skins before tromping down to the water. The bank on our side was a steep, three foot drop to the water, but there was a nice rocky slope on the other side, so I took my boots off and used the roots poking out of the bank to lower myself down. The water was chilly enough to give me goose bumps and perk my nipples, which was a welcome change to the stifling heat, once I adjusted to it. At the deepest part, the creek only came up to my belly, and the water was so clear I could see a school of fish no bigger than my thumb swimming by my toes.

On the rocky bank, I filled the water skins, and scrubbed out the skillet, then set my endless bag down and began pulling out clothes. Virtually everything I had was salt stained, and stank of sweat and horse. I'd long since quit worrying about wearing clean clothes and settled for whatever smelled the least disgusting. I scrubbed everything with the coarse soap until it was as clean as I could get it and, for about the hundredth time, wished Autumn had come with us. She'd have done a much better job.

Not knowing when my next opportunity would be, I stripped off the dress I was wearing and scrubbed clean it as well, laying everything out on the smooth rocks to dry. I dismissed the illusion spell before fishing Master Carter's mirror out of my bag and was delighted to see I wasn't quite as bone-thin as I had been, thanks to two weeks of regular meals.

The cool water was a welcome escape from the stagnant heat as I scrubbed myself clean. When I was finished. I laid back and let the slow gurgling water caress me while my clothes dried. It was so lovely, when I closed my eyes I could almost imagine I was on holiday, and all I needed to do was wave my hand for a beautiful servant to bring me a chilled glass of cider.

I'd almost dozed off when I heard splashing farther down the creek. Just my luck. Some peasant's come down here to fish and instead he's going to find a naked noble in the creek.

I was almost beyond caring.

There was a boulder poking out of the water blocking my view, so I stood up in to peer over it and immediately dropped back into the water. Three Turaggin rode their tall horses down the creek not fifteen yards from where I was. One of them bore burn scars, so there was no chance they were merely some other Turaggin who were just happening by.

My heart beat against my breast like a hammer on a blacksmith's anvil. I didn't know what to do. If I fled up the bank into the woods they'd be on me in a second. I might be able to take them all out with a well-placed gout of fire, but others had to be close by somewhere, and they'd almost certainly notice if their comrades suddenly burst into flames. If there was a fight, Darian would never get here in time to help, so I was naked in a creek by myself.

I searched about frantically for somewhere to hide. Across the creek, some ten yards down there was a sizable nest of branches that had gotten tangled up in the roots of the other bank. It wasn't great but it was the only option I had.

I drew a deep breath and slipped beneath the surface, hugging the bottom as I went. I'd always been a powerful swimmer and there was a strong urge to swim as fast as I could, but I forced myself to go slowly so as not to stir up the bottom or churn the water above me and draw attention to myself. I was positive one of the Turaggin had already spotted me in the shallow, clear water. I'd never felt so vulnerable, so utterly naked in my whole life.

Just as my lungs started to burn I saw the tangled nest of branches above me. If I'd been thinking clearly, I probably would have been terrified of coming across a snake or some other ghastly creature in that mess, but my only thoughts were of hiding from the Turaggin and the burning in my lungs. The branches snagged at my hair and scratched my exposed skin as I rose up to the surface in the middle of them but I hardly cared. As I breached the surface, I fought against the desperate need to gasp for air as I forced my body to breathe slowly, to keep from drawing any more attention to myself.

I could barely see out as I peered through the tangled web of branches. To my relief—and utter amazement—somehow they hadn't noticed me. They did however discover my clothes lying about on the rocks. They immediately started barking choppy, guttural statements at each other and searching about.

One of the men was scanning the bank when his eyes fell directly on my hiding place and lingered there. My heart froze in my chest and my breath caught. He'd seen me. It was over.

One of the other men grunted and pointed past my clothes into the tree line, and the one who was watching me turned and led his horse up onto the bank peering into the woods. One by one they went in a line up into the trees, searching about for me.

Where were they going? Realization rained down on me like Azava's light through parting clouds. My clothes were drying on that bank, so they thought our camp was over there. I could just wait here until they were out of sight, then climb up the bank behind me and run back to Darian. I'd be running nude through the woods but at least…

My heart sank as my eyes settled on my endless bag.

The Sarga Paza was in there.

I fought back tears as terror again rose in my chest again. I might need the book when I got to Vizipa, I couldn't leave without it. I could still hear the Turaggin crashing around just past the tree line searching for me, and only the Gods knew where the red-robed mages were. Panic was welling up inside of me but I forced my breathing to be even.

Why can't things ever be simple?

I knew what I had to do. There was no point mulling it over. It was never going to get any less scary. I took a few deep breaths, then finally one last gulp and disappeared beneath the water again. As before I stuck close to the bottom, but this time I wasn't worried about swimming slowly to avoid churning the water. I went as fast as I could.

My breast scraped painfully against the small sharp rocks as I came up the other bank. I could still hear their horses just out of my vision, no more than thirty paces away. I was shaking so badly I almost couldn't make it out of the water. I moved low and quiet, inch by inch, positive I was going to be spotted at any moment. Finally, my fingers found the smooth material of my bag and I snatched it up, clutching it to my chest like a childhood doll.

I retreated as quickly and quietly as I could, lowering myself back into the creek. I disappeared beneath the surface one last time, trusting the enchantment on my pouch to keep the water out of it. I swam so hard I almost crashed headfirst into the bank. As I came up out of the water I used the roots to pull myself up like a monkey.

When I felt the earth beneath me again I bolted, running with everything I had back to Darian. Rocks, roots, and sharp plants tore at my bare feet and legs, but spurred by my terror I paid them no heed. For about the hundredth time since I'd started on this journey I wondered if I was favored by the Gods, or cursed by them.

Chapter Twenty
Darian

The grass was soft beneath my back as Azava's light warmed my skin. The gentle wind brought with it the scent of wildflowers and distant rain. At least I had today. A day without stress, or fear, or worry. I decided I would be thankful for that. Then Samara came tearing through the woods naked.

"Samara, what's wrong? Are you hurt?" I asked gaining my feet. She was soaked and trying to catch her breath, but other than the scrapes and cuts one might expect to incur sprinting through the woods bare-ass naked, she seemed unharmed.

Between gulps of air she managed to get out, "Three…Turaggin…down by… creek…"

"Did they see you? Where were the rest of them? Where were the mages?" I demanded as I shoved one of my half-dry shirts into her hands.

"Didn't see me…don't know…" She said as she slipped the shirt over her head. It was large enough that it came to her mid-thigh.

"How in the..? Never mind," I said, shaking my head. "Bring the horses." I shoved my clothes and our meager supplies into the packs.

When she returned with the horses I saddled them and threw the packs on them in record time. "Tent?" Samara asked finally managing to catch her breath.

"No time. Leave it," I practically threw her on her horse and flung my surcoat on before jumping into my own saddle. We tore off at a gallop to the northwest, fleeing yet another camp.

I kept glancing behind us, expecting to see black turbans, red robes, or copper wasps, though thankfully I found none. We pressed on until our horses were exhausted and the waning sun cast long shadows through the trees.

We stopped at a small pond to let the horses quench their thirst. As Samara dismounted, she winced and grabbed the saddle to steady herself.

"What's wrong?" I asked.

"I guess the gashes in my feet are worse than I thought. Now that I'm not fleeing for my life, the pain's caught up to me," she said rotating her ankle to get a look at her bloody sole.

"Let's get those wounds washed out and closed. The last thing we need is you getting an infection out here. Though I did bring some Propolus just in case," I added with a sly smile.

"I'd almost rather you chop off the foot instead." She tried to take a step and winced again.

"Here, hold on to me." I knelt down a bit and she slid her arm around my neck, but it was still awkward with our height difference. "I think it'll just be easier if I carry you."

"I'm not helpless," she huffed.

"I know it goes against everything in your nature, but could you please not be difficult? Just this once?"

"Whatever. Just be mindful of wandering hands."

"I'll try to restrain myself," I said dryly. She kept her arm around my neck as I scooped her up like a child, one arm under her knees, the other at her low back. I carried her a few strides out into the pond and set her down on a large rock, then began gently washing her wounds. The water must have been spring-fed because it was shockingly cold. A couple of the cuts were pretty deep. It was a wonder she made it all the way back to camp with such tender feet.

"The cold water feels good," she said. "I seem to recall you saying there was no way they could track us."

I frowned. "They didn't track us."

"All evidence to the contrary," she said with raised brows. "Perhaps their noses are just better—"

"They could have the nose of a *black bear* and it wouldn't matter. There's no way they tracked us by scent over water. Period. They *must* be using magic to find us."

"We've been over this. You can't use magic to spy on people, only places. It's likely they simply followed us to the town and asked around until Captain Bjorn told them—"

"They wouldn't have caught up to us so soon," I countered, as I washed the cuts on her calf.

"We slowed our pace, and we took a day off. If they pushed hard the whole time…" she trailed off.

"It would have taken Bjorn at least twice as long to go upriver to town as it took us to go down. That puts them, at best, a full week behind us. We didn't slow down that much. Which means they must have exited the mountains from the east and then turned south, while somehow managing to track us through a hundred miles of forest." I blew out a long breath and splashed some of the cold water on my face. "It's not my pride talking, Samara, its experience. I'm telling you, the only way they could have found us is with magic."

"And **I'm** telling you the limitations of the magic. Perhaps there's some other way they're finding us we haven't considered yet?"

I bit my lip in frustration. *By the Gods, that woman would argue with her dying breath.* "Perhaps," I said, too weary to discuss it any farther. "Let me do a healing, then we'll see about fashioning something to cover your feet."

She glanced down at her bare legs poking out from beneath the oversized shirt. "And some pants would be lovely."

Despite my weariness I smiled. "Don't get all dressed up on my account."

Samara looked ridiculous, but at least she was clothed. Wearing my shirt and rolled up pants, she looked like a child playing dress-up in her parents' closet. I'd been able to fashion some shoes for her from a couple of grain sacks tied with twine. We'd had to leave some things behind, but it could have been much worse. At least it didn't rain.

The next morning, we were up with the first of Azava's rays. We hoped to rely on our previous tactics of just pushing our Manu mounts and outrunning our pursuers, but the dense woods slowed our progress. It was hard going, made even harder by our nearly exhausted dry rations, and the fact that we had one water skin between us. Still, at least we didn't see any turbans or robes. When we finally stopped it was well after dark.

We were just about to go to bed when Samara began frantically searching through her enchanted bag. "No," she pleaded, her eyes going wide. "Nonononono—"

"What's the matter?"

Tears welled up as she covered her mouth. "I left Master Carter's mirror on the rocks next to my clothes. Our pursuers must have it. "

"Damn it." I sat down and ran my fingers through my hair. We couldn't communicate with Master Carter anymore, but in the overall scheme of things it wasn't that bad. Just one more bump in the road. I looked up to see Samara's tear-stained face. "At least you remembered to grab your bag." I leaned over and put my hand on her back. "It's alright."

"No, it's not alright," she said wiping her face and brushing my hand off. "We need that mirror. What if he discovers something vitally important? What if he sends a message that tells them exactly what our plan is?"

"We have a plan?" I said dryly.

"This is *serious*. We have to try to go back for it."

"Have you gone mad?"

"We have to try to—"

"Absolutely not."

"Darian, despite what the Vija saw, I'm not sure I can do this on my own. I may need to draw on Master Carter's knowledge when we get to Vizipa."

I stood up and started pacing. I'd never known Samara to be particularly modest. If she said she might need to talk to Master Carter, I had no doubt she believed it. "What do you propose we do? Fight them all? Go back and ask them politely if we can have it back?"

She sent an annoyed glance my way. "Of course not. I can summon a demon to try and steal it back."

I just stared at her wide-eyed.

"What?" she asked.

"No."

"Look, it's no big deal."

"How could you even think about summoning a demon when we're up against people trying to open a gate to Hell?"

"Don't be so obtuse, most demons don't even—"

"You're not summoning a demon," I said. I couldn't believe I was having this conversation. I couldn't think of a better example to perfectly sum up the problem my people had with magic. I bent down to pick my saddle off the ground and said, "I'll see what I can do."

"By yourself? It's too dangerous," Samara said, her brows coming together. She actually looked worried.

"If I can't find the mirror, I'll just leave."

"I'm going with you," she said, climbing to her feet.

"We've already been over this, remember? If they get you they win. Anyway, with Tarka's gift I have the best chance of remaining unnoticed if I go alone."

"No," Samara said chewing on her lip. "No. We'll find another way."

"You said you need the mirror right?"

She glanced down at her feet for a moment. "I'll find a way to make do without it." Azava's gift told me she didn't believe that, at least not completely.

"Lie," I said, throwing the saddle back on Tavas, who didn't look happy about it.

"No, Darian. Don't you dare leave me here alone." With a jerky motion she wiped away tears that had started falling again.

"I'll be careful. I won't do anything reckless."

It was her turn to stare at me with arms crossed. "I suppose there's a first time for everything."

"I'll return. I promise."

She shook her head. "I don't like this."

I mounted Tavas and said, "If I'm not back by morning push on without me and I'll catch up." I turned and rode off before she could make some other objection.

We galloped for a mile or so, Tavas trusting me to be his eyes in the darkness, before slowing to a walk. We made our way cautiously after that, both of us alert to the slightest change in the environment. After perhaps another two miles the smell of cooking meat caught my nose. I dismounted and said quietly to the horse, "*Wait here.*" He snorted a reply and bent his head to graze the tender grass.

I called Tarka's gift and paced silently through the forest, following my nose until I could see the darting shadows cast by a camp fire. I took care to move with extra caution as I crept around until I was down wind. With the darkness and Tarka's gift, I was fairly certain none of the Turaggin would notice me, but I was far less sure about the tattooed mages. Either way, I was wary of startling the horses. I didn't forget to search the air above or keep my ears tuned for the buzz of wasps.

The Turaggin weren't being particularly quiet. I could make out their rough tongue as I grew closer. I approached the tree line from the side opposite the horses and took extra care with the last twenty yards or so, worried they might have set traps. I peered around a large oak and surveyed their camp.

The small clearing they'd set up camp in was cramped. Two large, hide-covered, dome tents dominated the clearing with a smaller Imperial-style tent off to the side. The Turaggin were spread out among the tiny camp. A few were chopping vegetables over a large bowed wok from which wafted the enticing aroma of cooking chicken. Several crouched naked around a shared water bucket and were washing themselves with rags, while others milled about stacking firewood or shuffling in and out of the tents. On the far side of the camp, two or three of them were tending to the horses. I noticed with surprise that one of the horses was the one that Marcus had been holding onto when he was killed.

Irrational anger sprang up in me at the thought of them claiming one of *my peoples'* horses, but I shouldn't have been shocked. What were they going to do, pass up a free horse? To the victor go the spoils, as the Zurans say. Still, it grated like sand in my eye. Then something occurred to me. I didn't see any other Manu horses, which meant there was a reasonable chance that Lucius and the houseguards had eluded them. I breathed a silent prayer that it was so.

An eerie green light emanating from the open flap of the smaller tent drew my attention. Two green blotches of coldfire illuminated the recumbent forms of Snake-Jaw and Waspgina, as they lay conversing on opposite bedrolls in a rambling, melodic tongue I didn't recognize. I couldn't see the mirror, but several packs lay strewn about the tent. It had to be in one of those if they had it with them.

There was no way I was going to be able to rifle through the mages' things while they were lying next to them. Waspgina laughed at something Snake-Jaw said like they were sitting in a café somewhere gossiping, rather than running Samara and I down to murder us. They looked so vulnerable that I thought again about putting an arrow through each of their necks. But I remembered how well that worked out last time I tried it, and it would definitely violate my promise to Samara not to do anything reckless. So, instead, I settled in to wait for an opportunity to sneak into the small canvas tent.

I'd hardly eaten anything in the last two days and the heady aroma of cooking meat permeating the area set my belly to grumbling. Maybe I could steal some food as well without them noticing it? My pulse quickened as a realization suddenly bloomed in my mind. There was only one large cooking pan, so everyone was going to be eating from it.

I quietly withdrew from my position, retreating back the way I'd approached, staying downwind of the horses. I was the son of a healer, and I'd been helping my mother look for medicinal plants since I was a child. The difference between a medicine and a poison was often only dosage.

I hurried down to a creek I'd crossed a few hundred yards back hoping to find some nightshade. There weren't any dark purple berries, but I did see something that would suit my purpose in a pinch. I harvested half dozen or so of the red-spotted mushrooms and used one of my daggers to dice them up, then made haste back to the clearing.

It looked like I'd arrived just in time. The meal was almost ready. I kept the fire between me and the cooks as I crept to the wok, hoping the smoke and haze would further camouflage Tarka's gift since I was right in front of them. The mushrooms would become visible as soon as I released them, so I had to stick my hand right down into the pot before I let go. Hot oil popped painfully against my knuckles but I managed to deposit my special ingredients without being spotted, which blended in immediately with the stir-fried rice, chicken, and vegetables. I smiled to myself as I retreated back to the tree line. One thing was sure, it would be a meal they wouldn't forget anytime soon.

Chapter Twenty-One
Samara

As weary as I was, there was no way I was going to find sleep even if I searched for it, so I didn't bother. Instead, I sat hugging my legs to my chest and resting my chin on my knees as Ananda's light peeked through the canopy. The thought of being left alone to complete my journey was utterly terrifying. I tried to keep my mind busy and stop my thoughts from wandering down a dark path. It worked for a while. Then I started thinking about all the things that could go wrong. How Darian could be injured or killed trying to steal back the mirror that I left behind.

I decided to pray to Arati and Ananda, Goddesses of darkness and the moon, to watch over Darian and keep him safe. Komala's head poked up from where he'd been dozing a few yards away and his ears perked forward. I'd picked up enough to know to pay attention to the horses. Darian melted through the brush a moment later and the knot that my stomach was balled into began to ease.

"By the Gods, it took you long enough. Did you get lost or something?" I said.

"I figured you'd be asleep."

"Like I could sleep with you out there risking your life. Did you get the mirror?"

"I waited around, but Snake-Jaw and Waspgina never left their tent, so I couldn't search it," he said as he dismounted.

"Damn." There's was something about Darian's demeanor that was off, the way he held himself, a slight pull to his lip. If I hadn't spent so much time around him recently I wouldn't have noticed. I crossed my arms and said, "Then why do you seem so pleased with yourself?"

Now he did grin. "I bought us a few days to get a good lead on them."

My eyes narrowed. "What did you do?"

"Don't worry, no one even knew I was there. I just added a special ingredient to their dinner. For the next few days they'll be too busy holding their bellies and squatting in the woods to chase us."

"Well, that's something," I said. Perhaps we'd gained a few days respite, but we still didn't have the mirror.

Darian unbuckled his saddle and sat it on the ground. "Don't fret. It's not as if they're going to give up the pursuit now. We'll likely have another chance to get the mirror back." He took a deep pull from our water skin and said, "Even if we can't, I have every faith you'll be able to figure out what needs to be done by yourself."

"That makes one of us," I said with a glower. "Did you learn anything else?"

"Perhaps..," he hesitated.

"What? Is it about Lucius?" My heart griped in my chest.

"I think Lucius and the guards might have escaped."

When he didn't continue I prompted, "Because?"

"The Turaggin claimed the horse Marcus was holding when he died, but they didn't have any others—"

My heart leapt. "Which means that Lucius might be alive!"

"It's not for certain but..."

"I'll take it," I said, hopping to my feet and throwing my arms around him. When I pulled away he flinched a bit. "What?"

"I was afraid you were going to slap me."

"You didn't do anything stupid or reckless did you?"

His eyes narrowed like he was searching for a trick. "No..."

I reached out and gave him a quick, easy pat on the cheek. "See? You're learning."

———————————

I felt lighter the next day, despite the lack of sleep, despite the grumbling from my belly, despite the fact I was wearing Darian's clothes with grain sacks on my feet, and despite the fact we'd lost the mirror. The tiny bit of evidence we had that Lucius might be alive lifted my spirits enough to push those other concerns to the back of my mind.

We continued on as though we were still being chased, trying to put as much distance between us and our hopefully-incapacitated pursuers as we could manage. We'd ran out of dry rations the day before however, and by midday the hunger gnawing at the pit of my stomach was too much to ignore.

"Alright, you have to hunt something," I said to Darian. "I'm in at least the third stage of starvation."

"There's no point in hunting until this evening when we can make a fire. Unless of course you're willing to eat it raw?" he asked with a sly smile.

"*Ugh,* I'm not that desperate," I said, wrinkling my nose. "Not yet, anyway."

"Then you can wait until tonight."

"If we stop for a quarter hour or so I can come up with something."

He twisted in the saddle to face me. "*You're* going to forage?"

I smiled back. "In my own way. Don't tell me you're not hungry."

"Starving. A quarter hour you say?"

"No longer."

"Fine, we can stop. The horses could use a break anyway."

We dismounted and I began rummaging through my endless bag for the things I needed. "Hand me one of those daggers," I said, gesturing to the blades crossed at his low back.

He drew one of the daggers, extending it to me handle first. "Careful, its sharp."

I took the blade and used it to dig a little hole, then dropped in a seed I'd held onto from a wild persimmon I'd eaten a week before, and pushed the dirt back over it. I knelt before the little mound and began casting.

Wispy, pale blue tendrils crept from my hands and snaked into the small mound. I brushed the dirt off my hands and stood up, extending Darian's knife back to him handle first as he'd handed it to me.

Darian pursed his lips as he accepted the blade back. "So, now what?"

"Now we wait."

After a pause he asked, "For how long?"

"Not long."

"You sure you know what you're doing?"

A tiny green shoot about a finger's length slithered out of the mound. Darian snickered saying, "Oh yes, that's truly a bountiful harvest."

"And you're always saying *I'm* the impatient one," I huffed. "Just wait a moment."

The shoot continued to thicken and reach skyward, sprouting branches as it went until the trunk was as thick around as my wrist and it was slightly taller than the horses. Thin leaves sprouted in every direction followed by green spheres that swelled and changed colors before our eyes, ripening to a reddish orange hue before dropping to the ground.

"Suravani's horns…" Darian said, staring wide eyed and slack jawed. "You could feed every hungry mouth in the world with this magic."

"Sadly no, it depletes the soil for several seasons, so it's not sustainable," I said kneeling to fill the burlap sack our dry rations had been in. "It is however, quite useful for feeding legions that have been cut off from their supply line." I took a bite out of one of the persimmons. As its sweet juice dribbled down my chin I added, "And hungry mages."

Darian shook his head picking up a piece of the fruit as if he couldn't believe it was real. "Zurans."

"Try one. They're delicious."

"I'm not sure…The elders warn—"

I rolled my eyes. "Again with the Manu superstition! It's not as if you were the one who cast the spell. You haven't stepped off your 'path of balance' or whatever."

"But…"

"Wouldn't it be wasteful if you didn't eat it?"

"I suppose…"

"It's not as if I'm going to force you to eat," I shrugged. "More for me if you don't anyway."

He sighed then took a tentative bite, then rolled his eyes back in pleasure, savoring the flavor. "It is delicious."

"You know, you're surprisingly easy to corrupt," I said with a wink.

"So it seems," he chuckled, flicking the juice that was on his fingers at me. The leaves of the little tree were already starting to turn yellow and flutter to the ground. Darian popped another of the ripe fruits in his mouth and said, "I don't suppose you can grow a salmon tree?"

I put one hand on my hip. "Find me a salmon seed and I'll see what I can do."

Over the next two days the forest thinned, giving way to farms and vineyards. As soon as we came across a road we took to it, favoring speed over stealth since it seemed our enemies could track us no matter what precautions we took, though I did recast the illusion spell. Long, neat rows of grapes stretched into the distance on one side of the road while fat goats and shaggy long-haired cattle grazed on the other side.

After crossing a rickety old bridge the road merged with a well maintained highway. Darian pulled out the map and studied it, trying to discern our location. "I think we just crossed over into Madhyama," he said. "Do you know anything about it?"

I wiped the sweat from my brow as I tried to recall my schooling. "It's a monarchy. If I remember correctly, the king's name is Tulic, or Tolmick, or something. I do remember they make pretty good wine, though not as good as the Empire's obviously."

"Obviously," Darian said with an eye roll. "Everything from the Empire *must* be better."

Ignoring his barb, I said, "Maybe we can buy some supplies from one of the locals?" I tugged on the oversized shirt. "And perhaps a dress?"

He let out an exaggerated sigh and said, "So needy." I started to quip back but his eyes held laughter. "I'd already planned on it. We need grain for the horses at the very least so we don't have to spend so much time grazing them."

The thought of warm bread made me salivate. "Grain for the humans wouldn't go unappreciated either."

Unfortunately we were gruffly turned away from a farmhouse and a vineyard without even getting a chance to explain we had coin to spend. "Not very hospitable, are they?" I said.

"They certainly risk Kavi's wrath," Darian said with a frown. "Perhaps there's been trouble with travelers in these lands. Hopefully third time's the charm."

We approached a group of five buildings set off from the road next to a large barn, but as we drew closer, Darian's gaze fell on a group of men working the fields and his expression soured. "We may not have any better luck after all. They're Kathoran." Despite the heat the men all wore slate gray coats and wide brimmed hats, and except for the children, they all sported full untrimmed beards.

"What does that mean?"

"The Kathora are very superstitious."

"This coming from a Manu?"

He shot me an annoyed glance. "Their superstitions direct how they dress, what they eat, when they should pray, what days they can do business, pretty much everything. And they're not too keen on outsiders. I tried to sell them some horses one time and they wouldn't even talk to me. We might as well just turn around and head back to the road."

"Are they dangerous?"

He considered that for a moment then shook his head. "No. Actually, I think they're pacifists."

"Well then we might as well talk to them. We don't have anything to lose from trying, do we?"

Darian shrugged. "I suppose not. Just don't let them know you're a mage, it might not go over well."

As we neared one of the houses a broad chested man with gray streaks in his long black beard stood in front of us with two younger men, likely his sons. He looked us over with discerning hazel eyes.

"Greetings and well met," Darian said, bowing from the saddle, "I'm Luca, and this is my wife, Ylsa."

He shifted uncomfortably. "Greetings. I am Thol, and these are my sons Vrak, and Sel." His gaze cast back and forth between us. "What do you want?"

I could see several pairs of eyes staring at us from the windows of the nearest house, which was painted the same slate gray as their clothes. "We just need some supplies," Darian said.

"What sort of supplies?"

"Grain for the horses mostly, and a couple of extra water skins if you have it." I cleared my throat and Darian added, "Oh, and a dress and some shoes if you've any to spare."

"We…we're just farmers, we have very little…"

Darian said, "We can pay, we have coin."

Thol's gaze rested on Darian's bow. "We don't have much to spare…"

"Please," I said. "We were forced to run from bandits and had to leave our supplies behind." It was close enough to the truth.

He took a deep breath and stroked his beard in contemplation. "I am not sure—"

"Thol!" a middle aged woman shouted as she stomped out of the house. She wore a full length, high collared dress with longs sleeves the same gray color the men wore, her hair covered in a matching scarf. "What are you thinking? Do they look like bandits to you?"

"Katja I was just—"

The woman looked right at Darian. "My husband will sell you whatever you need."

Darian seemed taken aback. "Th-thank you."

She turned to face me. "Now, you come with me child and we'll see if we can't find something for you to wear." I glanced at Darian who nodded. As I dismounted, Katja looked me over, "You and my oldest are about the same height. We should have something that will fit you."

"Thank you for your kindness," I said, "Truly."

"It's nothing, child. Sorry about my husband. Men can be bull-headed sometimes."

I glanced back at Darian. "Don't I know."

The dress that Katja found for me was an identical copy to the one worn by all the women. It was a bit loose in the chest but was otherwise a pretty good fit. The rough-spun gray fabric was hot and itchy but I was hardly going to complain. I had to squish my toes together to fit into the hard-worn leather boots I was presented with, but it was a far cry better than the grain sacks I'd been wearing.

It's amazing how quickly perspective can change.

———————————

Thol and Katja fed us a dinner of blackbird pie, which was a first for me, and offered to let us sleep in their house for the evening, but we declined, needing to gain distance on our pursuers and not wanting to bring danger to their home. We bid them farewell and took to the road again.

After we'd gone a mile or so I said, "You were wrong. They were very hospitable."

"So they were," he shrugged. "It happens every now and then."

"Kathora being hospitable?"

He smiled slyly. "Me being wrong."

"Do you really want me to start keeping count?"

"Go ahead, we can tally up who was right more often when this is all over. Or you could just go ahead and admit defeat now, it would be easier."

"Whatever, there's no way you're right more often than I am. Besides, what in our history together would make you think I ever do the easy thing?"

"You certainly have a point. First blackbird pie?"

"Was it that obvious?"

He chuckled. "I'm not surprised, it's not much of a highborn delicacy. How was it?"

"Delicious. Of course I was hungry enough I probably would've eaten hog slop and been grateful for it."

"So your culinary standards have lowered to hog slop now, eh? That was fast."

"All my standards have lowered," I said, glancing sideways at him. "Just look at the company I'm keeping."

"I'll bet you have line of smitten noble boys eagerly awaiting your return in White Harbor."

"Hardly. A few lovers perhaps, but I'm sure they've found someone else to warm their beds by now."

"There's no one special?"

"No, what would be the point?" When his brow wrinkled in confusion I continued. "A noble's marriage is arranged by their House."

"What?"

"Ah, so that isn't in your library is it?"

"No," he said looking away. "I'm sorry."

"Darian, don't be so dramatic. It's alright. It's not as if I'm being sold to a slaver."

His eyes met mine absent his usual bravado. "You're really alright with it?"

"Yes," I said, chuckling at his serious demeanor. "My parents grew to love each other very much."

We rode for a few moments in silence before he spoke again. "How does it work?"

I paused trying to think of the best way to explain it. "When my family thinks it's time, they'll try to arrange a marriage that brings honor to the House. Usually that means a match with a noble from one of the other great Houses, but sometimes it's different with women."

"Why?"

"When a woman marries she becomes a member of her husband's House. Though sometimes it brings more honor to the House to keep a woman within their ranks, so they'll usually marry her to a distant cousin within the house, or even a commoner."

His brows went up. "A commoner?"

"Usually someone the House owes a large debt too, or a very wealthy, influential merchant. The commoner is elevated into the House and the family doesn't lose the woman in question."

"That's what you want, isn't it?"

I considered my answer carefully. "I want whatever brings the most glory and honor to my house."

"Half-truth," he said.

I sighed, "Alright, I would prefer to stay with House Arga. If I somehow manage to pull this off I might even be able to arrange it."

"What if you're betrothed to some old, fat, hideous slob?"

"The House tries to arrange the best marriage possible. After all, it looks bad if they arrange a terrible match. Anyway, it's not as if I couldn't take lovers if it suited me. The House hardly cares as long as I give them two or three little noble babies and don't cause a scandal."

"What if they married you off to someone who beat you?"

I raised an eyebrow. "Assuming I didn't roast him the first time he raised a hand?"

He grinned. "Assuming that."

"I'd divorce him and leaved him shamed."

He shook his head. "The whole concept is just so foreign to me."

"Your people never had arranged marriages? It's always been love matches?"

"As far as I know. What of the commoners of the Empire?"

"Some of both, but usually it doesn't benefit a common family to arrange a marriage. Sometimes freemen arrange to have their daughters wed to citizens, but usually if they have the coin for that they can just pay for citizenship."

"You can *buy* citizenship? I thought the only way to become a citizen was through service?"

"It's expensive, but yes."

"Zurans," he said shaking his head. "What House is your mother from?"

The question caught me off guard. "What?"

"You said noble women took the name of their husband's House. Which one did she come from?"

I pursed my lips and looked down. "Paska."

"And she didn't mind leaving her family to join House Arga?"

"No, she knew her duty. And she loved my father."

He paused for a moment. "Loved?"

It was still hard to talk about it after all this time. "She was on her way to her cousin's wedding on an island off Galeswept when they sailed into a summer squall." I took a deep breath and continued, "Her ship broke apart. There were no survivors."

"That's the reason you don't like boats?" I nodded feeling my eyes tear up. Darian said, "I'm sorry. You don't have to talk about it."

I shook my head and rubbed at my eyes. "It's alright. I shouldn't still be this emotional after so much time."

"No, I understand." Pain so raw it hurt to look at crossed his face.

"Sitana?" I asked. He looked at me with questioning eyes. "I asked Pushpa about the carving in your house. I thought it was a statue of Ananda."

A sad smile graced his face, like he was reliving some private joke. "She would have laughed at the comparison."

"She was beautiful," I said.

"Aye," he answered, eyes gazing far off to the horizon. "Beautiful and stubborn. I told her she should have left sooner for her mother, but she wanted to wait for me to get back from Stonehaven." I must have looked confused because he explained, "It's a Manu custom that a woman bears her child in the home of her mother, and Sitana's lived in another village."

I felt tears come back to my eyes. "She was with child?"

He nodded, his lip quivering. "I told her it was too late, that she could send for her mother to come to us, but she wouldn't hear of it." He blew out a bitter sigh and shook his head. "She said she knew her own body, that we had at least a week before the child would come. So I relented. I just wanted her to be happy. We loaded up the wagon and left for her mother's. But after half a day she started having pains and went into labor." Tears slid from his distant gaze as he continued, "Something was wrong, it…It wasn't normal…There was so much blood. I couldn't…They…" He dropped his head in his hands and roughly wiped away the tears.

"Darian…"

"Maybe…Maybe I could have saved them if I'd been a stronger healer, more like my mother…"

His pain was a tangible thing, a great snake that wrapped around him, crushing the breath from his lungs. I felt horrible for making him relive it. I said the only thing I could think of. "You were strong enough to save me."

He inhaled deeply then let out a long, slow breath, seeming to regain his composure and said nothing for several minutes. I couldn't think of anything to say, so we rode in silence until he said, "What's the first thing you're going to do when you get home?"

The abrupt change of subject caught me off guard, but he obviously didn't want to talk about Sitana anymore. "Take a bath," I said. "A hot, rose-scented bath, with a gaggle of servants to attend me." I closed my eyes imagining it. "It might last days."

He shook his head and managed a slight smile. "Why am I not surprised?"

"What about you?"

"Well, a hot bath sounds nice, but first I'm going to have a nice cup of spiced tea with horse milk, and then a shot of whiskey."

I wrinkled my nose. "Ugh, horse milk?"

"What's wrong with horse milk?"

"It just sounds vile, drinking the milk that comes out of a horse."

He twisted in the saddle to face me and shot me an incredulous look. "How is drinking the secretions that come out of a cow or a goat any more disgusting than what comes out of a horse?"

He had me there I suppose. "I don't know, it's just icky."

"You didn't seem to mind it when you were recovering in my home."

"I didn't drink any horse milk."

His vexing grin spread across his face as he said, "Did you see any cows in Vana? Where did you think the milk for your tea came from?"

The face I made sent him into a fit of laughter that surely had the other travelers on the road thinking he was touched in the head.

"A *proper* cup of tea does sound lovely, and some wine."

"Zuran wine, of course," he said with an eye roll.

"That goes without saying."

Before I went to sleep that evening I pulled out the map and ran my finger along the distance we had yet to go to Vizipa. It seemed impossible that we still had so far to travel. I traced the path we'd taken, wondering where our pursuers were. The rest of the journey might not be very long after all if we couldn't find a way to deal with them. Definitively.

Chapter Twenty-Two
Darian

There was a long line of people ahead of us waiting to pay the toll and be on their way. After half an hour of listening to Samara huff impatiently, I'd gone up to the front of the line to investigate. When I returned she said, "Well?"

"A wagon load of chickens overturned on the bridge."

"How much longer do you think it'll be?"

"Well, the wagon is still on its side and chickens are running around everywhere."

She heaved a labored sigh and pulled at the neck of her dress as shimmering pearls of sweat beaded on her forehead. "Ugh, I'm roasting. How do those women wear these dresses in the summer?"

"You could always go back to wearing my clothes."

"At least these aren't falling off of me. When I get the chance I might cut the sleeves…off…" She trailed off, squinting back the direction we'd come from, then in a low urgent voice said, "Darian, *look*."

My chest tightened as I glanced back to see black turbans and red robes coming around the bend a half mile down the highway. I exhaled a long tired breath. "It's not like we didn't see this coming."

"What do we do?"

"We're going to get out of line and ride casually up to the front."

"But the bridge is still blocked off."

"Horses can swim remember? Just follow my lead."

Samara chewed on her lip but said nothing more. We walked our horses out of the column to the right, earning several jeers and sour looks from those waiting in line. I picked out a handful of silver coins from my pouch as we neared the bridge. A husky guard in rust-colored leather armor was standing in front of the bridge taking the brunt of the sweltering travelers' frustration. As we approached he said, "Back in line."

"You're collecting tolls, right?" I said.

"Yes, but you can wait like everybody else."

I tossed the handful of silver at him, easily twice what the toll would be, and said, "Keep the change," then spurred Tavas down the hill toward the river, Samara right behind me.

"Hey wait, come back! You can't just—"

His voice was lost as we plunged into the churning river. The water was deep and the horses immediately started swimming. The current was much stronger than I expected, sweeping us downstream even as our horses fought to make it to the far bank. I glanced back to check on Samara, her eyes were wide but she held on as Komala strained to get to the other side. By the time our horses gained their footing on the opposite bank we'd been swept over a hundred yards from the bridge.

"Sorry. I didn't expect the current to be so strong," I said.

"At least the swim cooled me off. What now?"

"Same plan as always," I said as we fled into the woods for what felt like the thousandth time.

We rode hard for several hours until the horses needed a rest. The forest was mostly old growth oak and ash so it was fairly open and it had a wildness to it, as if humans didn't intrude very often.

We stopped at a small pond to let the horses drink as we refilled our water skins. Samara knelt and splashed water her face, then took the skin and poured it over her head before refilling it. "I've just about had enough of this," she said.

"Can you imagine how frustrated the Turaggin are? We're running for our lives. They just want to get paid."

"Bloody Turaggin," Samara said, "They almost invaded the Empire a couple hundred years ago."

"I know, the Manu fought in that war."

"They're nothing but brutal thugs, and all their mages are all *necromancers*," she spat the last word out.

My brows went up in surprise. "Necromancy troubles you?"

"Of course. Doesn't it trouble you?"

"Well yes, but…"

She stood up putting her hands on her hips, "But what?"

"Samara, you summon demons. How is that better than necromancy?"

She stared at me with her mouth open. "It's disrespectful to the dead."

"So, to make sure I understand, in the Empire summoning demons is fine but raising zombies is taboo?"

"They're not the same thing at all," she huffed. "You realize without magic and demons that humans would never have won the Dragon War, right? We'd all still be kowtowing and making constant offerings to keep from being served up as a snack-rifice."

I started to respond when a faint, droning buzz caught my attention. I turned scanning the canopy for the source of the noise, and Samara followed my gaze. A coppery glint flashed a beam of sunlight that was filtered through the trees.

"Wasps?" Samara whispered.

"What else?" I sighed. "Come on, let's go."

As soon as we mounted, the wasps took notice of us, and buzzed down from the treetops. I could see half a dozen at least. Our horses were tired but we had no choice. We sped off at a full gallop. The little bastards were fast but we managed to make some gains against them.

"Wait," Samara said. I slowed Tavas to a canter and she came up next to me. "Do you feel that?"

There was a light prickle on my skin. I cast my gaze up into the trees to see a blue jay staring at me with seeming interest. It blinked three sets of eyes at me. "Bloody hell, we just rode into a *verge*."

"What do we do?" she asked glancing back to at the wasps a few dozen yards behind us.

"We can't go back, the wasps are right behind us. We'll have to try to go through."

"Are you sure that's a good plan?"

"No," I said honestly. "But we have nothing but bad options, and right now this seems like the least bad."

She gave a shaky laugh. "Does it seem like that happens to us a lot?"

"We're just lucky I suppose. Try to stay as calm as you can. If there's any Fae around maybe they'll be drawn to our pursuers instead of us." She nodded and we again galloped off, asking the horses to give us whatever they had left.

Eventually we lost the wasps. After a half hour with no droning or coppery flashes, we slowed to a walk. The horses were exhausted, nearly spent. I gazed through the thick ceiling of leaves trying to judge the sun's position. "We have maybe two hours of light left. Let's find a place to make camp."

"We're not going to push on until dark?" Samara asked.

I shook my head. "The horses are done. If we push them any further one of them will falter." I patted Tavas on the neck. "But that means that either their beasts are done for as well, or we have such a lead on them they won't find us before dark. Either way I need to get some sleep before night falls."

"Why?"

"Because, at the moment, we're in more danger from some Fae, undead, or verge twisted creature stumbling upon us in our sleep than we are from the people chasing us," I said. "Which means one of us is going to have to stay awake tonight, and it should probably be the one that can see in the dark."

"Fair enough," she said, pulling at the neck of her gown. "Lead the way."

We found a place that was mostly hidden from view and unloaded the horses. I gave them generous portions of our dwindling grain supply because I wasn't thrilled with the idea of them grazing in the verge, and they certainly needed to regain their strength. We didn't have a tent but I'd purchased a sizable sheet of canvas from Thol. We were able to tie it up to at least give us some overhead cover if it rained.

"Alright I'm going to sleep," I said. "Remember no coldfire, nothing that gives off light or—"

"I know. This isn't my first night hiding from bad guys, remember?"

"No, but unless I'm mistaken it is your first night in a verge. We need to do everything we can to keep from drawing attention to ourselves. The last thing we want is for some Fae to walk into our camp."

Something crossed her face. "I...I understand. When do you want me to wake you?"

"When it reaches full dark," I said, stretching out on my bedroll.

I'd closed my eyes for perhaps a minute when Samara shook my shoulder. "Darian," she whispered.

"What's wrong?" I asked, trying to blink the sleep out of my eyes.

"You told me to wake you."

"I told you to wake me at full dark, woman."

"It is full dark."

I looked around seeing everything in the grayish cast of Arati's gift. "Oh... sorry."

"It's alright," she snickered. "You were snoring so I could tell you were pretty far gone."

I sat up and my back popped, "Did you see anything?"

"A few strange animals, nothing more."

"That's good at least."

"Do you want me to stay awake with you for a while?"

"No, get some rest. You'll need it for tomorrow. But sleep with your boots on in case we have to leave in haste."

I sat back against an ash tree, my quiver next to me and my bow laid across my lap, an arrow already nocked on the string.

I woke Samara at the first rays of dawn. My eyes burned and my joints ached. It was going to be a long day.

"I take it there wasn't any trouble last night," Samara asked, slipping off the worn boots and rubbing her feet.

I shook my head. "I made a few tight patrols to stay awake in the middle of the night and the only thing I saw were some deer I startled, and a wolf that didn't seem at all interested in me."

"Perhaps this verge isn't all that dangerous?"

"There's no such thing as a safe verge," I said, shaking my head. "Some are just worse than others."

Compassion softened her features. "You look awful."

"Gratitude," I said with a smirk.

"I'm just worried. Are you going to be alright today?"

"Do I have a choice?"

She tugged at the collar of her dress and said, "There's something I need to do before we leave out. Let me see your knife."

As I drew one of my blades she slid the dress over her head, standing before me naked. A bolt shot through me despite my exhaustion. I stood there open-mouthed as she took the blade from my outstretched hand.

"What?" she asked at my expression, "You've already seen me naked twice, what's a third time?"

I had seen her naked two other times, but the first time she was gravely wounded and the second we were fleeing for our lives. Even dirty, ragged, and underfed she was stunning. Smooth creamy skin, perfect save the small scars from the crossbow bolts, covered long graceful limbs. Every feature was well proportioned, from her delicate collar bones, to her modest but perky breasts. Even her feet were perfect. For one of the few times in my life I was rendered speechless. I went about packing and saddling the horses while she attacked the garment with my blade, and despite my exhaustion, I stole a few surreptitious glances.

When she slipped the dress back over head, it stopped at her knees, and she'd taken off the sleeves and the high collar, cutting a V into the front. "There," she said passing the knife back to me. "I'm hardly a seamstress, but maybe now I won't die of heatstroke."

"It...definitely looks more comfortable." I cleared my suddenly dry throat. "Save those scraps of fabric, we may need them for something."

"Right," she said collecting the scraps and pulling her boots back on.

We climbed astride our mounts and rode on at a much less frenzied pace than the day before. I kept my bow across the saddle in front of me, wary of our pursuers and the myriad dangers of simply being in a verge. I did have to admit though, despite my earlier warning to Samara, this verge seemed fairly mild. At times it was easy to forget we were even in one, so subtle were the differences. Then we would come across a tree with feathers instead of leaves, or a toad the size of a chicken with tiny, dragonfly like wings flapping uselessly on its back. Gradually, the leaves on the old oaks bled to a beautiful lavender.

At least it was a pretty verge.

We munched on our dry rations as we rode, bolstered by some pecans grown using Samara's magic. The terrain was very hilly so at times it was difficult to manage. Not being able to see far in the thick trees, it was hard to pick a path. There were several times we had to double back because of a steep incline, which cost us some of whatever lead we had. There were no real discernible landmarks, so I could only guess where we were. I knew we were south of the highway so I kept us heading vaguely east-northeast, hoping it would take us out of the verge and keep us ahead of our opponents.

A few hours after midday we broke out of the trees to see a chasm before us, not unlike the one I'd almost fallen into a few weeks before, save there was no bridge suspended across. I pulled the map out and studied it. "This must be the Yohzee River. I don't suppose you have any magic that would help us get across?"

"Don't you think if I did I would have used it last time?" She glanced down the sheer drop to the river below.

"We'll have to find a way down to the water then." I focused the map down on the area where I thought we were and said, "Looks like north of us the river curves back to the west toward our friends, so I guess we'll follow it south until we find a place to cross."

"Fine, but I'm going to ride on the other side of you so I don't have to see down in that gorge."

We switched positions and followed the chasm south for a several more hours. We spoke little, both of us keeping our eyes and ears keened toward any threat. That probably saved us.

I heard what sounded like low murmur and brought Tavas to a stop. "Do you hear that?"

Samara tilted her head to the side and listened intently. After a moment there came the distinctive sound of a horse's whinny from the woods directly to our right. "I certainly heard that," she whispered.

"This way," I said, leading us just inside the tree line to behind a sprawling ash, large enough hide our horses. "Wait here," I said dismounting and calling Tarka's gift. I crept around the tree and searched in the direction the noise had come from. For a moment there was nothing, and then I heard low voices and the sound of brush being trampled. Then I saw a wasp. A moment after that a red robe and black turbans came into view. They were spread out loosely, searching for us cautiously, obviously wary of a surprise attack.

They knew we were over here. They didn't know where exactly, but they knew what direction. If they were following us, by either tracks or scent, they would have been coming from behind, not at an almost perfect perpendicular path. *I was right.*

I shook my head, putting those thoughts aside, and focusing instead on a plan as I went back around the ash tree where I'd left Samara and the horses. Her brow rose and she whispered, "Is it them?"

I nodded, whispering back, "They're spread out among the trees heading this way."

Her lip quivered and her eyes went wide just for a moment, then her mouth formed a determined line. "What do we do?"

"We ride right at them."

She blinked a couple times, in disbelief. "*That's* the plan?"

"They've got us against the chasm. It's the only way unless you have some spell that will let us escape?"

Her eyes cast back and forth for a moment. "We're on a verge...I could open a gate to Eather, but without an Elemental to guide us we'd be lost. We could wander for weeks before..."

"Before we starve to death or get eaten by the Fae?"

She nodded.

I shook my head. "We still have faster horses than they do. If we can hit them hard, maybe we can get past while they're startled."

"How?"

"I'll use Tarka's gift to hide us, and you hit one of the mages with a bolt of lightning, neither one of them have their shields up, then we'll ride past them back the way they came."

"Are you sure Tarka's gift will hide my spell-casting?"

"No."

She held my gaze for a long moment and chewed on her lip, then dismounted and said, "Let's do this before I lose my nerve."

I stepped behind her and slid my arms around her stomach, calling Tarka's gift. Straining with the effort of holding it over both of us I whispered in her ear, "Ready?"

"As I'll ever be."

As one, we moved around the tree. The enemy was still about two dozen yards away and approaching as a slow careful pace. I could see Waspgina now, but she was way in the rear, though Snake-Jaw was still out in front. Samara spoke in a low voice, "Too bad the mages aren't closer together. There's two Turrigan in front of Waspgina, I'm going to have to target Snake-Jaw."

That was disappointing. I was hoping to be rid of those cursed bugs, but there was nothing to be done. "Take what shot you think you can make, then mount up and ride past them. I'll be right behind you."

"Where do I go?"

"Just ride, it doesn't matter as long as it's away from them. I'll take the lead when we've lost them."

I felt her take a deep breath before she said, "I'm going to start casting now. Don't do anything to distract me."

I could feel when she began moving her arms to make the gestures but I couldn't tell if Tarka's gift hid the light from the casting. We'd know soon enough. I remembered to close my eyes against the flash but my ears rang with the deafening boom of her thunder. When I opened my eyes again a hot flash of grim satisfaction washed over me. Snake-Jaw lay blackened and twisted on the ground, crushed beneath his unfortunate horse.

I drug Samara back around the tree releasing Tarka's gift. When we reached the horses, I grabbed her by the waist and half-threw her in the saddle before I hopped up on my horse.

"*Move!*" I yelled.

As Samara rounded the tree at a full gallop with me right behind her, I took up my bow and nocked an arrow, guiding Tavas with my legs. Most of the Turaggin were still fighting the shock of the first attack, but a couple had recovered enough to act. One of them leveled his crossbow at Samara. My arrow hit him in the chest just before he released the trigger, causing the bolt to go wide.

One man with an ax moved to block Samara's path so I loosed my second arrow at him. He managed to get a buckler in front it, but it gave her enough time to get around him. I cut to the other side of him. He tried to change his momentum and swing at me but fell short.

I drew another arrow and first took aim at the Turaggin with the short bow. He'd dropped his arrow in the confusion and was fumbling with his quiver, so I shifted my focus to another man with a crossbow. He leveled his weapon at me and we had a moment, just before we both fired, where our eyes locked. There was a strange intimacy in that moment, as each of us loosed our missiles, trying to kill the other one. His arrow whipped through my hair as it passed, mine found his throat.

There was no one left close enough to strike as we rode out of their ranks, but Waspgina had raised her hands to start her spell casting. I sent my third arrow right toward her chest. As soon as I drew the string, she threw her body to the side, managing to dodge my arrow but fell out of the saddle in the process. The arrow clipped her horse's ear and it spooked. Unfortunately for the mage, her left foot was still caught in the stirrup. The beast tore away in fear, dragging the writhing, screaming mage as it went.

I turned my attention to trying to catch up to Samara, who had gained a sizable lead on me. Just as I'd caught up to within a few horse lengths of her an arrow flew by my head, narrowly missing me.

If I was still in archery range, then so were they. I drew an arrow and twisted in the saddle to fire back. The remaining Turaggin had rallied and were in pursuit, and they had taken up the dropped crossbows. It was nearly impossible to reload a crossbow on the back of a galloping horse, so the archer was still my biggest threat. I fired a shot at him, but it went wide.

As good an archer and horseman as I was, firing behind me on a galloping horse was difficult. If I took the time to slow and aim, they'd be on me before I got two shots off. So the Turaggin archer and I exchanged a few more shots to no effect, but when the one of the crossbows came up I immediately pulled to the side. The man wielding it obviously wasn't used to it however and the bolt came nowhere near me.

Samara cut hard to the left in front of me, so I followed and took the opportunity to shoot laterally instead of behind me. I fired three arrows in quick succession, hitting one of the crossbowmen in the shoulder, and a mace wielding-man in the eye, while the third shot caught a shield.

After that exchange, they fell back, putting some distance between us so I conserved my arrows, firing only when they got close. Samara zigzagged through the trees and they chased us for the better part of an hour, until their mounts began to tire. Eventually we gained enough of a lead that we could neither see them nor any of the wasps, so I passed Samara and took the lead.

I had no idea where we were but I led us vaguely southeast, hoping we'd get back to the Yohzee eventually. After another half hour or so I slowed our pace, giving our tired mounts a chance to recover.

Samara's eyes went wide. "Darian, you're bleeding," she said, pointing to the side of my head. I reached up to feel and my hand came away covered in blood. An arrow had caught my earlobe and I hadn't even noticed.

"It's just a scratch. You alright?"

"I think so," she said, looking herself over.

"Good, then we need to push on and find a place to cross the Yohzee."

She patted her panting horse's lathered flank. "You lead, I'll follow."

"You did good back there."

A smug smile drew her lips up, "I know."

Chapter Twenty-Three
Samara

It was nearly dark by the time we found a place to cross the Yohzee. We had to lead our horses up the steep, slag-covered slope. By the time we reached the top of the chasm, I was sweat-soaked and ready to collapse in exhaustion while Darian unsaddled the horses. The fighting, frenzied pace, sleep deprivation, and lack of food were catching up to him. Dark rings encircled red eyes and his limbs had a heaviness to them as he unloaded the horses, looking them over for injuries. He'd washed most of the blood off in the river but the wound on his ear was angry and swollen.

"I'll finish with the horses, you should tend to your wound," I said.

"It's just a scratch," he said

I groaned. "That's such a 'man' thing to say."

"I'll get to it eventually. First we need to talk," He said, aqua eyes burning with inner fire. "And I need you to hear what I'm about to say."

Why did I have a feeling this was going to be a tiresome conversation? I pulled my boots off and flexed my cramped toes. "I'm listening."

He drew in a deep breath and let it out slowly. "The only way they could be tracking us is with magic."

I was right. This was going to be tiresome. I rubbed my aching feet and said, "Darian, we've been over this. You can't—"

"It's the only explanation that makes any sense."

"There's no magic that lets you view an individual, only locations. And even then it takes time to prepare everything that's needed."

He ran his fingers though his hair in frustration. "Look, it's not that I don't believe you. But maybe it's something else? Maybe it's something you overlooked?" He started pacing back and forth, ticking off his fingers as he talked. "By the chasm today, they weren't reading our tracks, and they weren't following our scent. If they were they would have been coming up from behind us. Instead they were coming out of the woods at our flanks. How?"

"I don't know," I said, suddenly very tired.

"Well, just think about it. Mages must have a way of finding lost items?"

"Of course we do, but we have to put our sigil on the item first."

"Maybe someone put one of these 'sigils' on us?"

"You can't put it on a person…well, not without them being tattooed, or branded, or something. It's a literal mark."

"Perhaps it's on one of our things?"

"If a mage was close enough to do that, why not just kill us?"

"Maybe they couldn't do it without revealing themselves? Hell, maybe it's the noble who paid to have you killed?"

"Do you think me foolish?" I demanded. "We've been traipsing through the woods for weeks. Don't you think I'd have noticed a magical sigil at some point?"

"Maybe not. You've got a bunch of stuff in that special bag of yours. Can you tell me, beyond a shadow of a doubt, that it's not possible?"

I rubbed at my temples. "*Fine.* If it'll make you feel better I'll look through my bag."

I unrolled our makeshift shelter and started carefully pulling things out of my bag and setting them on the canvas until it was empty. It took me several deep breaths to clear my mind enough to cast the spell that let me see the threads of magic. The complex swirling pattern of the endless bag was distracting so I moved it behind me, then began looking over the items set before me.

There was substantially less than I'd started with, having left all my clothes by the river except the draa scarf. I had a few mundane things. A comb, a piece of chalk, a quill, a bottle of ink, some parchment, my mouth brush, but most of what was left was books. I'd brought several reference books I thought I might need, a work on magical theory, a few of my spellbooks, and of course both the translated and untranslated copies of the Sarga Paza. Even though it was pointless, I went over everything without seeing so much as a single thread of magic.

Darian hovered impatiently, arms crossed. "Well?"

"Darian there's nothing here, I told you…" I trailed off, frowning in confusion. Something was out of place. There was a page poking out of the top of untranslated Sarga Paza. I'd paid a small fortune to have it bound by the best bookmaker in White Harbor. I opened it to the page in question and the pattern of an active spell spiraled and danced before my eyes. There was a scrap of parchment the length of a finger and twice as wide shoved between the pages. On it was a scrawled sigil the color of tarnished copper. "Oh bloody Hell..."

There will be no living with him after this. He'll be insufferable.

"I *knew* it!" Darian said, kicking his saddle over. "From the very beginning I *told* you they were tracking us by magic. I told you."

I sighed, defeated. "You were right."

"Bastards, *that's* how they found us in Mystewood."

The full weight of it sank in as I blinked the spell away. "This had to have been with me before I left White Harbor."

"Did you ever loan the book out to anyone?"

"It never left my sight. My research was a secret. I didn't want anyone to beat me to the translation."

"Then whomever planted it had to be close to you. Do you have any idea who it could have been?"

"None," I said shaking my head. "I'll destroy the magic on this cursed thing." I closed my eyes and started to clear my mind.

"Wait," Darian said, a grim smile stretching his lips. "I have a better idea."

———————

As I watched the sigil float away down the Yohzee in the reed basket Darian had just woven I had to agree with him. "This is a better idea."

Darian grinned. "It'll probably buy us a day or two at least before they realize they've been fooled, and then they'll be forced to track us the old fashioned way."

"I hope they follow that bloody thing all the way to the ocean."

"Would that we were that lucky."

By the time we climbed back to the top of the chasm the second time, my calves were on fire. I filled my belly with enough of the dry rations to keep it from complaining and settled in to take my watch. I'd offered to take half the night so Darian could get some sleep. The question was, could I actually manage to stay awake? I couldn't summon any light, which meant reading was out of the question, so I settled for studying the stars.

It was a beautiful cloudless night and we'd camped near enough to the chasm that we had a clear view of the sky. I set my mind to finding and identifying the different constellations and tried to remember what they meant. Rocana was the God of both fate and the stars. It was claimed by his clerics that understanding the movement and interaction of the stellar bodies could give one insight to the future. I didn't know enough about the stars to divine the future, but I did know they were pretty, and they kept my mind occupied enough to stay awake until my shift was done.

When it came time to wake Darian, I shook him gently, having learned startling him was a bad idea. He blinked up at me. "Any trouble?"

"There's an owl with two sets of wings on a branch over there that's been watching me most of the night. Other than that, the only trouble I had was staying awake. But I managed."

"Good. Get some sleep. We're leaving at dawn again."

"Wonderful," I said unenthusiastically as I collapsed on my bedroll.

Darian seemed to have caught his second wind. The next day was spent zig-zagging, doubling back, creating false trails, and a dozen other counter-tracking techniques I neither understood nor cared to learn. By the end of it we'd covered barely half the distance we were used to, though he did let us make camp a bit early and I was able to wash up in a shallow, muddy stream.

The day after that, however, we pressed on with all haste, both of us ready to be out of the constant danger of the verge. We were satisfied that our remaining pursuers would have rough time tracking us. Our pace was brisk, but one the horses could maintain, stopping only to let the animals rest and check out bearings.

"Does this verge never end?" Darian grumbled.

"The Timira Forest is said to be three hundred leagues across in any direction."

"I guess we should thank the Gods we're not there I suppose," he said with a frown.

"It could be worse."

"It could always be worse."

I glanced down at my cut-up, hot, second-hand dress and my ill-fitting boots. "True, but at least—" We crested a hill and both of us froze.

The thing in the valley below us lacked any rational explanation. It was difficult for my mind to even focus on it so that I could make sense of it as it floated, suspended by no visible means. It was gray and mottled, shaped roughly like a potato the size of a horse. It had no discernible eyes, nor mouth, though circular patches of octopus-like tentacles sprouted from the front, rear, top, bottom and both sides. The thing looked like it would be more at home on the sea floor than nestled between the oak trees.

Darian eased his horse back down the slope and I followed. He said in a hushed voice, "That doesn't look like any verge-twisted creature I've ever seen. Is it a demon?"

I shook my head and whispered back, "I think it's a Forsaken, but it's rare to see one outside of Eather."

"Is it dangerous?"

"They're alien and unpredictable. Your guess is as good as mine."

Darian frowned. "As far as I'm concerned it can have that valley, we'll find another way around."

"Well, it didn't attack us. At least that's one thing we don't have to fight."

"Which is good because I only have two arrows left."

It took us a couple hours to work our way around the valley, and when we finally made it, it was nearly dusk. When we found a place to make camp, as soon as I dismounted, something charged out of the brush at me. It resembled a large bird, but instead of feathers it had scales and the head of a reptile. It looked like the lovechild of a viper and a duck.

I screamed and tried to back away but tripped over a root and fell on my rump. Komala reared up and tried to stomp the malformed little creature, but it just hissed and snapped at him. I was just about to cast a spell when a swipe from Darian's kukri took the creature's head off. But no one told the wretched little thing that. The body continued to run around for another minute or so until it finally fell over. The head continued to snap until Darian kicked it out into the brush.

I stood up, brushing the dead leaves off my dress. "I definitely preferred the four-winged owl."

"I told you there's no such thing as a safe verge," he said as he went over and nudged the body with his foot. "Too bad it's verge-tainted. It looks like it would have been a good meal."

I shook my head. "One day I'll be able to tell when you're jesting and when you're serious."

He gave his half smile and said, "Keep telling yourself that."

We switched shifts that night. Darian took the first and I took the second. It was getting progressively more difficult to stay awake at night and after a couple of hours, I caught myself starting to nod off. I decided to splash some water on my face. I took care to watch for snakes as I paced barefoot the two dozen or so yards to the little pond. The water was cold enough to be shocking and it helped to wash away some of the fogginess, leaving me a bit more alert.

As I stood up and turned to walk back to camp, I crashed into a woman with enough force to stagger her back a step and drop me onto my backside. "Oh, you startled me," the woman said in a high lilting voice. "Are you alright?"

The woman was about my size but I couldn't really make out anything else in the darkness. What was she doing out here?

"Here let me help you up," she said as she stepped forward to offer an outstretched hand, moving into the moonlight as she did. She was utterly beautiful, almost painfully so. Tiny trumpet-shaped flowers that matched the bright yellow of her eyes peeked out of chin-length green curls. They were a lovely contrast to her sea foam lips and creamy pale skin. She was clad only in a simple dress of lush green oak leaves. I'd never met one, but there was no doubt in my mind she was a nymph.

I started to shout, "Darian, Fae—" but then her fingers brushed the back of my hand. A palpable wave of desire cascaded through me, making all my other concerns seem insignificant. She languidly wrapped her long fingers around my hand and eased me to my feet.

"You poor thing," she said, reaching up with her other hand to caress my face. "It's been so long since you've been touched." There was a distant voice in the back of my mind that screamed at me. It told me that I was in danger, that I should run or fight, but it was drowned out by the softness of her touch. It called to me with both a soothing calm and a warm ember of promise. I nuzzled against her smooth hand. It *had* been a long time since I'd been touched…

She closed the distance between us, and cupped my face with her hands. She buried her face in my hair, exhaling her hot breath into my ear. She smelled like honeysuckle. "You have so much longing built up within you, so much desire."

I tried to reply but it came out as a low mumble that faded into a moan. She leaned back and stared at me, hunger naked in her golden eyes. The distant voice was speaking again, but I couldn't hear it over the hammering of my heart. The nymph chewed her lower lip as her other hand slid tantalizingly up my arm, leaving a tingling trail.

"It's plain you ache for release. Why do you fight it?" I couldn't think of a single reason. In fact I couldn't think of anything else. She was every lover I'd ever had, and every lover I'd ever secretly desired, rolled into one. All I wanted was her touch. I grabbed the hand that had wandered up to my neck and slid it down to my breast. "That's it," she breathed, gently squeezing and sending rippling waves of pleasure that only heightened my growing desire.

My eyes lingered on her full lips. I longed to kiss them, *needed* to kiss them. To take them between mine and explore her mouth with my tongue, have mine explored by hers.

Danger.

That was silly. How could lips be dangerous? I ignored the voice. I couldn't have stopped myself from tasting those lips if I wanted to.

I leaned in to kiss her and felt a finger on my lips. "No, not yet," she said.

"But...need..," I managed to say.

"You're not ready yet."

My need to kiss her was so great that I ached, so I brushed my lips upon the smooth skin of her neck. She tasted just like she smelled. Her leafy dress fell apart and fluttered to the ground like it had never been strung together, leaving her beautiful naked body bathed in Ananda's light. Her creamy skin was so pale it was almost translucent and I could see delicate green veins running just beneath the surface. I traced them with my tongue.

"That's it, my lovely," she purred. Her full breasts sported pert nipples the same color as her lips. I took one in my mouth, savoring it like a sweet. Her hand moved under my dress to find me already swollen and dripping. One long finger circled Ananda's mound, sending waves of pleasure radiating out. I let go of her nipple and threw my head back as I gasped.

I tried to kiss her again, and again she stopped me.

"Not yet."

I struggled to form words. "Wh...when?"

"When you beg for it," she said, sliding two long fingers inside me. Ecstasy sang through me as she moved expertly in and out of me. My breathing quickened and my pulse slammed through my veins as the pressure built. I quivered against her as my desire soared, driving my need to kiss her even higher. Just as my pleasure neared its climax, I leaned forward again.

"P...please...please..,"

A smile parted those lovely lips as she said, "Now you're ready."

No!

The voice screamed against screamed against the thundering storm within me. *If you do this you won't be able to save—*

A tsunami of pleasure slammed against me, wracking my body, washing everything but those lips from my mind. Their gravity propelled me toward them as though I was cascading back to earth. I fell toward the sweet release of her mouth and found only calloused fingers.

There was a pressure against my back and a glint of steel in the moonlight as Darian's dagger nestled under the nymph's chin. "Playtime's over," Darian said, his voice sounding gruff and hoarse.

I strained and pulled against his arm trying to get his hand off my mouth. I had to get to those lips...

"Now," Darian said, resting the blade against her creamy throat. The instant the knife touched her she leapt back with a yelp, rubbing at the red welt already present from contact with the iron.

"There's no need to be so rough," she said, her voice husky and dripping. "Unless you like it that way."

As soon as the skin contact between us was broken, her power drained out of me like water being wrung out of a rag, and my mind began to clear. My desire turned to horror when I realized how close I'd come to having my spirit fed upon. I tried to speak but Darian's hand was still covering my mouth.

"Sorry to interrupt your dinner, but I can't let you feed on her."

The nymph pouted with those full sea foam lips, still calling to me. "Not even a nibble? She's got plenty of ardor. She'll hardly even miss it."

"You'll have to find another meal tonight."

"What about you? You're all twisted up and turned around inside. It might even be good for you."

Darian eased us both back a step, his grip still firm over my mouth. I could still feel the Fae's power washing over me, stoking my desire, urging me to give in to her, but without the physical contact, I could fight it. It seemed Darian was feeling her power as well, judging from the hardness I felt against my backside. He swallowed thickly and said, "Not going to happen. I've had enough dealings with faeries to last a lifetime."

"You sure?" she said, sucking on the fingers she'd just had inside of me like it was candy. She sent a fresh wave of power cascading out.

"That's enough," Darian said, his body quivering. "Unless you want to get better acquainted with my dagger."

"That depends. Is it a large dagger?"

"You've just about discovered the limit of my patience."

"Oh lovely, put your weapon away. I'm a lover not a fighter." Predatory hunger still burned in her yellow eyes, but her features softened and the constant pressure of her power eased to a trickle. With a gesture her leaves drifted up and reformed into a dress. "Can't blame me for trying."

I tried to talk again, mumbling into Darian's hand. "Are you in control again?" he asked.

I nodded.

"Are you going to run over to her if I let go?"

I grumbled an indecipherable "no" into his hand and shook my head.

He released me and I turned a baleful gaze toward the nymph, anger replacing the desire I'd felt only a moment ago. I had to swallow twice before I could talk. "You almost had me."

She gave a tittering little laughter. "Oh lovely, I *did* have you."

Darian griped my shoulder, probably figuring I was thinking about throwing lightening at her. He was right.

"Where is your enclave?" Darian said.

"That way," the nymph pointed over her shoulder.

"How far?"

"I don't know," she said with a careless shrug and a mischievous smile. "That's such a human thing, gauging distance." Gods, even now I couldn't say if I'd rather kiss that mouth or smash it with a rock. *Cursed faeries.*

Darian cursed under his breath. "Run along. But I should warn you, if you're thinking about returning with your kin, she's a mage and I have plenty of steel."

"You needn't worry. I won't be back with anyone else," she looked at me and licked her lips. "I don't share." With that, she turned and started skipping back the way she'd pointed.

A thought occurred to me as she bounced away. "Hey," I shouted. "There are some people who might be following us in a few days. I'll bet they're quite lonely."

She beamed back a childlike smile just before she disappeared into the trees.

"You alright?" Darian asked.

I nodded, hugging myself and brushing my arms, trying to banish the tingling aftereffects. "I will be. Thanks for the help."

"I woke up when you cried out, but I didn't know where you were, or I'd have been here sooner," he said as we started walking back to the camp.

"How did you find me?"

"I…uh, followed the moaning." I was glad for the darkness then, because I flushed ear to ear.

We packed up camp and headed out, not trusting the nymph's word. When Azava's light softened the sky, I saw him sneaking curious glances out of the corner of my eye. "What?"

"Nothing," he said, but he had a smirk.

"Spit it out."

"I'm just surprised is all, I didn't know you were interested in women as well."

"That wasn't a woman. That was a Fae," I said. I might have been able to sell it better if I didn't blush when I spoke.

"So you're saying you're only attracted to men?" he asked with one eyebrow raised.

I thought about trying to phrase a response that could get past Azava's gift, but then I changed tactics and merely shrugged. "Sometimes you're in the mood for something savory, sometimes you're in the mood for something sweet."

His wide-eyed expression was priceless.

We traveled through the morning without encountering any more Fae. What we did encounter, however, was a swamp. A squishy, disgusting, smelly, bug-infested swamp. Darian was hesitant of the horses being in the shallow muddy waters, wary of snakes or whatever verge-warped horror might be in there, but unless we decided to turn back we didn't have any better options. Darian did his best to choose the path with the most dry land, but there was still a lot of slogging through mud. By noon, the horses were exhausted.

"Let's find a place to let the horses rest for a while. We need to see if we can find some drinkable water anyway," Darian said, mopping sweat from his brow.

I swatted at a fat mosquito, splattering a bloody mess on my arm. "Really? I'm ready to be out of this bog."

"As am I, but we have no idea how big it is. If don't let the horses rest we may be forced to camp here."

"Oh, nooo. No, no, no. Lead the way."

Darian led us to a sizable island in the marshy goop. We unloaded and unsaddled the horses, and Komala promptly laid down and rolled over on his back, wallowing in the mud.

"Stop that, you daft animal! I have to ride you later. Are you a pig or a horse?"

At being addressed, Komala stood up to come over and nuzzle me, smearing mud all over my shoulder. I stared at the mud for a moment. Once upon a time it might have bothered me, but right now I couldn't muster a single bit of care.

"When you're done playing with your horse, maybe we could go find some water?" said Darian.

"I haven't eaten or slept well for days, and was almost dinner for a faerie last night," I said giving him a glare. "Keep it up and I'll turn you into a toad."

His eyes narrowed to skeptical slits. "You can't do that."

"Want to find out?"

"At least if you did I'd get a day off."

I swatted at another mosquito. "And a bountiful feast."

As I followed Darian farther inland, I realized our little island was a peninsula. We'd seen more than a few snakes and some sizable crocodiles, but no Fae or verge-twisted nasties. Still, I was wary. If one were able to get past the reptiles, and the bugs, and the smell, the bog was actually rather beautiful. Algae that ranged from rust to cyan to leafy green covered the many ponds, while lily pads and brilliant lotuses bloomed in colors from the deepest black to hues reminiscent of the dawn.

"This place is really quite pretty," I said.

"If you say so. I can't stand swamps. The Zatru make their home in them."

That reminded me of something that had been bubbling at the back of my mind. "I'm surprised the Zatru are even a problem for your people. From what I saw, a small group of rangers made short work of them."

"The day you saw us we ambushed them. In small numbers they're only a threat to travelers and tiny villages. But in large numbers..." he trailed off seeming distant. "The Zatru are a clannish people, and they usually fight amongst themselves. But every so often the clans unite and it can be bad. The last time it happened they sacked Vana. My father died in that raid."

Thinking I'd touched on yet another painful subject, I stammered, "Oh, I'm sorry."

"There's nothing to be sorry about, you didn't know. He lost his life defending his family and his people. It was a good death."

"Doesn't make it hurt less."

"No, but I paid them back." His eyes darkened. "With interest."

"If the Zatru are so much trouble why don't you just drive them out?"

"The Empire tried. The Zatru are as at home in their swamps as the Manu are in Mystewood."

I saw a slight ripple out of the corner of my eye in the large algae-covered pond to my right, but when I looked I found nothing. Dismissing it, I continued, "The Empire? Really?"

"Twice. The first time they lost half a legion. The second time in they..." Darian utterly froze, eyes wide and mouth slack. I'd never seen him like that. I followed his gaze to the right to see a dragon.

A bloody *dragon*.

A long sinuous neck, sporting a double line of ridges like a crocodile, sprung from the pond, lifting a head larger than one of our horses. Terrifying predatory symmetry set off the graceful lines of its muzzle and the ridge of elegant spikes jutting from the jawline. Its skin was the same pale green of the algae with slightly darker stripes flowing across its body like a tiger. I stood frozen, transfixed as its yellow, vertical-slit eye focused on me. It was beautiful. It was amazing.

It. Was. *Terrifying*.

Time lost all meaning as I stood gazing into that eye, watching a keen mind stare back at me, studying me. If this creature desired our death there was nothing we could do to stop it. We stood unmoving, as the air from his breath blew my hair back. The dragon opened its mouth, revealing teeth the size of my thigh, and uttered a noise in a deep basso that I felt vibrating in my breastbone.

I stood there stunned, my mind lagging to comprehend the situation. I stood in the shadow of a dragon. A *dragon*. There hadn't been a dragon seen in the Empire since before the Causeway was built.

Some distant part of my consciousness realize that Darian was saying something, but I couldn't process it. I turned my head slowly, the barest amount necessary, and hesitated a moment before looking at him.

Darian was bent over in the formal bow he gave for nobles. He didn't straighten but his eyes found mine. "You speak draconic, don't you?"

It was required at the Academy but I hadn't spoken it in years. The sluggish wheels in my mind started turning enough for me to realize the sound the dragon uttered must have been it speaking to us. I gave the barest of nods.

"Well?" Darian said, his brows going up. "Say something."

My eyes shifted back to the great wyrm, as I frantically searched the vault of my memory. The words came to me one at a time as I struggled to form the difficult speech. "Greetings…honored…large one," I said at last. I reached not only for the words, but also what to say that might dissuade him from eating us.

The dragon again bellowed forth a noise that rattled my teeth. I'd never actually heard draconic spoken by, well a dragon, so I couldn't quite make it out. "Please forgive…great old one…not understand."

The creature made a sound that might have been either a growl or a chuckle and I jumped inadvertently. It spoke again, this time more slowly, drawing out each syllable.

"You are speaking wrong," the beast said, looking at me with what might have been amusement. "You must draw out the 'r' from the back of your throat. And put more breath in the 'h'." I stared up dumfounded. I was getting pronunciation lessons from a dragon. "Do you understand?"

I nodded slowly. "Yes…honored one…understand," I said focusing on making the changes.

The dragon rose up a bit as if pleased with itself. "That is improved." The great head swung back the direction we'd come from as if making sure we were alone. "I have not seen the young folk in some time. Only the fair folk, and the pure folk travel through here."

I struggled with the translation, guessing that young folk meant human. "Not know, honored large one. Mean no harm, no disrespect," I said, shaking my head frantically.

"Why are you here?" the behemoth asked, narrowing its eyes.

I didn't even know what to tell so we could get out alive, so I just spit out the truth. "Hunted…fleeing."

It canted its great head like a confused dog, "You must be desperate to come here. What did you do? Why do the young folk give chase?"

Again I cast about the vault of my mind, searching for the right words, trying to explain in a way that would persuade the creature not to eat us. I remembered the dragons fought with the Gods in the Divine War. "Fleeing... servants of Rajasa," was the best I could do with my limited vocabulary. It was difficult trying to read the dragon's serpentine expressions, but it seemed like he was trying to decide if he believed me. His scrutinizing gaze fell heavily upon me until something about his expression changed.

"You are a servant of Tarka?"

"Er, yes." I wondered how he knew I was a devotee until I realized his eye was fixed upon the silver medallion that was peeking out of my neckline.

"Then you have nothing to fear. Tarka provides for his followers," the great voice bellowed.

Of course. Tarka was also the patron of dragons.

The creature seemed to relax his posture. "What are you called?"

"Samara Arga," I said pronouncing it slowly, then gesturing at my companion's bent form. "Darian Wahya."

"What is it saying?" Darian whispered.

I ignored him, and asked, "What are you called?" before I even stopped to consider he might find it rude.

"Ardra'lub'dhaka."

"Ardra...lub...dhaka," I struggled. "Beautiful name." *The right combination of flattery and bribery...*

The giant head tilted back a bit and let out a low grumble. I wasn't sure what that meant but it continued, "Is Darian Wahya injured?"

I glanced over at his bent over form. "No, he shows respect of...of his tribe of young folk."

The beast made the grumbling noise again I still couldn't discern. "You may pass through this place, Samara Arga," rumbled the dragon's basso. My heart leapt. "With one condition."

I swallowed audibly, my pulse beating in my ears, "Of course honored large one. What...what is condition?"

"You will tell no one I am here."

That might end up being a difficult promise to keep, but I hardly had any other options. "As you wish, honored large one."

The dragon cast one more glance at each of us before the long neck started drifting back into the water. "Learn much, Samara Arga, follower of Tarka. All knowledge is sacred," were the dragon's parting words as it's head sank beneath the dark water.

My blood raced through my veins as we retraced our path back to the horses, moving as swiftly as we could without running. I tried to slow my breathing and steady my shaking hands.

"You alright?" Darian asked in a concerned tone. He was as pale as a cloud.

I blinked at him. "Do you jest? I'm *wonderful*. Do you know how many mages at the Academy have seen a live dragon? Barely a handful. I could write a treatise on what just happened."

His look of concern drifted into a scowl. "Had a nice conversation did you? What did you talk about, the weather?"

His jab might have been annoying under normal circumstances, but I was too excited. "He, at least I think it a male, just asked what we were doing here and I told him the truth. He said we could travel through his territory as long as we didn't tell anyone about him. He was really quite polite."

"Well, perhaps we should have stayed for tea then," he huffed.

When we made it back to the horses I riffled through my bag and came up with a quill and ink, then sat down with one of my journals.

"Are you serious?" Darian said with a look of disbelief on his face. "Surely that can wait."

I began furiously scribbling and without looking up I said, "I need to get it down while it's fresh in my mind."

"You do remember we're in a dragon's verge-twisted swamp, right?"

"Don't be so dramatic. If he gave us permission to pass, he's not going to suddenly change his mind and decide to eat us if I take a few moments to write some notes."

He shook his head, a look of exasperation on his face. "Zurans."

Thankfully we made it out of the swamp and onto higher ground before nightfall. This part of the verge lacked the rich purple leaves, but was instead littered with small rocks that glowed with a pale green luminescence. We made camp under a large ash tree whose limbs moved with the rhythm of some phantom current, and managed to get through the night without being attacked by anything other than mosquitoes.

After a breakfast of magically grown dates, we set out the next day at a much more leisurely pace, taking it easier on the horses that looked as ragged as we felt. We passed the day encountering nothing other than a few strange-looking animals and made camp in a small grotto that offered a bit of overhead cover.

Darian shook his head as he studied the map. "We've got to be getting close to the edge of this verge," he said.

I shrugged as I pulled my boots off. "I hope so. I could really use a full night's sleep and I'm sick of eating nothing but fruit and nuts."

"Seconded," he said rubbing red eyes with the heels of his palms. "You want first watch?"

"Well, since it seems I have bad luck with second watch, I suppose I'll take first."

"Wake me at midnight," he said, slipping off his surcoat and mail and crawling into his bed roll.

It wasn't so bad until the last bit of Azava's light faded, but once the darkness settled in my eyelids grew heavy. Very heavy. I used every trick I'd come up with to stay awake, but I was just so worn and tired it didn't seem to matter. There wasn't anything to focus on to stay awake, not even any of the tiny glowing stones. I sat up straighter, chewed on my tongue, did some memory exercises, but still my eyes drifted shut and my head would start to fall. I would jerk awake and look around guiltily. Several times I thought about waking Darian early but he was just as exhausted as me and I didn't want him to think I was weak. Despite my best effort, eventually I lost the battle and drifted into sleep. And I dreamed.

At first it was wonderful. I was soaking in a hot bath with rose petals drifting about me as Autumn rubbed my sore feet. We giggled and gossiped about nothing important as servants brought me cup after cup of wine. Then slowly the light in my dream dimmed until I couldn't see anything, and the water grew cold, painfully cold. The bath grew so frigid it became biting icy daggers digging at every inch of my skin. I tried to get out of the tub but I couldn't, my muscles locked up as I shivered uncontrollably. My mouth opened to scream but my lungs were robbed of air. I fought against the cold uselessly, like a toddler trying to escape her parents' firm embrace, until the pain started to fade, replaced by a soothing numbness.

The same part of my mind that had fought against the nymph screamed at me, telling me I had to stand up and get out of the life-draining water. With the last bit of my failing strength I gripped the edge of the tub and…opened my eyes.

Two dark, translucent humanoid forms floated above me, their hands reaching into me as they sapped my warmth. They looked like they could have been people made of black smoke, save for their glowing red eyes.

Shades. Undead that fed on the heat of the living. They were fairly harmless unless they caught you when you were helpless.

Or sleeping.

I tried to scream but my teeth were chattering violently and I couldn't seem to draw a full breath. I managed to roll off the rock that'd been my perch and onto the ground, breaking the shades contact with me. Four more dark forms were huddled around Darian who shivered violently on his bedroll, frost forming in his beard. Through chattering teeth I managed, "D-D-Darian…w-wake up."

His eyes blinked open then went wide with shock. He tried to squirm out of his bed roll, but he didn't seem to have enough control of his muscles to even get his blanket off. He bucked again, feebly trying to roll away, but couldn't even manage that.

A shadowy, insubstantial hand reached down to caress my face, leaving it numb and causing frost to form on my eyelashes. I fought back panic and a plan formed in my mind. *Light. Shades hate light.*

Every bit of my training was put to the test. I cleared my mind and began forming the spell as the other shade reached a dark hand into my thigh, stealing the warmth from my leg. It was only because I had cast this spell daily that I was able to form the needed mudras with my stiff, shaking fingers. I gave the spell power and pale blue coldfire sprang to life above me.

The shades around me recoiled as though burned and fled back into the corner of the grotto. Finally I could breathe. I sucked in a full breath and, with a thought sent the wisp of coldfire flying into the mass of shades hovering over Darian, scattering them to the night. Darian gasped and coughed as I sent the light around the grotto chasing away the few shades that lingered, leaving us alone bathed in blue light and warm night air.

I was still horribly cold, dangerously cold, and was considering trying to pull together a spell to create fire when I heard the horses give a concerned cry. I tried to gain my feet but my leg gave out on me and I landed in a heap on the ground. I drug myself along the ground on my elbows until I could see out of the grotto. Darian's horse was reared up, kicking at the incorporeal dark shapes to no effect. Again, I sent the coldfire into the black mass and sent them scattering.

After they were gone, I collapsed on my stomach in a shivering pile. Komala came over and nuzzled my hair with concern. His warm breath felt wonderful. I reached up and caught a handful of mane and used it to pull myself up. I wrapped my arms around his massive neck, drawing what warmth I could from his bay hide. Slowly, the numbness in my body faded to pins and needles. Feeling returned and my shaking grew manageable.

The muscles in my leg still didn't want to cooperate but I limped back into the grotto to find Darian curled in a ball, still shivering uncontrollably. It was hard to tell in light of the coldfire, but it looked like his lips were blue.

"Darian, can you stand? You need get up and move around."

He tried to speak, "F-f-f-"

"What?" I leaned down to try and hear him.

"F-fucking v-v-verge," he spat out between chattering teeth.

I wasn't sure I could lift him to his feet under the best of conditions, let alone in my present state. I hobbled over to our gear and grabbed the first thing I saw that looked expendable, which happened to be the canvas he'd gotten from Thol, and drug it over by him. Now that I was able to move my fingers, it was simple enough to call forth a gout of flame similar to what I'd used on our attackers in Mystewood, but much smaller. Once the canvas was alight I went back out into the woods until I found a sizable fallen branch and drug it back to the fire. I didn't even bother to try and cut it up, I just drug the whole thing onto the burning canvas, and then I grabbed our blankets and bedding and wrapped them around both of us we huddled together in front of the fire.

I slipped my arms around Darian and pulled him into my lap. Slowly his shivering abated. Eventually his breathing grew calm and he relaxed against me. "It would have been awfully embarrassing to freeze to death at the hands of a few shades after surviving a dragon," he mumbled.

I was too weary even to laugh.

———————————

As had become our norm, we left at first light. Neither one of us slept very much after I drove off the shades. I mounted Komala in a surreal, dreamlike daze, exhausted beyond measure. I could barely even focus on the path in front of me, using most of my strength just to keep my eyes open. I was worried I'd drift off to sleep and fall off my horse, but what really scared me was Darian.

His reactions were slow, his senses were dull, and his shoulders were bent as though he carried sacks of grain across them. Since we'd left the Empire he'd seemed stoic and unflappable, reacting and adapting to every challenge, always ready to take charge. It was easy to see why his fellow Rangers had made him their leader. Now he looked lost, just drifting with the current. I hadn't realized until that moment how much I'd come to depend on that strength, how much I leaned on him. That scared me more than anything.

We bumbled through the trees at a slow pace, and I hardly noticed where we were going. If anything had attacked us, the fight would have been over before it started. Neither one of us had the energy or will to fight or run anymore.

Late in the morning something started nagging at the back of my consciousness. I tried to pin it down through the thick fog in my head, but every time I reached for the thought, it slipped through my fingers like water. Eventually,

I realized the tingly sensation that had been a constant since we'd entered the verge was gone.

"Do you feel that?" I asked. He looked back at me, brows furrowed in confusion. "I think we're out of the verge."

It took another few moments for realization to dawn in his eyes. "Finally. By the Gods, let's find some water and a place to rest."

We followed a distant, churning sound to discover a small waterfall cascading into a sizable crystal pool. Both of us practically fell out of the saddle to drink the cool refreshing water. Large fish could be seen gliding beneath the glassy surface and Darian wasted no time hunting a couple for dinner, though in his exhausted state he lost one of his two remaining arrows.

It was delicious. I could hardly believe I'd been complaining about eating fish just a few weeks before. I stuffed my face well past the point of being full, into decadent misery. We collapsed onto our bedrolls under the willow branches. Just before I descended into an exhausted dreamless sleep, I realized I forgot to take my boots off. I just couldn't muster the energy so I slept with them on.

I had no idea how long I'd been sleeping, nor how long I would have continued to sleep if I hadn't been awoken by a *clack, clack, clack,* and a heavenly smell. The sun was high in the sky, and I might not have realized it was the next day if I hadn't woken once in the middle of the night.

A mouthwatering aroma hung in the air, drawing my attention to a large water fowl spit-roasted over the fire. There was a pile of wood shavings next to the fire, some feathers had been split to use as fletchings, and a dozen dowels cured in the sun a few yards away.

I stood up stiffly and stretched, eliciting several pops from my back, then followed the clacking sound down to the water. Darian sat on a stone by the shore, striking at a flaky white rock with a piece of antler, a row of neat flint arrowheads by his feet.

"I see you've been busy," I said. He just kept chipping away at the stone like he didn't hear me. "Darian?" Still no response. His eyes were dilated and his face was a mask of intensity. "Darian?"

He blinked a few times and his pupils shrank back to normal. He looked up like he was just noticing me. "Look who finally decided to wake up."

"Are you alright?"

"Do you jest? I've finally had a full night sleep and a real meal."

"Just a moment ago you seemed…"

"Ah." He grinned nudging one of the arrow heads with his boot. "Vastuvit's gift."

"Oh," I said catching on.

I picked up one of the sharp, well-shaped arrowheads. "I thought the Manu used steel arrow-heads. Why do you even know how to do this?"

"Ever heard of a Varaha?"

I shook my head.

"Nasty verge-twisted beast that sometimes gives us trouble. They have thick hides but they're vulnerable to obsidian, so we always keep a few special arrowheads for them."

"Huh, why are they vulnerable to obsidian?"

"No idea," he said brushing flecks off his pants. "You should try that crane."

"Oh, I intend to," I said feeling my belly grumble at the thought of it. "Are we traveling today?"

"No, I figured we could all use a day of rest."

"Sweeter words were never spoken. Well, since you've done everything else, I suppose the least I could do is laundry."

"You sure that's a good idea?" When I gave him a confused look, he smirked and explained. "Remember how much trouble you got in last time you did laundry?"

"It didn't work out so bad for you as I recall, you got to see me naked."

He tilted his head as if pondering the point. "Do all the laundry you like."

After a meal and laundry, I bathed and went for swim in the cool translucent water, then laid naked on the shore as Azava's warmth dried me. I hardly cared if Darian saw me. What did it matter at this point? The rest of the day was spent lounging, as the horses alternated between grazing and sleeping in the shade, while Darian finished fashioning his arrows. The small respite was enough to almost make me feel normal again.

Until night fell.

I'd just drifted off to sleep when I felt the shade's leeching icy fingers cover my mouth and nose. I tried to scream but only sucked in frigid arctic air that burned my lungs. More vampiric hands grabbed me all over, stealing my warmth and leaving only digging, piercing knives of pain.

I tried to roll toward Darian and rouse him, but my cold muscles betrayed me and all I could do was turn my head in horror. Darian stared back at me with cold dead eyes, his face a mask of terrified, frozen pain. *Darian, no. It can't end like this.*

Tears froze against my cheek as I wept. *It's my fault you're here. I'm so sorry.*

My body jerked violently. "Samara," Darian said shaking me by the shoulders, "Samara, wake up."

I blinked bleary eyes open to see him hovering over me in the moonlight. My face was wet with tears as I shivered. "Sh-shades?"

"There's no shades, we're safe."

"What?" I asked stupidly.

"You were having a nightmare."

A nightmare? What am I, a child? "Th-thank you for waking me," I said rolling over to turn my back to him in embarrassment.

"Are you sure you're alright?"

"Go back to sleep," I said as I squeezed my eyes shut tight. I couldn't stop crying, and despite the warm night air I was still shivering. *This is ridiculous. I'm a mage of the Academy, not an infant.* But I couldn't stop. My body refused to listen me, making me feel even more helpless. I just tried to keep from making noise as I wept, hoping Darian would just leave me alone and go back to sleep.

The blanket rustled as he got under it, wrapping his arms around me and drawing me against him. "What are you doing?" I demanded.

"Shh, it's alright," he said in soothing tones one would use on a child, which just frustrated me, causing me to cry harder.

"S-stop it, I'm fine," I said trying to wiggle out of his grasp.

His grip tightened has he held me firmly against him. "I know."

I struggled harder but his embrace was steel. "Are you daft? Let go of me."

"No."

"I don't need you to baby me, I'm a—"

"—mage of the Academy, I know. Everyone breaks at some point." His voice went ragged. "Trust me I know. Just relax."

I struggled one more time against his adamantine grip before giving up, my strength spent. I let go, melting back against his chest. He held me as I shivered and cried. Finally, I stilled and the tears ceased. Relaxed in his arms I found sleep, free from shades or other night terrors.

My body had become so conditioned to rising with the dawn that my eyes eased open as the first sparkling rays of daybreak warmed the land. We'd changed positions at some point in the night so that Darian was on his back and I was nestled up against him with my head pillowed on his shoulder, his arms still wrapped around me. In that moment I felt content and safe, watching his chest rise and fall with sleep.

Then I remembered how I couldn't stop crying the night before because of a silly nightmare and my shame returned, twisting into anger when I thought about how Darian had treated me like a child, and refused to obey me when I told him to leave me alone.

Like on the ferry? Said some distant part of my consciousness. *Just perhaps, he was actually trying to comfort you, not bring you shame?*

I was all set to argue with myself but then I thought about it. Darian could be tiresome to no end, but he was hardly unkind. In fact, I couldn't think of a single time he'd been intentionally cruel.

Perhaps it's not truly him you're angry at...

I hated the thought of needing someone else, of not being enough on my own. I'd always been that way, never wanting to ask for help, never wanting to be seen as weak. My aunt's voice rang in my head, "A lady of house Arga should always *look* like a lady of house Arga."

I blew out a sigh, letting my anger drain away and conceding defeat to the more reasonable part of my mind. I could admit when I was being irrational.

Every now and then.

Darian let out the barest hint of a snore as his chest rose. It was adorable. I readjusted a bit and in response his arms tightened around me, pulling me closer. I melted into the embrace and I had to admit that it felt good. I watched his chest rise and fall, reaching out to run a finger over the brown draa where I knew a small scar hid beneath, wondering what had caused it. My eyes wandered up to his face. His typical dusting of stubble had grown into a thick, soft beard surrounding his full lips. My heart quickened a bit as I wondered what it might be like to kiss them. *Oh bloody hell.*

I'd fallen for him.

Realization hit me like a slap in the face. *Just what I need, to fall for a commoner. Not even a citizen, an uncoined.*

Now that I realized it though, there was no denying it. One could fight gravity for a time, but eventually it brings everything back to the ground. I reached up and touched his fluffy beard noticing for the first time the soft red highlights in it. He nuzzled against my hand. It's not as though he wasn't handsome. In fact he was gorgeous in a rough way. He was just so...*vexing.* I'd never had anyone get under my skin the way he did.

What if he didn't feel the same about me? What if he only saw me as some weak, stuck-up noble who he was saddled with until we stopped the portal from opening? There was a weird fluttering in my chest I'd never felt before, accompanied by a strange vulnerability.

He had to care about me at least a little bit or he wouldn't have held me while I cried last night, despite my repeated attempts to throw him off. And it's not as if I hadn't caught his eyes lingering once or twice...

I let out a long sigh, remembering the philosopher Asiheti's words, "Let it be what it will be."

I slid over until I was on top of him and kissed his full lips, gently at first, until his eyes fluttered open questioningly.

"Samara? Wh—" he started to say when I kissed him again, this time with the longing the nymph had used her Fae powers to conjure, except this was genuine. For a long terrifying moment I stood on a cliff not knowing how he was going to respond. Then, like sparks catching on dry tenders, his flame sprung to life.

His arms tightened, pulling me into a kiss that burned to my core. A kiss that would have moved Ananda herself.

Chapter Twenty-Four
Darian

Something brushed lightly across my lips like a butterfly. My eyes fluttered open to see Samara's face above mine. Was I dreaming? "Samara? Wh—"

A wavy red curtain cascaded down around my face as her lips found mine again, this time with raw earnest passion. If this was a dream, then it was a good one. There was a question in the kiss though, and vulnerability in those crystal eyes.

Electricity arched through me as though I'd been struck by one of her lightning bolts. My arms tightened around her, pulling her against me as I captured and savored her mouth. A soft moan escaped her as she closed her pale eyes and surrendered against my embrace. She writhed against me as my tongue danced with hers.

The heat melted away a bit as our kisses became sensual and exploring. I buried my head in her hair and nibbled her earlobe, as her tongue traced a path down my neck. She squirmed, rocking her hips as she straddled me. I could feel her heat against me through the draa, and I was already swollen and ready, straining against the fabric.

She leaned back and in one graceful move slipped the dress over her head to sit astride me naked in the early morning light. I marveled again at her perfect symmetry, her creamy pale skin with its adorable dusting of freckles, every one of which seemed perfectly placed. My hands slid up her back, savoring the smoothness. She leaned in to kiss me again, the heat returning once more, the pressure building, but when she pulled away wavy red locks was replaced with straight black hair.

Sitana.

A fresh shock of pain and guilt cursed through me as that old wound was torn open. I squeezed my eyes shut and when I opened them, Samara again straddled me, fumbling with the drawstring on my pants. A miasma of conflicting feelings swirled about within me.

"Samara, wait…"

She smiled with flushed cheeks. "There's nothing to worry about. I've had the Maiden Tea, I won't be fertile again until—"

"Just wait…"

"Darian, it's alright. I want this," she said as she ground against the stretched fabric of my pants. "And from the looks of it so do you."

"I-I can't…" I said, grabbing her by the hips and sliding her off me. "I'm sorry."

Her lips quivered as her eyes clouded with tears, then her face twisted in anger. "I didn't realize I fell so far below your standards."

"It's not you—"

"Spare me the 'it's not you it's me' line, I've used it plenty of times."

I gained my feet, tears swimming in my own eyes. My throat felt swollen, and my tongue thickened in my mouth as I tried to speak. I only managed to get out one word before I paced away.

"Sita."

I made my way around to the far side of the lake until I was hidden by the rocks, then sank down against a boulder and cried. Emotions stormed inside me, cutting and tearing with their sharp edges. I felt horrible about hurting Samara, but I couldn't help but feel like I'd been about to betray Sita's memory.

"I wouldn't have minded when I was alive, how would you be betraying me?" Sita's voice rang through the air, vibrant and strong. I looked up to see her standing right next to me. "Jealousy? Ownership? This is not the way of the Manu."

"Sita…How? Is this a dream?"

"Of course it's a dream. I'm dead," she said reasonably.

I leapt to my feet throwing my arms around her. She was just as I remembered her, even her scent. "Is your spirit here? Or is this all just in my mind?"

"Does it matter?" she said, kissing me playfully. "Now, quit dodging the question. How does being lonely and miserable honor my memory?"

"I…"

"If I had died and you had survived, would you want me to suffer?"

I hung my head, ashamed to even look at her. "No, of course not."

"Then what makes you think I would want that for you?"

"I know you wouldn't, but if I slept with Samara…"

"It wouldn't just be pleasure," she said as she brushed a lock of hair out of my eyes. "You love her."

"I'm not sure that I—"

"Lie," the voice said. "You've known for some time. You just can't admit it to yourself. Why?"

I stared at my feet. "I don't know."

"Does the love you feel for her take anything away from the love you feel for me?"

"Of course not."

She smiled smugly at me. "Then I ask again, where is the betrayal?"

I opened my mouth to reply but nothing came out. I felt like an idiot, speechless in a conversation with a dream.

She held nothing but joy and compassion in her dark eyes as her fingers caressed my cheek. "My love, you don't have to hurt anymore."

"Do you forgive me?" I couldn't stop myself from asking, though I was terrified of her answer.

Her tittering laughter caught me off guard. "There is nothing to forgive."

"But, I couldn't save you."

"You can't fly either, am I to hold that against you? No one blames you for what happened, except you."

"I was supposed to protect you."

"Did you not do everything you could?"

"Yes, but I shouldn't have let you go in the first place."

Her hand caressed my face. "You're guilty of nothing other than loving me, and wanting to make me happy."

"Sita, I should have—"

"Darian," she said silencing me with a finger on my lips. "Do you truly wish to honor me?"

"More than anything," I said, my voice thick in my throat.

Her voice went soft, barely a whisper. "Then let go of your pain. Be happy." She kissed me again. It was firm and lingering. It was the goodbye kiss we never had.

And then she was gone.

My eyes blinked awake to harsh morning light. I leaned back against the rock and cried. My tears, my grief, my pain poured out upon the sand. For a moment I swore I caught the scent of Sitana's hair.

Perhaps I was finally going mad.

By the time I returned Samara already had our things packed and the horses saddled. Her lovely eyes were red and puffy, but a face was a neutral mask.

"We need to go," she said, her voice flat. "The season grows late. We've lost too much time running from our enemies."

I drew in a deep breath and let is out slowly. "Samara, listen—"

"Darian, there's no need to make this more awkward than it already is. We'll just go on like nothing happened."

"Let's just talk."

"Talk about what? I wanted a roll in the sheets and you didn't. It's fine." I didn't need Azava's gift to know the last part was a lie.

"There's more to it than that."

"No, there's not. I was lonely and you were kind to me last night. That's all there is to it," she huffed in a complicated mess of truths and falsehoods.

"I didn't mean to hurt you."

She let out a short bitter laugh. "Hurt me? Don't flatter yourself, you're just a commoner. It's not as if I have feelings for you. It would have been nothing more than a little comfort." More falsehoods.

I stood in stunned silence. Not because of what she'd said, but because of what Azava's gift had revealed. "You don't understand-"

"I understand *perfectly*, and I have no intention of competing with a ghost for the scraps of your affection," she said mounting her horse.

"Samara…"

"I'm through talking about this. Now let's be off, we've wasted enough daylight already."

Her tone left no room for debate, and I had no idea what I would say anyway. I mounted up and led us toward the rising sun.

The next four days went smoothly, though Samara was quick to snap at me and remained cold and distant when she wasn't yelling. We settled into a pace that was easier on the horses but still managed to cover quite a bit of ground. Now that we were out of the verge, we were able to have hot meals again and sleep through the whole night, though if it improved Samara's morale at all, she didn't show it.

The land drifted into smooth rolling hills sprinkled with trees and there were even herds of cattle or goats here and there. In the verge, the ubiquitous threat of danger kept me focused on my surroundings. Here, however, there were few dangers, which made for relatively easy traveling. It gave my mind room to wander, especially since Samara hardly spoke to me.

I thought about what I'd put my family and friends through after Sitana's death. At the time, I couldn't see anything but my own pain, but now I thought about how horrible it must have been for them to grieve for her, and see my suffering without being able to help me. I thought about Cayman's constant pushing, badgering me to focus on my horses, to go on patrol, when I could hardly imagine getting out of bed. I probably wouldn't have made it without him.

I wished I could apologize to everyone for how selfish I'd been. There was no guarantee I was ever going to get the chance to now. Thinking about home made me ache for Mystewood. The Manu were connected to it in a way few outsiders understood. I'd been away from it this long a few other times, but I'd never longed for it the way I did now.

I worried, too, about Lucius and the houseguards. I hoped that they'd escaped and were sitting in a tavern somewhere, singing a song and enjoying the watered-down wine Zurans loved so much. And if they didn't escape, I hoped they found a song and wine wherever they found themselves. I pondered Lucius's parting words to me. Despite what the clerics claimed, no one really knew what lay beyond the end, save the Gods. Were we reborn as some claimed? Did we dwell in the Realm of the Gods in a constant state of festival? Did we meet again the ones we'd lost? Was it something else entirely? I had no answers, but I liked to think the Gods were more merciful to us in death than they were in life.

I finally purged my thoughts and focused on the only things that mattered; keeping Samara alive and preventing an army of demons from ravaging the world.

And then finding a barrel of whiskey to crawl into.

"Could you hand me the hoof knife out of my saddle bag?" I asked as I inspected Komala's rear leg. Since we'd taken a break, I figured I'd take the opportunity to tend the horses.

"I'm sure I could," Samara said, but made no move to get up from where she sat combing her hair.

I sighed. "Are you going to?"

"I wasn't planning on it. Why? Is there something wrong with your legs?"

"There's about to be something wrong with your legs," I grumbled under my breath.

"What was that?"

"Nothing," I said as I walked over and fished the tool out of my saddlebag.

"Talking to yourself is a bad habit, you ought to watch that."

"It's not nearly my worst vice. Fraternizing with Zuran nobles on the other hand…"

"Are you counting bad jokes as a vice? Because then—"

"I'm sure glad you decided to start talking to me again," I said dryly, digging at Komala's hoof.

She shrugged. "I can only go so long without talking until my head implodes."

"I've noticed that is a common affliction among women," I said. I thought I heard a faint noise, but when I listened for it the wind picked up drowning it out. I looked around but didn't see anything, so I went back to work with the small hooked blade.

Samara huffed. "At least when women talk, they have interesting things to say—"

I heard the sound again…a droning buzz.

I snapped my head around to see a glistening copper wasp, descending toward Samara's head. "Wasp!" I shouted. "Get down!" She obeyed immediately, flattening out on the ground. The shimmering insect buzzed about and she squealed, squirming away from it and grabbing for the cloak she'd been using to keep the sun off of her fair skin. She flailed with the cloak, catching it in the billowing fabric. I ran over and stomped at the material until I was rewarded with a satisfying crunch.

"That was close," Samara said between rapid breaths. "Looks like our friends managed to track us after all."

"So it seems. The question is, how did they find us this time?" I said, pulling the cloak back and stomping on the flattened metallic body one more time to be sure. It looked no different from any other squished bug save for the green blood. "We need to go. Where there's one of those vile things, there's bound to be more."

We gathered out things and rode off at a gallop until reached the top of a narrow valley with a thick ridge of foliage. As I slowed us to a halt Samara asked, "Why are we stopping? Surely we're not making camp here?"

"I want to see how many still pursue us, and by what means."

Samara just nodded and we dismounted and left the horses grazing fifty yards back, before crawling under the low branches of a cedar that grew along the ridge line. After perhaps an hour of surveying the valley below, our enemies came into view. I counted only one red robe and five black turbans, but it's what preceded them that drew my eye. The creature looked like the misshapen lovechild of a tarantula and an iguana, and it was easily half again the size of my horse. Bristly hair and sharp-looking ridges ran along every plane of the fiendish thing and two long cockroach-like antennae patted along the ground ahead of it.

"I'm going to go out on a limb and say that cuddly-looking thing down there in front a demon, right?" I asked in a low voice.

She nodded and whispered back, "It's a Maksika."

"I suppose they're used for tracking?"

"Right on the first guess."

The bastard was fast at it too, it was way out ahead of the horses.

"Darian," Samara said touching my arm. Her lips were pressed thin and there was tightness in her jaw. "I'm done with running. I want finish this."

"Samara—" I started.

"Just listen. Even if we can stay ahead of them, with those wasps, it's only a matter of time before they get lucky or we get careless. And we've already lost so much time—"

"You're right."

"—running from them, we'll be lucky if we can even make to Vizipa on the main roads…wait, did you say I'm right?"

"Yes."

"Oh."

"By the Gods, you even argue when someone tries to agree with you," I said, blowing out a sigh. "I've reached the same conclusion."

"Well, if you would learn I'm always right then I wouldn't have to argue."

"Oh, you mean like with the sigil?"

"I wasn't technically wrong about…oh, never mind. What now?"

"We gain some distance on them and come up with a plan tonight."

We retreated from our hiding place and returned to the horses, pushing them hard until dark. Once we found a place to camp, we set about drawing up a plan. "I only counted five Turaggin left," I said as I sharpened my kukri. "I don't think they'll be a problem for me as long as we catch them by surprise."

"I can't believe they're still with Waspgina after all that's happened. Perhaps they're under some magical compulsion?"

"Never underestimate the power of greed," I said testing the edge of the blade. "Anyway, the real dangers are the mage and the demon."

"I can handle the demon by myself," Samara said. I could sense no lie but there was a hesitance in her voice.

"You sure?"

"Yes, but I'll have to be close."

"How close?"

"No more than a few paces."

"Alright," I said scratching the beard that had grown out well past my liking. "I'll work on that. What about Waspgina?"

"You hit her first, before she has time to cast a spell."

"And her bugs?"

"I'll handle them. Can you deal with everyone else?"

I nodded. "If we choose the right battlefield."

"Are *you* sure?"

"There's a big difference in being the hunter and being hunted." I felt my mouth curve up into a smile. "It's time they learned that."

I hardly dared to breathe as the last of the Turaggin passed a few feet beneath the oak branch I was perched on. He was so close I could smell his gamey stench as the sweat rolled down my face with the exertion of holding Tarka's gift. We'd left the horses a half mile away so they wouldn't give away our ambush.

Half a dozen copper forms hovered in the air near the tattooed mage as her demon wandered about, feeling the soft forest floor with its antennae, doubtlessly trying to make sense of the confusing scent trail I'd laid down for it. Waspgina spat something at it in harsh tongue that seemed to have far too many consonants, and the malformed creature replied in tone that sounded angry. Finally, it seemed to determine the correct path and tentatively wandered over toward a thick, oddly shaped bush. It was time. Our foes were in position.

I took a steadying breath and drew back on the bowstring slowly, hoping no one would notice the slight creak of the wood. I looked down the shaft of my arrow right at the center of Waspgina's back, issuing a silent prayer to any of the Gods that cared to listen that Samara survive unscathed.

The string snapped taught and time seemed to slow as the arrow hung in the air between us just before striking the tattooed woman between the shoulder blades. The mage made a choked sound as she jerked forward and fell hard to the ground. I released Tarka's gift and let out a whooping Manu battle cry to make sure everyone knew where I was.

The Turaggin spun their horses around as they drew their weapons, pointing at me and barking at each other in their choppy tongue. The demon seemed a little slow to catch on however, so I sent an arrow at its bristly, ridge-lined back. The flint arrowhead hardly penetrated the creature's thick hide, but it spun around, turning its reptilian head toward me and away from the pale blue glow coming from the odd bush.

Once everyone's attention was on me, Samara stepped out from behind her hastily constructed camouflage and a glowing blue symbol formed in air in front of the demon. The beast screamed a noise that reverberated in my bones before it vanished with a flash of green fire. In the following confusion, Samara managed to get back in her hiding spot before the any of the black turbaned heads spotted her.

The Turaggin cast about for a moment before returning their attention to me. I jumped back toward the trunk using another thick oak branch as cover from a Turaggin crossbow. After I heard the bolt smack the hard wood, I leaned back around and loosed another arrow, taking a bowman in the chest. The only ranged fighter they had left was the crossbowman, and I'd have him long before he reloaded.

Apparently he realized it too. He dropped the crossbow and drew a cavalry saber with glowing white runes etched along the blade and charged toward me. Was he going to try and attack me up in the tree? Maybe I'd given the Turaggin too much credit as professional soldiers. I loosed another arrow at the ax-wielding one I had a better angle on, taking him in the eye.

Only three left. Everything was actually going according to plan for once. I drew back and aimed at another black turban. Just before I fired, the one charging me reached my tree and there was a sharp noise. The tree shuddered violently causing my shot to go wide. I looked down to see the man with the glowing sword riding past and then the tree began to lean.

"There's no way," I said in disbelief.

There were loud cracks and groans as the tree began to fall. My mind scrambled to understand that he'd just cut through a decently-sized oak tree with one stroke of his enchanted sword.

I forced these thoughts away so I could deal with my immediate problem. I did my best to guess the falling speed and judge where the branches would be falling, then as I neared the ground, I jumped. There was a twang and a pop as my bowstring caught an errant branch, which didn't make much of a difference anyway because I lost most of my arrows in the fall. I landed in a jarring roll that rattled my teeth, but I managed to clear the falling branches and keep from turning an ankle.

I gained my feet, trying to shake the stars out of my vision, as another one of the horseman bore down on me. I cast my useless bow aside and drew my kukri and one of my daggers. I was in a bad place. A warrior on foot was at a huge disadvantage against a mounted one. But I was a Manu, and I knew horses.

I stood my ground against the Turaggin as he sped toward me with his spiked mace. At the last moment I called Tarka's gift and tossed my dagger to the left as I stepped to the right.

Warhorses were trained to trample men in battle. When I disappeared from the horse's view, he instinctively changed course toward the only motion he saw, my falling dagger. As the horse missed me by a hands-width, I struck at the rider, slipping just under his shield with the heavy blade, slicing him from navel to kidney. He was dead. It would just take him a moment to realize it.

The bastard with the magic sword was turning around to come after me, but there was a reason we'd chosen this location for the ambush. I used the thick trees to block his path then ran over some deadfall I knew he wouldn't chance running his horse through, forcing him to double back around.

Once I cleared the deadfall, I cast a glance at the other Turaggin, who seemed to be searching for Samara. I trusted she could hold her own against one mercenary, so I turned my attention back to the man with the enchanted sword.

I cleared the deadfall and stopped so that he had a clear line to charge me, then held out my arms issuing a challenge. "Come and get me," I shouted. The look on his face told me he wanted nothing more. I turned and sprinted away between two thick elm trees. He spurred his horse toward me, closing the distance swiftly and bellowing a harrowing Turaggin battle cry that was cut short as he struck the twine I'd strung between the trees.

Not even having time to cast a glance back I sprinted toward one of the slain men. The last remaining mounted Turaggin apparently decided I'd been enough trouble and moved to pursue. He was closing on me at a full gallop as I reached the body and found what I was looking for. I dropped my blades and took up the man's cast-off short bow, drew my last remaining arrow and fired. He caught the arrow in the mouth, and hit the ground with a crunch.

I looked around, trying to determine what threat yet remained. The man with the glowing sword paced toward me. His turban was gone and he moved with a limp, but other than that he didn't seem like he was too worse for the wear. I supposed it was too much to hope he'd broken his neck in the fall.

I wasn't at all interested in getting anywhere near that ghastly sword. I looked on the ground for more arrows but the archer's quiver must have been tied to his saddle, and most of the horses had panicked and fled. I'd never trained with any of the heavy Turaggin weapons, so I took up my kukri and drew my remaining dagger.

"Walk away. Just get on your horse and go," I said.

In reply, the man just laughed as he closed the distance between us. It was a bitter sound that held no mirth, only bloodlust and hatred.

I began to circle clockwise, forcing him to pivot on his injured left leg to stay facing me. It wasn't as bad as I'd hoped, but it might slow him down enough to give me an opening. After seeing what had happened to the oak, I didn't have any delusions that the rune-lined blade wouldn't slice through both my kukri and my armor like cheese. My best option was to try to force him to make a mistake, then close and finish him quickly. No easy feat when he had height, weight, and reach on me.

The Turaggin launched into a short flurry of attacks obviously intended to cause me to give ground. I acquiesced, retreating but also continuing to circle counterclockwise.

His form and timing were both good. This big man was no novice fighter. He paced toward me carefully, measuring the distance. I continued to circle but I let him close. There was nothing to be gained from forcing him to chase me, and I had no intention of letting myself get maneuvered back against a tree.

He burst forward with a dizzying flurry of strikes that forced me to give ground rapidly. For such a big man he was quick and graceful. This was no driving tactic. He rained down blow after blow trying to dominate and overwhelm me. Despite the onslaught, he didn't drop his guard or give me an opening I could exploit, but I did notice he was putting too much weight on his uninjured leg as he pushed off it to drive his attack forward. It wasn't much, but it would have to do.

I focused with everything I had, calling Tarka's gift around me for an instant, despite being driven back by the relentless attack. If he hadn't seen me use it before, my sudden disappearance alone might have given me the opening I needed, but he focused on my hazy form and continued forward, launching a powerful downward diagonal strike. What he didn't notice, was that I stopped retreating.

By the time he realized his mistake it was too late. I dropped to the ground, slipping under his attack and kicked with all my strength toward his uninjured back leg, the one he was putting too much weight on. It connected just above his ankle with an audible crack.

The Turaggin screamed and fell as his leg crumpled beneath him. Somehow he maintained a grip on his sword. I popped back up to my feet and swung at his sword arm with my kukri, hoping to take his hand off. He managed to twist just enough to take the blow on his thick steel bracer, but the impact jarred the enchanted sword from his grip.

He reached out with his other hand and grabbed my wrist that held the kukri in a vice-like grip trying to wrest it away from me. I twisted and jabbed my dagger into his belly with enough force to pierce the thick leather armor. He maintained his hold as his hate-filled eyes bored into me, until I drove the blade farther and gave a twist. The strength slowly bled from his white knuckles and he fell back, finally collapsing. I stepped forward with my kukri prepared to finish it, when I caught a green glow out of the corner of my eye.

Waspgina was on her side a dozen paces away, wispy green light building around her hand movements. I should have known better than to think one well-placed arrow would be enough. I flashed back to how the tattooed mage had still been trying to fight even after Samara's Elemental had bisected him. I wouldn't be able to reach her before she finished her spell, nor could I reach any cover large enough to protect me. There was nothing I could do.

I closed my eyes against the flame erupting before me, hoping Arati wouldn't let me suffer too long before she ended it.

Chapter Twenty-five
Samara

Flame bellowed from my outstretched hands, swallowing Waspgina and her coppery children as it had the first mage who'd attacked me. If she screamed it was lost in the roar of the flame. I showered her with fire until I was sure she didn't have any tricks left before I released the spell. The air smelled like roasting pork. A very short time ago it would have made me retch.

I glanced around looking for other dangers but only myself and Darian remained standing, his arm up shielding his face from the flame. "Are you alright?" I asked.

He moved his arm then looked down and blinked a few times as if unsure of the answer, then his eyes fell on Waspgina's unmoving form wreathed in flames. "More or less. You couldn't have cut that any closer?"

"You're welcome," I said. "Are you sure you're unhurt? I saw you fall out of a tree."

"Scrapes, bruises, and a bunch of sap in my hair," he shrugged. "I'll live."

The only enemy that was still moving was the one Darian had just been fighting. He drug himself feebly toward his sword with one hand as the other held his guts in. One of his feet turned outward, facing the wrong direction. Despite everything, a pang of sympathy rang through me. Even as I watched the man fell still, a pool of blood creeping out beneath him.

"We should search through their things to see if they have the mirror," I said, purposely averting my eyes from the Turaggin's body.

"Let me collect my weapons and I'll work on rounding up the horses."

As Darian went to find his discarded dagger and bow, I looked around at the devastation we'd wrought. It felt uncomfortably like what had happened to my houseguards in Mystewood, though I supposed there was a certain amount of poetic justice in that. Hopefully that meant we were done being dogged at every turn.

Darian strode toward me, fishing a spare bowstring out of his pouch. "Alright, I'll see if I can round up the horses, you start-*ow!*" He slapped violently at his left shoulder. His brows came together and his eyes widened. "Damn it."

"What?"

"Look like we missed one," he said, turning his palm to me so I could see the pulverized copper and green mess.

"Wh-what do we do?"

He wiped his hand off on the dead man's clothes. "We stay calm. Maybe it's not any worse than a normal wasp stin-*arg...*" his face crumpled into a mask of pain as he gripped his shoulder and sank to his knees.

"Darian..."

"By the Gods, it feels like liquid fire." He took deep breath, then relaxed a bit, some of the agony leaving his face.

"Irin's gift?"

He nodded. "Help me get this mail off."

I helped him take his surcoat off and shirk the sleeveless chainmail and draa shirt over his head to reveal an angry red lump already visibly swollen. "This looks bad. Does Ananda's gift work on venom?"

"Better...than on infection. But I have to drop Irin's gift to use it."

"You can't use both at the same time?"

He gave a look a teacher would use on a slow child. "The God of battle and the Goddess of compassion?" He shook his head. "I'm going to try to do a healing," he said through clenched teeth. He took a deep breath, swallowed hard, and nearly doubled over. His hand shook violently over the wound as his eyes squeezed shut in a mask of agony. After a moment his face relaxed and some of the tension eased out. "I can't...the pain is too much."

I blew out a shuttered breath, panic rising in my chest. "We'll have to go find a healer. Stay here. I'll go get the horses." He looked like wanted to argue, but finally just nodded weakly.

I took off at a run to where we'd hidden our mounts, and by the time I reached them, my thighs burned and I was gulping down air. I mounted Komala and led Darian's horse back to his master's shuddering form. I helped Darian onto the saddle, then gathered up his things and threw them in the bags.

"Which way?" I asked climbing in the saddle.

He blinked and looked around for a moment. It was clear that most of his concentration was being spent on maintaining Irin's gift. "Keep on northeast," he said inclining his head in that direction. "There's signs of grazing animals around. We can't be too far from a farm or some kind of settlement."

"Alright," I said, leading us off in the direction Darian indicated at a canter. We followed the path for nearly an hour before the trees thinned down and I could see signs of cattle. I kept looking nervously back over my shoulder every few moments to check on Darian. He was holding it together but the strain of maintaining Irin's gift was etched on his face.

Finally, we came upon a low wall of stacked stones that looked like it had been tended somewhat recently. After a few more moments, a small herd of cattle became visible. Sweat beaded on Darian's forehead with the strain of holding the pain at bay. A stab radiated through my chest at seeing him in such agony.

We passed the herd as the sun continued to sink lower behind us. I was beginning to doubt my decision until I caught a whiff of wood smoke. My heart leapt as we cleared a copse of trees and I could see a puffy line snaking up over the distant hill off to the right.

"Over there!" I said. As we crested the hill a modest thatched roof cottage with a small barn off to the side came into view. I clutched my amulet and mouthed a silent prayer of thanks to Tarka. I couldn't see anyone as we approached, but there was light flickering through the round windows, and black smoke curling out from the chimney.

We stopped at the wood rail fence that framed the house, meant to keep the cattle out of the garden. "Just stay here," I said. He nodded, sending beads of sweat rolling down his bare chest.

I strode through the fence and banged hard on the solid oak door. After a moment I heard a woman's voice through the door.

"Who's there?"

I didn't need to fake the earnestness in my voice. "A traveler in need of aid."

No response.

"Please, it's urgent," I pleaded.

After a moment's hesitation the voice said, "My husband will be back within the hour, you can speak with him."

"My husband may not have that long," I said, frustrating bleeding into my voice. "He needs a healer urgently." After another moment of silence, I added, "Please, *look* at us! You can plainly see we're not bandits."

I could hear what sounded like a heavy wooden bolt slide, then the door creaked open the width of two fingers. A middle aged woman's face appeared. Her eyes darted from me to Darian before returning. "Please," I pleaded again.

"Go north on the road 'til you get to the fork and go right, then over the bridge and left at the crossroads. You'll come to a temple with a healer."

"Wait, what road?"

She pointed a crooked finger over my shoulder and I squinted in the fading light to see a road about fifty yards past the barn. As soon as I turned my head, the door slammed shut and I could hear the bar sliding back into place.

"Wait," I shouted at the door. "What does the temple look like? How far is it?" When I didn't get a reply I beat my fist hard against the door. "Hey, how far is it?"

No reply. Apparently she decided she'd helped enough.

I slammed my hand against the door a few more times and shouted to no avail. I had the irrational urge to blow up the door, but I realized that wouldn't help Darian. It would only terrorize a middle aged farmer's wife. I stalked back through gate and mounted my horse.

"I take it that didn't go so well," Darian said through clenched teeth.

My nerves were starting to get away from me so I took a calming breath. "She gave me directions to a healer. She just neglected to mention how far it was."

Darian took a ragged breath. "Hopefully…not far."

I started to say something meaningless and reassuring but then I stopped myself, wary of Azava's gift. Instead I merely said, "Come, let's go."

We found the small, packed-dirt road that was marked with deep wagon ruts and followed it for several miles. It was nearing twilight when we came to the fork and Darian strained visibly, the veins in his neck popping out.

"Here, take some water," I said, passing him my skin. He drank in small controlled sips and in the fading light, I could see his wound had swollen up to size of a peach with green-tinged streaks radiating out in all direction, one of them reaching toward his heart.

We followed the right fork and encountered no one else. When the last of the day left us, I summoned coldfire to keep the darkness at bay. Tension built in my chest. I had no idea how far the temple was, no idea how long Darian was going to be able to hold on, and no idea what to do if his condition worsened. My instincts told me he wouldn't make it through the night without aid. I did my best to cast my worry aside and focus on the road before us. I had to keep my wits.

"Samara," Darian said weakly. "I…can't hold it anymore."

"You have to. Just a little longer," I pleaded. "The temple's just up ahead."

"Lie," he choked out, then doubled over in the saddle gripping his shoulder.

"Darian—"

"*Bloody hell*, it burns," he said, then leaned over and emptied his stomach on the road, barely managing to stay in the saddle. When it was done, he held himself shivering, his eyes shut tight in pain as tears crept out to trace their way down his cheek. My heart shattered to witness it.

"I know it hurts, just…just do your best to stay in the saddle, alright? If you fall out, I doubt I'm strong enough to pick you up."

He nodded wordlessly as he was wracked by quiet sobs.

My vision blurred as I wiped tears away from my own eyes. I took the reins out of his hand and led his horse back down the trail. We carried on down the dark road, the tranquil night only interrupted by Darian's occasional groan or light whimper.

After an eon, we came to a small wooden bridge that groaned and creaked under our weight, and I could make out the crossroads just up ahead. We turned left down a dirt road identical to the one we were on. Tall, thin cypress trees crowded the road and formed a canopy above us, blotting out the stars as the road meandered and wandered. I soon lost all sense of direction. Darian managed somehow to keep himself astride his mount, but could do nothing else but hug himself and shiver, though with pain or fever I couldn't tell.

We rode on and on through the darkness for what seemed like two eternities, seeing neither people nor buildings. I didn't know how much longer Darian could last before the hellish venom overtook him, but I knew it wasn't long. I refused to contemplate the possibility that the woman simply lied about the healer to get rid of us.

I was considering doubling back to see if we'd somehow missed it when I saw an old latticework archway overgrown with ivy and tiny white flowers. It bore a faded sign marked with the phases of the moon.

"This is it. We've found it!" I said.

Darian said nothing but his eyes eased open with a spark of hope.

I ducked my head as we passed through the arch to follow a path lined with well-tended hedges on either side to a squat, round stone building and a small stable. There was a corral attached to the stable and horses milling about in it, but no light shown through the slats of the shuttered windows.

I hopped down out of my saddle and ran to the building. I beat on the solid double doors with my fist as I had at the farm house. "Please, someone help!" I shouted, "I need a healer."

I heard murmuring inside, then after a moment a warm light flickered through the shutters. The door opened to reveal a pretty young woman with long black hair and light brown skin, wearing plain white robes and holding a flickering oil lamp. She looked like she might be Manu until she spoke with a thick rolling accent. "Plague or injury?"

"Injury. My husband was stung by," I hesitated. "Something."

She glanced at the coldfire still hovering above my head for a moment then her eyes darted back to me. "Show me," she said sliding through the door. Once she moved I could see the curious eyes of a half dozen or so children in the hall behind her.

She followed me over to Darian who was clutching his wound. "I need to see," the woman said gently moving his hand out of the way. Her eyes widened as she studied it. "Shiara," she called back over her shoulder, "Take Chochi and go light the candles in the healing room and draw some water. Suko," she said as she examined Darian's wound again with an unreadable look, "go wake Brother Vari." She turned to me. "Help me get him inside."

Between the two of us we managed to get him out of the saddle, though he nearly collapsed. One of the children ran up to take the horses to the stables. As the young woman led us inside, Darian leaned heavily against me. It was dark in the building and I could only just make out that we passed through a sizable chamber before entering a room with three stone tubs in the center and lit candles on every horizontal surface.

"Help me remove his clothes and ease him into the tub," the woman said. Working together, we got his pants and boots off. Darian was unable to offer either help or protest, though he did let out a small cry as we eased him down into the granite tub.

A man with thinning brown hair and a deeply-lined face entered the room wearing a robe identical to the woman's. Brother Vari I guessed. "What do we have, Siva?"

"A severe reaction to an insect sting."

"Let me take a look," he said, grabbing a candle and leaning down to examine Darian's shoulder. It was even worse than before. The sting had swollen to the size of an apple, and the wispy tendrils tracked even farther. "A severe reaction indeed," Brother Vari said. "The first thing we need to do is make an incision so that some of the fluid can drain. That should relieve some of the pain immediately."

"Less p-pain would be welcome," Darian said through clenched teeth.

Brother Vari laid a hand on Darian's head and said, "Just relax." He then went over to grab a bundle out of the cabinet and unrolled a canvas pack with little pockets for cutting instruments. He pulled out a thin blade that looked like a boning knife.

"Hold still, son," he said as he drew the blade lightly over Darian's distended flesh. Behind the sharp blade a line of blood mixed with coppery green puss that smelled vaguely of sulfur gushed out of the wound. Brother Vari's mouth dropped open aghast as the putrid mixture slid down Darian's arm. "This is no ordinary wound."

"Please, can you help him?"

"I've never seen anything like this," he said setting the knife aside and taking up a small wooden bowl. "We'll do everything we can, but his life is in Ananda's hands."

Sister Siva took up an identical bowl and they both dipped it into the cask of clear water that was between the tubs. Their faces became serene and their eyes narrowed to heavily-lidded slits as they began whispering prayers over their bowls in the Refined tongue. After nearly a minute the water in the bowls faded to an opaque silvery-white. One after the other, they slowly poured the water over the wound before going back to refill their bowls and start the process over again.

The first time I'd witnessed the healing waters was when I was a little girl and Lucius broke his arm falling off a horse. I'd been fascinated with it then, full of questions as I stared wide-eyed at the priests. Now I was petrified, unable to take my eyes off of Darian as he grimaced and squirmed while the water poured over his arm.

Darian reached out with his right hand and I squeezed his fingers. Time lost all meaning as one tiny silvery waterfall faded into another. I have no idea how long the ongoing cascade lasted, but I was vaguely aware when Sister Siva called for the children to bring more water for the cask. The tension in Darian's body slowly eased until at last he released his grip on my hand. My heart tightened in my chest before I realized he'd just fallen asleep, or more likely passed out.

Rosy light crept through the windows by the time the robed pair stopped their work. The wound had shrunk to the size of a nectarine, the streaks had vanished, and it no longer wept green ichor.

"I believe he will recover," Brother Vari said, mopping sweat from his brow with his sleeve.

"Thank you," I said, as tears I'd held back for hours slid down my cheek.

"Save your thanks for Ananda," he said rubbing the heels of his hand into his weary eyes. "It was her will that he survive."

Sweat glistened on Darian's bare torso as he, slowly and carefully, went through his morning exercises, light glinting off his daggers. "Well, you're obviously feeling better," I said as I entered the room, bearing a tray with warm bread and a thick gray cereal.

"Getting there," he said, his left arm trembling as he finished the last series of moves.

I ran my finger over raised pink tissue that had formed where the wound had been. In the three days since we'd arrived, the swelling had subsided and the wound itself was now a circular scar with streaks stretching away. It looked vaguely like a sun with rays of light radiating out. "What did Brother Vari say?"

"He'd prefer me to stay a few more days to build up my strength, but I told him we'd already been delayed too long. Eventually he relented." Darian flashed his half grin. "He's amazed at how quickly I've recovered."

"You didn't tell him about Ananda's gift?"

He shook his head as snatched the bread off the tray and took a bite.

"He's a priest of Ananda, what harm would it do?"

"It's not my secret to tell. It belongs my people," he mumbled around a mouthful.

I shrugged conceding the point. "Do you think the scar will fade?"

Darian glanced at his shoulder. "Perhaps some, but it will always be visible. It's no matter to me," he said, darting his eyes toward me. "I'm told women find scars fetching."

I rolled my eyes. "Come find me when you clean up and we'll discuss our next move," I said before slipping out of the small infirmary. The short respite of sleeping indoors and eating hot meals seemed to have lifted his spirits. It certainly had mine. My small canvas cot was heavenly compared to sleeping on the hard ground with the bugs for weeks on end.

The giggles of the children bounced off the stone wall as I crossed through the circular chapel, careful not to track through the area that had already been scrubbed. They made some kind of game out of their chores, seeing who could finish their section first. I'd come to learn they were all orphans taken in by the temple.

I glanced across the sanctuary, not grand by any definition, and rested my gaze on the statue of Ananda behind the altar, her arms outstretched and welcoming. I'd stood in much grander temples of course. The great domed Devalaya in White Harbor could house this whole building in its sanctuary with room to spare. However, it struck me that this place fulfilled its promise to the Goddess of love and compassion more than any other I'd ever encountered.

I thought of the petitioners who flowed into the temple during festivals and offered sacrifices solely so that Ananda might take notice and grant them the object of their desires. The priests and priestess here lived lives of service, healing the sick, and caring for orphans. For maybe the first time, I was truly humbled standing in a temple. I gave a silent prayer of thanks as I walked past the statue, and left the children to their scrubbing games as their laughter followed me down the hallway.

I'd asked Sister Siva if there was a place I could use to write a letter and she directed me to an old battered table in a storage roomed that served my purposes well enough. I pulled out my books out of the endless bag and began to pour over them.

After I knew Darian was safe and I had some time to think, I came to accept that Master Carter's mirror was lost to me. I was on my own when we arrived at Vizipa. I was buried in study and had my books and parchments scattered about my makeshift desk haphazardly, when Siva glided into the store room to rummage through some supplies.

"My, have you read all these books?" Siva asked in her pleasant accent, staring at the mess.

I stretched my back and was rewarded with an audible pop. "At one point or another, yes. I even wrote a couple of them," I said tapping my personal journals.

"You must be quite the scholar," she said, eyes widening. "Especially if you speak Bhagitan."

"Bhagitan? Why do you say that?"

She looked confused for a moment then pointed at a folded up missive with swirling characters lying at the top of one of my piles. It was the one we retrieved off the robed mage my Elemental had killed. Now I placed her accent. It was the same one my childhood geometry teacher had, the same one as the tattooed mages. I snatched the parchment up and unfolded it. "This is Bhagitan? Are you sure?"

"Er, yes."

"Can you read it?" I said, hope springing up in my chest.

"I am not sure," she said tentatively. "I have not read this script since I was a young girl."

"Would you mind trying? It might be important."

She glanced skeptically at the parchment. "I will try, but I can make no promises." She took the paper and gingerly flattened out its creases on the table. Siva's brow crinkled as she slid her finger along below the curvy foreign letters. "*Mahana o samucca sabuja agunera sahakari,*" she read slowly, then paused as if trying to decide how to translate it. "Acolyte—"

"Hold just a moment," I said, scrambling for blank parchment as I wet my quill. "Now, please continue."

"Acolyte of the great and exalted Green Flame…"

Chapter Twenty-Six
Darian

"It was Bhagitan," Samara said as she swept into the stable like a spring storm.

I glanced up from Komala's hoof and set my rasp aside. "What was?"

"The letter we pulled off the mage in Carvog. Sister Siva was able to translate it," Samara said with a wide grin.

It took a moment for the full implication of that statement to settle in my mind. "Well, what did it say?"

"It's a letter, sent from within the Empire to the 'Acolytes of the Green Flame'."

That struck some vague recollection from my schooling. "The Green Flame is a euphemism for the Rajasa right?"

Her brows went up like she was impressed. "It is."

"I don't supposed it's signed?"

"Afraid not."

"What else?"

"I was right. The 'Acolytes' were dispatched to Carvog to wait for us. The letter is dated before we left Stonehaven." She reached out to stroke Komala's neck, who in turn nuzzled her shoulder. "And the letter makes reference to an ally, just as the mage in Mystewood did."

"Likely the noble who's financing them. It was too much to hope they'd use a name, I suppose," I said, absently rubbing the dull ache in my shoulder. The edge of Samara's lip twitched just a bit, if I hadn't spent so much time around her I wouldn't have caught it. "What are you leaving out?"

"Oh..," her smile broadened slowly, "Just the location of all the places the Acolytes were dispatched to wait for us."

"You jest?" I asked, though Azava's gift told me there was no lie.

She nodded, "For once, we might actually be one step—"

"Shhh, don't say it out loud. You might curse it."

An hour later we had the map sprawled out on Samara's table with small pebbles marking the locations where letter indicated. I scratched my stubble as I studied it. "Lucius's original plan could still work. If we head up through Gopura and take the highway north to the Blood," I said tracing the route with my finger.

"We'd be backtracking."

"It's the safest way to avoid any tattooed trouble without going too far out of the way. And the equinox grows closer, we're pressed for time as it is. We'll make up weeks of travel on the river."

"Just what I was hoping for," Samara said with a frown. "More time on a ship."

"Look at the bright side, assuming we survive this ordeal, perhaps your phobia of boat travel will be cured."

"Sure, only to be replaced by new phobias of shades, nymphs, verges…"

"You know, I really admire your ability to always see positive side of a situation."

"It's a gift," she said, poking one of the pebbles. "Let's just hope they haven't changed plans since that letter was dispatched."

"Can you think of a better option?"

"Do you think I'd have been quiet about it if I had?"

"Not for a moment," I said brushing the pebbles aside and rolling up the map.

———————————

The next morning Brother Vari and Sister Siva came to bid us farewell.

"Thank you for everything," I said, "The healing, the lodging, the food, everything."

Brother Vari held up his hand shaking his head. "No thanks is necessary."

"What do we owe you?" Samara said.

"You owe us nothing," Sister Siva said, "We but held up our oaths to Ananda, we can accept no coin for that. Though if you wish to donate to the temple, anything would be appreciated."

Samara reached into her pouch and came away with one of the platinum pieces and pressed it into Siva's hand. Her eyes widened when she recognized what it was. "No, no, this is far too much."

"Too much for what? This is a donation to the temple," Samara said.

Siva just stared back at her wide eyed.

"I've seen how much those children can eat," Samara said.

"Thank you," the sister said. "May Ananda ever guide your heart."

"We need all the guidance we can get," Samara said before we rode off.

We followed the packed dirt road until it connected with a highway and followed its course west, northwest. My shoulder throbbed with a dull ache but it was tolerable, and Samara and I traveled with an easiness we hadn't had since before the morning by the waterfall. There was still tension between us but we ignored it. Samara avoided contact as much as possible, as well as any situation in which I might see her nude. At night she slept with her back to me, far enough away that we wouldn't touch. Once or twice I considered broaching the subject, but now that there was finally peace between us, I didn't want to jeopardize it.

We hoped to arrive in Gopura before nightfall, but we hadn't counted on the highway being so crowded, so the sun was straddling the horizon by the time the city's walls came into view. The city was roughly circular and rested atop a hill, with at least a dozen watchtowers rising above the reddish tan walls that surrounded it. By the time we made our way up the winding road through the olive groves the last of the Azava's light was quickly fading. We passed through the heavy iron gates just as they were closing for the day.

Despite the late hour the streets were quite crowded. The first few inns we tried were full, but we finally found one with a vacancy. According to the translated letter we didn't have to worry about our enemy lying in wait for us here, but even so I felt vulnerable, like eyes watched us from every alley.

"Does the inn have a bath?" Samara asked the porter as we were shown to our room on the second story.

"No, but there's a public bath just down the street," the young man replied.

"Heated?"

"Of course."

Samara's eyes practically glazed over in anticipation.

After thanking the porter and sending him away with coin, I said, "We've got other things that take priority over a hot bath—"

"Maybe for you, but a bath is at the very top of my priority list."

"Look, all I'm saying is—"

"You haven't been wearing the same dress for weeks," she interrupted again. "You can do whatever you like, but I'm taking a bath."

As a great general once said, choose your battles wisely. I heaved a sigh. "Fine, let's go."

The bath house was Imperial style with large communal pools only segregated by gender. I had to admit, the bath felt heavenly. I soaked in the hot water for a long while, knowing Samara would take her time, and some of the stiffness of traveling as well as the dull ache in my shoulder faded away.

When Samara finally emerged, dreamy eyed, I said, "How was it?"

She stared at me as if it was the stupidest thing she'd ever heard. "It was a religious experience."

The next day was largely spent shopping for supplies. We mostly just replaced the things we lost while fleeing from our enemies: tent, cooking pots and the like, and of course Samara's wardrobe. She bought new riding boots, a few dresses, skirts, stockings, and blouses in the flowing local style, and at my urging a pair of doe skin breeches and a matching vest. Some things are just easier to do in pants.

On the way back to the inn, we passed a large open-air slave market. Men, women, and children of all ages and nationalities were crammed together in crowded cages, while others stood upon the dais where they were to be auctioned from, naked but for their slave collars and the chains that fastened them in place. Some, it was easy to see, were new to their condition and yet to be broken. They resisted their jailers and held their head high in dignity or defiance, baring fresh bruises and lash marks. Others however, shuffled forward with downcast eyes, putting up no resistance, accepting their condition either because they'd been born into it or because it had been beaten into them. They had long since learned that defiance earned them the whip or a far worse punishment. My thoughts drifted back to the humiliations my friends had suffered as slaves of the Zatru, before being rescued or ransomed back to their families.

"Barbaric," Samara said, staring at the dais.

"There's plenty of slavery in the Empire," I countered.

"At least in the Empire, slaves are given enough to eat, and not chained naked upon a podium."

My brows went up. "So it's their nudity you object to, and not the fact that humans are being sold like horses?"

"It's not the same."

"Oh really? How is it different?"

"Well, first off there are laws that dictate how you can treat a slave in the Empire. Owners can inflict no permanent scars or do anything that inhibits their ability to work. There's heavy fines for those who violate those rules."

"*Fines?* I'm sure that's a real comfort for someone who's being whipped on a daily basis."

"It's far better than in most of the world."

"Let me ask you this," I said facing her. "Is it an uncommon practice for masters to force themselves on their slaves?"

Samara was quiet, her face drawn. "No, sadly it's not."

"And when was the last time a citizen was convicted of raping a slave?"

"I…don't know."

"I would say that leaves a permanent scar, even if it's not a visible one."

She turned her face from me and was quite for a long moment. Eventually she said, "At least in the Empire a slave automatically gains their freedom after seven years of service. That's a far cry better than any other slave-owning nation."

"Oh, so it's alright to sell a human being as property as long as it's only for seven years? How can you defend that?"

"I'm not," she said, her body shaking with frustration. "All I'm saying is slaves are treated better in the Empire than outside it. Why are you lashing out at me? It's not as if I own any slaves!" she shouted.

"I'll bet House Arga does."

"I am not my House. And I'm done fighting about this."

We walked the rest of the way back to the inn both quietly stewing and, after another trip to the baths, turned in early without saying another word. We left shortly after dawn the next morning on the wide and well-traveled highway that led to north out of the city. It took me about half the morning of curt one-word answers to realized we'd returned to the "not-talking-to-me" punishment.

At first I was annoyed, but then I thought about it. She had every right to be angry. I'd taken out my disgust and anger at the slave market out on her.

"Apologies," I said.

"For what?" Samara asked.

Uh oh.

Her words seemed innocuous enough but her tone held an edge. I'd been married once before. I knew that this was a test to see if I really knew what she was angry about. And failure would bring several more days of silence.

"Yesterday, the slave market made me angry and I took it out on you. That wasn't fair. I'm sorry."

Her expression softened and eventually she said, "Accepted." After a few more moments of silence she added, "You had a point. It was fairly hypocritical to defend the Empire."

"As you said, you own no slaves. You're hardly responsible for the actions of the

Empire or your House. It's not as if you set the policy." I took a long drink from my new water skin. "Gods know there's some of my leader's policies I'd like to change."

"Like what?"

I wasn't sure it was a conversation I wanted to have, but at least she was talking to me again. "Like how concerned we are at maintaining the status quo, even to our detriment."

"What do you mean?"

I chewed my lip. "Did you know the Manu have been subjects of the Zura for fifteen hundred years?"

She shook her head.

"My people lived in Mystewood long before the word 'Zura' ever passed anyone's lips. When the Empire started expanding, our elders consulted the Vijas, who saw that no amount of resistance would hold the land-hungry invaders at bay. So our elders decided to surrender to Zuran rule without a single arrow ever being fired."

"That decision probably saved countless Manu from death or enslavement."

"Probably, but that's not the point. Our elders were so worried about tipping the canoe and angering the Zurans that they acquiesced to every request. Even as the Old Empire broke apart and territory after territory slipped their leash, still we stayed loyal, never raising a hand."

"So what are you suggesting? That the Manu revolt? Darian, that's an awful idea!"

"I'm not suggesting revolt, I'm suggesting citizenship."

Her brow drew together. "What?"

"The Manu have been nothing but loyal. We've paid our taxes, fought in wars when asked, we even deal with the Zatru so the Empire doesn't have to. Hell, after a millennia and a half of service, we're still not allowed to own swords or metal armor."

"You seem to get along rather well without it," she said.

"Again, that's not the point," I said running my hands through my hair. "All I'm saying is we either deserve to be let into the Empire or out of it."

After a quiet moment she said. "You're right. That hardly seems fair. Have the Manu petitioned the Empire before?"

"No, the Guras are so afraid of upsetting the status quo that they're not even willing to take a chance at making things better. As it has ever been with my people."

She was quiet for moment. "If you can convince your leaders to sign off on it, I'll help you write a petition to Emperor Pulo and the Senate."

"Are you serious?" I said.

She smiled. "It's the least I can do for all the kindness the Manu have shown me. I'll not lie, it's a long shot at best, but perhaps I can gain some support for it within House Arga."

It was my turn to smile. "Long shots seem to be our specialty."

Port Feath was little more than a half-mile long dock with just enough buildings around it to legitimize calling it a town. The rust colored clay that gave the Blood River its sanguine appearance clung to everything, causing the wooden structures to look like an old iron skillet. Samara saw to our lodgings for the evening while I went to book passage.

"Any luck?" she asked upon my return.

"I booked passage on the fastest ship they had listed. All they had left was a luxury cabin."

Samara threw her hand dramatically over her heart and said, "How awful."

"Yes, I'm sure you're heartbroken. Just remember we're trying to keep a low profile. Don't get careless just because we don't have Turaggin in our shadow anymore. The Acolytes are still looking for us."

"Yes, *husband*."

"We should probably come up with new aliases, as well. Our Dezika disguises are getting a little stale." I scratched at the hair on my chin. "Too bad we didn't have Ganicus forge us some extra papers."

"I have it," Samara said tapping her lips. "I'll be a wealthy citizen on vacation, and you can be my man servant."

"How's that different than what we've been doing?" I quipped.

"A good man servant would do my laundry."

"You get what you pay for," I said dryly.

The next day we set out on the largest river vessel I'd ever seen, an enormous three-masted monster. "No wonder this boat is the fastest," Samara said. "It's got a Shipstone."

"Of course," I said.

"You don't know what that is do you?"

"Not a clue."

Her mouth quirked in a smile. "It's an enchanted item we make in the Empire that can produce wind," she said, gesturing to the twelve sided geometric stone covered in glowing white runes, nestled in its cradle at the back of the boat. "It probably cost nearly as much as the ship itself." She glanced over at me and said, "Do you still object to accepting aid from magic?"

I scoffed. "That rock could be handed down from one of the Rajasa and I wouldn't care, as long as it hastens our journey."

"As I said before, you're surprisingly easy to corrupt."

"Perhaps you just have a talent for it."

The vessel made for a smooth journey on the calm deep waters of the Blood, easing both Samara and Tavas's discomfort with boats. With the constant wind from the Shipstone aiding the downstream travel, hundreds of miles faded behind us quickly as we chased the rising sun. Not wanting to draw unwanted attention to ourselves, we said little to anyone and spent most of the time in our cabin.

Despite the close proximity Samara and I shared, we didn't talk much, though she was pleasant enough when we did. The awkwardness that had loomed over us since the morning by the waterfall seemed to be even more present in the cramped quarters. I didn't know how to make sense out of the storm of conflicting emotions within me, so I did my best to set them aside and focus on the task at hand. The most dangerous part of our journey lay before us, as our destination was no doubt swarming with more of our tattooed foes.

Five days filled with hot meals and, notably absent, long hours in the saddle did quite a bit to renew my strength, and our spirits. My shoulder was still feeling a bit tight but it grew a little looser with every exercise, and the ache had mostly faded.

Tension eased back into my shoulders as the massive vessel glided into port. We'd spent hours discussing the best plan to slip into Moravar unnoticed. Not only did we have to worry about the Acolytes, who were probably searching for us, the border was likely to be locked down fairly tight because of the war. Ultimately, we decided to take the Blood all the way to Diyati, then travel south and approach Moravar from the east, rather than from the west as the Acolytes probably expected.

As we led the horses down the ramp into the bustling port, Samara asked, "Shall we push on or find lodgings here for the evening?"

At my urging Samara had tweaked her illusion spell to change her red locks to a sandy blonde, and cover up her noble eyes with green ones. I wore my grandfather's cloak over my clothes despite the heat. Even with those precautions, as I looked around at the crowded dock, I felt vulnerable. "Let's put some miles behind us in case the Acolytes left someone here to keep an eye out for us."

"Do you think that's likely?"

"Better safe than ambushed."

"And I was just getting used to sleeping in a proper bed again."

"Just so that doesn't happen again, I'll take the bed whenever we sleep at an inn and you can sleep on the floor."

"Such a gentleman," she said with an eye roll.

The main highway was flush with summer trade, so we decided to attempt to seek anonymity amongst the throngs of travelers rather than take one of the smaller, less traveled roads. We proceeded cautiously, both alert for some sign of trouble or ambush, but we saw nothing. We spent the night a large roadside inn and left out the next morning an hour after dawn.

Chapter Twenty-Seven

Samara

It was one of those rare mornings that I'd risen before Darian. Not wishing to wake him, I slipped out of the tiny inn room and found the only place spacious and quiet enough for me to do my morning practices: the stables. As I sat down in an empty stall, the mingling scent of horse and straw drew my thoughts across time and distance to my hiding place at Father's estate.

Between my parents, brothers, uncles, aunts, cousins, and the servants, privacy was a hard thing to find growing up. Whenever I was upset, or when I just wanted to be alone, I would climb up to the loft above the stables used to store hay. It was the one place I could go and just...*be*, without having to live up to anyone's expectations. It was the one place I was totally free, the one place I felt completely safe. As I drew in a breath, I held on to that feeling of safety, wishing I was there. I took another breath and began my meditation.

A half hour later as I slipped out of the stall and brushed straw from my new clothes, Komala let out an excited whinny. He nuzzled against my neck, drawing a giggle out of me. His coat was in dire need of attention, so I grabbed a curry brush and a comb and went into his stall. His thick mane was a tangled mess, and I worked at it with a patience never had for my own hair. That done, I set about brushing his deep bay coat.

He'd held up surprisingly well, especially considering how much had been asked of him, but I could see the toll he paid as my hand passed over ribs that stood out noticeably. As I reached an area on his shoulder, he stretched his neck out with half closed eyes as he drew his lips back from his gums. It was about the most adorable thing I'd ever seen. "Oh, you like that?" I said scratching harder and sending him into horse bliss.

When I finished, his bay coat glowed warmly in the early light. I marveled at his strong flanks, muscles taut beneath his hide, which despite its thickness shuddered in response to the weight of a fly. I could see how Darian found enjoyment in raising these majestic animals. "Thank you," I said, placing a kiss on his velvety muzzle. I wasn't even sure what I was thanking him for, but in that moment I felt a profound sense of gratitude toward the gentle creature.

"Savor that 'thank you', Komala. She doesn't dole them out very often."

I glanced over my shoulder to catch Darian's half smile. "I give them when they're earned," I said.

"I'm fairly sure I've been slapped more times than I've been thanked."

"I dole those out when they've been earned as well," I said with a smirk.

The land was flat and open, the monotony of the landscape broken only by the small towns spaced along the highway every twenty or thirty miles, and the frequent stone bridges, all exact copies of the previous one. So it was for the next three days. All in all it was probably the most boring stretch of highway I'd ever been on. I'd never been so happy in all my life to be bored. We slept with a roof over our heads at night and hid among the masses of late-summer travelers during the day, all without any sign of trouble. I'd been a bit skeptical about Darian's idea of approaching from the east, but it seemed to be working pretty well so far.

On the fourth day out of port, we turned off onto a smaller highway and followed it toward the setting sun. The next four days went much as the previous four had, save that the plains gave way to low mountains. One morning we woke up to air that was noticeably cooler than the day before, a silent reminder that the equinox was rapidly approaching and our time grew short. As we neared the border to Moravar, we found lodgings in a walled settlement that was larger than any we'd stayed in since leaving the river.

After we finished our evening meal, Darian slipped out to take care of a few things and told me not to wait up, which suited my tired body just fine. So I went to bed, and laid there awake, unable to sleep without Darian next to me.

I'd gotten over the brush-off Darian had given me. It wasn't as if I was in love with him. It was a phase, just a silly phase brought on by all we'd weathered together, and the enormity of the task before us. It would pass.

So what if occasionally I wanted to lean in and kiss him? So what if sometimes, when his hand brushed mine, my belly flipped and my blood raced? I hadn't had a good roll in the sheets in months, and I couldn't deny that he was handsome. But that's all it was.

So what if when he pushed me away it felt like he had shoved his dagger in my chest and twisted? That was nothing but bruised pride. I'd have been happy to share my body with him, but that didn't mean I was in love. Besides, there was no way I was going to compete for any man's attention, even if it was with a ghost. And he was a commoner. What future could we possibly have?

When he finally did slip in I feigned sleep so that I wouldn't have to explain that I couldn't rest until I knew he was safe. He crawled into the room's only bed next to me and was snoring gently in just a few moments. I took a cleansing breath and willed my body to sleep, fighting off the urge to roll over and melt against his warmth.

As I did every night.

I was *not* in love. I just had to keep repeating it.

"Did you take care of everything you set out to do last night?" I asked when we rose the next morning.

"I procured a local map," he said with a yawn. "And I spent some time at a few taverns to see if I could learn anything."

"Did you?"

"The border with Moravar is pretty tight. The men I talked to said they were only letting citizens and those with current trade-papers through.'

"Well, that's a problem but hardly an unforeseen one. We'll figure something out." Something about his face made me ask, "Anything else?"

He chewed his lip and nodded.

"Bad news?" I asked.

"Bad news for some," he said. "Things have gotten worse between Zura and Moravar. There've been ships lost on both sides, and apparently the Empire's moved two legions onto the Pebble Islands." He shook his head. "Who would have thought so much would be put in jeopardy over arbitrary lines on a map?"

"So what do we do about the border?" I asked.

"I've been thinking about that." He rolled out the enchanted map on the bed and placed the local one above it. "The border is formed by the White River," he said, tracing the line on the map. "From what I was told, it's fast and dangerous, which means we'll need to cross at a bridge. There is a bridge at the border crossing on the highway, of course, but they're not likely to let us pass there. We've had a fair amount of luck so far sticking to back roads and pushing through the wilderness, so I figure we'll stick to what we know. South of the highway there's a verge—"

"No."

"Don't worry. My thoughts mirror yours," he said, the corner of his lips edging up. He traced another squiggly line on the local map. "It looks as though there's a small road here, with a bridge that leads to the northeast. We'll lose some time doubling back to the main highway once we cross, but I don't see any better options."

I studied the maps for a moment. "Nor I. And you're right, it's best to fall back on what's worked for us so far."

"Let's leave out then. Assuming we have fair weather the whole way, we'll only arrive a few days ahead of the equinox at best."

After stopping to ask directions, we found the gate that let toward the road we needed to take. As we approached, I felt the weight of someone's gaze upon us. Three men loading packs onto a flat-bed cart had their attention on us. One of the men was enormous, towering over the others. His bald head was crisscrossed with scars and there was a ratty patch over his right eye. The second was thin, twitchy, and missing most of his teeth. Their clothes were gritty and salt stained and neither of them looked like they'd bathed in weeks.

The third man seemed out of place next to the other two. The gold scarf tied elegantly around his neck disappeared down the front of his black damask doublet with silver stitching. His hair was slicked back with oil and he was clean shaven except for a meticulously trimmed mustache and triangle of hair at his chin. His eyes were firmly upon me.

He slid an assessing gaze over me, drinking in the details as one might view a hog you were considering buying at market. Then his eyes slipped over to Darian. "Nice horse you got there," he said.

Darian's gaze fell over the men, equally as assessing. "You have a good eye," he said stone-faced.

"You must not be from around here."

"Just passing through," Darian replied.

"I'd be careful going that way," the man said, inclining his head toward the gate.

"Why's that?"

"S'rough road."

"We've traveled rough roads before," Darian said, locking eyes with the man. "We'll manage. Thanks for the concern."

The oily man just smiled and nodded as we passed through the gate.

After we gained some distance I said, "They seemed a bit too interested in us."

"They certainly did."

"Do you think they're working with the Acolytes?"

"It's possible, though I think it more likely they were sizing us for slave collars. Either way, we should keep our eyes open and not dawdle."

"Agreed," I said, casting a look back over my shoulder at the city walls fading behind us.

Our road turned out to be more of a dirt path through the woods, barely wide enough for us to ride abreast. It seemed that the stifling summer heat had finally broken, ushered out by a gentle west wind. The breeze that washed over us brought with it the refreshing scent of the distant mountains, along with the realization of how close we were to the end of our long road, a prospect both elating and terrifying.

I finally gave voice to a thought that I'd carried with me for some time. "Darian, when we get to Vizipa…I want you to leave before I release Shakkar's demon."

"What?"

"I trust the Vija's vision…but we have no idea what the Anaviya will do once it's free. It could just decide to vent its anger at being locked up on everyone it sees. I've seen that sort of thing before when a demon escapes a binding."

"Samara—" he began, but I interrupted.

"Please, just hear me out. I certainly hope the demon doesn't decide to eat me or whatever, but there's no guarantee. At least one of us needs to survive to tell the Empire what we've learned about the Acolytes."

He made a noise that was neither agreement nor disagreement, then grew quiet, his face pensive as he apparently considered my words. Darian was stubborn but he was also practical, I was sure that once he really thought about it he would come to the same conclusion.

"No," Darian said, as casually as though I'd asked him if he wanted jam on his bread. I waited for him to elaborate, but he said nothing more.

"Darian, I've thought this through—"

"So have I. My answer is no."

"If I am to die, no purpose is served by you dying beside me."

"My mind is made up," he said, in that moment sounding exactly like my father. "I won't leave you."

The whirlwind of emotions swirled around inside me again, cutting and tearing. He wouldn't share a night in my arms, but he would die beside me for no cause? "So, you're willing to follow me to the end?"

"The end? No," he said, his aqua eyes meeting mine. "I'm willing to go beyond it."

"What does that even…" I started to say, but at that moment we came around a bend in the road to see the bridge before us. Or rather, what once had been a bridge. It had collapsed or been washed away some time ago by the look of it. All of the emotions swirling around inside me drained away, leaving me numb and tired. Both of us sat there in silence, staring at the broken bits of stone and the rushing white water beneath it. "Again?" I asked.

A scowl crept across his face. "It would be funny if it wasn't so sad."

"Clearly we've somehow offended the God that presides over bridges. Would that be Kavi or Vastuvit?"

"I'm not sure, but I say we make sacrifices of apology to both of them at the next temple we come across," he said. "Is it too much to ask for an accurate bloody map?"

"What are our options?"

"We can travel along the river and see if we can find a safer place to cross, but there are no other bridges anywhere close by other than the highway."

"Told you this was a rough road," said a voice from behind us.

We spun about to see the men from earlier standing in the road, oily-hair and twitchy, with crossbows leveled at us. I was *really* sick of crossbows.

"Now, be a good boy and toss that bow on the ground," the well-dressed man said. "Slowly"

Darian glanced about, doubtlessly coming to the same conclusion as me. The brush was too thick to ride through and we had the river to our backs. We were trapped. Darian slowly eased his bow from across his body and tossed it on the ground.

"Oh splendid, you're good at following directions," the man said, his lips drawn up in a wicked smile. "That bodes well for everyone involved. Now the knives." Darian unbuckled his belt and dropped it as well. The man walked confidently forward, keeping his crossbow trained on Darian as he kicked the weapons aside, while Twitchy pointed his at me, his lecherous eyes searching over my body. "Now get down, both of you."

"This is a foolish mistake," Darian said as he eased down from the saddle and I followed suit, dismounting to the right to keep Komala between me and my attackers.

"The only 'foolish mistake' here was hauling this lovely piece of fluff though the countryside without proper protection," the well-dressed man said.

Twitchy said, "With a face like that she'll bring a nice price at the Sarasi auction."

"Aye, brothel owners pay top coin for a ripe little peach like her," the oily-haired said with a wink to me. My breath caught in my throat as I imagined being chained naked upon some dais. Not that it would matter much if I didn't make it to Vizipa by the equinox. "Lefty, get the shackles and chains." The big man shifted his ax over one shoulder as he went to the wagon and rummaged about.

"He's pretty enough the brothel might take him too," Twitchy said, sucking his few remaining teeth.

"Maybe if he was a little younger," said Oily-hair. "But it's no matter. They're always looking for a strong back down in the mines."

I swallowed my fear and tried to get a handle on the situation. I knew as soon as those manacles went on, it would be very difficult for me to cast magic, limiting our options severely. Even unarmed, Darian was dangerous, and I had no doubt he'd either already come up with a plan or was close to one. I also knew he wouldn't try anything as long I had a crossbow pointed at me.

"Over there, both of you," Oily-hair said, gesturing toward the cart. Darian and I both started slowly walking toward Twitchy to the ominous—*clank-clank-clank*—of Lefty pulling chains out of the cart. "This really is a good-looking horse. Bet it'll fetch nearly as much as the girl."

Lefty lumbered next to Darian, grabbing his arm with one meaty hand and fumbling with the chains with the other, ax under his arm. Twitchy still had his crossbow trained on me. I needed to do something quick.

Now that the big man had a hold on Darian, Oily-hair lowered his crossbow and walked over to Darian's horse, running his hand along the stud's chestnut hide. "Who knows, I might even keep this one for myself," he said, walking around behind the animal.

A flash of cleverness sprang into my mind. I raised my hand to my face said, "I can't…Please…Stop…" I teetered once, then crumpled to the ground as though I'd fainted, hitting the road hard enough to send a jolt of pain through me. They had to believe it.

Twitchy nearly doubled over with laughter. "We 'av us a delicate flower here."

Without moving from the ground, I opened my eyes and caught Darian's gaze then glanced to the crossbow that was no longer pointed at me. I could see on his face he'd already caught on to my plan.

Three things happened almost simultaneously. Darian cried out in Manu and his horse kicked with both hind legs, catching Oily-hair walking behind him with a wet crunch. Then Darian twisted in Lefty's grip and slammed the point of his thumb into the towering man's good eye with all the strength he could muster. And Twitchy, caught by the surprise of the moment, squeezed the trigger of his crossbow.

A horse screamed in pain.

In a blur of movement, Darian reached for the only thing Oily-hair hadn't made him drop: his quiver. He drew an arrow and jammed it into Lefty's throat, transforming the tall man's cries of pain into a bloody gurgle.

Twitchy's eyes widened in shock with the gravity of what had just happened as Darian turned toward him. He dropped the now-useless crossbow and reached down for me, probably thinking to use me for a hostage, but he didn't realize I was conscious. I rolled away and scurried on my hands and knees to keep out of reach.

Darian drew another arrow, holding it by the shaft in his right hand, as he darted to get between me and my attacker. Twitchy, realizing he wasn't going to get to me before Darian, backed toward the cart and drew a dagger, waving it before him with a shaky hand. "L-look, this was just business. Nothin' personal."

Darian paced toward the man, armed with only his arrow. "You chose the wrong business."

As Darian closed on him, the man slashed and stabbed at him with a series of wild swings. He should have just turned and ran. Darian twisted and dodged the first few attacks then struck back, jamming the arrow into the arm holding the blade. As though it were a choreographed dance, Darian took the blade out of his hand and ended the man's cries with it. It was *so fast*. The whole fight from the time I hit the ground until it was over lasted the length of ten slow breaths. Without the immediate threat of violence, my nerves began to return to normal, and a whimpering sound accompanied by a small movement drew my attention.

A bay horse lay on his side in a growing lake of blood, a crossbow bolt protruding from his neck. "Komala!" I scrambled over to him. He tried feebly to lift his head but he didn't have the strength. I crouched next to him, laying my hand on velvet muzzle and his eye cast about in terror a moment before it settled on me, and he seemed to calm.

Blood soaked through my dress as I knelt, stroking him, "Shhh, it's alright I'm here. Just be still." He made one last low sound and stared right into my eyes, then went still. "Darian," I screamed. "Darian, come here. You have to help him."

Then Darian was kneeling beside me on the bloody ground, "There's nothing I can do. He's gone," Darian said, gently closing his eye.

"No," I said wrapping my arms around Komala's head. Tears filled my eyes and something inside me broke. The wall that I'd held all my pain and grief behind just cracked and shattered like a dam, a river of tears bursting forth.

I cried all the tears I couldn't shed for Harold, or Dirk, or Koto, or Marcus and all the other houseguards whose names I didn't even know. I cried for Autumn's loss, and all ordeals she had to endure. I cried for my brother's uncertain fate. I cried for Darian's suffering at the hands of the Fae and the wasp. I cried for my suffering.

It hurt. It hurt so bad. All of it.

It was a little girl losing her mother all over again.

I didn't even push Darian away as he tried to hold me.

I cried into his hair as we knelt there together in that lake of blood.

Why?

Why were the Gods so cruel?

Chapter Twenty-eight
Darian

I let go of the dying man and quickly turned to check on Samara. She seemed rattled but unharmed, so I went to make sure our enemies didn't have any surprises left in them. They didn't. The tall one was well and truly dead, and while the well-dressed one was still drawing shallow irregular breaths, he'd had half of his skull caved in and wasn't long for this world.

"Komala!" Samara shouted, scrambling to the gelding's recumbent form and collapsing next to him, stroking him. The twitchy little shit of a slaver had shot him with his crossbow. I'd killed him far more quickly then he deserved. Samara murmured to the wounded horse and stroked his face, giving him what comfort she could. What more could anyone ask for, horse or man.

"Darian," she cried. "Darian, come here. You have to help him." I could see from where I stood the gelding's injury was fatal. I crossed over and knelt down next to her in the bloody mud.

"There's nothing I can do. He's gone," I said, reaching out to close his eye in respect, remembering the wobbly-legged little colt I'd named "gentle".

"No," Samara said wrapping her arms around him and sobbing. It was different than when she'd cried after the nightmare. This came from the depths of her soul. We'd seen so much violence together in such a short time that it was easy to forget she was new to it. Very new. I'd seen some of my best friends killed in battle in front of me and held my wife as she drew her last breath. But until the ambush by the river, the Zatru attack on the caravan was the closest she'd ever been to battle.

I drew her to me gently, half expecting her to push me away, but she threw her arms around me as if clinging to a raft in the sea. I didn't try to soothe her.

I just held on.

When Samara's sobs were finally finished, I led her down to the river to wash off the muddy blood caked on both of us. We set up our camp a few hundred yards off into the woods from where we were attacked. Once Samara was passed out in the tent, I went back and searched the men, then laid them all out next to each other off the road and closed their eyes as was Manu custom, whether they deserved it or not. Then I tended to Tavas and the draft horse pulling the cart, before finally going to bed myself, wishing I could do more than lay a piece of fabric over Komala's head in respect.

Samara was quiet the next morning. I didn't know what to say, didn't know if there was something I could say that would help her, so I said nothing. Over breakfast she finely broke the silence.

"Thank you," she said. The dark rings under her eyes told of her exhaustion and weariness. "Perhaps you were right." At my questioning stare she added, "Perhaps I don't dole out thanks enough."

Not knowing what to say I just nodded.

She let out a tired sigh. "Were they really just slavers?"

"Looks that way. I found papers when I went through their things."

"At least that means the Acolytes probably still don't know we're here. What do we do now?"

I had an idea but I hesitated, casting about for a way to tell her. I was pretty sure it wasn't going to go over very well.

"You have a plan, don't you?" Samara said surprising me.

"Why do you say that?"

"You squint a little bit and chew on your lip when you have something you don't want to tell me." She smirked. "You have a plan, don't you," she repeated, but this time it wasn't a question.

I nodded.

"I'm going to hate it, aren't I?"

I nodded again.

An hour later when I locked the chain attached to her slave color to the iron hoop between her feet in the back of the cart she said, "You were right again. I do hate it."

"I'm not thrilled about it either."

"Believe me, if I'd have thought of something better I would have given it voice," she said with a frown.

I worked at tying the yellow scarf the way the previous owner had done it but I couldn't seem to get it. "Quit fussing with it and come here," Samara said, deftly tying it and tucking it under the doublet, then leaned back to examine her handiwork.

"How do I look?" I asked. Along with donning the dead man's clothes, I'd shaved and tied my hair back with a length of ribbon.

"Surprisingly sophisticated," she said, then added, "for a barbarian."

"Of course," I said with an eye roll.

Samara's eyes drifted to the spot on the road where Komala's still form lay. "I wish we had time to bury him."

"As do I."

She nodded and without another word we left, riding in silence save for the creak of the cart.

———————————

Apprehension rose in my chest as we approached the checkpoint, as well as on odd sense of symmetry. We'd crossed a border much like this when we left Zura, and with a similar deception, only under the pretense of selling horses rather than humans. At a glance, I saw that there were easily two or three dozen soldiers at the bridge. If it turned bad, it would be very bad.

"Remember, eyes downcast," I whispered to Samara. "You've got to show deference or they're not going to believe you're a slave."

"I know, we've been over this," she murmured back. "You worry about playing your part, I'll worry about mine."

I sighed. One would think at some point I'd accept the fact that every conversation was going to be like climbing onto the back of an unbroken colt.

"Name and papers," said a soldier when we reached the checkpoint.

I handed the man the travel papers I'd liberated off the dead slavers. "Oleg V'Arlen," I said hoping my pronunciation was passable since I'd never actually heard it spoken. The man looked over my papers carefully. Except for the captains with their brown, green, and yellow striped capes, all the soldiers looked identical in their polished breast plates, chainmail sleeves, and spiked helms. Most of them bore halberds. Only one carried no weapons or armor, and was instead clad in brown robes with green trim and a lavishly embroidered yellow cloak. He could only be some sort of nobility or a mage, though by his bearing I'd would guess the latter. Luckily, he seemed to be in some deep discussion with one of the other men and paid us little attention.

"Why's that horse saddled?" the soldier asked, pointing back at Tavas, who was on a lead line behind the cart.

I tried to think of a response other than needing a quick getaway. "Just bought him. He's only green-broke so I'm getting him used to my saddle."

"Huh. Where you been trading?" the soldier said.

"Pardon?"

He looked at the papers again. "Says here you're a flesh merchant. Where you been trading?"

I said the first thing that popped in my head. "Gopura." At least I could answer a few cursory questions about the slave market there, having seen it.

He looked up from his papers. "There are plenty of auctions closer. Why travel so far?"

"Specialized product requires a specialized market," I said, hoping it was oblique enough of a response. I was definitely not prepared for such in-depth questions.

"Why you bringing this one back?" he asked, gesturing to Samara on the bench behind me.

"Didn't get the price I was hoping for."

The man I was talking to seemed satisfied with that answer but a younger soldier next him chimed in. "How much you askin'?"

Damn.

I had absolutely no concept of what price a slave was worth. If he'd made an offer, Varga's gift would give a rough sense, but he didn't so I had nothing to go on. I needed a price that was high enough that he wouldn't buy her on the spot, but low enough to be believable. I made a crude guess based on what a high-end horse might sell for. "Three hundred and twenty five gold."

"Ahk, that's ridiculous. No wonder you didn't sell her."

I reached back and roughly grabbed Samara by the chin turning her to face him, "Come now, look at this face."

"Not bad, but she's got hardly any tits to speak of."

"She has other talents," I said giving my most lewd smile.

"She could have a gold-lined cooch, but she still ain't worth three twenty-five."

I glanced around to see we'd drawn an audience. The last thing we needed was more scrutiny, I had to wrap this conversation up before I got a question I couldn't answer. "For you my friend, two-eighty. One time offer only."

He looked like he might actually be pondering it, but the soldier holding my papers said, "Quit wasting the man's time. It's not like you have that kind of coin."

The other man spat on the ground. "She'd have to have wine coming out of her nipples for that price anyway."

The first soldier handed me back the papers. "You'll have to pay taxes on her since you're bringing her back."

"Of course," I said, paying him.

After counting the coins he waved us through. It was all I could do not to let out and audible sigh of relief. Once we'd cleared the massive stone bridge and put some distance between us and the border Samara said, "Tried a little hard to sell me back there didn't you?"

"I was just trying to ease suspicion."

"You certainly did a good job. You had me wondering there for a moment."

"Would you relax? I've dealt with enough customers to know he wasn't going to pay that price for you."

"Are you suggesting I'm not worth two-eighty?" she asked, brows raised.

I looked her over and stroked my chin as if considering. "Perhaps if you came with a gag."

"Trust me," she said, slowly licking her lips, "that would diminish my value."

I was going to quip back something cleaver, but I found suddenly that my throat was very dry.

Our slaver ruse held up better than I had expected, especially considering the rocky start at the border. But none of the other check points, toll collectors, or city guards seemed to suspect anything. The weather, however, was not so cooperative. The skies grayed over and a constant soaking rain plagued us for days. And to make it worse, each day the temperature dropped slightly. I was used to such conditions, but Samara looked miserable. We'd bought her a cloak in Gopura, but it was far too nice for a slave to wear, so all she could do was huddle under a sopping blanket. Perhaps her genuine misery was what made our deception believable. Eventually the rain moved on, though it had slowed us substantially, robbing us of valuable time.

"I don't know how people stand these things," Samara said, after I took her slave collar off behind the walls of the inn room where we were staying. "The *chafing*. Ugh."

"The people who find themselves wearing one don't have much of a choice about it."

"Fair enough," she conceded as she rubbed her neck.

"Can you point out exactly where Vizipa is?" I asked. "It's not marked on either map."

"That's actually not all that surprising," she said, studying the maps and pointing to a spot in the mountains, which then I marked. "It's been abandoned for centuries. A pity really."

"Why?"

"It sits on perhaps the most powerful ley line nexus in the world." She gave me a wry stare. "I'm surprised you didn't know that, as well-read as you are."

"What use has a Manu for ley lines?" I asked with a shrug. "The temple's just ruins now though, right?"

"Yes, but it's not as though that affects the nexus. Anyway, it was once one of the greatest architectural wonders of the world. It was the first structure to ever tap into a nexus and draw power from it."

"What happened?"

"It was destroyed by the Turaggin when they invaded a few centuries ago."

"If it was as amazing as you say, then why destroy it?"

"It was the home of one of the greatest schools of magic outside the Empire, the Enlightened Brotherhood of Magi. When the Turaggin invaded, the Brotherhood resisted and it took a heavy toll on their forces. Vizipa was targeted to make an example out of them. Though it cost the Turrigan dearly to do so."

"And the Enlightened Brotherhood?"

"It cost them even more dearly," she said solemnly. "Dead to the last man. Though they wiped out nearly a quarter of the invading forces. Afterward it was never rebuilt. One of my instructors made a pilgrimage there once. I remember her saying it was fairly isolated but the roads were good enough."

"Do we need to pick up anything before we head into the mountains?"

"Like what?"

"Special ingredients or something."

She smirked. "I'm not baking a cake."

"Well, how am I supposed to know?"

"I think I have what I need, but I'm hardly sure. It's not like I've ever done this before."

"Comforting."

A sardonic smile spread across her face. "Come now, where's your sense of adventure?"

"I'm pretty sure it's either back in that cave where the shades attacked us, or on the forest floor where I got stung by the demon wasp, but I might have lost it along with my dignity in Carvog when I was rolling around on the ground, wrapped up in magical thread."

"Well, at least you still have your sense of humor."

"Such as it is," I said as I scanned the maps. "Since it seems this is the last sizable city before we turn off toward the mountains, I'm going to see what I can learn."

"See if you can find a cloak that I can actually wear."

"Done. Be sure not to leave the room without your collar."

"I know," she said absently rubbing her neck again. "Be careful."

"Aren't I always?"

She just stared at me head cocked, hands on hips. "I'm not going to dignify that with a response."

When I returned near midnight, she was still awake with a dozen open books spread about the bed. "A little light reading?"

"Research," she said, stretching. "Any luck?"

I tossed her the rough woven brown cloak I'd found. "A bit."

She unwrapped the cloak and held it up like child on her birthday. "I never thought I'd be so happy to see such an ugly, coarse piece of fabric."

"Circumstance is everything," I said, sitting down and pulling off my boots. "Did you learn anything?"

"They make pretty good whiskey in Moravar."

Her mouth quirked in an unamused scowl. "Anything useful?"

"I learned that all my haunting brothels finally paid off. One of them remembers seeing a group of red robed individuals with green tattoos."

"Are they here now?" she said tensing.

"It was several weeks ago, and they seemed to just be passing through. But there was a bunch of them."

"That makes sense," she said, her gaze fixed and distant as though she were calculating a vast sum in her head. "They're probably headed the same place we are."

"That's where my thoughts took me," I said, taking off the doublet and undoing the complicated weave of the scarf.

"Did you learn anything else? News of the war?"

"Nothing new, which in this case is probably good news. Besides, we have plenty of worries before us without borrowing others."

"I fear that statement is all too true."

———

It was a good thing Samara had a new cloak. Between the late season and the steadily climbing altitude, the temperature continued to drop daily. After the heat we'd dealt with the past months, it was a welcome change. Though the mountains weren't nearly as tall or imposing as the ones around Stonehaven, they were still impressive. On our third day out of the city, we took refuge in the quaint little inn of a picturesque mountain village and restocked our supplies. I figured we were no more than three days from Vizipa, assuming the weather didn't turn bad and we encountered no trouble. With our history, however, I wasn't overly optimistic of either.

We left the village the next morning, headed along a road that threaded between the mountains. Unlike the highway we'd been on before, there were relatively few travelers along this route. Samara and I were chatting idly, discussing possible plans and contingencies, when we rounded a curve in the road to see soldiers.

Samara and I both froze, startled for a moment but quickly composed ourselves. I just hoped the soldiers were too far away to notice. "G'mornin'," I said, trying to force the shakiness out of my voice.

There was one of the yellow cloaked soldiers with a pointy blond beard, and three of the regulars wielding halberds. One of the regulars spoke up. "Mornin'. Papers, please."

Now that the surprise was wearing off I tried to slip back into the character of the slaver. "This can't be another toll," I huffed, making a show of jerking the papers out of my pouch. "I just paid one a few miles back."

"Don't get wound up mate it's just a checkpoint. Name?" Two of the regulars sidled up to the left of the cart, while the cloaked one and the last regular came around to the right.

"Oleg V'Arlen," I said, taking note that one that the yellow cloaked one seemed awfully interested in Samara.

"Coming back from market?" the soldier asked glancing at the papers.

"Yeah, hoping to get home before the weather turns. Looks like it might be an earl—"

"Why do you have that one?" the cloaked man interrupted, dragging his scrutinizing gaze over Samara.

"Got her in a favorable trade and decided to keep her for a season or so," I said glancing over at him. "I like variety." Samara, for her part did her best to keep her eyes downcast and shoulders slouched.

He opened his mouth to respond, but by then his eyes settled on something. I followed his gaze to Samara's Tarka amulet. It was far nicer than something a slave would own, and we should have realized it. I had no desire to harm any of these men simply for doing their job, but I couldn't let them take us into custody either. Wishing I hadn't packed my bow and quiver on Tavas, I shifted slightly to slide my hand under the blanket. "You wanna take a closer look at the merchandise?" I said, trying to sound frustrated rather than tense.

"Somethin' the matter, lieutenant? His papers look right," the man holding the documents said.

"It's probably nothing," the man said, then he started making the hand movements I'd come to associate with spell casting.

Bloody Hell.

The yellow cloaked mage's hands glowed with orange light for a moment, then his eyes went completely black. "Something's wrong! There's an illusion spell—" That was as far as he got before I jerked the crossbow out from under the blanket.

I leveled it at the man holding the papers and sent a bolt into his shoulder, hoping I missed the major vessels, then leaned forward and swung the crossbow at the man next to him like a club, catching him across the side of the face and breaking off several pieces of wood in the process.

"—on the girl," the mage finished as I turned and threw the now-broken crossbow end over end, slamming into his nose and laying him out on the ground.

The one uninjured soldier reacted faster than I would have figured, thrusting his halberd at me and catching me in the ribs. In that moment I was thankful Lucius had insisted on the chain shirt. A bad bruise was better than a gaping wound any day.

I drew one of my daggers and hurled it at him. It chinked harmlessly off his breastplate but he did retreat a few steps. I drew my kukri and my remaining dagger and jumped off the cart to rush him, hoping to catch him off guard and slip within the reach of his polearm, but he recovered too quickly, thrusting and swiping to keep me back.

I was in a bad position. I could tell just from the short exchange we'd had this man knew what he was doing, and he was wearing armor while wielding a weapon that had huge reach on me. As long as he wasn't reckless and fought defensively, I was at a huge disadvantage. He could hold me off for a long time, assuming he didn't get a good hit in on me and end the fight there. Time was not my ally. I had no idea how injured the other soldiers were, or if there were others around, or if another traveler would come along and decide to fight against me. The Rangers had a term for this situation—a clusterfuck.

Out of the corner of my eye I noticed a pale blue glow I'd become distinctly familiar with. Samara's spell-casting. I might not be comfortable with magic, but at that moment I had to admit it was welcome.

"No you don't, bitch," the yellow cloaked mage said, blood dripping down his beard as he stood. He grabbed ahold of the chain attached to her collar and yanked. Samara let out a scream that pierced the depth of my soul as blue lightning arced along her body. She collapsed bonelessly into the back of the cart.

My world stopped spinning.

I had to reach her.

The flash drew the attention of the soldier I was fighting. I drew Tarka's gift around me for but an instant as I slipped within the reach of his halberd. I flipped the grip of my kukri around and brought its wide spine across the bridge of his nose, sending him to the ground hard.

Then I turned and rushed the mage, no longer caring about his well-being. He saw me just in time to catch the pommel of my kukri in the teeth. I pounded him with it again, and again, until I was sure he was no longer a threat. By that time his face was a bloody mess. I dropped him and leapt up into the back of the cart to see Samara wedged supine between the benches.

The illusion spell was gone, revealing her as she truly was. And she wasn't breathing.

"Samara!" I yelled as I fell down next to her and started shaking her. Nothing.

"No," I pleaded. "You have to wake up." Gone was the thought that the world hung in the balance. In that moment all I could think of was her. I pleaded and bargained with the Gods that if they let her live, I would do whatever they asked. And if she died, even they would fear my wrath.

She let out a low moan and then a cough as her eye lids fluttered open for a moment.

A wall that I'd built up when Sita died crumbled, sending a flood of emotions through me. Tears blurred my vision as I tried to pull myself together.

"Samara?"

"W-what?"

"Are you…are you alright?"

"I think so, other than the badger trying to claw its way out of my skull."

The reality of our present situation returned to me. "We have to leave now. Can you ride?"

She nodded then squeezed her eyes shut as though doing so hurt. I drew her to her feet, and then guided her on wobbly legs to the back of the cart where she was able to get astride Tavas. I retrieved my bow and quiver then followed suit, mounting in front of her. "Hold on tight," I said, drawing her arms around my stomach and tearing off at a gallop down the curvy road deeper into the mountains. Only the staccato of hoof beats betrayed our passing in the serene morning calm.

Chapter Twenty-Nine
Samara

I tentatively opened my eyes, discovering to my relief that the vicious throbbing pain in my head had faded to a slight annoyance. A crackling fire cast shadows that chased one another across the walls of a large, musty-smelling room. I had dim memories of a barn next to a burnt house, which was where I was assuming we were. I slowly sat up, testing my bearings.

"How are you feeling?" Darian asked, concern etched across his face.

"Much better," I said, gaining my feet and brushing some hay out of my hair. "I haven't had a backlash hangover like that since I was a student. How long have I been out?"

"Just a few hours. Hungry?"

"Famished," I said after a moment's consideration. "Though my over-full bladder is of more pressing concern at the moment." I rose to go outside and Darian stood up as well.

"Do you need help?"

Why was he acting so strange? "No, I'm fairly certain I can handle it," I said before heading out of the barn to take care of my business. When I returned, he'd warmed a loaf of bread with some melted cheese over the fire. Now that there was food in front of me I was ravenous. While I ate my meal, Darian kept staring at me with a strange look. "Is there something you're not telling me?" I asked as I finished.

"What? No, why?"

"You're doing that thing with your face again."

"I just…I was worried. You said before that backlash could be lethal."

As with most things with Darian, his concern was touching while somehow managing to be frustrating. "I told you I'm fine," I said. "Luckily it was just a binding spell. If I'd been a lightning bolt or something I could have been in real trouble."

He let out a deep breath and again his eyes squinted a bit as his mouth tightened.

I huffed out a sigh. "Look, obviously there's something you're not telling me. Spit it out."

He ran his fingers through his hair. "Remind me never to play cards with you."

Now I was starting to get frustrated. "You know I'm not going to leave it alone. You might as well come clean n—"

Suddenly the distance between us was gone as his lips covered mine, strong arms wrapping around my body. Shock gave way to desire as I yielded to that kiss, then my senses returned to me as though through a distant fog. I took a step back out of his grasp. "What are you doing? You pushed me away remember?"

"I know," he said simply. "I'm sorry." Then his lips found mine again.

Part of me wanted nothing more than to drink in those lips until I was intoxicated, but the pain of rejection was still too close to the surface. Again I pulled back.

"You don't just get to decide to cast me aside one minute and then the next—"

He kissed me again but it was gentle and yielding, with no demand behind it. That almost had me, but I wasn't going to be made a fool of again. I shoved him away at arm's length. "Stop it! Look, I know about Sitana. I'm not going to compete with—"

"Samara, I do love Sita and I always will, but she's gone," he said, closing the space between us again and reaching up to gently stroke my cheek with the back of his hand. "There is no competition. I choose you."

"But—"

"Every frustrating, stubborn part of you," he said with his irritating half smile.

If he'd kissed me I would have pushed him away again, but he didn't. He just cradled my face and stared at me with those aqua eyes. In them I saw nothing but vulnerability and longing. He just stood there waiting for several long moments, yielding to my decision.

Damn vexing barbarian.

I dug my fingers into his hair and pulled him to me, falling into his kiss, into him. In that moment there were no walls between us. No pain, or pride, or fear. Just need. The same need a fire has of air, or crops have of water. Clothes fell aside as hungry hands tore at them until nothing separated us. All senses left me except the scent of his skin and the warmth of his touch.

We made love.

It wasn't with the tentative, searching care of new lovers. It was with the aching need of water rushing to fill a submerged bowl. We filled the empty space in one another. It may have been nothing more than the sum of our shared experiences, the fire we'd been forged in together, but with him my fear was gone. When we found our shared release we held on, pulling each other even closer, as though, if we held on tight enough, that feeling, that moment, might last forever.

The sunrise shined between the old wooden planks, casting long golden lines across the dirt floor. In the light of a new day, the glow from the night before faded, only to be replaced with the shadow of fear and doubt.

What if last night had only happened because Darian thought I'd nearly died? What if he just said what he did to comfort me, and didn't really mean any of it? All the warmth and safety I'd of the night was replaced with an all-too familiar vulnerability. What had seemed simple last night was hard and complicated this morning. I let out a deep sigh.

"Uh oh," Darian said.

I rolled over to face him. "What?"

"That sigh means you're agonizing over something you've got bouncing around in your head."

"It's nothing, I'm…just worried about how much time we've lost."

"Lie," he said, running his fingers through my hair.

Damn Azava's gift. "Darian—"

He silenced me with a finger on my lips which would have angered me to no end if hadn't followed it by saying, "You were torturing yourself because you're afraid I don't share your feelings, but I do."

"And what feelings would those be?"

"Love," he said.

Hearing it spoken so plainly was jarring. "I do *not* love you," I said, trying to extract myself from the tangle of limbs and blankets.

"Lie," he said, pulling me back toward him. "Come here and I'll show you that I meant what I said last night."

I did.

And he did.

Our morning roll in the sheets was less urgent than the night before but no less intense. When we were spent, I laid my head on his chest trying to catch my breath. "Pushpa was right," I murmured to myself.

"Hmm?"

"Nothing," I said.

His ego was big enough already.

We washed up in a stream that was cold enough to set my teeth chattering and then left, making our way toward the road. Now that our slave ruse had been discovered, I dressed in my new clothes and happily donned the warmer cloak. Darian also retired the bloody torn doublet, taking back up his surcoat and bracers. There wasn't very much room behind him on the saddle, and the ride wasn't all that comfortable, but I made do.

The events of the last day seemed dreamlike and surreal. The distance that had been present between Darian and I since our fight by the waterfall was gone. It was difficult to make sense of the emotional eddies swirling around inside of me, so I decided not to try. This one time I wouldn't dissect, or label, or analyze every little thing. There would be plenty of time for that if we both survived. Besides, I felt light and buoyed, with a renewed since of optimism.

Unfortunately the afterglow didn't last very long.

We came around a ridge that overlooked the road we were bound for to see a long column of soldiers on horseback.

"Think we made them mad?" Darian said.

"Bloody Hell, there must be a hundred of them down there."

He nodded. "Looks like a whole cavalry unit."

"I thought you said you didn't kill any of their friends yesterday."

"Well, two of them were pretty banged up but they were alive when I left them," he said scratching his light stubble. "Though killing them may have been the wiser choice. At least then they wouldn't know who they were looking for."

"No, you did the right thing," I said, tightening my grip around his abdomen. "Anyway they're looking for a blond woman and a clean-cut merchant."

"Mmm, I imagine if they find us they will err on the side of caution and take us into custody anyway until it's sorted out."

"We probably shouldn't get caught then."

He glared back over his shoulder at me. "You're just full of helpful suggestions this morning."

"What can I say? I didn't get a lot of sleep last night. Do you think you can find a way to cut through the woods and find the road we need to take off this highway?"

"Aye, it's just more time lost."

"Then we shouldn't waist any more discussing it."

"Yes, *m'lady*," he said with a smirk.

"That's a good barbarian," I said, returning it.

It took far longer for us to reach the road than Darian had figured, mostly because we had to climb half a mountain to do it, at times moving along ledges so narrow we had to walk single file as Darian led his horse. We lost nearly an entire day when it was all said and done. Now I *was* truly starting to worry. Unless my count was off, we were but one full day and night from the equinox. I shared my thoughts with Darian as we lay curled up together in our little tent just after sunset.

He blew out a deep breath. "I share you concern. Just as a factor of distance we should reach Vizipa before tomorrow night..."

"But?"

"Well, assuming we don't run into the cavalry unit that's looking for us, I find it nearly impossible to believe the Acolytes have left Vizipa unguarded. Having seen how they operate, I would guess they've probably left mages along the road."

"They might assume we're lost, or dead, or delayed at the very least," I said. It didn't sound very convincing even to me.

"That's possible, but the bastards have been fairly methodical up to this point, and they must have had these plans in motion for some time. Even if they're not expecting trouble we have to assume they've prepared for it."

"So what are you suggesting? Keep off the road and make through the wilds? We've barely enough time as it is." Not to mention we didn't know for sure what we'd be dealing with when we got there.

"No, you're right. Time is our greatest foe. If we don't make it by the equinox then it's all for naught. We've no choice but to chance the road. We'll just have to be alert for an ambush."

"It's a pity we don't have any practice at that," I said with a smirk. "Where's the waterskin?"

"With the saddlebags."

As I crawled out of the tent, the cool night air rose gooseflesh along my naked body. I hastily located the skin and retreated back with Darian under the blanket.

"I love your freckles," he said.

I stared at him incredulously, trying to decide if he was jesting. "Seriously?"

"They're adorable."

"You just saw me naked and it's my freckles you're commenting on? I don't know if that means there's something wrong with you, or with me."

"There were many things I found desirable. Shall I list them?"

"Yes, please do."

"I fear it might take all night."

"You're pretty good at this flattery thing," I said, snuggling up next to him. "Next we shall have to teach you about bribery."

"I *was* married once. Remind me to tell you the story sometime about when I was courting Sitana."

"Oh, I heard." When his eyes widened in surprise I said, "Pushpa and your sister told me."

"Figures. Remind me instead to tell you every embarrassing story I can think of about Nia."

We took to the road an hour before dawn, taking advantage of Arati's gift and the dark empty roads to cover as much distance as possible. After sunrise we were much more cautious, paying careful attention to our surroundings and the other travelers we came across. We hurried past the few tiny villages we encountered using Tarka's gift, wary of Acolytes or their agents. Just before midday, the flattened top of the volcano where Vizipa lay could be seen in the distance. "That must be it," I said pointing.

"What? The volcano?"

I nodded. "Vizipa lies in the crater at the top."

His shoulders hunched a bit. "I see…"

"Don't worry, it's been dormant for millennia."

"It's not that, I just didn't realize we were going to have to summit a mountain. It will take yet more time and leave us—"

A gentle feather-on-my-skin sensation washed over me. Darian went rigid and faded into muted colors as he called Tarka's gift around us and brought us to a stop.

The question that was on my tongue died as I saw what prompted his actions. Four figures in red robes stood casually chatting in the road some yards ahead. We froze as statues for several moments, barely breathing, but the quartet kept chatting amongst themselves showing no sign that they'd noticed us.

Slowly and quietly, Darian eased us into the tree line. Once we were a safe distance away, he released Tarka's gift, obviously exhausted from the strain. "Well," I said, exhaling the breath I'd been holding. "As ambushes go that could have been worse."

"I'm fairly sure that was a road block rather than an ambush, though I'm certain it would have turned into one if they'd recognized us. They're probably just turning away all traffic to keep prying eyes from what they're doing. I'd wager two mares there's more behind them patrolling the road."

"Maybe we'll get lucky and those soldiers who are chasing us will come along and run them off?"

"Does that sound like our luck? Besides, we don't have the time to be sitting around here waiting."

"What now? We go through the woods the whole way?"

"Do you have a better suggestion?"

I dug the heels of my hands into my eyes in frustration. "If the Acolytes just keep stealing sand from our hourglass they'll succeed in stopping us without ever lifting a finger."

"Our time grows short but, so far as we know, we still have the element of surprise. That's no small thing." he said, easing into a trot through the thick trees. "The Imazighen have a saying, 'The elephant may be great, but when it stumbles, it does not easily rise.'"

Chapter Thirty
Darian

Skilled as I was at navigating in thick forest, it was difficult to keep my bearings once we got into the valleys. We were forced to cut a curving, meandering path between and around the low mountains. In the thick trees there were times we lost sight of the volcano for hours at a time. We soon came to a juncture and I had a difficult time finding the right way. As I tried to orient myself, Samara closed her eyes for perhaps two breaths then pointed and said, "That way."

I blinked at her. "You've had a compass in your head this entire time and you're just now speaking up about it?"

"I can feel the lay lines building toward the nexus."

"And you're sure it's that way?"

She closed her eyes again for a moment then said, "Positive. You can't feel it?"

I followed suit and closed my eyes for a moment, concentrating. I sensed neither the prickly feeling of a verge, nor the warm feeling that sometimes accompanied holy places. "Nothing."

"Mages are taught how to feel for lay lines, though some people can do it naturally. I figured with all your Manu gifts you'd be able to as well."

"Apparently not. Since you seem to know where we're going, let me know if we get off course."

"Oh, so let me make sure I understand this. The great woodsman needs help from the little city mage to find his way through the trees?"

I glanced back over my shoulder with a smirk. "The little city mage should be careful, or she'll find herself bound, gagged, and thrown over the saddle."

"Work before play," she said, patting my cheek with a wicked smile.

The sun hung heavy in the western sky as the volcano finally loomed above us. We had at most two hours before we lost Azava's light, and the darkness made it much more difficult to ascend the mountain, especially for Samara and Tavas as they lacked Arati's gift and coldfire would draw attention. We followed the twisting game trail toward the base of the mountain when suddenly Tavas's nostrils flared and he let out a whine.

"Whoa," I said pulling back on the reins.

"What's the matter?" Samara said.

"He smells something nearby. It could just be a bear or—" Then the smell hit me as well. It was a charnel-house odor, as if something nearby had its bowels torn open and was left to rot in the sun. "By the Gods…"

"No," Samara said, wrinkling her nose. "By the Rajasa. I'm fairly certain that's an Azuchi."

"Demon?"

She nodded. "They're often summoned as guards."

"Smells like it's already dead."

"It's worse up close."

I could hardly imagine that. "Alright, you stay here with Tavas, I'll scout ahead and come back."

She shook her head a bit too fast, betraying her fear. "We should stay together."

"I can't keep Tarka's gift up around you and Tavas very long, but I can maintain it easily on just myself. I'm just going to scout a path up the mountain. If I see any trouble I'll come right back." I glanced toward the west. "Time grows short."

She sighed, setting her jaw. "Be careful."

Realizing that was about the closest thing to an agreement I was going to get out of her, I gave her a quick kiss. "Stay hidden behind that deadfall over there," I said, pointing. "I won't be long." With that I called Tarka's gift and took off at a light jog along the game trail.

I didn't have to scout far.

The foul stench grew stronger the closer I got to the mountain until I found its source. Two creatures paced along the trail, barking back and forth at each other in their guttural demon tongue. From behind they could almost be mistaken for gaunt panthers, save for their slimy green hide and the spines trailing down their back that ended in a barbed tail. Seeing them from the front banished any idea that these were creatures of the natural world. Dead white eyes stared out above a large hawk-like beak that looked like it was made of some sort of black metal. Long hooked claws of the same substance scored the ground as the creatures paced along with feline grace. As I stood watching, two more of the demons glided into view from the bank of a small creek that intersected the trail.

Fantastic.

I'd been, to my misfortune, downwind of the creatures but the breeze shifted, blowing from behind me. One of the closer demons cocked its head as though sniffing the wind then turned in my direction muttering a string of consonants to the other.

I wondered idly how the thing could smell anything over its own stench as I quietly withdrew. It continued to scan the area for a moment, then again muttered something to its companion before lurching back to patrol.

I retraced my steps to find Samara where I'd left her and described to her what I'd seen.

"Yeah, those are Azuchi," she sighed. "And there were four of them?"

"Four that I could see, but there could be more. We're going to have to see if we can find another way up. Unless you think we could take them?"

"Not without making a lot of noise."

"No point in wasting any more breath talking about it then," I said climbing into the saddle in front of her.

We made a wide arc around, not wanting to cross the path of any of those patrols, and took a more eastern approach to the sleeping volcano. As we neared its base, the rank odor again assaulted our noses. After a quick exchange with Samara, we fell back and circled wide, trying yet another approach.

A third time we were confronted with the odor. "We're going to have to change our tactics," said Samara. "We don't have time to keep circling the mountain looking for a way up."

The sun was barely a finger's width above the horizon. "We're either going to have to fight them or try to find a way to sneak by them, which will be difficult considering they seem to have a keen sense of smell."

Samara took a deep breath as if to steel herself. "I have an idea."

A strained note in her voice gave me pause. I twisted to see her face. "Am I going to hate it?"

"Without a doubt. But I think it's our best shot."

I braced myself. "Let's hear it then."

She glanced down for a moment seeming to collect her thoughts. "I'll summon a demon to scout the path and guide us up."

I ran my palm slowly down my face. "Summoning a demon is your solution to every problem."

"The Acolytes will be opening the gate in barely twelve hours. We're out of other options. I can call a small, fast demon that can find us a clear path and return quickly—"

"Samara," I said, tightness building in my chest, "The things we're up against are demons. How do we know it won't just betray us to them?"

"It won't," she said evenly.

"As far as we can tell, the Acolytes are working for the Rajasa. Why would a demon go against its makers?"

"I don't have time to explain why. This is our best chance, but we must decide now, because the only practical time to summon a demon is at dusk or dawn."

"I can't believe we're even discussing this"

"Darian," she said calmly, staring into my eyes. "Do you trust me?"

I started to say, "Yes, but..." However, what I saw in her eyes stopped me. She'd thought this through. This wasn't the same young, proud, arrogant noble I'd met by the hippodrome in Stonehaven. She had a quiet, calm confidence in her plan, but there was also a vulnerability there. She believed in her plan, but she needed me to believe in her. As uncomfortable was I was with the idea, I did trust her.

"Yes," I said, adding no qualification.

"Thank you," she said. The barest of smiles gracing her lips. "This will work."

I shook my head. "You're such a bad influence."

Samara took my dagger and drew a circle with a five pointed star in the center roughly a yard wide, into the patch of dirt we'd cleared. She then drew another circle around it and began inscribing symbols into the space between. By the time she was done, the sun was almost completely lost behind the horizon.

As she handed my dagger back to me she glanced at my face and said, "Try to relax. I know what I'm doing."

I gave her a skeptical look.

"I've worked with this demon several times before."

"I trust you, but that doesn't mean I have to like this, and I'm definitely not going to relax."

"Fair enough, I suppose," she said. She turned to face the circle and took a deep breath, then began her casting.

I nocked an arrow.

Samara started a low chanting along with her mudras, and the circle began to glow with a soft blue light. It went on for several minutes, longer than I'd seen any other spell take. I held a lookout for trouble while keeping one eye firmly fixed on the center of the circle. As Samara's chanting built to a crescendo there was a bulge in the circle as there had been when she'd summoned the Elemental. With a flash of green flame, the minion of Hell appeared in the circle.

After all the build-up it was actually kind of disappointing.

The demon was roughly the same size and shape as a small monkey, though instead of fur it had shiny black scales like a snake. It sported bat-like wings on its back and all its limbs, including the tail, ended in three clawed digits. Comically large, wide-set eyes looked about frantically as if trying to orient itself, while the creature's needle-toothed mouth was constantly mumbling a stream indecipherable words in a high, squeaky voice.

"Niggli'po," Samara said in an authoritative voice. "Do you yield to my will?"

"Niggli'po?" I said, putting my arrow back in the quiver. "The creature spawned from the depths of Hell is named Niggli'po?"

The demon squeaked something back in its demon language and Samara said, "In the Common tongue please."

"Yes, yes," the thing replied in broken Common. "I submit. How I serve you?"

"Good," Samara said. With a wave of her hand the glowing lines of the circle faded. "Do you see that volcano?"

"I see," Niggli'po said nodding vigorously, setting his large ears flapping.

"We want to get to the top, but there are demons guarding the way." Samara paused and closed her eyes for a moment as if organizing her thoughts. "You will find a path that is unguarded and safe for us to take to the top of the mountain, and then return and lead us. Do you understand?"

"I undra...undrastine...I get it."

"You will do this without being detected by anyone. If you are found, you will not reveal who summoned you or what your task was."

"I got it."

"Good. You will perform this task and return as quickly as you can. Do you have any questions?"

The little creature canted its head to one side, large eyes closed to slits. "No."

"Very well, then. You may go perform your task," Samara said, then drummed her fingers on her forehead as if remembering something. "Oh, and harm no living creature."

The demons ears and wings drooped in obvious disappointment. "As you wish," Niggli'po said dejectedly, then with a flap of his leathery wings disappeared into the trees as quickly and silently as a shadow in the night.

"That…was not what I was expecting."

"Not all demons are vicious, slavering monstrosities."

I shook my head looking towards the mountain. "And you're sure he won't betray us?"

"Not intentionally at least. Bound demons must comply with their summoner's commands to the best of their ability, which is why I took such care with my phrasing." Her brows went up. "You said you trusted me."

I shook my head looking toward the volcano. "I do trust you, it's the scaly little Hell-monkey I'm wary of. Come, let's eat something while we have the chance."

We dined silently on biscuits and jerky as the shadows lengthened and settled into full darkness. The moon rose casting but a thin sickle of light. As I watched it, the weight of the moment settled firmly upon my shoulders. It seemed unreal to think that after months of journey and struggle we had only a single night to complete our task. I knew whatever weight was on my shoulders, Samara's burden was twice as heavy. Once we reached Vizipa her task was only beginning.

"You should probably change into your doeskin leathers," I said.

"Because some things are more easily done in pants?" she said, playfully entwining her fingers in mine.

"That, and it gives you at least a little extra protection."

"I'm not sure pants are going to aid me in jail-breaking a demon."

"Shows how much you know."

"I think you just want to see me naked one more time before we climb the mountain of almost-certain-doom."

I felt the corners of my mouth drag up into a smile. "Guilty."

"As I told you, I'm good at seeing through men's schemes," she said, planting a lingering kiss on my lips. She rose and slipped her dress off over her head, the chilly night air raising goose flesh along her body. She stood there a moment longer, reveling in me reveling in the sight of her, before shimmying into her leathers and wrapping the cloak around her shoulders.

Nearly an hour after darkness settled, the flapping of leather wings heralded Niggli'po's return. "Found it," the impish little demon said, plopping down in front of us and looking pleased with himself.

"And you weren't detected?" Samara asked.

"Course not," he creature replied, looking as indignant as a he could manage.

"Very good. Now you will lead us there without being spotted."

"Yes. Is no prolem," he said, puffing out his tiny chest. Even I had to admit, for a Rajasa-spawned creature from the depths of Hell, it was kind of adorable.

We mounted up and followed Niggli'po as he led us through the dark woods, moving with an uneven hopping gait that made him look even more ridiculous and simian. Every so often he would take to his wings and scout ahead, only to return a few moments later to assure us the path was clear. As he led us to the northeastern slope of the mountain, we smelled the stench of the Azuchi but Niggli'po assured us there were none nearby. At this point we had no real choice but to trust him. We made it to the foot of the mountain and started ascending without seeing any Acolytes or other demons.

The slope wasn't too rocky, and in daylight we probably could have ridden most of the way up, but at night, with nothing but starlight and the sliver of the moon, I figured it wasn't worth taking the chance of Tavas missing a step and tumbling. So we walked. The temperature fell until I could see my breath, but we encountered no trouble as we followed the winding path Niggli'po chose for us. It was difficult to tell in the darkness, but I guessed it took us about two hours to reach the top.

"Look down there," Samara whispered as we neared the top. Our path had meandered around to the north side of the mountain and far down at the base a swarm of green lights danced like fireflies.

"Is that..?"

"Coldfire," Samara nodded. "Those are Acolytes."

"There are dozens of them down there."

"That must be where they're performing the ritual to open the gate."

"Let's clear the summit and be out of sight before someone sees us."

"You think they could spot us all the way up here in the dark?"

"After one of them squeezed wasps out of her twat? I'm not up for taking any chances."

As we crested the lip of the dormant volcano, Vizipa materialized into view dominating the summit. The massive rectangular structure was covered in black marble shot through with golden veins. The majority of the roof and several sections of the wall had either partially or completely collapsed, but the face of the building, with its colossal columns the width of a redwood trunk, remained untouched. Even though it lay in ruins, it was impressive.

There were several rocky outcroppings and enough trees to give us easy cover. We slipped around the building to find a place to leave Tavas where he would neither call attention to us nor get spooked by whatever waited for us beyond the half-broken walls.

"Niggli'po," Samara said in hushed tones. "Do you think you can get a look in there without being spotted?"

"Yes. I go look around and tells you what I see," he said, ears flopping as he nodded.

"Then do so."

With a few beats of leathery wings the demon disappeared into the night sky.

Something dawned on me as the creature departed. "He's awfully used to working with you. This isn't the first time you've used Niggli'po as a spy, is it?"

"A good mage never reveals all her secrets," Samara said flashing an enigmatic smile. After a moment, however, she closed her eyes and began massaging her temples, taking slow deep breaths.

"You alright?"

"Yes it's just…my teeth are practically buzzing with the power of the nexus."

"Really?" I said still not sensing anything.

"I can't believe you don't feel it. I mean, I knew it was one of the strongest in the world but…the reality's a bit overwhelming."

"Is it going to be a problem?"

Her hair whispered as she shook her head. "No, I think I just need a moment to acclimate." She closed her eyes again and looked like she was going through a series of breathing exercises.

I gave her space and took the opportunity to check my weapons and stretch out some of the stiffness from the climb. After a few minutes she opened her eyes and she seemed more comfortable. "Better?"

"Better."

"Good," I said, reaching out to gently take her shoulders. "Are you ready to face what's behind those walls?"

She took a shaky breath. "I guess I have to be."

There was hesitance in her voice and she trembled slightly beneath my touch. "You sure?"

She took a deep steadying breath and squeezed my arm. "I'm ready. Let's go trip the elephant."

The enormous bronze front doors had never been breached. They had some sort of unfathomably powerful enchantment on them that even today protected them from virtually all damage. Unfortunately for the Enlightened Brotherhood, the other doors had no such magic upon them and had long since been destroyed. It was through one of these small side doors that I slipped in.

More than half the structure was a large open hall or cathedral of some sort. We knew from what Niggli'po had reported that the imprisoned demon we were here for was in a smaller chamber in the rear section. We also knew it was far from unguarded. An Acolyte and half a dozen demons stood sentinel against interference.

Considering how much of the roof and walls had been destroyed I expected there to be quite a bit of rubble, but the valuable marble had long since been scavenged leaving the room mostly clean and open. The eight monolithic midnight columns that once supported the ceiling gave silent testament to the grandeur this place once had. Each column had been carved from a single piece of marble, and they reached seventy yards high to where the ceiling once stood. Several of them bore deep gouge marks from where chains had been used to try to topple them, but despite their best efforts, the looters had been unable to bring the columns down. I took inspiration from that.

Other than the stars twinkling through the open roof the only light was the sickly green pall of coldfire coming from the far end of the massive hall. One of the Acolytes had apparently claimed the corner as his, and had set up a small pavilion. The mage reclined on his side in a nest of pillows, reading from a large tome and puffing leisurely from a hookah.

Scattered throughout the hall between us were three demons. One I recognized as an Azuchi, which looked indistinguishable from its cousins at the base of the mountain. The others were new to me. One might have been recognizable as a large man were it not for the slouched posture, jutting tusks, and covering of shaggy, matted, gray fur.

The other shared the size and rough proportions of a man, but that's where the similarity ended. It was half again taller and broader than any human, with massive bulky muscles covered by reddish-black armored skin than made me think of a lobster, while swirling horns reminiscent of an antelope sprung from its head. Its arms alone were the width of my torso. It carried over its shoulder a massive club wrapped in thick iron bands. Unlike Nigglipoo, all of these demons seemed like they'd been chosen for their fighting ability and I wasn't very keen on getting in a wrestling match with any of them.

I withdrew silently back through the door I'd entered from and let go of

Tarka's gift long enough to give Samara a single nod. She swallowed, then returned it. Squinting, I could barely make out Niggli'po perched atop the wall. He was supposed to let us know of reinforcements. I was just hoping Samara's trust in the little Hell-spawn wasn't misplaced. I took one last deep breath and pulled Tarka's gift around me once again, retracing my steps back into the large chamber.

I made my way silently around to the opposite wall and began slowly creeping along it back to where the tattooed mage rested on his pillows, thankful the black background would make it harder to spot my outline. I watched the demons carefully as I slid down the hall, silent as a shadow, paying careful attention to the Azuchi, remembering how the one at the base of the mountain had caught my scent. At least the high walls blocked most of the wind. The large red one made a slow circuit around the hall walking a guard route, but it never took him near me.

Green light washed over me as I approached the Acolyte's corner. Rarely in my life had I felt more exposed and vulnerable than I did then, sliding inch by inch down the wall not two paces from the tattooed mage. I expected him to catch some faint sound or see my hazy silhouette in relief against the wall, but the bald man simply puffed on his hookah and periodically reached down to turn the page. I continued past until finally I stood behind him.

The whisper made by the kukri as it slipped from its well-oiled sheath sounded like thunder to my ears, but the Acolyte didn't so much as twitch. Given how hard they'd been to kill in the past, I wasn't going to take any chances. I planned on taking his head off. I raised my blade and looked at the red robed man reclining on his side…and felt a moment of conflict.

Samara and I had agreed that the Acolyte was the greatest threat and needed to be taken out first, definitively. And yet, I couldn't help but feel like what I was about to do was wrong. I'd killed from ambush before. Hell, I'd shot Waspgina in the back, but I had been pursued and the danger was apparent. This Acolyte was just laying here. Yes, he served the Rajasa. Yes, he would doubtlessly try and kill me if he knew I was here. But killing a man just laying sprawled out on pillows felt like murder, which would definitely violate my Amani.

But it didn't matter.

This man was standing between us and stopping the gate from opening. He had to die. This was war. War was dirty, and ugly, and messy. I just hoped that the Gods would see it that way.

The blade sang through the air, sending his bald head rolling down the pile of pillows, and the fountain of blood from his neck soaked the tome. I jammed my bloody blade back into its sheath and whipped my bow into position.

I expected to see three demons rushing me, but none of them immediately reacted. It wasn't until a moment later when the coldfire snuffed out that they even looked toward me. By then my first shot was already in the air. It took the Azuchi through what would be the heart and lungs in a normal beast. The demon cried out a surprised squawk as it sank to the floor. The next arrow sailed toward the shaggy one but it reacted with surprising speed, getting under the shot by throwing itself to the ground. The red one stared dumfounded for a few seconds before reacting, giving me a chance to send two arrows his chest. Both had about the same effect of a normal arrow on a Varaha.

The red demon looked down at the arrows protruding out of its chest and slapped them away as one would a mosquito, then shouted something at me in infernal and launched into a lumbering charge, club held high. The shaggy one joined him a moment later. Having no desire to be trapped in a corner with the hulking monster, I leapt over the Acolyte's headless corpse and sprinted back down the wall the way I'd came.

Once the red demon got going, his long powerful strides carried him deceptively fast. I changed course and darted behind one of the huge columns and wrapped myself in Tarka's gift, then reversed course back toward the wall. Both the demons chasing me fell for my deception, and the ruse bought me a few precious seconds. I fired an arrow into Shaggy's ribs, and ducked behind another massive column for cover.

A guttural shout alerted me to a new presence in the hall as three more demons flooded out of a large door in the rear. One looked like a man-sized midnight blue bird with a lizard's head and tail. Another was mostly humanoid with coal black skin, wearing tarnished copper armor and brandishing a matching sword and shield, while the last one appeared to be a mass of maggot-colored tentacles arranged in a roughly quadruped shape.

I summoned all my speed and made for the side door I'd entered from, with the three new demons following on my heels and the big red one stomping and intercepting course. The only one not chasing me was Shaggy, who was too busy trying to pull my arrow out of his ribs.

I almost made it to the door. I would have if not for the flying one. The thing dove low, trying to hook me with its curved talons. I fell into a roll that sent arrows flying from my quiver but I managed to get under the creature's claws as it passed me by. I used my momentum to get back to my feet with little more than a stumble. The bird-demon let out a cry and banked about to come back for another pass.

I put all my energy into my legs, pushing me toward the door that was my salvation. I could hear the clanking of armor just behind me as well as the thundering footfalls of Red just off to the side as I reached the door, and ran right past it. If the demons thought my behavior was odd it gave none of them pause as they passed in front of the door a moment later and were bathed in a cone of fire.

Close as I was, the heat against my back felt like a furnace and I was fairly sure I lost a bit of hair. Half a dozen strides later, I looked back over my shoulder to see the gout of flame fading and the two following me writhing on the ground in agony. Red however, never even slowed. He was blackened and smoking but otherwise seemed completely unaffected by his jaunt through the inferno.

Of course.

He was going to be on me in two or three of his massive strides so I did the only thing I could do and made for the closest column. I darted around it just as he swung. His massive club smashed into the black marble, sending a stinging spray of debris across my neck and face, mercifully missing my eyes. Red tried to round the column to get a clean swing at me, but I kept moving, keeping it between us like a child trying to avoid an angry parent's discipline. The demon growled in frustration and tried to go the other way but I just changed course as well.

It might not have been the most brilliant or dignified plan, but I didn't have a lot of other options. The ease with which Red brushed off the arrows led me to believe my blades wouldn't be of much use, and that was assuming I could get inside his massive reach without getting splattered like a melon. The only thing I could do was buy time until Samara could deal with him, as was the plan, but we'd already ruled out Samara using lightning for fear the thunder would bring reinforcements, so her range and options were severely limited.

"It's getting away," cried Niggli'po's high pitched voice. The bird-thing was flapping its great wings as fast as it could to gain altitude and clear the wall, having seemingly realized it might be outmatched. I couldn't allow it to escape and warn the Acolytes. I broke away from the column, running toward the center of the hall and reached for one of the few arrows I hadn't lost in the roll. I nocked it on the run, hearing the thunderous footfalls of Red pursuing me. I knew I was only going to get one arrow off no matter what, and realistically I didn't like my odds.

When I had a clear shot I slid to a stop, drew back, took aim with a lead, and fired. I didn't even have a second to see if my arrow struck true. I threw myself ungracefully to the side, feeling the rush of air as the iron-banded club passed right through the space I'd just occupied. I rolled and kicked getting briefly tangled in my surcoat as the club came down again, slamming a deep gouge in the marble right next to me, again spattering sharp chips across me.

I backpedaled and stumbled and somehow managed to gain my feet at a run with Red practically breathing the same air as me. Distantly, I was aware of a thud as the bird-demon crashed into the wall, and another a few seconds later as it slammed into the ground, but my thoughts were on Red as he closed on me. I sprinted with everything I had, managing to stay just out of the club's reach. I didn't realize until a moment too late that I'd been chased right into Shaggy, now free of my arrow and staring at me with malice-filled eyes.

He was directly in my path and I had no time to change course. I crashed into Shaggy and we went down hard in a tangle of limbs. I rolled and squirmed, trying to extricate myself from the gray demon, but he had about a hundred pounds on me, and from the feel of him, it was all muscle. We rolled and fought but it became immediately clear he was much stronger than me and I ended up on the bottom. He smelled like a yak that had wallowed in its own feces.

Shaggy hit me hard enough to rattle my teeth and fill my mouth with blood. His next blow bounced the back of my head of the marble, filling my vision with white flickering stars. As Shaggy pounded me again and again, I managed to throw my arms up, blocking some of the hits with my bracers.

I was rattled, but I had enough sense left to realize that if I was going to do something to keep Shaggy from beating me to death I had to do it quick. A moment later I realized just how bad things really were.

Red loomed over us, club raised overhead in both hands and nothing but unfathomable rage in his face. He was about to splatter us both. At least Shaggy had the comfort of not knowing it was coming.

Then Red stiffened and fell as straight as a tree trunk, cursing out in his guttural language as he slammed into the ground. The sound of the impact caused Shaggy to turn and look, granting me a moment's reprieve. I couldn't reach any of my weapons with him straddling me so I did the only thing I could think of. I jammed two fingers as far as I could into the arrow wound in his ribs. The demon managed to scream and growl at the same time as it reeled away from me.

But I didn't let go. I curled my fingers getting a grip on the inside of his rib, slipped my dagger out with my left hand and sank it to the hilt in the creature's furry gut. Again and again I withdrew the blade only to slam it home, never letting go of his wound. Finally, the demon sagged in my grip, sliding to the floor and leaving me covered in his sticky, blackish blood.

A stream of guttural curses drew my attention to Red's prone, writhing form as he fought against the shimmering silvery thread that bound him. I knew from experience, the harder he fought it, the tighter the thread became. "Frustrating isn't it?" I said. A blue rune lit the air above Red for an instant before he vanished in a flash of green flame.

Samara threw her arms around me. "Darian, are you alright?" she asked, her voice thick with concern.

My nose might be broken, my vision was still a bit wobbly, and my head felt like it was going to explode, on top of the symphony of other pains coursing its way through my nerves. I ran my tongue along the inside of my mouth, doing an inventory. A few teeth felt loose but it seemed like they were all present, though my mouth was filling up with blood. I drew upon Irin's gift to numb the pain. Samara needed to worry about the task at hand and not me.

"Fine," I said, spitting out a mouthful of blood, "Why do you ask?"

Chapter Thirty-one
Samara

We'd sent Niggli'po to scout the hallway while Darian recovered what arrows he could and finished off the demons that were still twitching. Still, we were cautious as we made our way down the long corridor. I glanced again at Darian; it looked as if a fountain of blood had poured from his nose, his left eye was half-swollen shut, and his face was a mess of cuts.

"I told you it's just scrapes and bruises," he said, catching me looking. "The only thing you need to worry about is dealing with this demon. Are you ready?"

No. Actually I was terrified. I was afraid of dying. I was even more afraid of failing and condemning others to death. A cold lump of doubt had settled in my belly. But there was a sense of excitement fluttering in my chest as well. That combined with constant pressure of the nexus and the fact I was still coming down from the battle we'd just been in, my nerves were a tornado of conflicting sensations.

But none of that mattered. I was ready because I had to be.

"Yes."

"Good, because I think this is it," he said, gesturing to the soft golden glow bathing the corridor through the archway of the chamber up ahead.

I took one last steadying breath and banished my fears as best I could, drawing myself to stand tall. I was Initiate Mage Samara of House Arga, noble of the Empire of Zura. I would face what was on the other side of that archway with my head held high. Before my courage had a chance to flee, I walked through the archway, with Darian Wayha, Ranger of the Manu, by my side.

The chamber was a plain square perhaps ten yards on each side, and was utterly empty except for the four-yard diameter summoning circle dominating the center of the room. The circle and all the diagrams had been etched into the ground and filled in with gold, as was required to summon and bind an Anaviya. I only took a cursory glance at these details, for it was the being inside the circle that held all of my attention.

The demon stood up on broad cloven hooves as we entered, easily twice the height of either of us. He was as he had been in the Vija's swirling vision, though that hardly did him justice. Huge leathery wings, too large to fully open in the confines of the circle, jutted gracefully from his back. His jet black skin was spider-webbed with cracks from his hooves to the elegantly curved ram horns adorning his head. From each of these fissures, black smoke bellowed and an orange glow issued forth, as though his blood was molten and about to erupt from his body. He had no true eyes, only the same orange glow pouring forth from deep-set sockets.

I cleared my suddenly dry throat and said in the Infernal tongue, "Greetings, Anaviya." The demon's glowing eyes widened and he tilted his head slightly to the side. I continued, "I am Samara Arga, Mage of—"

"You are Zuran?" the demon interrupted in Common. I'd half expected his voice to be a deep basso that rattled my breastbone like the dragon's had been, but instead it was a rich baritone.

"Er…yes, I am," I fumbled back in Infernal.

"Unless it displeases you, I would prefer to converse in the Common tongue."

That was strange. I'd never, not once, had a demon speak to me in Common without being ordered to. "Whatever you prefer," I said making the switch.

"Samara," the Anaviya said, seemingly rolling my name around in his maw. "I am At'Mavat." After searching so long for the demon's name, a surge of unbridled excitement vibrated through me at finally knowing it. "You are obviously not aligned with the mages who imprisoned me here. So, that begs the question…" His gaze of inner fire shifted back between Darian and I. "Why are you here?"

I swallowed. "You are the Anaviya who taught Shakkar, are you not?"

His gaze narrowed on me again and for a long moment he just stared, seemingly studying me. After what felt like an eternity he said, "I am."

"Then I am here to free you."

The demon's eyes went wide as his lips pulled back from dagger-like teeth. For a moment I thought he was about to growl at me, but then I realized he was smiling. "Free me?"

I'd played this conversation out in my head many times since the night in the cave, and so I phrased the next statement very carefully. "Yes. Though I would request a favor in return for doing so." Darian shifted uncomfortably next to me.

The demon crossed his arms in front of his broad chest and stared down at me in what was either contempt or amusement, or quite possibly both. "Oh? What favor?"

"The mages who imprisoned you here seek to open a portal to your Realm. I ask only that you stop them from doing so."

"Ahhh," the demon said rubbing his square jaw. "That brings much into clarity." The Anaviya closed his ember eyes as he tapped his chin. It was a strangely human gesture for a demon. He was silent for perhaps half a minute, during which time my heart hammered in my chest like a drum, then he opened his eyes and spoke. "I will do as you request, Samara," the demon said. "In exchange for a favor of my own."

Uh oh. "What favor?" I asked, swallowing nervously.

"In order to stop the portal, I must return to my Realm. For helping you, I ask you summon me back to Acala after I am done," his gaze bore into me. "And release me with no binding."

I swallowed my heart back down in my chest as Darian stared at me with nervous eyes. An unbound Anaviya loose in the world could be bad, but I couldn't imagine a scenario in which one Anaviya would be worse than the legions of demons that would flood through the gate otherwise. Making the deal was the only rational choice, I had no other options. There was only one problem.

"That is agreeable." I saw Darian wince at those words. "But I lack both the skill and the knowledge to summon an Anaviya such as yourself."

"I can impart what knowledge you need," he said, waving a clawed hand dismissively. "Swear to me you will summon me as soon as you gain the power to do so, and we have a bargain."

Darian caught my gaze and gave a slight nod. When I furrowed my brow at him, he mouthed the word "truth". Apparently Azava's gift worked on demons.

"I will summon you to this Realm and release you without binding as soon as I have the power and skill to do so safely. As I swear it," my throat was so dry I had to swallow twice before I could finish, "so mote it be."

"Very well, mage. It seems we have an accord."

So there it was. My deal with the devil.

"I will need a moment to prepare."

The demon gave his dagger-laced smile again and gestured to the golden glow radiating from the floor. "I have nothing but time."

I caught Darian's gaze and he followed me out into the corridor. Once we were out of sight, I slid my arms around him and leaned my head on his shoulder. His arms tightened around me. "Darian…"

"No."

I leaned back far enough to see his face. "You don't even know what I was—"

"You were about to ask me to leave again. The answer is no."

"Just wait with Tavas until—"

"I'm not going anywhere. Besides, that demon was telling the truth. And it seems to me it's putting as much trust in us as we are in it."

"Just in case—"

"Not going to happen."

"Listen here you scruffy, irritating barbarian," I said jamming my finger in his chest. "I'm trying to do the reasonable thing, *and* keep you safe by the way. The least you could do is let me finish a sent—"

His lips silenced mine with a kiss as his arms tightened around me. Yes, it was infuriating, but I melted into it anyway. I was trying to send him away because I cared about him, so I couldn't get mad at him for staying for the same reasons. Though, this silence-me-with-a-kiss thing was not going to become a regular occurrence. "Are you finished?" he asked pulling away just enough to talk.

"I'm *not* in love with you."

"Liar."

"Barbarian."

"Pest."

"Let's go release the demon into the world so he can stop the other demons from being released into the world."

He rolled his eyes. "There's *no way* this plan could go horribly wrong."

"None at all," I echoed as we crossed back through the archway.

At'Mavat seemed to swell and give off even more smoke as we entered the chamber. "Are you prepared?"

"I am, though I have one question to ask, if I may?"

"Ask," the demon said with what seemed like an amused smirk.

"Why did you give your name to Shakkar when he asked for it?"

The demon again shut his eyes, stroking his chin with a midnight talon. When his fiery eyes opened again they were filled with an unreadable expression. "Curiosity."

I nodded. That, at least, was an answer I could understand. "I'm going to dismiss the circle now." As I took a deep breath and began summoning my power, At'Mavat's head canted to the side again. I shaped the spell in my mind that would unravel the magic of the circle, gave it power and released it. My light washed over the glowing circle and diagrams…and did nothing.

"I thought you were aware," At'Mavat sighed. "This circle is drawing power directly from the nexus. It cannot merely be dispelled."

I hadn't noticed before but the circle containing At'Mavat wasn't exactly the same as the one in the book. It was surrounded by two extra rings with script in between them. One tapped into the power of the nexus, while the other made the circle itself invulnerable to damage, both magical and mundane. My heart sank to my feet. I walked the perimeter of the whole circle looking for some flaw or loop-hole to exploit but there was nothing. Archmage Valerius couldn't have designed a better circle.

"Samara?" Darian said.

"He's right, it's tapping directly into the nexus. I can't dispel this."

"Alright. What do we do?"

"I…I don't know," I said, fighting the panic welling up in my chest.

"The mages who trapped me here were thorough," At'Mavat said in a low rumble only slightly more than a growl.

"What if we damaged the engraving?" Darian said.

"The spells renders it indestructible. Perhaps if we destroyed the marble around it down to the foundation that might work, but we hardly have time for that."

"There must be something?" Darian said.

But what? The spells worked into the outer rings were flawless. Dozens of Masters working together might be able to overwhelm the protections, but one lonely Initiate would have better luck trying to empty a lake with only a tea cup.

"I thought all I would have to do when we got here was dispel a simple summoning circle. This," I said, gesturing to the intricate arcane sigils of the outer ring, "is way beyond anything I've ever dealt with." I buried my face in my hands. "If only I hadn't lost the mirror, Master Carter might know—"

Darian gripped my shoulders. "Master Carter's not here. You are the only one who can figure this out."

"I don't have the training."

"Aren't you supposed to be some sort of prodigy? Figure something out."

"Darian, I don't know *everything*."

"So what? You're just giving up? Where's the stubborn woman I've been traveling with for the past six months?"

"No, I'm not giving up. I just don't know what to do."

"Perhaps," At'Mavat interjected, "you could find a way to temporarily deplete the power of the nexus?"

"Maybe if this nexus were smaller," I said, shaking my head, "or there was a Causeway gate built on top of it or something, but this nexus is so strong that…" I trailed off as my brain began connecting the scattered dots. I was approaching this all wrong. The problem wasn't the summoning circle. *That* I could handle easily. The problem was the power being channeled to it from the nexus. I sat down and began pulling books out of my endless bag.

Darian said, "Samara, what are—"

"Quiet," I said, as I flipped open one of my journals to an empty page and furiously scribbling with my quill. I had an idea that was theoretically possible, but as far as I knew it had never been done, likely because there had never been a reason for it. A diagram began to take shape. A very complicated diagram. When it was finished I looked it over, compared it to the golden glow on the floor before me, and then looked it over again. It might work.

I held the picture up before Darian. "Do you think you could copy this around the circle, exactly as drawn here, using Vastuvit's gift?"

He took the journal from my hand and studied it. "Yes, but it will take some time."

I glanced at the sky through Vizipa's broken roof. "Unless I'm reading the stars wrong, you have less than two hours, so you should get to it," I said, thrusting a piece of chalk into his hand. "And remember it needs to be exact."

"What happens if it's not?"

I thought about it for a moment. "Either my spell won't work…or it might cause the volcano to explode."

He looked at the chalk in his hand with a frown. "No pressure."

Without further words, Darian took the journal and the chalk and went to work, slipping into the intense almost trance-like state indicative of Vastuvit's gift.

At'Mavat folded his huge leathery wings around himself like a cape. "You obviously have a plan."

"Yes," I said, thumbing through several of the reference books I'd brought and arranging them open on the ground around me. "Though there's no guarantee it's actually going to work."

"Indeed," was the demon's only reply.

Now all I had to do was figure out how to cast the most complicated and difficult spell I'd ever attempted, while drawing on enough power to cook me to a cinder if I lost control.

While I poured over texts of magical theory, Darian continued to copy my diagram with long even passes of his hand, his face a mask of concentration. At'Mavat watched Darian with a silent intensity until the diagram was nearly half complete then he spoke, drawing me from my studies. "Clever." When I glanced wide eyed up from my books he continued, "You're going to try to pull the energy of the nexus away from the summoning circle."

"It's the only thing that came to mind," I shrugged.

The demon canted his head at me again, "You remind me of him."

"Who? The mage that bound you here?"

He shook his great horned head. "Shakkar." His fiery eyes and stared past me as if remembering. "You are as curious, and clever, and bold as he was."

"Me?" I said in disbelief. "You're comparing me to Shakkar the Wise?"

A chuckle rumbled out in his rich baritone from deep in the Anaviya's chest. "You know him only as a legend, a story from the distant past. I knew him as a man, arrogant and ambitious."

It was true. I'd never really thought about him as a real person before. "You said that you gave him your name out of curiosity, but how did he trick you into helping him?" As soon as I said it At'Mavat's expression changed and I realized I'd probably offended him. "I'm sorry, that was a rude question…"

"Shakkar did not trick me into helping him," the Anaviya said, chuckling again. "He asked me."

"He…just asked you?"

"Yes. Did you think he threatened me?"

"Well…"

"If he had, I would have simply broken through his clumsy circle and torn him in half."

A shudder ran down my spine at the matter-of-fact statement. "Why didn't you?"

"He gave me no cause to. In fact, he was very courteous."

"So why did you agree to help him?"

"The answer should be obvious young mage," the demon said narrowing his pyroclastic eyes. "I wanted to."

"But why would a demon—"

"Want to help a human entrap other demons?" At'Mavat interrupted. "I suppose I never cared for my 'brethren' very much. And Shakkar offered me something that no other being ever had."

"Freedom?" I said hazarding a guess.

"Friendship."

I stared, mouth agape.

He canted his head at me again. "Is that so hard to accept?"

"Well, I um…I've never…" I stumbled.

"I suppose I understand your reluctance to believe me."

"I just wasn't expecting to hear that. There's not even a word in the Infernal tongue for 'friend'."

"I was the same as the other children of the Rajasa once," he said with a look of what might have been pity.

"What changed?"

"Are you familiar with Chaya'zveta?"

"Yes," I said, trying to remember back to my demonology class. Chaya'zveta was the Rajasa also known as The Shadow Of The Flame, one of the hardest to understand in terms of human thought.

"Chaya'zveta is the one who made me," At'Mavat said, another unreadable demon expression crossing his face. "After the Gods forced them into Hell, the Rajasa raged and railed against their prison. But despite their unfathomable power, the walls of their new Realm held them in check. They could neither reach, nor even see out to the Realms that they had once so coveted. But, at some point they realized that a mouse may slip through the bars of a cage meant for a tiger. With this understanding, the Rajasa created legions of new creatures with the hope that they might find a way into the other Realms."

"Yaviyas."

At'Mavat nodded. "But though the Rajasa rival the Gods in power, they lack their vision, their order, their understanding of cause and effect. And the Yaviyas shared the flaws of their creators. So, seeing how well the Devas served the Gods, the Rajasa sought to copy them."

"They made the Anaviya," I said catching on.

"Very good," the demon said, inclining his head towards me. "The Anaviya's were more powerful, more intelligent, and able to do something even the Rajasa could not. Think in the abstract, plan beyond the moment."

"Then why did the Rajasa only make seventy-two?" I asked, voicing a question that had always troubled me.

"They agreed that each of them may only make nine."

"Why? Surely they possess the power to make more."

At'Mavat smiled. "The Rajasa felt that if they made too many of us, we might one day find a way to subjugate them. After all, they created us for the purpose of scheming. And they couldn't simply take away our free will, or we couldn't adequately serve them when we were in other Realms."

That actually made sense. "But that doesn't explain why you are different."

"I wasn't, at first. Chaya'zveta created me with an abiding hatred for the Gods and all those loyal to them. And for a very long time I did hate," he said as his glowing eyes narrowed to slits. "But my creator also made me to learn, and to reason, and to question. And so I did.

"I learned all I could from demons who had found their way to your realm and back. But the more I learned, the more I came to admire what the Gods had created, and the more I began to see the flaws in my creator and the other Rajasa. After several millennia I became disillusioned with both my maker and my role."

A momentary softness came to At'Mavat's hard features. "And then a demon showed up asking for permission to give my name to a human mage. I was intrigued, both by the mage's boldness and his cleverness, so I sent my name and allowed myself to be summoned. When I arrived, he greeted me courteously and immediately dismissed the circle."

"He dismissed the circle?" I said in disbelief.

"He knew that his weak little circle couldn't hold me, so he released me and humbly asked for my assistance. If he'd tried compel me or trick me I would have walked through his clumsy barrier and ended him, but he simply asked me to teach him. So I accepted. I began to teach Shakkar, and in so doing I came to realize that I far preferred the company of humans, to that of Yaviya, Anaviya, or Rajasa. So I stayed by Shakkar's side for the rest of his days."

"Why did you return to Hell?"

"I didn't."

"Wait…you've been in our Realm the entire time since Shakkar summoned you?"

"Well, I spent some time in Eather, but the majority of my time has been spent in Acala, yes."

I stared dumbfounded. That certainly explained why A'vish couldn't find him. "But no one's seen you for nearly three thousand years."

He smiled. "I have been among those that know the value of discretion."

"Wait…if you were in our Realm, how were the Acolytes able to summon you?"

"They did not summon me." His inner flames flared when he spoke, and more smoke bellowed from his fissures. "They tricked me into coming here, then trapped me in this circle."

"So, what do the Rajasa seek to gain from opening the gate if they can't get out?"

"Have you not been listening? The Rajasa lack what they would need to conceive of such a plan. This must be the scheming of men."

"But the Acolytes are working for the Rajasa."

At'Mavat waved one clawed hand. "Doubtless they are, the Rajasa have offered power and promises of greatness to such humans for ages. But the Rajasa lack both the understanding and the foresight needed for this."

I rubbed my temples as I tried to process everything. "So why did they even bother trapping you here?"

"They must have known I would have stopped them as soon as I felt a gate between our Realms start to open."

"Oh, that makes…what? You would have shut the portal anyway?"

"Without you making the bargain? Yes."

"Why?"

"I've already told you, I prefer the company of humans to that of demons. If the minions of the Rajasa managed to conquer this world, everything that I love about it would be destroyed. As I said, I've come to admire what the Gods created." His eyes narrowed. "Do not think this revelation releases you from your bargain. If you fail to follow through with your obligation to summon me, when I do make it back to this Realm, I will hunt you down and destroy you on principal."

I swallowed. He might be an unusual demon, but he was still a demon. "I've sworn it. I will keep my word."

"Good, you seem an interesting human. It would be a shame to kill you."

"Um, thank you. You're certainly an unusual demon."

"I will assume that is a compliment," At'Mavat said. "There is one thing I am curious about. How did you know I was here?"

Knowing what Darian's objections would be I considered my question carefully. I held up the untranslated copy of the Sarga Paza. "This was recently discovered in some ruins, and it has the diagram of your circle that's missing in all modern copies. But I wasn't able to translate it from Vikatan, so I took it to a seer who pointed me here," I said sticking as close to the truth as I dared.

"Nothing stays buried forever, it seems," the Anaviya said as he stared at the diagram of his circle. "I suppose it is serendipitous that is was discovered when it was."

That was rather serendipitous…

I ran my fingers through my hair, trying to absorb everything. The Vija's vision finally made sense. And she got that vision by using Rocana's gift. Rocana was the God of time and fate. Perhaps we'd received more aid from the Gods than we realized.

Pre-dawn light glowed through the broken sections of the eastern wall by the time I finished checking the diagram. It matched my drawing down to the smallest details. The inner ring surrounded the entire circle and the outer ring had three spokes leading out to smaller circles with various geometric shapes and magical script filling the empty spaces. "This is flawless, Darian. You're officially hired to draw all my circles."

"I'm out of your price range," he said with a wink. "Are there any other preparations?"

"No, I'm ready."

"Good, because we only have a few minutes before dawn."

"Do you think I'm unaware of that?" I huffed.

Darian ran his fingers through my hair. "You can do this, I have faith in y—"

This time is was my lips that did the silencing.

"You talk too much," I said, pulling away from him. "Now try not to do anything to distract me. This is, without a doubt, the hardest spell I've ever attempted."

"Yes, m'lady," he said giving the smile I'd once found vexing.

I sat in the lotus position with my various magical texts arranged around me, and took a deep breath, about to clear my mind when At'Mavat spoke. "This may sound self-serving under the circumstances, but I hope you survive this."

I figured that was about the best compliment I was going to get out of an Anaviya. "Thank you, At'Mavat. So do I."

So with that, I cleared my mind of demons, portals, summoning circles, and Darian. I released everything, letting it all fade away until there was nothing but calm. Then I began to construct the spell.

Putting it together was like holding a dozen needles and trying to thread them all at once on the first try. The problem was it wasn't really a spell, it was several spells all woven together. I had to try several times before I could picture it all in my mind, and when I finally did, holding onto it was like trying to balance a house of cards in my palm. Several times it collapsed and I had to start over, all with the constant pressure of the nexus buzzing in my head, and the understanding in the back of my mind that every second I delayed brought the world closer to catastrophe.

After a half a dozen tries, I was finally able to hold the spell in my mind. I waited for a few moments like that to make sure I was able to maintain the image. Once I was as certain as I could be, I gave the spell power. The energy began to build slowly, least I overwhelm myself and topple the house of cards. What seemed like an eternity passed before I began to form the mudras with a level of care and detail I hadn't had since my early days in the academy. The spell was beginning to come together, when I distantly heard Niggli'po's frantic, high-pitched shouting. My delicate and perfectly balanced spell began coming apart.

I pushed the outside world away, ignoring everything but the delicate forces warring within me. I used every bit of my training and concentration to keep the image of the spell whole in my mind, while still feeding it power. The image wobbled and wavered, tipping like a ship to and fro, threatening to capsize. Finally the wavering stopped and I again had the spell under control.

Again something, some sort of noise…perhaps fighting, tore at my concentration, but this time I kept the spell together and continued feeding it power. The power built until my head ached and my chakras burned. I had to overcome the ambient current of the nexus for a moment in order for my spell to enchant the diagram and bring it to life. The problem was that I had no concept of how much power might be required, so all I could do was feed the spell as much energy as I could while still maintaining my concentration. I had to go right to the line, but if I stepped one toe over, that was it. I lost. I died. And millions died with me.

As a battle raged nearby and my body burned and ached, I found a strange sense of detached calm, as if I watched myself from above. Mages called this state Satori. I'd heard others talk about it but I'd never experienced it myself. Finally, the power running through my meridians reached the point I could take no more.

I released the spell.

Chapter Thirty-Two
Darian

Samara sat with legs crossed in front of the circle. I might have thought she was doing her morning meditations were her face not squeezed with concentration. My chest tightened with every second that passed as I watched the eastern sky grow rosy through the broken wall. I wished there was something I could do to help, but this was her trial, not mine. I felt about a useful as a pitchfork with no tines.

"Lookout, demon coming!" screeched Niggli'po from his perch atop the broken wall. One of the Azuchi guarding the base of the mountain must have gotten suspicious and come to investigate. I snapped my bow into position, drew an arrow back and aimed for the archway. Unfortunately, that's not where the demon came from.

The Azuchi's polished beak peaked over the wall an instant before it leapt. I whipped my bow toward it and fired, trying to correct for the path of the creatures jump, but it happened too fast. My arrow struck the hellspawn, but it was a grazing shot that slid just under the slimy skin of the creature's back leg and emerged out the other side. The creature landed gracefully on the black marble, its claws gouging furrows into the ground.

It hesitated but a moment as it took in the scene, then its dead white eyes locked onto where Samara sat facing the circle with her back to the demon. It charged. I had no time for another shot, so I did the only thing I could think of. I tackled it. It was a bad plan—I realized it as I was doing it—but I simply had no other option. A demon spawned for the sole purpose of battle it might be, but I still had at least fifty pounds on it.

Apparently a body slam wasn't what the demon had been expecting, because I caught it completely off-guard. I crashed into the Azuchi and we went sliding across the smooth marble in a tangle.

I thought they smelled bad before, but up close it was all I could do not to retch. As we came to a stop, I wound up on top of the creature who was pinned under me on its side. The spines on the creature's back gouged and dug at me but I managed to get an arm around its neck, keeping the vicious beak pointed away from me. It was short lived. The slimy substance that gave it its awful stench was slicker than oil, and the creature managed to squirm its head right through my arms. It attempted to snap at me but I smacked its beak aside with a bracer.

I tried to roll away but the demon was faster. It managed to get a swipe off at me with its vicious claws. Steel rings chimed across the marble as the creatures black claws sliced across my chest in a downward arc from my breastbone to my floating ribs, cutting to the bone. I bit back a cry, kicking with all my strength into the gaunt creature's ribs, and was rewarded with a satisfying crack. The demon wailed and cursed at me in his infernal tongue as it scampered a few steps back.

I rolled back to my feet, blood soaking my shirt and surcoat, and drew my kukri and dagger. The creature was limping and moving a bit slower, but it had definitely gotten the better of me in that exchange. If it had ever been in doubt, I could confirm tackling a demon was a bad idea.

The Azuchi's white eyes again locked on Samara and it hunched as if getting ready to try another charge. I quickly moved to step between them, trailing blood as I went. The creature barked something at me in Infernal.

"Very well, I accept your surrender," I replied in Common. The creature's eyes narrowed and it spat something back at me that needed no translation. Apparently it understood Common.

It started to circle around me in a slow arc and I moved to keep myself between it and Samara. I couldn't give ground without moving and the creature realized that. Without warning it came at me, snapping and clawing. Immediately I spotted the creature's error. It came at me viciously, hoping to overwhelm my defenses. It wasn't a bad plan, but the thing had overextended. I shifted my stance subtlety to the left, and launched a back-hand swipe with my kukri to decapitate it. If it had been just a beast, the battle would have ended there, but the demon spotted the shift in my stance and dodged at the last moment so that my blade just nicked its neck.

The gouge along my ribs burned with just that small effort, but I pressed my advantage by launching into a flurry of slashes. The creature gave ground as I advanced, barely staying ahead of my attacks. As it retreated it angled itself sideways and whipped its tail at me. I spotted it just in time and dodged, the tail's barb coming so close that it clipped my trailing hood.

The creature came at me aggressively again, and I retreated a few steps. It lacked any advantage of range on me, so by moving back just a bit, I was hoping to lure it into over-extending again. The Azuchi didn't disappoint me. As it overextended a second time, I changed stance for the counterattack again, then shuffled back a step. The demon seemed fairly smart and I figured it was expecting the same maneuver from me as before. I was right. Halting its lunge halfway through, it snapped the tail barb at me. But now I was now out of range. The kukri cleanly severed the end of the tail, sending it clacking along the ground.

The demon wailed in pain, charging me again. This time there was no plan or battle strategy, just unbridled fury. I tried to find an opening but it came at me too fast. Unwilling to give ground, I tried to keep the demon at bay with attacks of my own, but slowed by blood loss, pain, and exhaustion I couldn't keep up. The creature caught my kukri in one of its swipes, and sent it sliding across the room.

The demon knew it had me. As it crouched to pounce, I used the one trick I had left and pulled Tarka's gift around me. I hoped to throw the demon off long enough to at least draw my other dagger, but my hazy form did nothing to confuse the Hellish beast.

The Azuchi leapt upon me and dragged me to the smooth floor. I managed to angle sideways and avoid the rending claws, but I lost my dagger as we slammed into the ground. All I could see was the creature's skinny forked tongue as its beak lunged forward to tear my face off. I threw my hand out, catching the creature by the throat. It squirmed and writhed against my grip, its beak snapping angrily again and again not three fingers from my nose. I managed to get my other hand on its neck as well, but despite my weight advantage, the thing was just stronger than me. As much as I fought and struggled, the demon's beak was slowly descending. I could see in its dead eyes it knew.

I knew.

I couldn't win. I couldn't defeat it. But I knew something the demon didn't. I didn't have to. All I had to do was keep it occupied until Samara finished her spell. I just prayed my strength held out that long.

A burst of light, brighter than a flash of lightning, filled the room. For a moment the creature pulled back blinking rapidly against the sudden light. I hadn't been looking that way but the demon had been blinded. It pulled its head back, giving me a precious moment's respite. Then creature's eyes snapped open wide and it moved as if to leave me and rush Samara. But I still had both my hands on its throat, and as long as I still drew breath I was not going let go.

Chapter Thirty-Three
Samara

I sank to my knees, spent with the release of the pent-up energy and blinded by the explosion of blue-white light. I was lightheaded and wobbly, unable even to stand. I blinked for several seconds before I could see anything. When my vision did clear I noticed two things. The first was that Darian was soaked in blood and pinned to the ground wrestling with an Azuchi. The second was that the circle holding At'Mavat still glowed at its full intensity. My heart fell to the floor.

I'd failed. Darian was about to die because of it. I was about to die because of it. Millions were about to die because of it. Vija Saptarsi had been wrong, I couldn't stop it. And the fact that I'd tried my best would comfort no one. All we'd done, all we'd suffered, all we'd endured, it all meant nothing. How could the Gods let this happen?

The chalk lines on the floor began to glow. First in pale blue, then in the purist white. The script and diagrams flashed to life, drawing the power of the nexus and feeding it to the three Anaviya summoning circles, imbuing them with life. The fact they held no demons meant nothing, the only thing that mattered was that they fed on the power being siphoned from the nexus, diverting it away from At'Mavat's circle. The glow began to fade from the outer rings, the ones drawing from the nexus and protecting the circle, until all that was left was the plain sheen of the gold engraving.

"Samara, *now!* Dispel the circle!" At'Mavat bellowed.

I felt drained like I never had before, yet I began to reach for the power to shape one last spell. It was like trying to fill a sieve, but I hadn't come this far to fail. I drew the energy through my ragged chakras, ignoring the pain until there was just enough power for the spell, then I released it.

The enchantment on At'Mavat's circle faded.

A roar issued forth that shook the very foundation of Vizipa, echoing off the broken walls as At'Mavat rose to his full height, wings extended. The circle must have been holding back more than I realized, because heat like that of a furnace now blasted away from his body.

"Save him," I pleaded, but the Anaviya was already moving. One great flap of his wings closed the distance between him and the bloody, writhing forms. At'Mavat snatched the Azuchi up and ripped it in half with no more effort than a child would spend on a caterpillar.

"You must continue to keep her safe," At'Mavat said to Darian as he carelessly tossed the halves of demon across the room. "I yet have need of her."

"Darian," I said, dragging myself over to him. A row of cuts had gouged through his chainmail, slicing deep wounds across his ribs. "How bad are you hurt? Talk to me."

"Women...always fussing," he said with a cough.

I huffed with a small amount of relief. "Will you ever cease to vex me?"

"Depends on which one of us lives longer," Darian said, angling his body so I could put pressure on the wounds.

"Fare thee well until we meet again," At'Mavat said, actually bowing toward me.

"Wait, I still can't read—"

The smoke billowing forth from the Anaviya moved to swirl around me in a black vortex the next instant. As I inhaled the acrid vapor, I felt as if fingers were moving around inside my brain. Suddenly I understood Vikatan as if I'd always known it.

"I look forward to our next meeting, young mage." And with a few great flaps of his massive wings the demon was gone.

"Can you walk?" I asked.

He nodded and I tried help him to his feet but found I was rather unsteady on mine as well. "Can you walk?" Darian countered.

"Yes, I'm just a bit wobbly. Now come on, we need to go."

We collected Darian's discarded weapons and made our way down the corridor, through the sanctuary, and back toward the door we'd entered through. "Niggli'po," I called out. "Are there any other demons around the building?"

The demon glided down to join us. "I don see any."

"Alright," I said as I reached the ancient doorway. "I'll go get Tavas, you wait here and see if you can stanch the bleeding with Ananda's gift."

I jogged on shaky legs to find the chestnut right where we was supposed to be, and rode him back to Darian. "How's the bleeding?" I asked

"It'll probably open up again but it's stopped for now."

"Do you need help mounting?"

"I'll manage," he said, climbing up behind me.

I rode to the trailhead and said to Niggli'po, "Check the path we took up to make sure it's clear."

"Yes'm," the demon said taking onto the wind.

"Samara," Darian said, gravely. "It's starting."

The sun had just crested the eastern horizon and I stared down the north slope to where we'd seen the coldfire a few hours earlier. Three dozen red-clad figures, arranged in two neat brackets, were visible at the bottom. A sickly green glow emanated from all the Acolytes and in the space between them the air began to shift and deform. A vertical slit opened ten yards high, as if the air just bent in on itself. The split began to gradually widen.

Then a demon came through.

Darian and I sat in stunned silence, transfixed by what we were witnessing as the portal to Hell widened. Dozens of demons began to stream through the rift. "What's going on? I thought At'Mavat was going to stop this," Darian wheezed.

"He will." I don't know what the source of my confidence was, but I said with a surety.

"What's he waiting for?"

"I don't know."

Demons poured out of the widening gate by the scores. There was no uniformity to them at all. Some flew, while others walked, and still others slithered. Some were smaller than Niggli'po; others were larger than an elephant. As the gate reached its zenith, a massive demon with four arms and one huge glowing red eye stepped through. I gasped.

"What?"

"That's Nir'guna, one of the Anaviya."

"By the Gods…"

A black blur fell from the sky trailing a smoking swath. At'Mavat landed on one Acolytes crushing him, then grabbed the man nearest and threw him into one of the tattooed mages in the other bracket. Then, before anyone else could react, he streaked across the field slamming into Nir'guna and tackling him back through the portal.

Green lightning danced among the crowd as nearly a third of Acolytes' power backlashed. The portal started shrinking, but the mages who were still standing managed to recover and stabilize the portal, at least for a moment.

Then the portal started closing again, this time faster.

"He's dealt with the mages on the other side," I said.

The sounds of battle erupted as dozens of armed men on horseback flooded into the valley, cutting into the demons while the glow of lightning and fire spells bloomed through the hordes. The cavalry that was looking for us found the demons instead. The valley before us erupted into chaos. Despite the frantic efforts of the Acolytes, the gate slammed shut and disappeared into nothingness, crushing the unfortunate demons that were still coming through.

"It…it's over," I said, awestruck.

"There's still scores of demons down there, and I think we'll have a hard time convincing those soldiers we're on their side," Darian said. "We should go before we're noticed."

"Agreed," I said, casting one last look at the carnage below.

In the daylight we made it down the mountain in a fraction of the time it'd taken us to climb it. At the base, we turned south and beat a hasty retreat. We encountered no one, but the sound of battle could be heard echoing off the mountain behind us.

Once all the noise faded into the distance, we stopped to rest and give Darian the chance to do a proper healing. His wounds were deep and he'd lost a lot of blood, but nothing seemed to be life threatening. I was even able to clean and repair his surcoat with the same spell I'd used on the wagon axle, though the chain shirt was missing too many rings.

Once we were finished tending to Darian, I turned to Niggli'po. "You've served me well, but it's time to send you back to your Realm."

"No." The demon's eyes grew wide. "Don send me back. I be good, I be good!"

I shook my head. "You'll call too much attention."

"No, I stay hidden. No one see. Don send Niggli'po back!"

"Why do you want to stay here so bad?" Darian asked.

His large eyes turned to Darian. "Hell not so good a place for someone my size."

"I will call you back later," I said.

The tiny demon's ears fell. "Yes, master." he said, looking dejected but resolved.

I was still exhausted but I managed to draw myself together enough to cast the banishing spell. Darian shook his head and said, "You know, for a demon, that little monkey wasn't so bad."

"Well, I wouldn't trust him alone with my cat, but he's fairly harmless. He certainly served me well this time. When I get home I'll…" And then it hit me, all at once. We'd won. We'd done what we came here to do. And we both survived. All the emotions I'd brushed aside and locked away came flooding out, washing over me and I started crying pent up tears of joy and relief. Why did I always have to cry?

I just prayed to the Gods that Lucius and the houseguards survived as well.

Darian pulled me gently against him and held me. As I wiped my eyes and stared up at him, I noticed tear stains marking his cheeks as well. He kissed me on the forehead and said, "Let's go home."

———————

I lost my Tarka medallion somewhere in Vizipa and I felt strangely naked and vulnerable without it during the ten days it took to reach Sivat. As much as we wanted to rush home we still had to be careful. We traveled back roads as much as possible and did everything we could to keep from calling attention to ourselves. After the frenzied pace of our journey eastward I had to admit, taking it slow and easy was a welcome change.

Sivat's gates were tightly guarded, but with Tarka's gift and a bit of ingenuity, we found a way through without having to answer any uncomfortable questions or present papers we didn't have. When at last we made it inside the walls, we found the city abuzz with stories of demons to the north, though tales ranged widely and details were sketchy at best. There was also another, most welcome piece of news. The Empire and Moravar had declared a temporary truce. Whether the two were related or not I couldn't say, but it seemed an awfully big coincidence if they weren't.

We made our way through the twisting streets of the large city and found the contact by the river Master Carter had told me about before I'd lost the mirror. At the mention of a Vesuvian Teakettle we were hurried inside by a thin woman with long black hair that was shot through with silver. She cast the same transportation spell that Master Carter used to sneak us out of Stonehaven, though it seemed much more taxing on her that it had on him, and she had to cast it several times to cover the needed distance, leaving us at a port town past the blockade.

I shook my head. It'd taken Darian and I nearly five months to travel the miles we'd just covered in a quarter hour. Surreal didn't even begin to describe how I felt.

———————

My heart fluttered as Zenith grew on the horizon before us. I still wasn't very comfortable on the water, so we'd spent most of the three-day voyage below decks in our berth. Fortunately Darian had managed to keep my mind off the water and occupied with, well, other things. However, as I stood on the deck watching the city of my ancestors grow closer, all my apprehension vanished. I was home.

"Are we giving our true names to the harbormaster?" Darian asked. An abundance of coin had caused them to overlook our lack of papers when we booked passage, but that wouldn't work in the Empire.

"Why wouldn't we?"

"There's still the matter of the noble who's in league with the Acolytes and wants to kill you."

"We've already foiled their plot," I said. "Why would they risk further exposure trying to hurt me now?"

"Revenge is a powerful motivator."

"Fair point. At least I have a big strong Ranger to protect me," I said, taking his arm.

"Hey, my job was to get you to Vizipa and back safely, which I did. If you expect me to protect you now, it'll cost you," he said in a serious voice, but his eyes betrayed the jest.

"I'm sure we can work something out," I said, rising to my tip toes to kiss him.

A few hours later we found ourselves standing in line waiting to see a port authority officer. The short line to the left us was reserved for citizens and nobles, but since Darian was neither, we were both stuck in the much longer line for the uncoined.

"Names?" the Port Authority agent said.

"Darian Wayha and Samara Arga," I said.

"Is Darian spelled with a…I'm sorry, what was the second name again?"

"Samara of House Arga."

"May I see your coin?"

"I lost it."

"Right." The agents shared a glance. "You know impersonating a noble is a serious offense?"

Darian caught my eye and moved his hand in a circle in front of his face. Oh right, I'd forgotten about the illusion. I dismissed the spell and both the agents snapped to attention as my eyes and hair returned to their true color. "M'lady, I apologize. I…I meant no disrespect."

"You have given none. You're only doing your jobs," I said. There was a quick conversation between the men in hushed tones and one of them took off at a quick jog.

"We'll get everything sorted, m'lady. You and your companion can have a seat over there," he said indicating some chairs under a canopy.

"Actually, I'm quite anxious to be on my way. Someone from the palace could verify my identity."

The man looked uneasy and he fumbled for words. "I'm sure you are m'lady, but I'm afraid you and your friend are going to have to wait. I could have some refreshments brought—"

I sighed. "No, that's not necessary." We took a seat in the plush chairs bearing my house coloring and waited.

"Does this seem amiss?" Darian asked after a moment.

"No, it seems like bureaucracy." I didn't even know what the protocol for was for a noble trying to reenter the empire without her coin, but I was sure several trees had to die for the paperwork.

The agent who ran off returned with the burly harbormaster, four legionnaires, and a graceful, clean-cut man bearing the unmistakable purple riding cloak of an Imperial Courier. "You are Lady Samara?" the courier asked in the cultured voice I would expect from a noble, though his brown eyes said differently.

"Yes," I said, a self-assuredness in my voice I didn't feel.

"Then this is for you," he said as he opened his scroll case and bowed, offering a rolled missive bearing the Emperor's dragon seal.

I swallowed and took the scroll. There was a flash of purple light as I broke the magical wax and unrolled it.

Lady Samara of House Arga,

Your presence is requested at the Imperial Palace at the earliest possible point upon receiving this letter. You are to speak to no one, nor send any letters, nor transfer any information by any other means, magical or mundane, beforehand. Please proceed with the Imperial Courier who presented you with this directly to the Causeway.

Sincerely,
Emperor Pullo Divias Cario Vima.

I swallowed again and passed the parchment for Darian to read. "Shall we depart, m'lady?" the courier asked.

"I need to collect my horse," Darian said.

The courier looked at the Harbormaster who nodded. "Your horse will be brought along after it's unloaded." Darian didn't look happy about that but he didn't say anything else.

"May we stop by Arga Palace for a moment on the way?"

"I have orders to take you directly to the Gate, m'lady."

"I just want a bath and a change of clothes."

"I'm sorry, m'lady."

"What harm is there in letting me take a bath? We've already missed the morning Gate opening. Are we just going to sit in the Gateroom until this evening?"

"No, m'lady," the courier said in a calm, even tone. "The Gate will be opened specially for us." That silenced me. I couldn't remember the last time the Gate had been opened out of sequence. "Shall we be off?"

The courier had phrased it as a question out of courtesy. The legionnaires didn't move to take Darian's weapons or take us into custody, but it was clear we didn't have a choice. I had no doubt that if we resisted, we'd be shackled and chained before they hauled us unceremoniously through Kardama. I glanced over at Darian and nodded slightly.

"And m'lady shall encounter no harm while in your care, correct?"

The courier's brow furrowed a bit. "Of course not."

Darian nodded back to me. "Let us be off then," I said.

An hour later we sat in a parlor of the Imperial Palace being served food and wine by a flurry of attentive servants. If we were under arrest, it was the nicest arrest one could hope for.

A man strode into the room clad in the gold and white of House Vima, with skin the color of ebony and eyes the exact same hue of Autumn's. "Lady Samara, Freeman Darian, thank you so much for joining us," he said in the same jovial manner as a host might at a dinner party. "The Emperor sends his regards. He regrets that he can't be here to greet you himself, but he is busy negotiating an end to this little skirmish."

"Of course, Aquilinius. It's good to see you again," I said mustering all the poise I could, sitting there unbathed, in salt-stained clothes. Aquilinius's official tittle was the Minister of Public Information, though he was unofficially known as the Councilor of Propaganda. Most Emperors tended to hire members of their own House for important positions, but Emperor Pullo had a falling out with several high ranking members of House Vima and he'd done the opposite, excluding most of his family from those posts. Aquilinius was an exception, which meant one could be assured he had the job for only one reason. He was very good at it.

"A pleasure, as always," he said, kissing my cheeks in greeting. "Freeman Darian, do you find the food and wine to your liking?"

I half expected some sardonic comment from Darian, but apparently he knew better. "It's wonderful, m'lord, especially after the meals we've eaten lately. Gratitude."

"It's the least we could do. Please, sit," he said, perching elegantly on the sofa across from us. "Now, down to business—"

"M'lord, might I ask if there's been any word of my brother, Lucius?" I asked, terrified of what the answer might be.

"You are unaware? Your brother is well, he returned a few weeks ago. We've sent word to your family. They'll likely be in Imperia by morning."

Lucius was alright. The boulder that had been sitting on my chest since we'd parted finally fell to the ground. Relief washed over me in a palpable wave leaving me light-headed.

"First, on behalf of the Emperor, I want to thank you," Aquilinius continued. "You've done a great service for the Empire, and for the world."

You're bloody well right we have. "I simply did the only thing that seemed reasonable under the circumstances," I said. "As any loyal citizen of the Empire would have."

"More than most, I'd say," he chuckled. "I'd be very interested in hearing the story of how you did it," he said, motioning to the servants. A dark haired young scribe came and sat next to him with a tablet and parchment.

I'm sure you would. "It's a long story."

"I have nothing but time," he said, his expression unreadable. "Please, humor me."

I didn't feel much like playing the bard. Exhaustion pulled at me, and I ached to see my family, but it didn't seem like we had much of a choice. So I told him the whole story, starting with what we learned from the Vija and ending with the summons from the Imperial Courier. I left out nothing, save the parts about the Manu's gifts and the dragon, as I'd been sworn to secrecy in both those cases. Aquilinius listened intently as the scribe's quill flew furiously, interrupting only to ask a few clarifying questions. Darian remained silent the entire time.

"What a fascinating story," Aquilinius said when I finished, then he turned to Darian. "Is that how you remember the events transpiring?"

"Yes, m'lord."

"Is there anything you wish to add?"

"Just one thing," Darian said glancing over to me. "The noble who betrayed Samara remains unknown. Until that individual is found, she will never be safe."

"I assure you we're looking into the matter."

Darian gave a short bow. "Very good."

Aquilinius stared off into the distance for a moment as if lost in thought. "As you can imagine," he said as his golden eyes returned to me, "this incident has caused quite a stir, both inside and outside of the Empire. Right now the details are still sketchy, but you sent letters to quite a few people when you first returned from the seer—"

Including the Emperor…

"—it's only a matter of time before someone pieces together what happened. It would be embarrassing for Emperor Pullo, and frankly for all of Zura, if it were to come out that we knew about the portal ahead of time and took no action to stop it."

Which is exactly what happened.

"Therefore I have a proposition—"

Here it comes…

"—we feel it would be best if it were thought that you were carrying out a secret mission, acting under order from the Emperor."

"I see…"

"The Emperor would be *most appreciative*," Aquilinius said raising his eyebrows. "And after all, it's what's in the best interest of the Empire."

I'd been so preoccupied by everything else I hadn't even given it any thought, but I should have seen this coming. Aquilinius was right, after all. If it came out that I'd warned the Council and the Emperor and they'd done nothing, it would be a huge embarrassment. It would hurt the Emperor's standing, both at home and abroad.

Perhaps it was my exhaustion, but I had a very difficult time mustering up a single ounce of concern. They had ignored me, and if I hadn't gone off on my own the Acolytes would have succeeded. Darian, Lucius, and I were the ones who had taken all the risk, and who had starved, and bled, and suffered, and fought. And now, the Emperor wanted to swoop in and share in the credit?

I almost told Aquilinius exactly what Emperor Pullo could do with his "appreciation." But then the part of me that was capable of rational thought kicked in. I could refuse the offer, but assuming that didn't get me "lost" in the dungeon, it would certainly earn me the Emperor's ire. On the other hand, accepting the offer would endear me to the Emperor of Zura, which would bring honor to both me and my house. All it would cost me was a measure of pride.

And then the Emperor would owe me a favor.

I glanced over to Darian, who had remained silent, taking his cues from me. There were many things such a favor could buy.

"Of course," I said to Aquilinius. "If that is what's best for the Empire."

Aquilinius's smile broadened. "It's what is best for everyone."

After we'd agreed upon what our story would be and promised to return with Lucius, Ganicus, and Master Carter, we were dismissed. We were sent on our way in a gilded purple carriage with an escort of Imperial Guards for the absurdly short trip to the Arga estate. I melted into Darian's arms resting my head against his shoulder. "Do you think I made the right decision?"

He was quiet for a moment. "It think, as we have done many times in recent months, you took the option that was the least wrong."

"That's not exactly the reassurance I was looking for," I pouted.

"If there's one thing this journey has taught me, it's that the world isn't black and white. And we can't afford to be either." He squeezed me closer. "Not if we wish to live in it."

I drew a deep breath of the damp night air, savoring the scents of the city. Some were pleasant, some weren't, but it smelled like home to me. "I suppose you might have a point."

He pulled back just enough to see my face. "Does it physically hurt you to simply say 'you're right'?"

"Yes," I said, planting a kiss on his full lips. "It does. I would think you'd know that by now."

The carriage rolled to a stop and we exited onto the steps of the Arga mansion. After Darian was reassured by the Imperial Guards that his horse would be brought to the stables, we strode up the white marble stairs. I was already envisioning the longest, hottest, most luxurious bath of my life, but Aquilinius had been wrong about one thing. My family had managed to catch the evening Causeway.

"Otter," I heard as I entered the foyer, just before my twin swept me up in a crushing hug that left my feet dangling. I squeezed him back as hard as I could. After so much worry it seemed unreal. "I knew you would do it."

He lowered me so that my feet touched the ground, but I still clung tightly to him. "Gods, it's good to see you," I whispered. "What happened after we separated?"

He pushed me back at arm's length and looked me over as if to make sure I was alright, the same way he had when we met on the road returning from Mystewood. "They followed us for a several hours, then all of a sudden turned back."

"They were tracking me by magic," I said.

"How did you finally deal with them?"

"We…I'll tell you the whole story later."

"Of course," Lucius, said planting a kiss on my forehead. "There's time."

"M'lord, it's good to—"

"Don't you 'm'lord' me you tough, wily bastard," my brother said, silencing him with a rough embrace. "It's Lucius to you."

"Lucius, it's good to see you."

"Likewise. Now come," Lucius said, facing me again. "Father is waiting."

We followed Lucius to the manor's vast atrium where I didn't see my father, but I did find another welcome face. "Mistress," Autumn said, leaping off the couch where she'd been sitting. We embraced and I squeezed her so tight she squealed.

"I told you to call me Samara." I said.

She laughed despite her tears. "I missed you."

"I missed you. More than you'll ever know." We finally released each other, both of us wiping at our eyes. "Where's Father?"

"He went to speak with Councilor Decias, but he should be back any moment. By the Gods, you're even thinner than when you left," she said, sliding the chain with my citizenship coin over my head and looking me over. "You're practically skin and bones."

"A situation I plan to remedy in short order." After my time on the road I definitely would never miss another meal any time soon.

Autumn went over and kissed Darian on the cheek murmuring in a low voice I could barely make out, "Thank you for keeping her safe."

"It was my honor, Lady Autumn," Darian said with a bow.

I noted Autumn was dressed in her normal clothes instead of mine. "Father saw through your disguise?"

"I can only be played the fool for so long," a voice came from behind me. "I do know my only daughter, after all."

I turned to see my father standing only a few paces behind me. His posture was stiff, his face unreadable. I could only begin to imagine how angry he was at me. After all, I'd directly disobeyed him, tricked him, and lied to him. He stood unmoving, his face a mask of neutrality, but after a moment a single tear slid from his rich purple eye. Whether it was from anger, or pain, or disappointment I didn't know, but it was a dagger to my heart. "Father, I…I'm sorry I…I couldn't think of any other way to—"

"Shh," my father said, putting his hand my cheek. "You did the right thing." He shook his head. "I should have known from the beginning. You're too much like your mother." He embraced me, and for perhaps the first time as a grown woman instead of his little girl. "She would be so proud of you."

"Thank you," I said. The words sounded hollow and inadequate, but they were the only ones I could find.

"Freeman Darian, words cannot express my gratitude to you," my father said, when we finally released each other. "I am in your debt."

"There is no debt, m'lord, it was my honor to escort Lady Samara. Though

I do have one request."

"Name it."

"I wish to send a letter with one of your couriers to let my family know I'm alive."

"Done." My father tapped his lips then after a moment said, "You trade in horses, do you not?"

Darian's brow wrinkled. "Yes, m'lord."

"I believe House Arga is in need of some new horses." A slight smile traced my father's lips. "A great many horses."

I finally got my bath. And as imagined it was the longest, most wonderful one I'd ever had. I luxuriated in all the small things I'd taken for granted before. Hot meals, clean laundry, warm water, good wine—it was as though I was experiencing everything again for the first time. I wondered if I would ever take those thing for granted again. Probably, I concluded, though I might be a bit more appreciative of them in the meantime.

I was hoping to have a chance to rest and recover, but the next two weeks flew by in a flurry of activity. Once Aquilinius had met with my co-conspirators and released the official story of what happened in Vizipa, I was a celebrity. Everyone in White Harbor was eager to speak with or merely just be seen with me. Not at all ready to wade into the viper's nest of noble politics, I mostly declined, choosing instead to spend time with Darian and my family, which only seemed to increase my celebrity status.

It made it easier to stay in when the six new houseguards I was assigned were under strict orders to go with me *everywhere* outside the gates of the estate. I made a point to learn all their names and to know if they were married, and where they were from, and how many children they had. I was never going to take the houseguards for granted again.

Emperor Pullo reached an agreement to sell the disputed islands to King Thaddeus, which ended the conflict and allowed both leaders to save face. After Aquilinius put his spin on it, the people all thought the Emperor was a genius, selling a tiny rock Zura didn't want for a premium price. The Councilor of Propaganda was, in fact, very good at his job.

When the Emperor finally did return, he held a small ceremony where he presented me, Darian, Autumn, Lucius, Ganicus, Master Carter, and the surviving houseguards who'd accompanied us, with the Imperial Exemplar medal, an award rarely doled out. He also presented Darian with a citizenship coin, completely oblivious to the fact that a Manu would never wear it because it was magical.

I'd never been so close to the Emperor before and I was struck by how old he looked. Since he'd been on the throne long before I was born, he was the only Emperor I'd ever known. To me he'd always been some larger-than-life figure. But as I stood before him all I saw was a man in purple robes bent by age, wearing a gold laurel wreath on the wispy silver remnants of his hair. An old man who'd cut a deal to share in glory he had no right to. Still, he was the Emperor of the most powerful nation the world had ever known…and now he owed me a favor.

Darian had been given one of the largest guest rooms in the manor to stay in, though he didn't sleep a single night in there. There was no telling what the White Harbor gossip mill was churning out, but I hardly cared what anyone thought. There might be some things I was ashamed of, but Darian was not one of them.

I was *not* in love.

I wasn't.

Alright, maybe.

Chapter Thirty-Four
Darian

"We have to get up," Samara said again as we lay entwined naked on her enormous silk-covered bed.

"You keep saying that," I said as I kissed the back of her neck.

"I mean it," she said between giggles. "I have a meeting with Master Carter."

"Just a while longer."

"No, I'll not keep him waiting," Samara said, disentangling her limbs from mine and stretching. "It's funny how you were the one who was always prodding me to get up when we were on the road."

"It figures you'd become a morning person *after* we finished rushing across the continent."

She slid out of bed, and much to my disappointment, slipped on a robe. "Are you going to lay in bed and complain all day?"

"I haven't ruled it out."

She smiled despite herself. "If you're coming with me, you'd better get up."

I just stared at her still not moving.

"Well? Are you coming?"

"You'd have to come back to bed for that," I said.

She let out a labored sigh and tossed trousers at me.

Staring out the window of the carriage as we rode the short distance to the Imperial Academy of Magic, I had to admit, White Harbor was impressive. The city was so vast, and there were so many people, it was difficult to get my head around. It was both beautiful and glorious. I could understand why Samara liked living here, though I could never be content in such a place. I longed for greenery and open spaces, but more than anything I ached for Mystewood. I missed my family, but it was more than that. Those ancient trees sang to my soul, begging me to return. There was only one siren whose song I heard more clearly, the one with the adorable freckles.

I had no idea how we were going to make it work. Her life was here and mine was with my people and my horses in Mystewood. That, and I knew one day her family would try to auction her off for marriage like a piece of livestock. But it didn't matter; I needed her. I burned for her. And she was a balm for my spirit. And anyway, we had a track record for doing impossible things.

I didn't know how a Zuran noble and a Manu horse trader would ever share a life together. I just had to have faith that Ananda made the right decision in leading our hearts to one another, faith that the Gods had a plan. And for the first time since Sita's death, I did.

After Samara led the way through the labyrinth of ancient stone buildings that made up the Academy, we climbed what seemed to be an endless flight of stairs to reach Master Carter's large office. When we reached the open door, Samara seemed taken aback to see the two people Master Carter was conversing with. One was a short, pale, brunette woman wearing a gray cloak with the symbol of the Academy on it. The other was a tall blond nobleman with crimson eyes, wearing robes of Imperial purple trimmed with gold.

"Master, are you busy? Shall I come back?" Samara asked in a hesitant voice.

"Ah, Samara there you are. Come in," Master Carter said in his soothing tone. As we entered, the mages stood.

"So this is the arrogant young mage I've heard so much about," the noble said.

"Archmage Valerius," Samara said, bowing to the blond noble, then she turned to the woman. "Master Flaviana. This is a most unexpected honor."

"Please, no need for such formalities," Archmage Valerius said. "And you must be the Manu that escorted her to Vizipa."

"Darian Wahya," I offered with a bow.

Master Carter cleared his throat. "This is the Imperial Archmage Valerius Paska, and Master Flaviana Varella."

"A pleasure," I said.

"Charmed," the Archmage said, then faced Samara. "Did you really create a diagram on the fly to siphon the energy from the nexus?"

"Yes," Samara said, recovering from her momentary shock.

"Show me," the Archmage said narrowing his red eyes.

Samara shuffled through her endless bag for a moment and produced the original she'd drawn for me to work off of. "Pardon the ink stains at the bottom.

It was done in haste."

The noble studied it for a long moment in silence then handed it to Master Flaviana. "You're right, Carter. She is clever."

"As I said," Master Carter said, not bothering to hide a smug smile.

The Archmage turned to Samara again. "Congratulations, Adept Samara."

"What?" Samara said mouth agape. "Adept? Don't I need to take the practical exam first?"

"I'd say this will suffice," Flaviana said, handing the diagram back to her. "We'll have the pinning ceremony next week."

"I believe that make you the youngest Adept in the history of the Academy, does it not?" Valerius asked.

Samara just stood there with a dumbfounded look.

"Yes, it does," Master Carter volunteered.

"Hmm, fortunate for House Arga. I'm sure I'll be seeing more of you, Adept Samara. Carter, Flaviana," he said nodding to each in turn before striding out the door.

"Always been a charmer that one," Master Flaviana said, shaking her head and turning to Master Carter. "You know how to spot the talent, Delias. I'll give you that."

"Every now and again I get lucky," Master Carter said, beaming.

Once we were back in the carriage, Samara gazed out the window as if a fog, unusually quiet. "What's the matter?" I asked.

"Hm? Nothing's the matter." I leveled my gaze at her, brows raised. "I don't know," she admitted with a sigh.

"Isn't this what you wanted? Wasn't that what started you on this path?"

"It was what I wanted," she sighed. "Once. The honor, the prestige, the attention..."

"It isn't what you thought it would be?"

She shook her head. "After meeting a dragon, and freeing At'Mavat, and stopping the Acolytes..."

"It felt a bit flat?" I offered

She nodded. "And if I'm being completely honest, I was driven by solving mystery of the unknown diagram as much as I was anything, and I already did that. It's just...after everything, being the youngest Adept just feels like less of a goal and more of a consolation prize. Though perhaps I can use it as a bargaining chip within house Arga. I mean, you'd think that after all the bloody work I went through..." Samara trailed off as she focused on something outside the window for a moment. She slapped the heel of her palm into her forehead.

"The Sena estate."

"What?"

"I keep forgetting to talk to Master Tertias."

"Who?"

"The man who…hold on," she leaned out the window and called to the driver, "Reginald, turn into the Sena estate." She returned her attention to me. "Master Tertias is the linguist who tried to help me translate the manuscript. He asked that if I managed to decipher Vikatan I would share it with him."

I nodded, vaguely recalling the conversation. It sounded like the recipe for a boring afternoon, but at least her momentary melancholy seemed to be replaced with genuine excitement.

A few minutes later, a House Sena servant led us down a long line of town homes that framed the estate. To my surprise there were a number of well-fed peacocks strutting along the property. "Are they pets?" I asked.

"Not exactly," Samara said pursing her lips and seeming to ponder for a moment. "More like decorations."

I shook my head. "Nobles."

Samara just smirked.

When we reached the house near the corner of the estate our guide knocked on the door. After a long silence, he knocked again. The door cracked open just wide enough for deeply lined face with bushy black eyebrows to appear. "What is it?" the man asked.

"You have visitors, m'lord."

The man squinted past the servant, then his eyes went wide and he blinked a few times as if trying make sense of what he was seeing. "Lady Samara?" he finally asked.

"Good afternoon, Master Tertias. I'm terribly sorry to drop by unannounced, but I have news I believe you'll find exciting. Do you have time to speak with me?"

The man seemed unsure for a moment, then his features lifted and he gave a charming smile. "Of course I have a moment for you, child. Please come in."

As I started through the door behind Samara, he looked at me and said, "They have food and refreshments at the guardhouse on the other side of the estate."

"Oh no, Master," Samara said, "he isn't a houseguard. This is my friend, Darian." Samara nudged me with her elbow. "He's quite scholarly was as well."

"M'lord," I said with a bow.

"Ah, I see." The man smiled in a grandfatherly way that didn't quite seem to reach his cyan eyes. "I'm always interested to meet a fellow scholar. Come, let us go to the study."

As we climbed the stairs, I was surprised how graceful Master Tertias was despite his slouched posture. At the top of the stairs was a sizable room with a long table in the middle and bookshelves lining every wall. The high-set stained glass windows made the room seem stuffy to me.

"Please have a seat," Master Tertias said, gesturing to the table. As we took seats across from him he fumbled some books closed he'd apparently been reading when we arrived. "Is this in regards to what we discussed last time?"

"Yes, Master."

"The word is you've had a bit of excitement since then," he said, bushy eyebrows raising.

"Just a bit," Samara said with a smirk.

"Come now, I heard you made quite the journey. Was it dangerous?"

"It had its moments."

"Well," Master Tertias said with his grandfatherly smile again, "I'm glad to see you safe before me today." *Lie.*

That surprised me. I'd only been half listening to the conversation up to that point, but now he had my full attention.

"That's kind of you to say, Master. The reason I stopped by was that on my journey I managed to find someone who spoke Vikatan."

"Truly? But that's not possible, the language is dead," Master Tertias said. Neither his expression, posture, nor voice, betrayed him. But Azava's gift told me he didn't have any idea whether or not what he said was true, which didn't make any sense for a renowned linguist.

"I was surprised as well," Samara said, being deliberately vague. The details of our interaction with At'Mavat weren't common knowledge.

"It sounds as though you have quite a lot to tell," the old man said. "Why don't I trade you a cup of tea for the story?"

Varga's gift pinged though my consciousness more strongly than I'd ever felt it. It told me that accepting that trade would be very unfavorable for us. Samara must have seen something in my face. She furrowed her brow for the briefest moment, then returned her attention to Master Tertias. "Um… certainly."

"Splendid. I just brewed a fresh kettle of Kalikara tea. This batch is simply wonderful." *Lie.* I studied him as he stood up and crossed the room. People who have as profound a slouch as him tended to shuffle their feet as they walked, but his gate was even and graceful. He stood in front of the little nook where the tea kettle was and poured with his back to us. As soon as he wasn't looking Samara shrugged her shoulders at me. I shrugged in response and reached across the table to quietly ease open the book he'd closed when we came in. It was written in the same script as the letter we'd pulled off of the Acolyte.

"Cream or sugar?" he called back over his shoulder.

"Th-thank you, no," Samara said.

"I'll take cream, Master Tobias," I said

"The name is Tertias, not Tobias." Lie.

"Oh, I'm sorry." I caught Samara's gaze and shook my head. "I've met so many new people recently it seems I'm getting the names confused."

"It's quite alright," he said turning with a tray bearing tea cups.

I drew in a quick breath, which Samara picked up on. If I hadn't been watching him like a wolf stalking a deer, I would have missed it in the defused light from the stained glass.

The man standing before us cast no shadow.

I was really regretting letting myself be talked into leaving my bow behind.

Chapter Thirty-five
Samara

Something was off with Darian. It was subtle. I wouldn't have noticed it if we hadn't spent the last six months breathing the same air, but his body held a tension I didn't understand. I tried discreetly to get his attention in a lull in the conversation, but he didn't seem to notice. Then when Master Tertias turned his back I shrugged at him, but he just shrugged back then peeked in one of the closed books across the table. I was certain he suspected something. I just hoped he tread carefully. Master Tertias was a well-respected noble, and if Darian offended him, it could cause a real mess.

As the steaming cups were placed before us, Darian made a two quick jerky slashes with his hand under the table, which I took to mean not to take a drink. Darian took up his cup and made a show of smelling it. "This tea certainly has a lovely aroma, m'lord."

"Yes, I've always been partial to it."

"I can understand why." Darian's gaze burned into the other man over his cup. "The floral notes must make it easy to hide the smell of poison."

Well, so much for treading carefully.

Master Tertias stared blankly for a moment then gave a genial smile. "Young man, I'm afraid your foreign sense of humor is lost on me."

"I'm not jesting," Darian said evenly.

Master Tertias's smile faded into a scowl. "Falsely accusing a noble is a serious crime."

"What did you use?" Darian said, swirling the liquid in the cup. "Nightshade?"

"How *dare* you?" Master Tertias said, rising to his feet.

"Darian," I cautioned.

"No, nightshade's a bit too obvious," Darian continued. "Yew seed? Doll's eye?"

"I'll have you flogged, you insolent *commoner*!"

"Darian…"

His gaze bore into Master Tertias. "When you summon the guards maybe they can help you find your missing shadow."

Darian was right. In the soft light I hadn't noticed, but Master Tertias didn't have a shadow. "Master Tertias? It was you?"

"That's not Master Tertias," Darian said.

The scowl faded from his face, replaced by an annoyed snarl. "If you had just taken tea the first time you came here you would have died quietly in your sleep."

"She doesn't do anything quietly," Darian said.

"She certainly proved to be far more trouble than I originally anticipated. I should have heeded the Ally's warnings more closely."

"What Ally?" I said.

The imposter gave a mirthless chuckle. "If you think I'm going to stand here and discuss my plans with you, then perhaps you're not that clever after all."

"Mind the hand," Darian warned. The man's left hand had started to slip into his robes.

The next moment was a blur of motion. The imposter's hand moved impossibly fast, darting into his robes and sending a glint of metal singing through the air quicker than a viper strike. But Darian had already started moving. He shouldered into me hard, sending me off the chair and sprawling onto the floor. He slammed his forearms together and the long thin blade pinged off his steel bracers and clattered along the table.

The imposter was already reaching into his robes again when Darian snapped his dagger out of its sheath to send it tumbling end over end through the air. The man tried to get out of the way but only managed to dodge enough to take the heavy knife in the shoulder instead of the throat. He let out no cry of pain, but hatred burned in the man's eyes as Darian drew his kukri and remaining dagger.

"It didn't have to go this way," the man said in a deeper voice than the one he'd been using. "But I'll not lie and say I'm not going to enjoy it." The face that I'd known as Master Tertias started to stretch and deform. For a moment it looked as though it was just going to melt off, but then the skin faded into a wispy, black film and parted to reveal a young man with dark eyes and honey colored skin. And a tarnished coppery-green symbol upon his brow. The black film slithered and draped about him like a shawl floating in water. My mind raced to make the connections.

It was his shadow.

When the Acolyte spoke again he had the same lilting accent as the others. "How many of my Brothers and Sisters did you kill?"

"I lost count," Darian said, moving to make his way around the long table.

"You *will* suffer!" the Acolyte said as his shadow wrapped around the handle of the dagger and yanked it out.

"Don't worry, you'll be joining them."

"Not any time soon." A bit of shadow rushed into the wound to staunch the bleeding as the blade chimed against the floor. A wispy tendril shot over the table and wrapped around Darian's throat. Eyes wide with surprise, he slashed and hacked at the black tentacle holding him, but the wispy arm reformed behind the blade even before it had passed all the way through. "Yes, do struggle. It makes this ever so much more rewarding."

Darian made a gurgling noise in response as he sliced again and again at the shadow, face growing red. I scrambled to get my feet under me, still partially using the table as cover. The tattooed man's dark, hate-filled eyes were so focused on Darian that he didn't seem to be paying any attention to me. That was foolish. He was hurting someone I cared about. And Darian was not the most dangerous person in the room. Not by a long shot. I drew a breath and cleared my mind.

Drawn by the glow of my spellcasting the Acolyte's dark eyes snapped over to me an instant before I finished. The black tentacle released Darian and swirled in front of the man to form a spiraling shield as I released the spell. Realizing that lightning or fire would have been a bad idea in such confined quarters, I'd opted for something different. Death rained from between my outstretched palms in the form of razor sharp, obsidian shards the length of my hand.

The rolling shadowy mass managed to deflect most of the larger pieces but a few of the smaller ones got through. One such piece found his eye. This time he did scream. By the time the spell ended, a dozen or so pieces the size of my thumb had made it past he the dark shield, and no telling how many had shattered against the bookshelf behind him and ricocheted smaller shards into his back. His one remaining eye burned balefully at me.

"We shall meet again. I promise," the man said as the spiraling shadow reshaped itself into gauzy black wings that sprouted from his shoulders. A few quick flaps sent him through the window over my head. I dove under the table as shards of stained glass rained down to join obsidian scattered all over the room.

I crawled under the long table and carefully made my way out from the far end near where Darian was coughing. I came to my feet and wrapped my arms around him as he caught his breath. "Are you alright?"

"Aye, I'm fine," he said in a gravelly voice.

"Good," I said taking a step back and slapping him hard across the face. The look he gave me was one of utter shock. "What? You thought that just because we share a bed now I wasn't going to slap you when you do something reckless?"

"But…he was the one who hired the mercenaries," Darian said, shaking off the surprise and rubbing his cheek. "He was the noble who betrayed you."

"Firstly, he wasn't a noble, he was just impersonating one. I've no doubt the real Tertias Sena is dead. Secondly, the moment you figured that out, you should have made some excuse for us to leave. Then we could have returned with dozens of soldiers and battle mages. Instead, you decide to handle it yourself and almost get killed," I said, punctuating my point by poking him in the chest.

"You're right. I'm sorry," he said, putting his hands on my shoulders. "I should have handled it the way you said, then perhaps he wouldn't have escaped."

I was so sure he was going to argue I almost shouted at him again. "Well… yes," I sighed letting my anger slowly evaporate. "Eventually you'll figure out I'm always right and you should just agree with me. It saves time."

"Like when you said it was impossible for them to be tracking us by magic?"

"You sure you want to bring that up right now?"

"No," he chuckled. "Gratitude for the save. Again."

"You're welcome," I said, feeling suddenly exhausted. "Anyway, you saved me from the knife first." I couldn't stop myself from adding, "Which wouldn't have been necessary if you hadn't provoked a fight."

"I know, I know," he said rolling his eyes. "How many times do you figure we've barely escaped death since this all started?"

I looked around surveying the damage, feeling a small pang of guilt for all the books I'd destroyed. "I've stopped counting."

I stood holding Tavas's reins in the Gateroom with a feeling of tightness in my chest, fighting the urge to cry as Darian said his farewells to Autumn and Lucius. Once all the excitement about the revelation regarding "Master Tertias" had died down, things faded into some semblance of normalcy, and a month passed almost in the blink of an eye. Now Darian had to leave for Mystewood before the pass closed for the season. My head knew he needed to go, needed to tend his horses and see his family, but my heart was heavy with sadness. I don't know why, after all he was taking it with him.

"Safe travels on the road, my friend," Lucius said.

Darian clasped his outstretched arm saying, "After what I've been through, I think Kavi owes me a smooth journey."

"Take care, Ranger Darian," Autumn said, giving him a warm hug and a kiss on the cheek.

He took a step back and gave her his formal bow. "You take care as well, Lady Autumn." She blushed and giggled as she always did when he addressed her so.

"Can you give us a moment?" I asked my brother and Autumn.

Lucius nodded and Autumn said, "We'll be in the courtyard."

"You as well," I said to the houseguards. They'd eased up a bit since we'd discovered who was behind the plot, but not much.

Apparently Reginald decided the Gateroom was safe enough. "As you wish, m'lady."

Once they left, I pressed the reins into Darian's hand and slid into his arms, embarrassed and slightly terrified at how vulnerable I felt. I stayed like that for several minutes, just breathing in his scent and soaking up his touch, oblivious to the stares of the other people in the Gateroom.

He broke the silence first. "You could come with me and spend the winter in Mystewood?"

It wasn't the first time he'd asked, and believe me, I'd given it serious thought. "I can't. I have obligations at the Academy."

"I know. But I had to ask again."

"When will you be back?"

"Just before the vernal equinox, when the pass opens again."

"No."

"I beg your pardon?"

"That's too long. I'll need to see you before then."

He chuckled. "The pass will be covered with ice, what am I supposed to do?"

"Well, if you're not clever enough to figure out a way, I'll just have to visit you then."

"What are *you* going to do about the ice?"

"Have you forgotten I'm an Adept mage? I can make fire and whatnot."

"Right."

I leaned back and stared into his gorgeous aqua eyes with their inner ring of gold. "Do you doubt the vastness of my power?"

"Not for a moment," he said with a half-smile. "And if your magic isn't enough, you can always pester the ice until it gives in and lets you by."

"Remind me why I'm going to miss you again?"

"Because you're madly in love with me. Just as I am with you."

My heart did a flip-flop in my chest when he said those words. I fought valiantly not to smile. "You flatter yourself. You may be the bravest man I know, and better than average in between the sheets, but so what? That doesn't mean anything."

"It doesn't?"

"No it doesn't," I said. "I am not in love with yo—"

He silenced me with his kiss and I melted into it, devouring his lips.

"Liar," he said when he finally pulled away.

"Vexing barbarian."

Epilogue

Footfalls echoed off the windowless sandstone walls as the man strode into the circular room illuminated only by the harsh green coldfire above his head. The bandages that covered his left eye partially concealed the mark upon his brow as the man stiffly knelt in the center of the room, which was empty save for the round black mirror mounted to the wall.

The man swallowed heavily once before speaking. "Contact the Ally."

The words etched along the edge of the mirror began to burn with the same hue has the coldfire until the entire rim was aglow. For a few heartbeats nothing happened. The kneeling man fidgeted uncomfortably. Black faded to give way to an image within the glowing script and the room was awash in purple light that clashed with the hovering coldfire.

The silvery-blue face that filled the center of the mirror was painfully beautiful. Eyes that seemed crafted of polished platinum stared dispassionately from features too perfectly symmetrical to belong to any man. The entity's voice was a haunting symphony that filled the small space with the Refined tongue. "Could you have failed any more spectacularly?"

The kneeling man wiped at a line of pink fluid that wept from beneath his bandaged eye before he spoke. "There were…unforeseen events."

The face in the mirror angled down, bringing into view metallic fire that burned in place of hair. "The events were not unforeseen, I warned you of them," the symphonic voice boomed, "You merely underestimated your opponent. I gave you all the information you needed to succeed, yet still you managed to fail."

The man grimaced and lowered his eyes. Again he cleared his throat and said, "I am sorry. You warned us of the girl, but we never imagined—"

"Silence," the voice said. "I care not for your excuses or your apologies. You are after all, but a human. I should not be surprised by your failure." The man's shadow quivered at the words, but he said nothing. The entity in the mirror continued, "The path forward is what must be considered now. How many of the Acolytes were lost?"

The man's face twisted into a scowl as he said, "More than half."

"Focus on recruitment and training. When your numbers again swell, a new course of action will be set upon."

"What of Samara Arga?" the man said, his shadow twisting and writhing as if in pain.

"Leave her be for the time." Platinum eyes narrowed. "We may yet have use for her."

The end.

ABOUT THE AUTHOR

MATTHEW MITCHELL

As a dreamer and an avid fan of all things fantasy and sci-fi, Matthew began writing his own stories at the age of twelve. He honed his storytelling skills running tabletop roleplaying games, and later, live-action roleplaying games. After a decade as a pediatric nurse, he decided to pursue a full-time career in writing, his first love. Matthew has been practicing a variety of martial arts since he was nine, and is generally considered to be an encyclopedia of useless knowledge. He lives in Arlington, Texas with his wife, twin boys, three dogs, a wolf, and the wolf's fluffy cat.

For mor info about the author, visit the author's website:
www.author-matthew-mitchell.com

www.ingramcontent.com/pod-product-compliance
Lightning Source LLC
Chambersburg PA
CBHW050902250626
47155CB00001B/63